THE KINGS OF WILLOWS PEAK

A VAMPIRE REVERSE HAREM ROMANCE

CASSANDRA DOON

A Note From The Author

Well, well, well… we meet again.

For some of you, that is. This book was originally published back in 2022, and if I'm being brutally honest, it didn't do very well. My writing style was… let's call it choppy. It needed a lot of work, and the story I was so passionate about just wasn't shining through the way it deserved.

Instead of simply unpublishing it and pretending like it never existed, I decided to give it the glow-up it deserved. I've taken the original story and completely rewritten it in the style I've learned to love—and I hope you will, too. The story itself hasn't changed. It's still the same three infuriatingly hot kings and our girl, Willow. But it no longer sounds like I wrote it in my sleep.

To all of you who read the original version and still loved it, thank you. Your support meant the world to me then, and it means even more now. I promise you're going to love this version even more. And to all the new readers, welcome! I'm so excited for you to step into this world for the first time.

WELCOME TO WILLOW'S PEAK.

Chapter 1

Willow

The universe, as it turns out, has a sick sense of humor. And timing. It's 2:04 AM on my seventeenth birthday when I'm unceremoniously yoinked from my bed. Not that I'm looking at the clock. My face is currently being introduced to a cloth that smells like a regrettable chemical romance between almonds and old pennies. My last coherent thought isn't 'Oh no, I'm being kidnapped!' but rather, 'Damn it, I left a half-full can of La Croix on my nightstand. That's gonna leave a ring.' Then, the world snaps off like a bad fluorescent bulb in a high school hallway.

I come to with a gasp, my lungs filling with air that's suspiciously clean. It's the kind of clean that smells expensive, like a freshly unwrapped Apple product mixed with the distinct, high-quality scent of premium interior latex paint. I know that smell. That's Benjamin Moore's 'Aura' line. My dad's a contractor, and I've spent enough summers mixing paint to know the good stuff from the cheap crap that gives you a headache. My kidnapper, it seems, is a kidnapper of taste. And a recent decorator.

My cheek is pressed against a floor so polished I can see the blurry, funhouse-mirror version of my own face staring back. I push myself up, my limbs feeling like over-cooked spaghetti. The room is… vast. And empty. Like, 'We just bought this mansion and haven't furnished it yet' empty. Tall arched windows line one wall, and outside, a forest presses in, a solid wall of spooky, impenetrable black. The moonlight spills through, painting long, skeletal shadows on the floor. very gothic. Ten out of ten for atmosphere.

It's when I try to stand that I notice the new accessory. It's a sleek black plastic band clasped around my ankle. It's not a Fitbit. A single, pulsing red light winks at me, a steady, rhythmic beat that feels like it's mocking my own frantic heartbeat. Well, isn't this just the latest in high-tech abduction chic? Panic, cold and sharp, finally decides to join the party, clawing its way up my throat. I take a deep breath, the fancy paint smell doing little to calm my nerves. Okay. Don't freak out. Assess the situation. You're in a freshly painted, unfurnished mansion, wearing a mystery ankle bracelet. This is fine.

My first instinct, naturally, is to get the hell out. I scramble to my feet, my bare feet cold against the ridiculously clean floor, and I run. I don't know where I'm going; I just pick a direction and haul ass. I find a long, dark hallway lined with… nothing. No portraits of creepy ancestors, no suits of armor. Just more pristine, freshly painted walls. This place is a blank canvas. I finally spot a set of heavy oak doors and burst through them, expecting freedom, or at least a well-manicured lawn. I get a face full of night air, thick with the smell of pine and damp earth. And then, as my foot hits the soft ground, a jolt of pure, white-hot agony shoots up my leg. It's like being tasered by a very angry, very precise god. I scream, a sound that the forest just swallows whole, and I'm on the ground, my leg twitching, the smell of ozone sharp in my nostrils.

After a minute, the pain fades to a dull, angry buzz. I lie there, gasping, the taste of blood and dirt in my mouth. So, that's the deal. The ankle bracelet isn't just for show. It's a leash. A very, very effective leash. I crawl back to the stone steps of the manor, defeated and humiliated, and sit there, shivering in my stupid, unicorn-print pajama shorts. I hug my knees to my chest, my mind racing. Who does this? Who kidnaps a seventeen-year-old girl, puts her in an empty, freshly painted mansion, and slaps a geo-fence ankle monitor on her? And why 2:04 AM? It's all so… specific. So… extra. Whoever my host is, they're a planner. And they have a flair for the dramatic. And, apparently, a subscription to Architectural Digest. I can't decide if I should be terrified or impressed. Maybe both.

Okay, new plan. Running is out. Hiding and waiting for the psycho-with-a-good-decorator to show up seems like a solid option B. But first, reconnaissance. And maybe some pants. Shivering in my PJs on a cold stone step is not a good look, even for a kidnapping victim. I push myself up, my leg still tingling, and head back inside. The heavy oak door closes behind me with a soft, expensive-sounding click.

The house is eerily silent. I start walking, my bare feet making soft padding sounds on the polished wood. Room after empty room, all smelling of that damn Benjamin Moore paint. It's like wandering through a high-end furniture showroom before the furniture arrives. Then, I find the kitchen. And I stop dead. It's… perfect. A massive marble island, stainless steel appliances that look like they've never been touched, and a fridge the size of a small car. I pull the handle, half-expecting it to be empty. It's not. It's stocked. Like, 'prepping for a zombie apocalypse but with artisanal cheese' stocked. There's organic milk, cage-free eggs, a frankly intimidating amount of kale, and a whole drawer dedicated to different kinds of cheese. My kidnapper might be a psychopath, but at least I won't starve. And they have good taste in cheese. Points for that.

I keep exploring, my curiosity now warring with my fear. I find a grand staircase that sweeps up to the second floor. More empty rooms. Then, at the end of a long hall, I find a closed door. It's the only one. I push it open, and my jaw drops. It's a bedroom. A fully furnished, looks-like-it's-straight-out-of-a-magazine bedroom. There's a huge bed with a fluffy white duvet that looks like a cloud, a cozy-looking armchair, and a walk-in closet. I step inside, and the closet is full of clothes. My size. Jeans, sweaters, t-shirts — all new, all with the tags still on. It's a shopping spree I never went on. This is getting weirder by the second. My kidnapper is not only a foodie decorator but also my personal stylist. Creepy. And also, these are some nice sweaters.

My tour of this bizarre, five-star prison continues. I find a room with towering, built-in shelves, and my book-loving heart does a little flutter of hope. A library! Maybe this won't be so bad after all. I rush inside, my eyes scanning the shelves, and the hope dies as quickly as it came. The shelves are empty. Not a single book. Just rows and rows of empty, mocking wood. It's a special kind of cruel to build a library and not put any books in it. This, more than the kidnapping, more than the ankle monitor, feels like a personal attack. This psycho is a monster.

My brief, sweater-induced good mood evaporates. The fear comes back, cold and sharp, but this time it's mixed with a healthy dose of pissed off. Okay. No more exploring. No more admiring the cheese selection. It's time to get serious. I march back down to the kitchen, my bare feet slapping against the floor with purpose. I yank open a drawer, then another, until I find what I'm looking for. A block of professional-grade kitchen knives. I pull out the chef's knife. It's heavy, perfectly balanced, and wickedly sharp. This will do.

Now, where to wait? I need a spot with a good view of the front door, but where I won't be seen right away. I find it in the grand, empty living room, behind the sweeping curve of the staircase. It's dark, and if I crouch down, I'm completely hidden. I settle onto the cold floor, the handle of the knife clutched in my hand, my back pressed against the wall. And I wait. And wait. And wait. The sun starts to rise, painting the empty room in shades of orange and pink. My stomach growls, a loud, obnoxious sound in the dead quiet. You know what? Screw this. I'm not going to be murdered on an empty stomach. I creep back to the kitchen, grab a hunk of what looks like a fancy aged cheddar from the cheese drawer, and sneak back to my hiding spot. And damn, it's good cheese. Salty, sharp, with those little crunchy crystals. My kidnapper may be a monster, but he's a monster with an excellent cheese guy.

Hours pass. I take a few risky, high-speed trips to a downstairs bathroom, the knife held out in front of me like a deranged Olympic fencer. The sun crawls across the sky, and my adrenaline-fueled rage slowly fades into a bone-deep boredom. By late afternoon, I'm half-convinced I've been forgotten, left to rot in this beautiful, empty house with a lifetime supply of kale. Then, I hear it. The sound of a key in the front door.

My heart leaps into my throat. I flatten myself against the wall, my knuckles white around the knife handle. The heavy door swings open, and a man walks in. And he is… stunning. Annoyingly, breathtakingly stunning. He's just over six feet tall, with messy brown hair that looks artfully disheveled, and he's wearing a tailored suit that probably costs more than my car. He's carrying a single paper grocery bag. This is it. I take a deep breath, and with a scream that's more of a squeak, I launch myself from behind the staircase; the knife aimed at his ridiculously expensive suit.

I get maybe two steps before a blinding, electric pain shoots up my leg, and my whole body seizes. The ankle monitor. I'd forgotten about the damn ankle monitor. The scream dies in my throat, my muscles lock up, and I go down like a sack of potatoes, the knife clattering uselessly on the floor. I'm just a twitching, silent heap at the feet of my gorgeous, well-dressed captor.

He doesn't even flinch. He just looks down at me, then at the knife, then back at me. One of his eyebrows quirks up in mild amusement. He calmly steps over my still-twitching body, places his grocery bag on the kitchen island, and then turns back to me. He crouches down, and I get a full blast of his eyes. They are the brightest, most impossibly blue eyes I have ever seen. He effortlessly plucks the knife from the floor with one hand, his other still resting on the grocery bag. "Now, now, Willow," he says, his voice a low, calm murmur that sends a shiver down my spine. "I'm here to cook your dinner. I nearly dropped the eggs."

My body finally unlocks, and I can breathe again, sucking in a huge, ragged gasp of air. The anger comes roaring back, hot and fierce. "Who the hell are you?" I manage to get out, my voice raspy. "I want to go home! I want my parents!"

He stands up, turning his back on me to start unpacking the groceries. "You won't be going home," he says, his voice casual, like he's discussing the weather. "And they're not your parents. More like… handlers. Your real family is dead." He pulls a carton of eggs from the bag, the ones he almost dropped, and places them on the counter. He turns to look at me, his blue eyes unreadable. "Look, I know you have questions. A lot of them. so how about this? Give me twenty minutes to cook, and I'll explain everything. Deal?"

CHAPTER 2

WILLOW

Three years. It's amazing what can change in three years. For starters, I'm twenty now, which means I can legally drink in most of the world, not that it matters when your only social companion is a 170-something-year-old vampire who thinks wine coolers are a modern marvel. The ankle monitor is still my least favorite accessory, a constant, humming reminder of my five-star incarceration. But the library… the library is no longer a cruel, empty joke.

It's my sanctuary. My fortress of solitude. My hoard. After my initial… let's call it a 'disagreement'… with Caleb about the definition of 'basic human rights,' which apparently do not include access to literature, he caved. Big time. Now, the towering shelves are groaning under the weight of thousands of books. It's a glorious, chaotic mess of fantasy epics, trashy romance novels, dense historical texts, and the occasional weirdly specific manual on 18th-century shipbuilding. It smells of old paper and dust and contentment.

I'm currently buried in a ridiculously comfortable armchair, my legs slung over the side, halfway through a chapter that's just getting to the good part. The hero is about to make a monumentally stupid decision involving a cursed sword and a princess with questionable motives, and I am so here for it. That's when I hear it. The familiar solid thunk of the heavy oak front door closing.

Caleb's back.

A moment later, his voice echoes through the house, warm and familiar. "Willow! I'm home! And I come bearing gifts, mostly of the edible variety!"

I don't even look up from my page. "Ten minutes!" I yell back, my voice muffled by the high back of the chair. "The fate of the entire Western Kingdom is hanging in the balance, and I can't just abandon them now!"

I hear his low chuckle from the hallway. "Of course. The Western Kingdom takes precedence over your weekly grocery supply. I'll start unpacking." The sound of his footsteps fades toward the kitchen, followed by the telltale rustle of paper bags and the soft clink of glass bottles. It's a strange domestic noise that has become the soundtrack to my life. My kidnapper, my jailer, my personal chef, and, against all odds, my friend. It's a weird, complicated relationship that would probably make any therapist's head explode. But it's mine. And right now, he's interrupting a very important moment of literary idiocy. The nerve.

True to my word, ten minutes later, the hero has predictably gotten himself captured, the princess has revealed her evil-but-tragic backstory, and I've slammed the book shut with a satisfied sigh. I stretch, my joints popping in protest, and wander out of my book cave and toward the kitchen. The smell of fresh bread and something citrusy hangs in the air. Caleb is standing at the marble island, arranging vegetables on the counter. He's traded his tailored suit for a soft grey Henley that makes his shoulders look even broader, and his messy brown hair is catching the afternoon light. For a terrifying creature of the night, he's ridiculously domestic.

"Did you remember the yellow cheese this time?" I ask, leaning against the doorframe.

He glances up, and his ridiculously blue eyes crinkle at the corners. "Yes, Willow, I got your gross, plastic-y, an-offense-to-dairy-everywhere yellow cheese." He gestures with a carrot to a block of bright orange cheddar on the counter. "It's sitting right there, contaminating the brie."

"It's not an offense; it's a classic. It melts better on toast," I argue, snagging a grape from a bunch he's just washed. "And don't you dare let it touch the brie. That's a war crime."

He shakes his head, a smile playing on his lips. "You're a strange girl." He pauses, a mischievous glint in his eyes. "Speaking of strange, I have something for you."

My eyes light up. "Is it the second book? Please tell me it's the second book. The hero just got captured by the Shadow King, and I need to know if the princess is going to rescue him or just steal his sword."

Caleb laughs, a deep, warm sound. He reaches into one of the grocery bags and pulls out not one but three new books. The rest of the series. My heart does a little happy dance. "I figured two weeks was a long time to wait to find out," he says, handing them to me.

I launch myself at him, wrapping my arms around his

waist and hugging the books to my chest. "You are the best kidnapper-slash-jailer-slash-friend a girl could ask for," I gush into his shirt.

He pats my back awkwardly. "You're welcome. Though I still don't understand your taste in literature. Or cheese." He gently disentangles himself and gestures toward the back door. "Now, before I get started on dinner and you disappear into your book cave for the next two weeks, how about a walk? I thought we could go check on those nests in the sycamore tree."

I agree instantly, my mood lifting. I slip on a pair of boots and follow him outside. The air is cool and crisp, smelling of damp earth and the faint, sweet scent of heather. It's a far cry from that first day, when stepping over the threshold meant a body-wracking jolt of electricity. A year ago, Caleb extended the range of my ankle monitor. A reward, he'd said, for not trying to stab him again. Now I can wander the grounds, sit under the ancient sycamore and read, or just walk to the edge of the tree line and stare into the dense, mysterious woods. We're in Scotland, he'd told me. And against all odds, I've fallen in love with its wild, rugged beauty.

That first night feels like a lifetime ago. The info-dump to end all info-dumps. Finding out my parents weren't my parents, but 'handlers.' That my real family was dead, killed by rogue vampires. That Caleb, my ridiculously handsome captor, was also a vampire, and old as fuck. And, in the most crushing blow of all, that vampires don't glitter. It was a lot to swallow. The prophecy was the weirdest part. Apparently, I'm the lynchpin of some cosmic prophecy, and the fate of the world depends on me living a long, boring, human life and dying of old age. No pressure.

"It would be safer if you just turned me," I'd argued one night, after a particularly vivid nightmare about rogue vampires. "Then the prophecy would be moot, and I could help you fight."

He'd just shaken his head, his expression unreadable. "No." Just… no. Rude. But whatever. It's not like I can force him.

We reach the sycamore tree, and I point up at the nests. "See? I told you there were three." I lean against the rough bark, looking up at him. "You know, for a terrifying creature of the night, you're surprisingly good at this whole guardian thing. You're like my fairy god-vamp."

He throws his head back and laughs, a genuine, unguarded sound that makes my chest feel warm. "A fairy god-vamp? I wish. I don't have the glittery wings to live up to that title."

"That's too bad," I say with a dramatic sigh, a real smile spreading across my face. "I've always wanted to fly." We start walking back toward the house as the sky begins to blush with the first hints of sunset. "So, this fancy vampire meeting in London. What exactly does a 'mediator' do? Do you have to use a spray bottle when the ancient ones start hissing at each other?"

He chuckles, kicking at a loose stone on the path. "It's not quite that dramatic. Mostly, it's about navigating egos that are even older than I am. My sire… he's a visionary, but he's not always the most… diplomatic. I'm there to be the calm, rational one. To translate his grand ideas into something the more… traditional members can stomach without throwing a tantrum."

"So you're a vampire guidance counselor," I deadpan. "Do you have a little office with a couch and one of those desktop Zen gardens?"

"Ha. No. My office is usually a stuffy, windowless room with a lot of scowling vampires who still think the printing press was a mistake," he says, a wry twist to his lips. "But it's important. My sire is trying to build a better, safer world for our kind, and someone has to wrangle the grumpy old men who are stuck in the past."

"Well, I'm glad it's you and not me," I say, bumping his arm with my shoulder as we reach the kitchen door. "I'd probably tell them to get over it or turn to dust already."

"And that, my dear Willow, is why you are not the mediator," he says, holding the door open for me.

The kitchen is warm and smells of garlic and herbs now. Caleb gets to work, moving with an easy, practiced grace that's mesmerizing to watch. He's making pasta from scratch, because of course he is. He hands me a head of garlic and a knife. "You're on garlic duty."

"My greatest culinary skill," I say, taking the knife. I start chopping, my technique more enthusiastic than precise. "So, are you nervous? About the meeting?"

He's kneading the pasta dough, his movements strong and sure. "A little," he admits, not looking at me. "It's a lot of responsibility. And the kings will be there. They're… intense."

"Intense as in 'stare into your soul and judge your every life choice' intense, or intense as in 'might rip your throat out if you use the wrong fork' intense?" I ask, my hands now covered in sticky garlic juice.

"A healthy mix of both," he says, with a serious note in his voice. He finishes kneading the dough and starts rolling it out with a speed and precision that's just showing off. "Just stay out of trouble while I'm gone, okay? No trying to escape, no trying to fight any rogue vampires that might wander by."

"Hey! I only tried to stab you that one time," I protest, holding up my garlic-y hands in surrender. "And you have to admit, you were being very kidnap-y."

He cracks a smile. "Fair enough." He puts the pasta through the cutter, and perfect little ribbons of fettuccine fall onto the counter. "Now, are you going to help me with the sauce, or are you just going to stand there and critique my life choices?"

We eat at the massive dining room table, which usually feels cavernous and lonely, but tonight, with two plates of fresh pasta and a bowl of salad between us, it feels almost cozy. The food is, as always, incredible. We talk about the book I just finished, about the new nests in the tree, about nothing and everything. It's easy. Comfortable. And the whole time, a little knot of dread is tightening in my stomach. Two weeks. It's going to be a long two weeks.

"You'll be okay, you know," he says, as if reading my mind. He's leaning back in his chair, a glass of red wine—for him, blood-red and probably from some ancient, priceless vintage; for me, a non-alcoholic sparkling cider that he insists on serving in a fancy wine glass—held loosely in his hand. "You have a fortress of books and a fridge full of cheese."

"I know," I say, pushing a piece of pasta around my plate. "But I'll still miss my fairy god-vamp."

He smiles, a real, soft smile that reaches his eyes. "I'll miss my snarky, cheese-obsessed human, too. Now eat your dinner. It's a long two weeks, and you'll need your strength for all that reading."

CHAPTER 3

THEODORE

The grandfather clock in the hall is ticking. Loudly. Each tick is a tiny hammer blow against my last nerve. We're late. Not 'fashionably late' like my brother Oscar probably thinks is a thing, but actually, offensively late. The car has been idling on the gravel drive for seventeen minutes. I know this because I've counted every single agonizing second. We live in a castle just south of London. It's not a long drive to the annual meeting. But at this rate, we'll be lucky to get there by next Tuesday.

My fingers are drumming a frantic, silent rhythm against the handle of my suitcase. This whole place is a monument to wasted time. Centuries of dust and memories clinging to every stone. I hate it. It's drafty, it's pretentious, and right now, it's the cage holding my ridiculously slow brother hostage. Probably by his own reflection.

That's it. I've had enough. "OSCAR!" My voice echoes through the grand hall, bouncing off the ridiculously high, tapestry-covered ceilings. "If your perfectly coiffed ass is not down here in the next ten seconds, I am leaving you behind to explain to the entire council why you were too busy contemplating your own navel to attend the most important meeting of the year!"

The silence that follows is almost more infuriating than the ticking clock. Then finally, a sound from the top of the grand staircase. Not the sound of someone rushing, of course. But the soft, measured tread of someone who doesn't have a single care in the world. He appears, and I swear to God, he's moving in slow motion. His black hair is perfect. His tailored suit is immaculate, not a single crease. The intricate black ink of his tattoos peeks out from the cuffs of his crisp white shirt as he adjusts a cufflink, a look of serene concentration on his face. He's a walking, talking personification of my last nerve.

He glides down the stairs, his movements fluid and unhurried. He reaches the bottom, stops in front of me, and gives me a slow, deliberate once-over. A small, infuriating smile plays on his lips. "Theodore," he says, his voice as smooth as the silk lining of his jacket. "Calm down. You'll give yourself an aneurysm."

"I'll give you an aneurysm," I snarl, snatching his suit bag from his shoulder. "We're late."

"We're kings," he retorts, his voice infuriatingly placid. He turns and, as we walk toward the door, he pauses to straighten a painting on the wall that is already perfectly straight. His fingers, covered in the same black ink as his arms, ghost over the frame, checking for dust. My jaw clenches so hard I'm surprised my teeth don't crack. This is what he does. His anxiety manifests in these tiny, maddening acts of control. Straightening paintings, aligning his cufflinks, alphabetizing his goddamn sock drawer. It's his way of holding himself together. It's also my personal hell.

"Jasper is already in the city," I say, my voice tight, as I yank the heavy oak door open. "Probably charming his way through the junior council members and leaving a trail of broken hearts and empty blood bags."

"Someone has to have fun," Oscar says, stepping out into the weak morning light. He winces, pulling a pair of sunglasses from his pocket and sliding them on. "And it's certainly not going to be you."

He's right, of course. Fun is a luxury I can't afford. Not when the fate of our entire species rests on us finding one girl. A girl we've been hunting for nearly two centuries. A girl who is supposed to be the cure to the curse that made us what we are. The one who is supposed to fill the gaping, aching void in our souls. The one Oscar obsessively searches for on his phone, the one Jasper tries to forget in the arms of a different human every night, and the one I… I just carry. A constant, heavy weight.

The driver, a silent man named Arthur who has been with us for decades, holds the car door open. I slide into the cool leather of the backseat; the tinted windows instantly shield me from the irritatingly cheerful morning. It's not that we're allergic to the sun. That's a ridiculous myth, probably started by some dramatic idiot in the 1600s. We don't burn; we don't sparkle—thank Christ. The truth is much more boring. The sun just… sucks. It's a low-grade fever on the skin, a constant, draining hum of energy. The world is too bright, too loud, too much. We keep to a nighttime routine because it's quieter, more efficient, and frankly, less noticeable when you can move faster than the human eye can track. It's just nicer. But for this annual dog and pony show, we endure.

Oscar gets on the other side, his phone already in his hand. "I still don't see why we have to attend in person," he mutters, his thumb starting its rhythmic, obsessive swipe across the screen. "It's the same self-congratulatory bullshit every year."

"It's called tradition, Oscar," I say, my voice dripping with sarcasm. "Something you might appreciate if you ever looked up from that damn phone. We go, we smile, we remind everyone who's in charge, and then we come home. It's a performance. And you, my dear brother, are an excellent actor."

He doesn't answer, his attention completely absorbed by the glowing screen. He's searching. Always searching. For her. The girl. Our mate. The one who is supposed to be the cure for this cursed existence. The one who is supposed to fill the gaping, aching void in our souls that was carved into us the night we were turned. For nearly two hundred years, we've been hunting for a ghost. A whisper. A prophecy. And the waiting is a poison that has seeped into my very bones. She is mine. Ours. She belongs to us, and the fact that she is out there, somewhere, living a life that doesn't involve me, is a constant, burning insult. I want her. Not just want. I need to possess her, to own her, to finally have the one thing that is rightfully mine. The frustration is a living thing inside me, a caged beast that claws at my ribs.

"Anything?" I ask, my voice tight.

Oscar doesn't look up. "The usual. Dead ends.

Corrupted data. A thousand faces that are close, but not right." He sighs in frustration. "It's like trying to find a specific grain of sand on a beach that spans the entire globe."

"Then search harder," I snap, the beast in my chest roaring. "She's out there, Oscar. I can feel it. And I'm done waiting."

"We're all done waiting, Theo," he says, his voice quiet, but with an edge of steel. "Jasper is already in London, running his teams ragged. He's got his hunters sweeping for any sign of rogue activity that might lead us to her, and his security team is turning the hotel inside out, making sure this meeting goes off without a hitch. He deals with his frustration by doing. I deal with it by searching. And you… you just get angry."

He's right. And I hate him for it. I turn to look out the window, the English countryside a blur of green and grey. He's right. Jasper throws himself into action, into violence and fleeting pleasures. Oscar throws himself into data, into patterns and possibilities. And I… I just let the anger burn. It's the only thing that feels real anymore. The only thing that fills the void, even for a moment.

The car pulls up to the curb in front of The Corinthian, its gleaming glass and steel facade a monument to modern excess. A bellboy in a crisp uniform rushes to open the door. He's young, his face a mixture of awe and terror. Good. A little fear is healthy.

"Welcome back," he says, his voice trembling slightly.

I just grunt and get out. Oscar gives the driver his instructions. "We will be returning to the castle in two weeks. Tuesday. Be here at seven am. On the dot."

"Yes, sir," Arthur says, his face impassive.

The bellboy has already loaded our bags onto a golden trolley. He follows us into the lobby, the wheels of the trolley silent on the plush carpet. We don't stop at the main check-in desk. We walk straight to a discreet, unmarked door at the back of the lobby. Our private lift. The bellboy slides the trolley into the mirrored interior, his hands shaking slightly. He doesn't move to get in. He knows the rule. He's not allowed. No one is.

I press the button for the penthouse, the doors sliding shut with a soft hiss, leaving the terrified bellboy behind. It's a good rule. It's our rule. After all, we own the hotel. The whole damn building. A fact that no one, not even the poor, trembling bellboy, knows but us.

CHAPTER 4

JASPER

The air in the underground car park of The Corinthian is cold, sterile, and smells of concrete dust and expensive exhaust fumes. It's a nice change from the cloying scent of old money and desperation that permeates the lobby upstairs. I'm leaning against the hood of my Aston Martin, a beautiful, sleek beast of a machine that's currently gathering dust while I'm stuck here playing security guard. Around me, my team is assembled. Ten of the meanest, fastest, most loyal bastards you'll ever meet. They're all dressed in sharp, dark suits, looking more like a high-end security detail for a pop star than a clean-up crew for supernatural messes. Which I guess is kind of the point.

"Alright, listen up, you ugly bastards," I say, my voice echoing slightly in the cavernous space. I push off the car and start to pace in front of them, my own suit, a custom number I had made in Milan, moving with me like a second skin. "Theodore and Oscar are upstairs, probably arguing about the correct way to breathe.

Which means the annual 'Who's the Dustiest Vampire?' convention is about to begin. And that means we're on duty."

A few of them crack a smile. They know the drill. This meeting is the biggest pain in my ass all year. A bunch of ancient relics in a room, pretending they don't hate each other while they posture and preen. It's my job to make sure none of them gets any bright ideas.

"Standard formation," I continue, pointing to different members of the team. "Liam, Anya, you've got the lobby. Look mean, look bored, try not to snack on the bellboys. Marcus, rooftop perimeter. You see anything with wings that isn't a pigeon, you let me know. The rest of you, service entrances, hallways, and mingling. You know the drill. Look intimidating, be charming, and for the love of God, don't let any of the old-timers corner you. They'll talk your ear off about the good old days of the bubonic plague."

I'm about to continue when Liam's phone buzzes. He pulls it from his pocket, his brow furrowing as he reads the screen. He looks up at me, his expression grim. "Boss," he says, his voice low. "We've got a problem."

I stop pacing. The playful energy in the air evaporates, replaced by a sudden, sharp chill. "What kind of problem?"

"A new one. Sloppy. Feeding in the middle of Camden Market. Left a witness, hysterical but alive."

I close my eyes for a second, a muscle in my jaw twitching. A new one. A rogue. Some idiot who got turned and wasn't taught the rules. And now it's my mess to clean up. This is what I do. I'm the janitor of the vampire world.

While Theodore broods and Oscar analyzes, I'm the one who takes out the trash.

"Idiot," I mutter, opening my eyes. They're all looking at me, waiting. "Anya," I say, my voice flat, all traces of humor gone. "You're with Liam. Go to Camden. Find it." I look them both in the eye, my voice dropping to a low, cold whisper. "Put it down. Be discreet. No more witnesses. And for God's sake, don't make a mess. I just had this suit dry-cleaned."

They both nod, a silent, perfect understanding passing between them. They're good. The best. They turn and head for one of the black sedans parked in the corner, moving with a silent, deadly grace. In a moment, they're gone, the only sound the soft purr of the engine as they disappear up the ramp.

I turn back to the rest of the team, a wide, easy grin spreading across my face. The fun-loving mask is back in place. "Now," I say, clapping my hands together. "Where were we? Ah, yes. The art of looking intimidating while being bored out of your minds. Let's continue."

I wrap up the briefing, sending the rest of my team to their posts with a final warning not to drink all the good stuff from the blood bar before I get there. They disperse, melting into the shadows of the car park, and I'm left alone with the low hum of the ventilation system. I check the ridiculously expensive watch on my wrist. Four pm. The main event doesn't kick off until nine pm. Five hours. My brothers just rolled in, fresh from their beauty sleep in the castle, but I've been up since five am. For these big events, I switch to a human schedule. It's a necessary evil. It means I'm on the ground, running my teams, and dealing with messes like the Camden idiot while the rest of our kind are still tucked into their coffins, or whatever the hell they sleep in. It's also exhausting. The sun doesn't hurt me, not really, but being awake during the day feels like walking through water. Everything is just a little bit harder, a little bit slower. And it makes me hungry.

There's a strict 'no biting' rule once the event starts. It's a sensible precaution, really. You get 200-plus vampires in one spot, many of whom have the self-control of a toddler in a candy store, and things can get messy. One little nibble leads to another, and before you know it, you've got a bloodbath in the ballroom and a PR nightmare on your hands. So, from nine pm. onwards, it's blood bags only. O-negative in a pouch. It's like drinking a cold, metallic smoothie, and it's just as appealing as it sounds.

But it's not nine yet. I have a five-hour window. And I am not going to survive a night of political bullshit and my brothers' brooding on an empty stomach. I need a real meal. Something warm, something fresh. Something with a pulse.

I take a back elevator up to the ground floor and slip out a side entrance into a bustling London alley. The city is loud, the rumble of a double-decker bus vibrating through the soles of my shoes, the smell of fried onions and diesel fumes clinging to the air, the overwhelming cacophony of a thousand heartbeats thrumming around me. I straighten my tie, run a hand through my hair, and melt into the afternoon crowd, a shark gliding through a school of fish.

A group of tourists, loud and laughing, their blood thrumming with the cheap sugar of their sodas. Too sweet. I pass them by. A businessman, his heart a frantic, stressed-out jackhammer, barks into his phone. His blood would taste of stale coffee and anxiety. Bitter. I keep moving, my senses cast out like a net. I'm looking for a different rhythm, a different flavor in the air. Something to savor.

I turn down a quieter side street, the roar of the main road fading to a dull hum. Cobblestones replace pavement, and the frantic energy of the city gives way to a slower, more deliberate pace. Bookshops and little cafes line the street, their windows glowing warmly in the late afternoon light. The individual heartbeats are clearer here, each one a distinct note in the quiet air.

And then I hear it. A slow, sad melody. A heartbeat that's heavy with a sorrow that's almost… beautiful. I follow the sound, my eyes scanning the tables outside a small cafe. And there she is. A book is open on the table in front of her, but she's not reading. Her gaze is fixed on something far away, her shoulders slumped. As I watch, a single tear escapes and traces a slow, glittering path down her cheek. The scent of her blood hits me then, carried on the breeze. It's a complex bouquet—the sharp tang of sorrow, the sweetness of youth, the rich, dark notes of a deep, unspoken pain. It's perfect.

A slow, predatory smile spreads across my face. This is the game. This is the hunt. I smooth the lapels of my suit, adjust my cuffs, and start walking toward her, my footsteps silent on the cobblestones.

I'm halfway to her table, my mind already playing out the next hour, when it hits me. It's not a sound, not a sight. It's a scent, but that's not the right word. It's an explosion. It's the sweet, intoxicating aroma of rain-soaked earth after a long drought, the warm, comforting scent of old books and vanilla, the sharp, electric tang of ozone in the air just before a lightning strike. It's everything, all at once, bringing me to a dead stop in the middle of the cobblestone street.

The girl at the cafe — her sad, pretty face, her perfect, tragic scent—she's gone. Wiped from my mind. The world around me dissolves into a dull, grey, insignificant blur. Nothing matters but this. This scent. This feeling.

My fangs drop, a painful, aching pressure in my gums that I haven't felt with this kind of intensity in over a century. I clap a hand over my mouth, a strangled groan escaping my lips. My skin is on fire, every nerve ending screaming. I spin around, a desperate, frantic circle, my eyes wide, my senses stretched to their absolute limit, trying to catch another wisp of it. People jostle past me, their faces a blur of annoyance, their own scents a foul, cloying miasma that only highlights the impossible purity of the one I'm chasing. My heart, a long-dormant organ, is hammering against my ribs like a trapped bird.

And then, just as suddenly as it appeared, it's gone. Vanished. The world rushes back in, loud and garish and utterly, painfully empty. The void in my chest, the constant, dull ache I've lived with for two hundred years, rips open, a searing, white-hot agony. That was it. That was her. Our mate. And I lost her.

For a long moment, I just stand there, frozen, the weight of two centuries of fruitless searching crashing down on me. The hunger is still there, a low, angry growl in my gut, but now it's twisted with the bitter taste of loss and frustration. The girl at the cafe is still there, oblivious, but the thought of her now, her simple, sad scent, is like ash in my mouth. I can't. Not now.

I turn on my heel, my movements jerky and uncoordinated, and head for the nearest dark doorway, a pub called The Gilded Cage. How fitting. I need noise; I need a distraction; I need to fill this howling emptiness with something, anything, even if it's just for a few hours. I need blood, and I need a shag. And I need to forget the scent of everything I've ever wanted, disappearing on the afternoon air.

The noise hits me first as I push through the heavy wooden door. A wall of loud, boisterous chatter, the clinking of glasses, the dull thud of bass from a jukebox in the corner. My eyes, already adjusted to the dim light of the evening, scan the room with a predator's cold, detached efficiency. And there she is. A beautiful redhead, sitting alone at the bar, nursing a glass of amber liquid. Her posture is relaxed, confident, but there's a slight tightness around her eyes that speaks of a long day, of stress she's trying to drown. Perfect. A perfect distraction. A perfect temporary oblivion.

I make my way over to her, my movements smooth and silent despite the heavy boots on my feet. I slide onto the empty stool beside her, close enough that she can feel the coolness of my body, the subtle shift in the air. "Would you like another drink, love?" I ask, my voice a low, intimate purr that cuts through the noise of the pub and lands directly in her ear.

She turns to face me, her green eyes, flecked with gold, studying me with a careful, assessing gaze. She's not immediately bowled over. Good. I like a little bit of a challenge. "Depends," she says, her voice a little coy, a little challenging. "On who's asking."

I reach up and push back the hood of my jacket, letting her get a good look. I offer her a slow, lazy smile, the one I know makes women's knees weak. I feel the familiar, subtle shift in the air as my glamour, the supernatural allure that's both a gift and a curse, settles over her. I see the slight, almost imperceptible drooping of her eyelids, the soft, involuntary hitch in her breath. It's a power I hate, and yet, I use it without a second thought when the hunger or the emptiness becomes too much to bear.

"I'll have whatever you're having, love," I say, leaning in close, my lips brushing against the shell of her ear. I watch with detached, clinical satisfaction as goosebumps rise on the pale skin of her arms.

"Jameson," she replies, her voice a little breathy now, the challenge gone, replaced by a dawning fascination.

I signal the barman, a harried-looking man with a weary face, and order two. I hand him a fifty. "Keep the change," I say, my tone dismissing him before he's even taken the note. He doesn't argue.

I grab my drink and down it in one smooth, burning swallow, the alcohol doing nothing to numb the raw, gaping ache in my chest. I look over at the redhead, whose name I still don't know. "What's your name?" I ask, my voice soft, intimate.

"Sophie," she says, holding out a hand that's not quite steady. I take it, my fingers cool against her warm skin, and turn it over, pressing a light, lingering kiss to the back of it. Her breath hitches again.

"A pleasure to meet you, Sophie," I say, my eyes

holding hers, drawing her in. "Would you like to get out of here?"

She doesn't hesitate. Not for a second. "Yes," she breathes, and slams her own drink back in one go, the whiskey making her gasp.

It's only a short, five-minute walk to her apartment, and she fills the silence with a string of breathless, eager questions. I give her a shortened version of my name, "Jas," and a vague, plausible story about visiting family for an annual meeting. She seems to buy it, her mind already clouded by the glamour and the promise of what's to come, her focus narrowed to me and me alone.

When we reach her door, she fumbles with the key fob, her hands trembling slightly with anticipation. She walks straight in and then turns to look at me, still standing on the threshold, a silent, hooded figure in her brightly lit hallway.

"Well?" she says, a playful, inviting smile on her lips. "Are you going to come in?"

"Are you inviting me?" I purr, playing along with the age-old, ridiculous ritual that is, for some reason, still a part of our nature.

"Are you a vampire, Jas?" she teases, her voice light and flirtatious. "Do you need an invitation?"

"No," I reply, my voice dropping, losing its playful edge and taking on the true, ancient cadence of my real voice, a sound that holds the weight of centuries. "But call me old-fashioned. I like to be invited."

"Well then, kind sir," she says, her eyes wide and dark and full of me. "I would like to extend a formal invitation for you to enter my humble abode."

"Why, thank you, kind lady," I say, stepping over the threshold and closing the door behind me, shutting out the rest of the world, shutting out the memory of the scent I had lost.

I cup her face in my hands, my touch gentle but firm, and guide her lips to mine. The kiss is an obligation, a means to an end, a desperate attempt to fill the howling void within me, but she responds with an eagerness that's almost pathetic in its intensity. Her arms wrap around my neck as my hands roam down her body, the soft fabric of her blouse a thin, insignificant barrier between my skin and hers. I deepen the kiss, my mind a million miles away, and lift her into my arms. She wraps her legs around my waist, and we stumble toward her couch in a clumsy, desperate dance.

Her skin is warm and smooth under my touch as I dispense with her clothes, my movements efficient and practiced, my mind detached. I nip and suck at her nipples until they're hard, pebble-like points, my hands tracing every curve and dip of her body with a reverence she hasn't earned and I don't feel. It still doesn't feel right, this empty, physical act, but I push the thought away, giving in to the mindless, fleeting act of it.

"Oh, Jas, that feels so good," she moans, her head thrown back, her eyes closed in ecstasy.

I free myself from my jeans, and she immediately reaches for me, her hands closing around my length. I pull her down onto me, and she cries out, a loud, unrestrained sound that I hope her neighbour's can hear. The thought of being listened to, of being watched, is a small, cheap thrill that always manages to heighten the experience, a pathetic substitute for the real connection I crave.

"Fuck me, Sophie," I instruct, my voice a low, guttural growl.

She moves with a newfound intensity, her body flush against mine, her hands braced on my chest. I grip her hips, guiding her, urging her on, matching her rhythm. The heat between us is palpable, the tension building, but it's a hollow, meaningless heat, a fire with no warmth. I can feel the climax approaching, the familiar, tingling build-up, and with a final, deep kiss, I guide her head to the side, baring the long, elegant column of her neck. I plant small, teasing kisses along her skin, a predator playing with its food, searching for the perfect spot, the place where her pulse throbs just beneath the surface with a frantic, bird-like rhythm. And when I find it, I sink my fangs into her.

She shatters around me, her body convulsing, her orgasm a tidal wave that's a direct result of my bite. My own release is a distant secondary event, a footnote to the main event. My thirst, now that it's awakened, takes over, and I drink deeply, pulling long, hard draughts from her neck until the frantic beating of her heart begins to slow to a steady, rhythmic thump. Then, with a final, lingering lick, I run my tongue over the marks, the supernatural saliva sealing the wounds as if they had never been.

I lift her off me, her body limp and pliant, a beautiful, empty doll, and gently lay her down on the couch, covering her with a soft throw blanket. I look into her dazed, unfocused eyes, her pupils blown wide, her mind a blank slate.

"I want you to forget my face," I say, my voice firm,

the compulsion settling over her like a thick, impenetrable shroud. "All you will remember is going to the bar and meeting a mysterious, handsome stranger. You came back here and had the best, most mind-blowing sex of your life. After it was over, he left. You will not remember my name, my voice, or anything else about me. When you try to picture my face, all you will see is a blur."

I lean in and give her a gentle, meaningless kiss on the cheek before letting myself out of her apartment, the click of the lock echoing in the silent hallway.

As I make my way back toward The Corinthian, a familiar, fleeting twinge of guilt pricks at me. But it's a necessary evil, a small price to pay for our survival, for the secrecy that keeps us safe. Besides, she'll wake up feeling satisfied and happy, with no memory of what truly happened between us. She'll have her perfect night, a fantasy to replay in her mind. And I… I'll have this gnawing, relentless emptiness, an emptiness now made a thousand times worse by the memory of a scent that promised everything and had left me with nothing. A fair trade, I suppose. A fair trade.

Chapter 5

Oscar

The penthouse is quiet. Too quiet. Jasper was supposed to be here an hour ago, but the air is still, empty, and worst of all, beginning to feel stale. I can almost feel the particles of dust settling on every surface, a slow, invisible contamination. I don't need to run a predictive algorithm to know what's delayed him. After two centuries, my youngest brother's patterns are as predictable as the tides. A pretty face, a fleeting dalliance, a momentary, messy oblivion from the gnawing emptiness that plagues us all. He's lucky our particular affliction prevents procreation and the transmission of human diseases. Otherwise, he'd have a brood of illegitimate offspring scattered across the globe and be riddled with something unpleasant, like syphilis. The thought makes my skin crawl — an itch I can't scratch.

I retreat to the sanctuary of my own quarters, my fingers already twitching with the need to straighten, to organise, to control. The suit for this year's conference—a magnificent creation of midnight-blue wool and silk—

needs to be hung properly. I open the doors to my wardrobe, and the familiar, comforting scent of cedar and lavender washes over me, a balm to my frayed nerves. Inside, my suits are arranged in a perfect gradient of colour, from the darkest charcoals to the palest greys. But my gaze is drawn to the left, to the section for formal occasions, and my jaw clenches. Seven suits, each worn only once for this same tedious annual event, hang in their protective bags. And on the shoulders of those bags, a fine, almost imperceptible layer of dust has settled. An unacceptable film of neglect. A prickle of irritation crawls across my skin, spreading like a rash.

Theo, in his infinite, weary pragmatism, always tells me it's perfectly acceptable to wear a suit more than once. He fails to comprehend that it's not a matter of practicality, but of data. Each year, this conference represents another rotation of the wheel, another marker of our endless, unchanging existence. Each unworn suit is a data point of failure. To wear the same one twice would be to accept a null result, to admit that we are no closer to our goal than we were the year before. It's a small, perhaps foolish, rebellion. But it's mine.

With a sigh that's less about the physical effort and more about the mental weight of it all, I gather the seven heavy bags over my shoulder, the weight of them pulling at my muscles. The fabric rustles, a dry, whispering sound that sets my teeth on edge. I carry them out to the opulent lounge and carefully drape them over the back of the cream-coloured couch, my fingers smoothing out each bag, taking great care not to disturb the perfectly arranged decorative pillows. I pick up the telephone, the cool plastic against my ear, and call down to the lobby, my voice calm and measured as I arrange for a concierge to retrieve the bags for donation. They are to be left just outside the main penthouse door, a door we never use. We have our own private lift, a silent, gleaming box that ascends directly from the secure parking garage to the heart of our apartment. It's a necessary precaution. Guests on the rare occasions we have them use the external lift. I place the bags outside, the corridor beyond feeling alien and contaminated, the air thick with the scent of strangers and their germs. I scurry back inside, the click of the lock a satisfying sound of security, and make my way back to my room. The weekly cleaner has been, but I can't shake the nagging, persistent feeling that things are not truly clean unless I attend to them myself.

I begin with the dusting, my cloth moving over every surface with a practiced, meticulous grace, each stroke deliberate and precise. I change the sheets on my bed, stripping away the old ones and folding them into a perfect square before placing them in the linen bag. The crisp, cool scent of freshly laundered linen is a small, profound pleasure as I smooth the new sheets over the mattress, tucking in each corner. I vacuum every inch of the plush carpet, the machine's hum a soothing, monotonous song, watching the dirt and dust disappear into the canister. How can I ever be certain that the cleaner was as thorough, as dedicated to the eradication of every last speck of dust? I can't. And that uncertainty is a germ in itself, a nagging thought that burrows into my brain and refuses to leave.

Once my own sanctuary is restored to a state of perfect order, I step out, intending to see if Theodore requires anything. A pile of crumpled sheets lies discarded on the floor outside his open door, a small, chaotic heap that makes my fingers twitch. Inside, I can see him diligently wiping down each piece of furniture. He knows me. He knows I won't be able to rest until the entire apartment is spotless. A silent understanding passes between us as I scoop up the abandoned linens and add them to my own.

"Thank you," I say quietly.

He pauses, glancing up at me, and a small, mean smile tugs at the corner of his lips. "Don't mention it. Though I'm surprised you haven't already disinfected the entire hallway."

I feel my jaw tighten. "I was getting to it."

"Of course you were," he says, his voice dry. But there's no real malice in it, just a weary understanding. He turns back to his task, and I continue on to Jasper's room.

Jasper's room is next. His door creaks open to reveal a scene of predictable, almost charming, chaos. A messy, unmade bed, the sheets tangled and twisted, clothes strewn about the floor in haphazard heaps, the lingering scent of some fleeting, feminine perfume mixed with the metallic tang of blood and the musky, unmistakable smell of sex. It's no surprise. He was turned just as he was emerging from the throes of puberty, and though he now possesses the physical appearance of a man, his domestic habits remain stubbornly adolescent. With a deep, resigned sigh, I begin the familiar ritual. I strip his bed, gathering up the dirty laundry, the pungent scent of his exertions filling my nostrils and making my stomach turn. I deposit the discarded clothes into the hamper, holding them at arm's length, before moving on to cleaning and dusting every surface. I make his bed with fresh linen, my hands smoothing out every last crease. For a brief, fleeting moment, everything is in its proper place.

"Theo? Oscar?" Jasper's voice calls from the lift, echoing off the polished marble of the foyer. Speak of the devil, and he shall arrive. A small, rare smile touches my lips.

"In here," I call back, my voice calm and even.

The sound of his footsteps approaches, a confident, unhurried stride. And then he appears in the doorway, and the full force of his recent activities makes the room smell gross. He's still in his suit, but it's rumpled now, the tie loosened and hanging askew, the top two buttons of his shirt undone. His black hair is even more disheveled than usual, sticking up in places where fingers—not his own—have clearly run through it. There's a faint, telltale smudge of lipstick on the collar of his shirt, a dark red stain that stands out against the crisp white fabric. And the smell. God, the smell. It's a chaotic, unhygienic cocktail of his own familiar cologne, the cloying, floral scent of a woman's perfume, the musky, unmistakable smell of sex, and underneath it all, the faint, metallic tang of blood. It's overwhelming, invasive, and it makes my skin crawl.

A mischievous, self-satisfied grin is plastered on his face, his deep brown eyes sparkling with unrepentant amusement. His steps are light, utterly devoid of guilt or shame. He looks like a cat who's just devoured a canary and is very pleased with himself.

"I see you were… delayed," I say, my tone dry, one eyebrow raised in a silent, well-practiced expression of disapproval. My fingers twitch, wanting to reach out and straighten his tie, to button his shirt, to restore some semblance of order to his appearance.

"What ever gave you that impression?" he grins back, his voice a low, playful purr.

"Oh, I don't know," I reply, allowing a hint of my own amusement to colour my voice despite the discomfort crawling across my skin. "Perhaps the lingering scent of a perfume I don't recognize, or the thoroughly self-satisfied look upon your face. Or the lipstick on your collar. Or the fact that you smell like you've been rolling around in a… a… a petri dish of human fluids."

Theodore's voice cuts in from his room, sharp and mean. "A petri dish? Oscar, that's generous. He smells like a brothel."

Jasper throws his head back and laughs, a genuine, unguarded sound. "You're both just jealous."

"Jealous of what?" Theodore calls back. "Your complete lack of standards?"

"My ability to have fun," Jasper counters, still grinning.

Theodore appears in his doorway, leaning against the frame, his arms crossed. "Fun. Is that what we're calling it now?" His voice is cutting, but there's a faint, almost imperceptible softening around his eyes. He understands. We all do. It's Jasper's way, this relentless pursuit of sex. His coping mechanism.

When we first learned of her existence, Jasper was adamant, almost puritanical, in his insistence that he would remain faithful. But after fifty years of waiting, of a hope that dwindled with each passing decade, he gave in. Now, he seeks physical interactions wherever he can find it, a temporary balm for an eternal wound. Even Theodore succumbs now and then, though it's a rare occurrence, and one he always seems to regret with a profound, self-flagellating guilt. As for myself, I have been fiercely, unshakeably loyal to the idea of my mate since the moment I discovered her existence. It has been one hundred and ninety years, give or take, since I last shared my body with another. The data is clear. It is an inefficient, messy, and ultimately unsatisfying solution to the problem.

"Thank you for taking care of my room," Jasper says, his grin softening into something more genuine as he looks at me.

"It's no problem, little brother," I reply, a genuine affection warming my tone despite the lingering discomfort. "Though I cannot comprehend how you could even consider sleeping in that bed."

"The cleaner changed the sheets just two days ago," he sighs, a familiar note of exasperation in his voice. "They still smelled of washing powder."

"That does not necessarily mean they were clean," I counter, unable to help myself.

Theodore snorts from his doorway. "Oscar, if you had your way, we'd all be living in a sterile bubble."

"At least a sterile bubble would be clean," I mutter.

"Let's just agree to disagree, shall we?" Jasper says with a chuckle, clapping a hand on my shoulder. The touch is warm, solid, and despite the chaos he brings with him, it's comforting. He then strides into his en-suite bathroom to shower off the lingering evidence of his earlier activities. The scent of his conquest — a mixture of musk and sweat and satisfaction — fills the small space as he walks past me. It is, to my finely tuned sensibilities, the very essence of chaos.

I sigh again, a long, slow exhalation, and turn my mind to the unpleasant evening that lies ahead. The conference, the politics, the endless, wearying dance. At least for now the apartment is clean.

Chapter 6

Jasper

The first meeting of the annual conference from hell is scheduled for nine o'clock, but I've been awake since seven this morning, and I am, to put it mildly, bored out of my goddamn mind. I'm currently lying sprawled on my bed, a study in calculated indolence, my legs propped up against the ridiculously ornate headboard, my arms stretched outwards like a scarecrow that has given up on scaring crows and decided to take a nap instead. The atmosphere in the room feels stagnant, heavy with the weight of my own boredom. Every year, I promise myself I'll finally adjust to a proper night routine for this tedious conference, embrace the darkness, sleep through the day, and become the nocturnal predator I was always meant to be. And every year, I find myself unable to tear myself away from the alluring light of day. The sun is loud and distracting, and right now, I'd kill for a little distraction.

I hate this conference. It's the most dull, soul-crushingly uneventful function we're forced to attend, and yet, paradoxically, it also holds the greatest potential for danger. A single misstep, a single misplaced word, and the intricate web of lies that constitutes our existence could unravel. I'd suggested we hold the event at the Manor, our ancient, sprawling castle south of London. Eighteen rooms, a ballroom, a dining hall that could seat a small army. It would have been so much easier. But Theo shot down the idea before I could even fully articulate my brilliant, time-saving plan. The Manor, he'd reminded me with a weary sigh, was a cherished family heirloom, our sanctuary, not a bloody conference center. I, on the other hand, despise the place. It's frigid and lifeless, a stone mausoleum devoid of any hint of warmth or joy. The gnawing emptiness in my chest where my mate bond should be is somehow more pronounced within those ancient walls. I don't share the same sentimental admiration for that pile of rocks that Theo and Oscar do.

"Jasper, are you ready?" Theo's voice, laced with its usual weary patience, cuts through my thoughts. He pokes his head through the doorway, his expression one of long-suffering amusement as he takes in my dramatic, sprawled-out position on the bed.

A slow smile tugs at the corners of my mouth. I pop the 'P' in my response, drawing out the sound with a soft, satisfying plosive. "Yep."

Theo raises a single, perfectly sculpted eyebrow, his dark eyes glinting with a familiar, mischievous light. "Well, let's go, then," he says, his voice trailing off as he holds that one raised eyebrow for maximum dramatic effect. He's getting better at my games.

With a soft, theatrical laugh, I swing my legs over the

side of the bed and sit up, making my way toward him with a confident, rolling gait. My black Armani suit, tailored to absolute perfection with a crisp, white pinstripe, feels like a second skin. It's my go-to suit for this particular brand of misery, a familiar armor for a familiar battle.

"Is that last year's suit?" Theo asks, his gaze sweeping over my outfit before settling on his own, a classic, impeccably tailored navy suit that fits him like a glove.

"Sure is," I reply with a grin, turning around to show off the suit with a little, flamboyant twirl. "What can I say? It's a classic. A vintage, even."

Theo chuckles, a low, rumbling sound, and shakes his head, but I can see the hint of admiration in his eyes. "You could have bought a new suit, you know. Oscar would have a fit if he knew you were re-wearing formal attire."

I flash him another grin and a wink. "But why fix what isn't broken? Besides, it's good to have traditions. This suit and I, we have history. It would be a betrayal to abandon it now."

Theo just shakes his head at me again, a gesture that's equal parts exasperation and affection. "So, let me get this straight. I'm not allowed to wear the same suit, but you tell Oscar that buying a new one every year is a foolish extravagance and he should just re-wear his?"

Theo rubs his chin thoughtfully, a slow, deliberate gesture that means he's playing along. "I'm fairly certain," he says, his voice laced with mock seriousness, "that this particular suit was worn more than just last year. And the year before that."

A wide, triumphant smile spreads across my face as I nod in agreement. "You're right," I say, my voice filled with amusement. "This year will mark its fifth trip to this ridiculous, mind-numbing conference. We're practically a double act."

With another shake of his head, Theo turns and begins walking toward the lift. As always, we've 'rented' out the function room in this very building for our meeting. Aka owns it, but again, no one knows that but us. It saves us from the inconvenience of travel and, more importantly, helps to limit any unwanted attention.

"Oscar has already descended," Theo mutters as he presses the button for the lift, the small, illuminated circle glowing like a malevolent eye. "He scurried off twenty minutes ago to ensure that the correct, and no doubt tragically bland, menu was being served."

"Please tell me you had some say in the menu this year?" I grumble, a genuine pang of disappointment echoing in the pit of my stomach. "I need something substantial. Something that once had a face."

"Oh, I made suggestions," Theo chuckles, the sound dry and humorless. "But I am almost certain he scrapped every single one of them the moment I turned my back."

"So, it's going to be yet another sad little watercress salad with a few slivers of organic beetroot and a light dusting of some obscure, gluten-free grain," I sigh, the picture of culinary despair.

"I doubt it," Theo responds, a glint of amusement in his eyes. "Feta has been banned from the manor for the past month, if you haven't noticed. Apparently, Oscar did some extensive peer-reviewed research and discovered that the milk used in its production is not heated to his preferred, and frankly obsessive, temperature. This, he claims, results in higher levels of bacteria in the cheese, which could, and I quote, 'rot his insides'." He rolls his eyes in exasperation. "As if anything could rot our insides."

With a dramatic sigh, I run a hand down my face. "Oh, for fuck's sake. I liked feta," I say, the disappointment in my voice entirely genuine.

"So did I," Theo replies with a look of shared, sympathetic suffering.

"Please tell me you arranged to have the fridge in the apartment filled so I can at least eat something that doesn't taste of righteous indignation when we get back," I plead, my voice taking on a desperate, wheedling tone.

"Yes, I did. It will be stocked while we are in this meeting," he reassures me. "I had to wait until Oscar had performed his ritualistic cleansing of the entire appliance when we first arrived, of course."

"Thank God," I say with a palpable sense of relief. "I cannot live on rabbit food and moral superiority. My body is a temple, and it requires regular, delicious sacrifices." My smile at Theo is half genuine gratitude, half pure cheek.

"You do know you are perfectly capable of arranging to have the fridge filled yourself," Theo says, giving me a pointed, meaningful look.

"Not my job," I smirk at him, my grin wide and utterly unapologetic.

"How in the world is that not your job?" he asks, his voice a mixture of incredulity and amusement.

"Because," I explain, holding up a finger as if about to impart a piece of ancient, profound wisdom, "forty years ago, you, in a moment of weakness or perhaps uncharacteristic generosity, started filling the fridge and pantry with food for this event. You have continued to do so without fail every year since. This, according to the ancient and sacred laws of sibling delegation, solidifies it as now being your job, and your job only, for all eternity."

The lift door pinged, its cheerful sound compared to the grim reality of the evening ahead, and we step out into the lobby. As we make our way toward the conference room, the low murmuring, hustle and bustle of the hotel lobby surrounds us.

"That is not very sound logic," Theo states, a hint of laughter in his voice.

"Perhaps not," I retort, winking at him before confidently striding toward the conference room doors. "But it has served me well for the past forty years, so I believe I will stick with it."

This year, Oscar has chosen a sleek, almost painfully modern, black and white colour scheme for the event. With a proud, theatrical gesture, I spin around to face Theo, my arms spread wide to showcase my perfectly coordinated suit. "See this suit?" I declare. "It was made for this occasion. It is destiny."

"What must it be like to be perpetually nineteen?" Theo laughs, a genuine, warm sound that makes the evening seem slightly less dreadful.

"Hey now, you're only six years older than me, Grandpa," I say, playfully pointing a finger at him before turning on my heel and making my way toward the large, round table that is situated, with infuriating symmetry, in the exact center of the room.

I can never understand Oscar's insistence on a round table. It's a tactical nightmare, leaving everyone's backs exposed. As we take our seats, I can feel a familiar prickle of irritation at the thought of having my back to the door. "Come on, Grandpa," I mutter under my breath as I settle into my designated chair, my name proudly, and a little too formally, displayed on a small, engraved placard. "Let's just sit down and pretend like we give a damn."

Chapter 7

Willow

Caleb has been gone for a week. One whole, entire, seven-day week. And I am, to put it mildly, bored out of my skull. I'm twenty years old, a grown-ass woman by any reasonable standard, yet my entire world is confined to this beautiful, lonely prison with really great water pressure. My only companions are the ridiculously cheerful birds that chirp outside my window, their oblivious little songs a stark, almost cruel, counterpoint to the quiet, aching boredom in my own chest. It's like living in some twisted, forgotten fairytale, except I'm not a sleeping princess waiting for true love's kiss. No, I'm wide awake, I'm caffeinated, and I am desperately, achingly lonely.

Deep down, in the quiet, terrified corners of my heart that I try to ignore, I get it. I understand the whole prophecy deal, the weight of the burden that was dropped on my shoulders without so much as a 'by your leave.' The fate of the entire Vampire world, a world I had never asked to be a part of, apparently rests on me living a long, boring, human life. It's a terrifying, suffocating responsibility, and most days, I want nothing more than to tell the universe to go screw itself. I find myself wishing, with a fierce, selfish desperation, that Caleb would finally just bite me. Let someone else carry this curse. Let someone else be the lynchpin of their salvation. I did not sign up for this cosmic jury duty, and I am selfish enough, desperate enough, to hope for an easy way out, even if it means damnation and a sudden aversion to garlic bread.

The weight of it all, the constant, crushing pressure to save a species that I both fear and, in the form of Caleb, have come to care for, is suffocating. I'm curled up on the plush velvet couch in my library, the sound of the birds a distant, mocking echo of the freedom I crave. The book Caleb brought me, the third in a series I've become utterly lost in, is sitting on the cushions beside me. I devoured the first two with a hunger that bordered on desperation, and this one is proving to be just as addictive. It's about a girl kidnapped by a group of dangerous, morally grey criminals who, against all odds, end up falling in love with her. They even, in a twist that made my heart ache with a strange, vicarious longing, agreed to share her. Imagine that. Four hot, dangerous, tattooed men, all doting on you, their lives revolving around your happiness and safety. It sounds like a dream. For someone like me, even one man's genuine, uncomplicated affection seems entirely out of reach. My kidnapper is my best friend, and he's currently off playing vampire guidance counselor in London.

My days have fallen into a predictable, monotonous

rhythm. Breakfast outside with the birds if the sun is shining, a rare and precious treat in the Scottish highlands that makes me feel like a Disney princess, minus the singing animals and the prince. Or, more often, watching the rain droplets race each other down the glass roof of my sunroom, a small, beautiful conservatory Caleb built for me after I complained about the lack of natural light for my succulents. It's a life of quiet desperation and really, really good books.

Last year, in a fit of restless ambition, I asked Caleb if I could enroll in an online study program. I had visions of earning a degree, of having something to show for these lost years besides an encyclopedic knowledge of romance novel tropes. But he'd refused, his expression a mixture of regret and unyielding resolve. He blamed our lack of an internet connection — a practical, insurmountable obstacle. But I knew the truth. There was electricity here, enough to power this entire sprawling manor. The real reason was that he, or perhaps his mysterious boss, Mr. Whitten, deemed it too risky. I was a secret, a precious, dangerous secret that had to be protected at all costs. No Facebook for the harbinger of vampire destiny, I guess.

As a compromise, he'd started bringing me books on literature and art history, subjects he deemed to be of the utmost importance. After reading Wuthering Heights, I became utterly, hopelessly obsessed with the dark, brooding passion of it all. I was captivated by its brooding, tormented protagonist, Heathcliff. And I couldn't help but wonder, with a fierce, frustrated passion, why Catherine didn't just run away with him at the very first opportunity.

Why she had chosen a life of comfort and convention over a life of wild, untamed love. The tragic, self-destructive nature of their love story still haunted my soul, a beautiful, painful melody that played on a loop in my mind.

I find myself sitting on the wide, cushioned ledge of my bedroom window, staring out at the stormy sky, the dark, bruised clouds mirroring the turmoil in my own heart. I can't help but dream of a dark and brooding man of my own, someone who would do anything for me, someone who would, like Heathcliff, be willing to burn down the world for my love. But I know, with a certainty that's as cold and hard as the stone walls of the manor, that my reality will be far from that romantic fantasy. The Kings, the powerful, ancient vampire rulers who are hunting me, are not searching for their long-lost love. No, they want my bloodline; they want the power that's locked away in my DNA. Caleb warned me about them, how they would sweet-talk me, how they would whisper promises of love and devotion, how they would make me believe that I was their one true mate. It's a term that sends a shiver of revulsion down my spine. They would "mate" with me, and in doing so, they would gain incredible, world-shattering powers, the ability to destroy their enemies with a single, devastating glance. And once they had what they wanted, once they had drained me of my power and my purpose, they would kill me without a second thought, discarding me like a piece of rubbish.

But sometimes, in the deepest, most secret corners of my heart, in the wildest of my daydreams, I allow myself to imagine a different outcome. I imagine that one day, they would come to truly love and cherish me, that they would see me not as a means to an end, but as the end itself, just like the heroines in the romance novels I escape into. Of course, deep down, I know it's all just wishful thinking, a foolish, childish fantasy.

Caleb's boss, Mr. Whitten, was one of the original vampires, one of the few who had been there when the prophecy about my bloodline was first uttered. He knew the truth. He knew that the Kings saw me as nothing but a curse, the bane of their existence, a threat to be neutralized. And yet, he had been incredibly kind to me. He had provided me with this luxurious, beautiful home, a gilded cage to be sure, but a comfortable one nonetheless. I feel a strange, complicated gratitude for all he has done. Perhaps, I think, a new idea taking root in my mind, perhaps I could request a pet. A kitten, maybe, or a small, fluffy dog. Something warm and alive that I could confide in, something to talk to in the long, lonely hours of the day. Something that wouldn't try to save the world or suck my blood.

Loneliness is my only true ruler, the undisputed tyrant of my small kingdom. But everything else, I suppose, is manageable. I've never seen myself as someone with grand aspirations, no burning desire to conquer the world. I'm content, I think, with the idea of having someone to take care of me, of being a devoted, cherished housewife. The topic of having children had never really crossed my mind before now. In the books I read, it's either a topic that's studiously avoided, or it's used as a neat, tidy way to give the main characters their happily ever after. But it wasn't something that I actively sought out in my reading material. And now, standing here in this place where parenthood is not an option, where my future is a blank, terrifying canvas, I can't say that it makes me feel any particular emotion. It's just another impossible choice, another path not taken, in this already impossibly conflicted situation. At least a dog wouldn't care about prophecies. It would just care about walks and treats and belly rubs. And right now, that sounds like heaven.

CHAPTER 8

THEODORE

The low murmur of conversation from the assembled vampires fills the cavernous function room, a sound that grates on my already frayed nerves like nails on a chalkboard. I reach for the crisp white napkin laid out beside my plate and, with a practiced, almost unconscious movement, lay it gently across my lap. It's a small, insignificant gesture, a relic of a bygone era, but it's as ingrained in me as the very marrow of my bones. Centuries have passed since my mortal days, since a time when such niceties were not just expected, but were the very fabric of civilized society. Now, in this loud, brash, modern era, where polite behaviour seems a quaint and forgotten art, I often find myself longing for the strict, comforting etiquette lessons of my youth. It seems most people today, human and vampire alike, have no idea what the word "etiquette" even means. They're all just animals pretending to be men.

The minutes tick by, each one a small, leaden weight.

The rest of the eight — the original, ancient vampires who, along with my brothers and me, form the reluctant ruling council of our kind — begin to arrive. I rise from my seat, a mask of polite cordiality firmly in place, and greet each one with a forced smile and a firm handshake that I'm sure feels like a threat. Thomas Henry and his wife Isabella, their faces a study in aristocratic boredom, are the first to arrive. They're followed closely by Yvonne Eccleston and Edith Cottam, their conversation a low, conspiratorial buzz that I'm sure is about me. Edmund, with his perpetually grumpy expression and an air of arrogant self-importance that's almost comical, is, as always, the last to make an appearance. He moves through the room as if he believes himself to be the most important person in it, a belief that I know, with a weary certainty, is not shared by anyone else. One of these days, I'm going to put him in his place. Permanently.

Oscar, clad in a sharp, impeccably tailored suit, his face a mask of determined focus, has been meticulously planning this event for months. He's delegated tasks to each of us with his usual obsessive efficiency. I, as the eldest and, arguably, the most level-headed, have been given the unenviable responsibility of organizing the night's agenda and acting as both litigator and judge for the endless stream of petty disputes and requests that will inevitably arise. As the guests begin to take their seats, I can feel the weight of Oscar's expectations, and the even heavier weight of my own responsibilities, settling upon my shoulders like a shroud. It's a weight I'm used to carrying.

As soon as the eight of us are seated at the large, round table that Oscar, in his infinite wisdom, has insisted upon, the rest of the lower-class vampires are ushered into their seats. The term "lower class" is another relic of a bygone era, a term that has been used since the very beginning of our existence. I've never questioned it. It's simply tradition, and in a world that's constantly, dizzyingly changing, I find a strange, cold comfort in the unchanging nature of our traditions. If it ain't broke, as the modern parlance goes, don't fix it.

I uncross my legs and lean to the left, my gaze sweeping over the crowded room. My eyes meet Jasper's, and I raise my eyebrows in a silent, questioning gesture. He gives a subtle, almost imperceptible nod. I lean closer to him, my voice a low murmur that would be lost in the general din of the room. "There are at least fifty more vampires here than there were last year."

"We only approved around ten new turnings last year," Jasper replies, his own voice a low, concerned whisper. "So this is a very significant and very worrying increase."

"I'll ask Oscar how many chairs we booked last year compared to this year." I murmur, my gaze fixed on the sea of unfamiliar faces. I turn to Oscar, who is already engrossed in the leather-bound notebook that is his constant companion. I tap him on the shoulder to get his attention — a sharp, impatient rap of my knuckles. "How many chairs did we book last year, and how many this year?" I ask, my voice low and urgent.

He quickly flips through the pages of his notebook, his brow furrowed in concentration. "Two hundred and thirty-nine last year," he answers, his voice crisp and precise. "Two hundred and eighty-seven this year."

My eyebrows shoot up in surprise. "Fuck," I mutter, the curse a harsh, guttural sound in the refined atmosphere of the room. "That's forty-eight new vampires since last year. I do not recall approving that many."

Oscar nods, his expression grim. "A few couldn't make it last year due to work conflicts and requested to skip the event," he says, his pen already scribbling furiously in his notepad. "But still… the numbers seem off. very off."

The night wears on, a tedious, mind-numbing parade of endless requests for turning new vampires and ongoing, petty land disputes between the established vampire houses. Oscar's idea from one hundred and thirty years ago to divide them into individual houses and appoint a head of each was proving to be a stroke of genius. It means that we, the elders, no longer have to handle every single insignificant conflict and issue that arises. With one vampire in charge of each house, we can simply enforce the rules we've put in place. It's a system that took a great deal of effort to establish, but now it allows me to only have to deal with the teeming masses of our kind once a year, during this single, excruciatingly long gathering. And for that, I am eternally grateful.

As the clock on the far wall strikes four in the morning, we finally wrap up our work for the day. I stand up from my chair, my body stiff and weary, and reach for my jacket, which is draped over the back of my chair. On my way out, I pass Edmund, who has, with his usual lack of decorum, left a few minutes before the official end of the proceedings.

In the middle of the opulent, deserted foyer, he stands with another man, a man whose hair is a dark, rich brown, and whose face is unfamiliar to me. I assume he's one of Edmund's innumerable lackeys. Just as I'm about to pass by them, an unfamiliar, intoxicating scent hits my nostrils. It's a scent that's both sweet and earthy, a scent that speaks of rain-soaked forests and old, leather-bound books, a scent that's so utterly compelling that my fangs, with a will of their own, involuntarily extend. Panic, cold and sharp, lances through me. I quickly close my mouth, my jaw clenched tight, and fight to will my fangs back into submission. I turn on my heels, my heart hammering against my ribs, and walk back over to Edmund, a polite, meaningless smile plastered on my face. I extend a hand to his associate.

"Hello," I say, my voice a smooth, calm façade that belies the turmoil raging within me. "I don't believe we've had the pleasure of meeting before."

His hand clasps mine, his grip firm and confident. "No, I don't believe so either," he replies, his voice a smooth, melodic baritone. "Caleb Bampton, at your service."

"A pleasure to meet you, Caleb," I say, my smile feeling stiff and unnatural on my face as I inhale deeply, surreptitiously drawing his scent into my lungs. It's intoxicating, a heady, complex perfume that makes my senses reel and my cock stir in my trousers with a sudden, shocking urgency. I want to fuck him. I want to own him. I want to drown in that scent.

I turn to face Edmund, my eyes narrowed, my voice sharp with a suspicion I can no longer conceal. "And what role does Caleb play in your life, Edmund?"

Edmund's smug, self-satisfied smile widens. "Caleb here runs my investment properties," he says, his tone dripping with false casual nonchalance.

"Oh, really?" I raise an eyebrow, my gaze shifting back to Caleb. "And how long have you been doing that?"

His smile falters for a split second, a barely perceptible flicker of uncertainty in his eyes, before it returns in full force. "About twenty years now," he replies, his voice smooth, but with a hint of something I can't quite place… hesitation, perhaps?

I maintain eye contact with him, my gaze steady and unwavering. "It must be a very boring job," I comment, my tone casual, conversational.

To my surprise, a genuine, unguarded smile widens his lips, and his eyes, a startlingly clear shade of blue, sparkle with a sudden, genuine amusement. "No, in fact," he answers, his voice warm with a sincerity that seems utterly out of place in this den of liars and sycophants. "I very much enjoy my job."

This man, this Caleb Bampton, has my full, undivided attention. But I cannot, will not, let it be known. I give him a curt, dismissive nod and turn back to face Edmund, making some inane small talk before saying my goodbyes and heading back to the elevator.

As soon as the polished steel doors close, my mind begins to race. There was something about this man that was… off. Not only did he smell like my every wet dream, a scent so potent and alluring that it had almost brought me to my knees, but there was an air of mystery surrounding him, a sense of something hidden just beneath the surface. I need to get back to the apartment. I need to discuss this with Jasper and Oscar immediately. There is only one person, one being in all the world, who could possibly smell that way. And if I'm right, if my instincts are not deceiving me, then everything, absolutely everything, is about to change. And I will have what is mine.

CHAPTER 9

JASPER

I'm sprawled on the ridiculously long, white leather couch, my tie loosened and hanging around my neck like a silken noose I'd given up on tightening, a glass of whiskey sweating onto the chrome coffee table beside me. The conference was, as predicted, a soul-crushing exercise in futility, and I'm now enjoying the subsequent blissful silence of the penthouse, a silence that's only broken by the soft clinking of ice in my glass.

I'd managed to slip past everyone the second we were dismissed, practically sprinting for the private lift like a man escaping a burning building. Which, in a way, I was. The sound of the lift door sliding open — a smooth, almost silent hiss — catches my attention. I watch, my interest piqued, as Theo strides into the apartment, his usual mask of weary control replaced by something else, something wild and untamed that glitters in the depths of his dark eyes. He looks like he's seen a ghost, or maybe just realized his favorite suit has a wrinkle.

"Where's Oscar?" he demands, his voice sharp and urgent, a discordant note in the quiet harmony of the room.

"In his room, I presume," I reply, my voice a lazy drawl. "Probably engaging in his nightly ritual of colour-coding his sock drawer or some other equally thrilling activity." I raise my eyebrows at Theo's agitated demeanor, a slow, curious smile playing on my lips. This is new. This is interesting. I sit up straighter, swinging my legs off the couch, and remove my tie entirely, coiling it around my hand before placing it on the coffee table. "What happened?" I ask, my voice losing its lazy edge, replaced by a genuine curiosity. I gesture for him to come and sit next to me on the couch. "You look like you're about to spontaneously combust."

He ignores my invitation, his gaze fixed on the hallway that leads to our bedrooms. He calls out to Oscar again, his voice a sharp, commanding bark that echoes in the cavernous space. Then, as if his legs can no longer support the weight of his agitation, he makes his way over and sinks onto the couch beside me. The air between us is thick with a palpable tension, a heavy, charged silence as we wait for our brother to emerge.

Oscar's presence fills the lounge just thirty seconds later, a whirlwind of disheveled elegance. His trousers are half-undone, his shirt unbuttoned and draped carelessly over his shoulders, revealing the intricate, vibrant tapestry of ink that covers almost every inch of his smooth, pale skin. He's a walking work of art, a beautiful, chaotic masterpiece of anxiety and control. He stops in the middle of the room, a confused, almost wounded expression on his face as he takes in our intense, focused stares.

"What?" he asks, his voice a mixture of confusion and irritation, his hands immediately going to smooth down his already perfect hair. "Did someone touch my collection of antique, leather-bound first editions? I swear to God, if one of you has left a fingerprint on my pristine copy of Dracula…"

"I smelt her," Theo finally speaks, his voice a low, guttural sound that seems to be ripped from the very depths of his soul. "I fucking smelt her."

My entire body goes rigid, the whiskey glass in my hand forgotten. Theo's words hang in the air, heavy and sharp and full of a terrifying, exhilarating promise. The memory of my own experience from the day before — the sudden, overwhelming scent that had brought me to my knees — rushes back. My heart, that useless, dormant organ, begins to hammer against my ribs with a frantic, wild rhythm.

"What did it smell like?" I whisper, my voice barely audible, my gaze locked on Theo's wild, desperate eyes.

"Like my very own wet dream," he replies, his voice thick with a raw, visceral desire. "It was a mix of every scent I have ever loved, every memory of a time when I was still human and capable of feeling joy, all tangled up into one single, intoxicating aroma."

I know that smell. I know it with a certainty that's as terrifying as it is absolute. Mine had been the same. "Where?" I ask, my voice still a whisper. "Where did you smell it?"

"The scent was coming from a vampire named Caleb Bampton," Theo states, his voice now laced with a grim, dangerous gravity. "One of Edmund's lackeys."

"I do not believe our mate is a male," Oscar chimes in, his expression lost and confused as he stands, a beautiful, half-naked statue of bewilderment, in the middle of the lounge. His fingers are twitching, a sure sign he's about to start cleaning something to cope with the stress.

"The smell was not coming from him, you idiot," Theo clarifies, his patience clearly wearing thin. "It was emanating off of him. It was on his clothes, his skin. He had been with her. Recently."

"I smelled something similar yesterday," I confess, the words tumbling out of me, my own experience suddenly cast in a new, terrifying light. "While I was out... hunting."

"Hold on," Oscar declares, with a sudden, sharp clarity in his eyes. He springs into action, a blur of motion as he darts back to his room. He returns a moment later with his laptop, his movements precise and economical as he joins us in the lounge once again, settling into the armchair opposite the couch. He's already muttering to himself, a low, anxious stream of data points and variables.

"Where did you smell it?" he fires off, his voice a rapid-fire staccato of questions, his fingers already flying across the keyboard with a speed that's mesmerizing to watch. "When? What time? What was the ambient temperature? Was there a breeze? From which direction?"

My mind is racing, trying to piece together the fragmented memories of the day before. "I remember looking at my watch," I begin, my voice gaining strength as the details come back to me. "It was around five o'clock. I recall thinking that I still had plenty of time before the conference started. I wanted to go hunting, so I went for a walk down High Street." I take a deep breath, the memory of what happened next still vivid, still raw. "As I was walking, the scent hit me. My fangs extended; my senses went into overdrive. I couldn't resist the urge to follow it, but just as quickly as it appeared, it vanished into thin air."

"The same thing happened to me," Theo admits, his voice a low, incredulous murmur. "I was walking to the lifts, and Edmund was there, talking to this Caleb in the lobby. As I walked past them, I caught the scent, and my fangs came out instantly."

"What did you do?" I ask, leaning forward, my elbows on my knees, my entire being focused on his answer.

"Hold on," Oscar says, his voice sharp, commanding. "Let me handle one thing at a time." He mutters to himself, his eyes scanning the screen in front of him, his brow furrowed in intense concentration. "So, High Street, around five o'clock," he confirms with a nod before turning his piercing gaze on me. "What were you wearing? I can't remember."

I think back to the evening. "Charcoal suit," I say, my voice steady. "I had just finished with the tactical teams. I remember passing by a pub with a bright, garish green sign."

Oscar types away, his fingers a blur of motion. The light from his computer screen casts shifting, dancing shadows on his face, making him look like some ancient, arcane sorcerer casting a spell. "Okay, just going to search now," he says, his voice a low, focused murmur. After a few moments of intense, silent typing, he exclaims, "Got it!" He leans forward, his movements quick and precise, and grabs the TV remote off the coffee table. He flicks on the large wall-mounted television and changes the input to HDMI 3.

The screen flickers to life, mirroring the display on his laptop. "There you are," he says, pointing a long, elegant finger at the screen where a grainy, black-and-white image of me is walking up High Street.

"Shit," I confirm, my voice a breathy whisper as I watch my own ghostly image move across the screen.

"I am assuming this is when you smelled it?" he inquires, his tone dry and clinical. I watch, a strange sense of detachment washing over me, as my on-screen self suddenly stops in its tracks and begins to frantically turn in circles, walking back and forth like a man who has lost his mind.

"Okay, hold on," Oscar says, his fingers flying across the keyboard again. "I am going to get another angle, see who was walking past you at that exact moment."

I watch as the camera angle on the TV changes, shifting to a bird's-eye view from a camera mounted on a nearby building. I can see everyone who I had walked past, a sea of anonymous, unsuspecting faces.

"Right there," Oscar says, his voice sharp with discovery. The video playback pauses, freezing the moment in time. "That is when you catch the scent," he explains, gesturing toward a figure in a dark coat who is passing me on the pavement. "I can't see their faces from this angle. I will need to try another." With another flick of his finger, he switches to a different camera, this one from a shopfront across the street, revealing a clear, unobstructed view of a man's face.

"That's him," Theo states, his voice a low, dangerous

growl. He leans forward in his chair, his hands gripping the armrests so tightly that his knuckles are white. "That's Caleb."

A heavy, profound silence falls over the room as all three of us stare at the screen, studying every detail of Caleb's appearance. The only sound is the soft, almost inaudible hum of Oscar's computer as he navigates through more footage, his expression one of intense, focused determination.

"We need to follow him," he declares, his voice a low, resolute command.

My thoughts are racing, with a thousand different scenarios playing out in my mind. "I'll dispatch one of my men to shadow him while we are here for the conference," I say, my voice a hushed, urgent whisper. "And when it's over, I'll take over the surveillance myself. I will not let him out of my sight."

This conference — this tedious, meaningless charade — cannot end soon enough. Every moment we waste, every hour we spend locked in that room listening to the petty squabbles of our kind, is another opportunity for our mate, for the woman we've been searching for two centuries, to slip through our fingers. But as one of the Kings, I can't just abandon my duties. I have to stay to play my part, to maintain the fragile illusion of order.

Though my body trembles with a desperate urgency, a need to run, to hunt, to find her, my mind knows that we have to maintain our composure. We cannot, will not, let Edmund catch wind of the fact that we're onto his schemes.

Chapter 10

Oscar

The seven days of the conference haven't so much passed as they have congealed, each hour a thick, slow-moving river of suspense and frustration that threatens to drown us all. Time itself seems to have taken on a viscous, almost physical quality, each minute stretching out into an eternity of waiting and watching. A palpable tension has settled over the three of us, a heavy, suffocating blanket woven from the fine, sharp threads of our shared anxiety.

The name 'Caleb' has become a forbidden word, a specter that haunts the silent, cavernous spaces between our conversations. We speak of him in hushed tones when we speak of him at all, as if saying his name too loudly might somehow alert him to our interest, might somehow cause him to vanish like smoke. It has even infiltrated the sanctity of my dreams, a place I once considered my own private, orderly domain. Now, his unfamiliar face and the intoxicating, impossible scent that clings to him replay in an endless, tormenting loop, a constant, maddening reminder of what's at stake.

I've thrown myself into the only task that offers any semblance of control, the only thing that can quiet the frantic, chaotic screaming in my own mind. With almost perfect precision, I've constructed a complex and beautiful architecture of facial recognition software, its algorithms a delicate, intricate web I've spun across the city's sprawling digital consciousness. My fingers fly over the keyboard, the soft, rhythmic clicking the only sound in the otherwise silent penthouse, a steady, reassuring counterpoint to the frantic, irregular beating of my own dormant heart.

I've designed the system not only to follow Caleb's every move in real-time, a digital shadow that will cling to him wherever he goes, but also to scan through countless terabytes of historical footage, a painstaking digital excavation of his past. I am going to unearth his origins, to map the constellation of his life, to discover where he frequents, what his daily routine looks like, and, most importantly, who he associates with. My curiosity drives me forward with almost manic intensity. I scour through surveillance cameras from every corner of the city, hoping for a glimpse of his face, a clue to his whereabouts, a single thread that I can pull to unravel the entire mystery.

He has to have been near our mate recently; it's the only logical, rational explanation for the lingering trace of her scent upon him. Every moment I spend lost in the cool, clean, beautiful logic of the code feels like a step closer to unraveling the mystery, a step closer to her.

Despite my tireless, obsessive efforts, we've gained nothing of substance. The digital breadcrumbs lead nowhere, disappearing into dead ends and encrypted files I can't crack. Caleb, with his frantic, ceaseless movements between Edmund's various properties and the far-flung, scattered members of his flock, resembles a nimble, almost invisible carrier pigeon, delivering messages back and forth with a tireless, almost manic energy. Theo, in a moment of uncharacteristic and rather grim poetry, compared him to one of the rats used in human wars, a creature that carries a bomb into an unsuspecting building, only to watch it explode in a shower of chaos and destruction.

The analogy, I have to admit, seems all too fitting for this volatile, unpredictable situation. The tension in the penthouse grows heavier with each passing day, a ticking time bomb waiting for its inevitable, violent explosion. It feels as though we're walking on eggshells, just waiting for the moment when everything will come crashing down around us, each of us lost in our own private, silent hell of anticipation and dread.

The weight of this impending discovery, this final, desperate hunt for our mate, is a crushing, almost unbearable burden. We all know, though we never speak of it, what failure would mean. We would be driven to a unique form of insanity, a madness born of a severed bond, a soul forever, irrevocably incomplete. And in our tightly controlled, unforgiving society, to go insane means a swift and permanent end. It's a fate akin to being put down like a common, rabid dog, a final, ignominious solution to a problem that could not be solved. The thought makes my blood run cold, sending a shiver down my spine. It's the ultimate power play for a man like Edmund, whose ambitions know no bounds. What atrocities would he commit if he were to be given free rein at the top? He's already a despicable, power-hungry creature, a vampire who revels in his own cruelty, and he's as high up as one can get without being a king.

He revels in his power, turning mere mortals into immortal beings with a casual, almost flippant disregard for the sanctity of the act. But with this gift of immortality comes a heavy, unspoken price—absolute, unquestioning loyalty. Disobedience, even the slightest hint of it, means certain death at his hands. As one of the esteemed eight, he holds the authority to create new vampires without seeking permission from the rest of us, a privilege that is supposed to be exercised with the utmost care and discretion. Instead, he simply fills out the necessary paperwork to inform the others — a mere formality.

However, while his colleagues, the other original vampires, use this power sparingly, perhaps once or twice a decade, with the gravity and respect it deserves, Edmund seems to do so on a weekly basis, his creations a steady, growing army of loyal, unquestioning soldiers. His actions have raised suspicion among the group for years, their concerns voiced in hushed, private conversations over glasses of aged whiskey and behind closed doors, but without him breaking any of the sacred accords we had written ourselves, they are powerless to help us stop him. The tension among the eight is palpable, a simmering resentment that threatens to boil over at any moment, as they grudgingly accept Edmund's unchecked power.

We try our best to keep a watchful eye on him, but there's only so much control we have over his actions. If he is interfering with the search for our lost mate, if he is the one who has been hiding her all these years, we know we will have to take drastic measures. Theo had written it into the accords long ago, a precaution against rogue vampires who are trying to destroy her bloodline. And yet, despite their efforts, despite our efforts, she remains elusive and untraceable, a ghost we've been chasing for two centuries.

It makes me wonder, in the darkest, most despairing hours of the night, if the prophecy we were told was even real, or if it was just a ploy by Edmund to manipulate us, to keep us chasing shadows while he consolidated his power. Edmund was the only one present when it was foretold, the only one who had heard the words from the lips of the ancient seer, which only heightens Theo's anxiety about whether it was real or not.

The prophecy itself is burned into my memory, each word a brand upon my soul. I can recite it in my sleep, and often do, the words a haunting refrain that follows me through my waking hours and into my dreams.

With the ascension of the three kings, a fourth will rise to join them.
However, it will not be another king who stands beside them.
No, a queen will step into their midst.
With her arrival, a great divide shall be created.
She carries within her a power so immense.
It will shake the very foundations of the world.
Her mere presence can incite fear and awe in equal measure.

This queen holds within her grasp.
Ability to fracture the vampire world as she transfers this power to her very mates.
Her existence threatens to tear apart everything that once seemed stable and unshakable.

Theo could never shake the feeling that something was missing, that there was a piece of the puzzle we had not yet found, like a puzzle with a few pieces still scattered across the table, hidden in the shadows. When he had first learned of his prophesied powers, he had been giddy with excitement, his eyes alight with a fierce, almost frightening ambition. He had dreamed of controlling the masses, of bending the world to his will, of becoming the most powerful vampire who had ever lived.

I do not share his enthusiasm. Yes, I want the power, the strength that will come with finding our mate, but I long for a simpler life, a life without the burden of such great responsibility. The weight of fulfilling this destiny weighs heavily on my shoulders, a constant, crushing pressure that I can never quite escape. I yearn for days of something simpler and less complicated, for a time when my biggest concern was not the fate of the entire vampire world, but something mundane and ordinary.

Being a king is my greatest burden, a role I had never wanted, a role I had never intended to have. As the second born, I was always meant to be the spare, the one who stood in the shadows while my older brother Theo shone in the spotlight, basking in the warmth of our father's approval. Our father, the king of Willows Peak, had made sure we were groomed for our future roles from a young age, his expectations clear and unwavering.

While Theo thrived under the pressure, his shoulders broad enough to carry the weight of a kingdom, I couldn't help but shy away from it, recoiling from the suffocating expectations. We often joked, in the rare moments of levity we allowed ourselves, that Father only had Jasper as a backup plan, fully aware that I would run away if given the chance to rule, that I would disappear into the night and never look back. The weight of the crown feels heavy on my head, like a cage trapping me in a life I never wanted, a gilded prison from which there is no escape.

Theo's voice, sharp and commanding, cuts through my thoughts like a knife, jolting me back to the oppressive, stifling reality of the conference room. I had been lost in a spiral of memories, of the prophecy, of our endless, fruitless search for our mate, of the life I had once dreamed of before all of this, and it takes a moment for me to refocus on the here and now. The air in the room is thick with the scent of old paper, stale coffee, and the cloying, artificial fragrance of the hotel's air freshener, a sickly sweet smell that makes my stomach turn.

"Oscar, have the paperwork drawn up and ready for tomorrow," Theo repeats, his tone firm and businesslike, his gaze fixed on some distant point beyond the walls of the room, his mind clearly already on the next task, the next battle, the next impossible challenge.

I nod, my mind still lingering on the bittersweet nostalgia that had consumed me, on the memories of a simpler time. "Of course," I reply, my voice a low, steady murmur as I make a mental note to attend to the task, to add it to the ever-growing list of responsibilities that weigh me down. I look over at Jasper, and I can see that he is in the same state I had just been in, his gaze fixed on a spot on the polished mahogany of the table in front of him, his expression distant and unseeing, his mind clearly a million miles away, lost in his own private maze of hope and fear. Looking over at him, I can see he is not engaging in the daily monotonous tasks we are supposed to be doing, his mind clearly elsewhere.

On the third day, we finally, mercifully, surpassed the tedious, mind-numbing proceedings involving the lower-class vampires, sending them all back to their respective homes and territories with a mixture of relief and thinly veiled condescension. Now, only our table — the eight of us, the original, ancient, and deeply dysfunctional family — remains. Leaving only our table to remain.

Yvonne's normally composed, almost regal, demeanor appears flustered as she fidgets with her silverware, a small, repetitive, almost frantic movement that betrays her inner turmoil. Throughout the week's events, she has seemed to be the quickest to anger, her opinions sharp and often unsolicited, always eager to offer her thoughts on matters that require delicate handling. Despite this, despite her abrasive nature and her tendency to speak before think-ing, she remains my favorite among the group, her fiery passion and unwavering loyalty a welcome, if sometimes exhausting, change from the staid, boring company of the others.

In the council meetings, Thomas and Isabella are always the quietest; their voices are rarely heard unless a unanimous vote is required. They are a matched set, two halves of a silent, watchful whole, their expressions unreadable, their thoughts their own. Edith, on the other hand, is like a loose cannon, a mischievous, unpredictable force of nature. She chimes in with her opinions on every issue, even, and perhaps especially, when they are in direct opposition to the rest of the group. It's as if she enjoys throwing a wrench in the works just to keep everyone on their toes, to stir up trouble for the sheer, perverse pleasure of it.

The cheeky old sod. And old she is indeed.

She had been turned into a vampire at the ripe age of sixty-five, the very first of our kind, her transformation a desperate, last-ditch effort by our sire to save her after she had been viciously attacked by wolves while traveling home one night. Her body had lain on death's door, her life slipping away with each labored breath, until our sire came upon her and made her his guinea pig for his newly formed coven, his first experiment in creating immortal life. She became the cornerstone on which the rest of us were created, immortalized by her willingness to be the stepping stone for our kind, her courage and her pain the foundation upon which our entire world was built.

The woman has no filter whatsoever and regularly gives her opinion on personal matters without hesitation, without any sense of decorum or propriety. Jasper adores her, constantly seeking her company and valuing her as the cleverest and most charming of the group, his face lighting up whenever she enters a room. However, in my observations, she seems to be a mischievous instigator, a trouble-maker who delights in chaos, which only adds to Jasper's admiration for her.

"Ladies and gentlemen, the hour is four a.m.," Theo declares, his voice echoing in the now-silent conference room, a sound that is both weary and resolute, the voice of a man who has carried the weight of the world for far too long. He rises from his seat. "Tomorrow marks our final day here, and I expect every one of you to be punctual and fully prepared. We cannot afford to waste any more time on avoidable issues." His voice echoes off the walls of the conference room, a mix of fatigue and urgency evident in his tone, a desperate plea wrapped in a command.

With a silent, shared understanding, each member of the group rises from the table and makes their way back to their respective hotels, a slow, silent procession of ancient, powerful beings, each lost in their own thoughts, their own private worlds of worry and hope. I remain seated for a moment longer, the weight of the last seven days, the weight of the last two centuries, pressing down on me. The room grows quiet, save for the distant hum of traffic outside, the city just beginning to stir, to wake up to a new day, oblivious to the ancient, secret world that exists in its shadows.

CHAPTER 11

THEODORE

Every day, I watch Oscar perched on the couch like some neurotic gargoyle, his fingers dancing across the keys of his laptop in a frantic, desperate rhythm. His eyes are focused, each tap a tiny, insignificant prayer to the digital gods. But as the days bleed into one another with no breakthroughs, I can feel frustration clawing its way up my throat. All we do is watch this 'Caleb' character flit back and forth like a dutiful messenger pigeon, and our search for the one thing that matters feels stagnant and fucking hopeless. The anticipation of finally meeting our mate, of finally claiming what is ours, looms over my head like a black cloud, and I wish it would just fucking rain already.

Oscar is taking this the worst, of course. He hasn't smelled what Jasper and I have. All he has to go on is our fumbled, inadequate descriptions of a scent that defies words, a scent that promises to complete us. I can see the weight of it crushing him, evident in the way he paces back and forth every night before we descend into the conference room from hell. The creases on his forehead have deepened, and his eyes are bloodshot from lack of sleep. It's clear he hasn't even bothered going to bed, consumed by his obsessive determination to uncover something—anything—on Caleb that could provide us with the answers I demand. His unwavering focus is impressive, I'll give him that, but his self-destruction is starting to piss me off.

As the sun begins to set on our final day, my mind is consumed with thoughts of returning home and shedding this year's ridiculous attire. No matter how much I appreciate the power that comes with a well-tailored suit, my heart, or what's left of it, longs for the comfort of my everyday clothes. These tight-waisted jackets and excessive embellishments are a cage, and I'm ready to be free.

Jasper, of course, is a master of casual style, effortlessly pulling off tracksuit pants and t-shirts with an infuriatingly charming swagger. He often teases us for spending thousands on intricate tattoos that we keep hidden under our professional armor. "What's the point of having a masterpiece if you never let anyone see it?" he'd asked once, a wicked grin on his face. But who the hell would we show them to? We live secluded in our castle, working. Even our blood donors are always masked, their faces a blur of anonymity. My body is a roadmap of my life, a history of battles won and enemies vanquished, and I'll be damned if I share it with anyone but the woman who is destined to be mine. Jasper's body, on the other hand, is a chaotic canvas of spontaneous, meaningless designs. Thanks to the witches on our payroll and their spell-infused ink, these tattoos are as permanent as we are.

Oscar, like me, keeps his colourful ink hidden. I suspect it's for the same reason. He wants to share it with her, and only her.

I turn to Oscar, my patience worn thin. "Have you finished the paperwork for today?"

"Yes," he replies with a sigh of relief that grates on my nerves. "All done and printed." He gestures toward the stack of neatly organised papers on the kitchen counter.

"I even took the extra step of printing out copies for everyone to take home," he adds, his voice laced with frustration. "I don't understand why they can't just join the rest of us in the digital age and use laptops instead of making me convert everything into digital form for them."

Jasper strolls into the room, his black-and-white striped suit impeccably tailored to his tall frame. As he does up the last button, he muses, "I think Edith still uses a quill."

Oscar nods in agreement, a faint smile playing on his lips. "Oh yes, she does. I often find splotches of ink that have dripped onto her paperwork," he chuckles, a sound that's surprisingly light.

Jasper grins mischievously at Oscar. "I think she uses it just to annoy you."

Oscar lets out a hearty laugh. "That wouldn't surprise me one bit."

As Jasper adjusts his cufflinks, Oscar asks casually, "Will you be traveling back with us?"

Jasper shakes his head, his eyes glinting with a predatory light. "No, I think I'll head straight to following Caleb. I want to get a closer look at our little messenger boy. Maybe see what he smells like up close."

Oscar nods, his fingers already flying across the

keyboard. "I'll send you all the information I have now on where he goes daily, what he has been doing, and any other relevant details. He shouldn't be difficult to locate when it's time to pack up, especially with the tail you still have on him," Oscar says confidently. "I'll also provide a link to a page where I will post regular updates on my findings after today concludes."

Jasper gives a grateful nod, his playful demeanor gone, replaced by a cold, focused determination that I rarely see.

With a frustrated grumble, I express my desire for a smooth and efficient day, eager to leave this fucking city behind. "Can we please just get this over with?"

"Can you please hand me a blood bag?" Oscar's voice interrupts my thoughts. "I haven't fed yet," he sighs.

Jasper, ever the helpful one, heads to the fridge and retrieves a blood bag. "Do you want it poured into a cup, Your Highness, or do you prefer to drink straight from the bag like a commoner?" Jas asks with a sly grin.

"Do I appear like a savage to you?" Oscar retorts, his voice dripping with disdain. "A cup, as always."

Playful teasing erupts between them. Jasper, with a hint of mischief in his voice, pokes fun at Oscar's refinement. "God forbid that delicate mouth of yours should touch plastic." His infectious laughter echoes through the apartment.

Oscar, not one to back down, retorts with a snarky comeback about how washing a cup doesn't hinder his life like it seems to for him. I roll my eyes at their silly banter, the sound of their voices a dull roar in my ears.

Thankfully, once we get home, there will be no more need for bags. I share Jasper's disdain for them, but in a city like this where hunting is dangerous and could easily expose us, using bags is a necessary evil. The thought of all of us gathered in one place, fangs bared and bloodlust taking over, is a tempting one, but it's a risk we can't afford to take.

Jasper lets out a heavy sigh, the frustration clear on his face. "I can't take much more of this. I'm dying for some fresh blood," he mutters under his breath. "Something warm and willing."

I chuckle, a dark, humorless sound. "Well, we better get moving then, before you pass out from hunger," I tease as I clap my hands together, the sound a sharp crack in the tense silence. I grab the stack of paperwork off the kitchen counter, ready to tackle the last day of this fucking charade, and head toward the lift. The sooner this is over, the sooner the real hunt can begin.

CHAPTER 12

WILLOW

For the past two long, soul-crushingly boring weeks, I've spent my days sitting outside the grand manor on the cold stone steps, talking to the birds that flutter around me like I'm some kind of weird, lonely Disney princess. The anticipation of Caleb's return today has a frantic, fluttering bird trapped in my ribcage. He's always due back on Fridays at 3 pm with the groceries, but it's been well over three hours since his scheduled arrival, and my internal monologue has officially entered the 'he's dead in a ditch somewhere' phase of anxiety. The sun is starting to dip below the horizon, casting a pale pink glow over the ground, and despite the peaceful surroundings, my heart is racing with a potent cocktail of impatience and dread. Maybe he's not coming. Maybe he finally got tired of his weird, codependent relationship with his pet human and decided to ghost me. I wouldn't blame him. I'm a lot to deal with.

Shivering in the chilly autumn air, I finally retreat

inside to the warmth of the crackling fire. I take a seat in my favorite armchair, the one that's perfectly molded to the shape of my ass after three years of dedicated service, and reach for Wuthering Heights for what feels like the hundredth time. Despite having read all the books Caleb has left me, I always find myself drawn back to this time-less classic of toxic relationships and dramatic scenery. As I delve into their tumultuous relationship once again, the sounds of nature outside fade away and I'm transported into their world of passion and heartache. It's a welcome distraction from my own passionless, heartache-adjacent existence.

As I'm deep in the details of grave-digging, a faint but familiar sound catches my attention. The rhythmic thud of boots striking stone echoes through the door, causing me to bolt up from my chair and make a beeline for it. My heart races as I reach for the knob, knowing that it can only mean one thing: Caleb has returned. Without hesita-tion, I fling open the door and launch myself into his sturdy arms, eager to feel his warm embrace once again. His rich scent of old books, clean laundry, and something uniquely, wonderfully Caleb fills my nostrils, and I cling to him tightly, overwhelmed with a tidal wave of emotion at his return.

"Oh dear," Caleb exclaims, his voice tinged with amusement and worry as he quickly wraps his free arm around my waist to support me. With a gentle but firm grip, he leads us into the room while I cling to him like a designer handbag he's just purchased.

"Well, I missed you too, Willow," he chuckles, his eyes crinkling at the corners. As we stumble toward the center of the room, he deftly kicks the door closed with his booted foot. Bending down slightly, he carefully places my feet on the ground and meets my gaze with concern in his warm brown eyes.

Tears are streaming down my face, unstoppable in their flow. The sight of Caleb standing before me is like a lifeline, pulling me out of the abyss of loneliness that has been eating away at my soul. In his presence, I feel alive again, whole and complete. He's the only one who understands the depth of my longing for human connection, reminding me of what it feels like to truly be seen and heard. As we embrace, I can feel the weight of my emptiness dissipate, replaced by a warmth that spreads through every inch of my body. It's moments like these, with Caleb by my side, that I find solace in an otherwise lonely existence.

With a gentle voice and a rushed stride, Caleb hurries into the kitchen, setting the bags down on the wooden bench with a thud. He turns on his heel and rushes back to my side. With loving care, he wipes away the tears that stain my cheeks, using his thumbs to gently brush them away. His touch is warm and soothing, like a soft breeze on a summer day.

The words tumble out before I can stop them. "I missed you," I blurt, feeling foolish for stating the obvious.

Caleb's face lights up with a smile as he pulls me into a tight hug. "Now that I can see, Willow," he says, his voice a low, comforting rumble.

As we separate, Caleb motions toward the island bench in the kitchen. "Why don't you sit down and relax? I'll make you a hot chocolate."

My body sinks into the stool, grateful for the support

after a long day. The rich aroma of cocoa fills my senses as Caleb expertly prepares my drink. "Would you like to hear all about my adventures while I was away?" Caleb asks, his eyes twinkling mischievously.

A grin spreads across my face as I eagerly reply, "Oh yes please, I am desperate to know." As Caleb begins to recount his stories, the room fades away. His voice fills with excitement as he regales me with tales of driving through the bustling city streets, gazing at the towering skyscrapers and lavish buildings. He describes the delicious dinner feasts they indulged in, surrounded by the Kings at their round table, discussing important matters with the other illustrious members of the Originals. It's like a scene from a fairytale, where luxury and power intertwine in a dazzling display.

My curiosity can't be contained any longer. "What did the Originals wear?" I ask my fascination with clothing becoming more and more apparent.

Caleb chuckles at my question. "Well, Mr. and Mrs. Henry have always had a thing for old-fashioned attire from the 50s era. They never seem to update their wardrobe, even though they have all the money in the world to buy anything they want," he explains.

I can't help but picture Mrs. Henry in a soft pink dress, twirling around in it as she speaks to guests. The thought of it makes me smile.

Caleb leans in, his voice low and excited. "Miss. Eccleston was always so put together. Every day, she would grace the conference in a perfectly tailored pantsuit, the deep shade of navy accentuating her elegant figure, and blonde hair." I can't help but be intrigued, Caleb sounds like he has a small crush on Miss Eccleston. "What exactly is a pantsuit?" I ask. With enthusiasm, Caleb describes it as a stylish and functional suit for women, complete with attached pants that create a seamless look. My imagination runs wild at the thought of such sophisticated attire. "It sounds absolutely beautiful," I dreamily sigh, wishing for one to call my own. The image of Miss Eccleston in her pristine pantsuit stays with me, an embodiment of poise and confidence. And maybe a little bit of 'I could step on you and you'd thank me for it' energy. I'm into it.

"But what about Edith? What was she wearing?" I inquire curiously.

Caleb chuckles, "Oh, she wore a stunning red dress that made her grey hair shine, and added a real fur shawl. I'm sure she received plenty of scorn from passersby while walking the streets."

"My favorite colour is red," I declare. "Why would anyone hate a fur shawl?"

"It's the way of the world these days," Caleb shrugs. "Everyone is pro-animal rights and rejects the use of animals for food, fur, or leather." Despite his nonchalant tone, I can sense a hint of sadness in his explanation.

I furrow my brow, curiosity piqued as I ask, "So what do they do with the skin and fur from the animals they still kill for food then?"

A thoughtful expression crosses Caleb's face before he responds, "I suspect they still use it, but I also imagine it doesn't sell as well as it did with all the alternative options now readily available."

A warm mug of hot chocolate is placed in my hand by Caleb, breaking the tension of our conversation. The rich aroma of cocoa and cinnamon fills my senses. "This is so fascinating," I say, taking a sip of the hot liquid.

Caleb chuckles, "It's not a dinner table topic."

Startled, I turn to him and cock my head. His words hang in the air like a warning, heavy with caution. "What do you mean?" I inquire.

His expression becomes somber as he leans in closer. "Well, there are certain topics that are best left untouched during dinner conversations with friends, family or even acquaintances," he explains, his voice low and filled with wisdom. "Politics, someone's sexual preference, and now animal rights - these subjects will always stir up strong opinions at the table. And it only takes one person's personal views to ignite a heated discussion or even a fight."

A chuckle escapes his lips as he continues, "It's always safer to avoid these topics altogether."

I can't help but join in his laughter, knowing full well that I don't have any future dinner plans to worry about. But his words stay with me, lingering like a subtle reminder to tread carefully when it comes to sensitive matters like these.

Caleb's voice breaks through the comfortable silence, pulling my attention away from the book I was reading. "Have you eaten?" he asks, shifting the conversation. "Nope," I admit with a sheepish smile. "I was waiting for you." He chuckles, knowing me too well. "Well, I'm going to assume you haven't cooked since I left, and we need to restock the fridge?"

"Yes, please," I nod, grateful for his help. "Well then, let's not waste any more time. Grab your trusty apron and let's get to work," Caleb says with a mischievous glint in his eye. As always, his energy is infectious, and I can't help but feel excited to tackle the task at hand.

The hours fly by as we work diligently in the kitchen. Together, we concoct seven delectable dishes, filling my fridge to the brim with tantalizing aromas and mouth-watering flavors. The time spent with Caleb is a balm to my soul after the two weeks of longing for his presence. But as the clock strikes 1 am, he announces that it's time for him to go home. My heart sinks at the thought of being alone again.

"It's okay, Willow," he reassures me, noticing my tears. "I'll come back tomorrow. I even bought you some books that I forgot to bring today. I'll pop back in with them."

With a warm smile and a comforting hug, Caleb leaves, leaving behind a lingering sense of warmth and happiness in his wake. And the promise of more books. Which is almost as good as the promise of more him.

ONCE CALEB HAS LEFT, I roll up my sleeves and set to work scrubbing every nook and cranny of the kitchen. Our cooking always results in a massive mess, but it's worth it for the delicious meals we create together. As I spray down the counters and wipe away the splatters of sauce and flour, I can't help but smile at the memories of Caleb's mischievous antics. He always seems to conveniently disappear when the time comes for cleaning up, his excuse usually something along the lines of "Oh, I just remembered I have to check on something in the car." But that's just part of his charm, and I wouldn't have it any other way. The smell of lemon-scented cleaner fills the air, and I let out a content sigh as I admire the sparkling clean kitchen before me.

The clock in the kitchen reads 1:58 am when I hear a faint rustling outside, the sound of footsteps echoing off the cobble path. My heart races with excitement, hoping it's Caleb returning with the books he promised to bring. Without a second thought, I fling the kitchen towel I was using to dry dishes onto the counter and rush out to greet him, a wide, probably embarrassing smile already plastered on my face.

But as I step onto the porch, my hopes are shattered. The figure standing before me is not Caleb, but a dark silhouette against the moonlit night. A chill runs down my spine as I realize it's not Caleb at all. It's a man. A very, very attractive man. LikeLike the kind of attractive that should come with a warning label.

He's strikingly handsome, his features so perfect it makes my knees weak and my brain go a little fuzzy. His jet-black hair is styled to perfection, framing his chiseled jawline and dark eyes that seem to hold a mysterious depth, the kind of depth that probably hides a lot of secrets and possibly a body count. He's dressed in an all-black suit that hugs his tall and muscular frame like it was sewn directly onto his body, with the first few buttons of his shirt undone, revealing a tantalizing glimpse of smooth skin. As he turns slightly, I catch a glimpse of intricate black tattoos peeking out from under the fabric around his collar and neck, winding up like vines or shadows.

Towering over my 5 foot 10 height, he exudes a sense of confidence and power that makes me feel like a small, insignificant thing.

feeling suddenly self-conscious, and acutely aware that I'm wearing my ratty old apron and probably have flour in my hair, I nervously ask him, "Can I help you?" My voice is slightly trembling as I try to maintain eye contact with this enigmatic stranger, which is proving to be surprisingly difficult because his eyes are doing something to me that I don't entirely understand.

A devious smile stretches across the man's face, revealing a mouth full of sharp fangs. Oh. Oh shit. "Yes, dear," he replies with a sinister tone that sends a shiver down my spine, and not the good kind. "I think you can." My heart races as I take a step back, my survival instincts finally kicking in, but my foot catches on the uneven cobblestone path, and I tumble backward onto the hard ground, landing on my back with a thud that knocks the wind out of my lungs. The man's dark figure looms over me, his eyes glittering with something that could be malice or could be amusement — I can't quite tell — as he advances closer. Panic sets in as I realize there's no escape from this predatory creature. This is it. This is how I die. Killed by a stupidly hot vampire on my own front porch.

As he looms above me, his hand is held out in a gesture of assistance. I can't help but notice the muscles that ripple beneath his skin, a reminder of his strength and the fact that he could probably snap me in half like a twig if he wanted to. "Let me help you up ... Mate," he says with an air of authority, and I feel a chill run through my veins at the word. It carries so much weight and significance, a word Caleb has explained to me in hushed, reverent tones, and I am suddenly acutely aware of the importance of this moment.

They found me.

Fuck.

Chapter 13

Jasper

Tracking Caleb is surprisingly easy. The man doesn't seem to be making any effort to stay inconspicuous, which is either arrogant or stupid. I haven't decided which. Once the conference from hell finally ends, I relieve Mike from his week-long surveillance duty and take up the task myself. It's time for the fun to begin.

Once Edmund dismisses Caleb, I trail behind him with an ease that's almost boring. It's as effortless as slicing through a freshly baked pie, and I find myself wishing for a bit more of a challenge. As I follow his confident strides, my heart races with a potent cocktail of anticipation and curiosity, wondering where he'll lead me next. He travels through the winding roads of Scotland, a place that is not considered part of Edmund's territory, which makes my vampire senses tingle with suspicion.

After hours of driving, he finally reaches an apartment just over the border and quickly changes into more casual attire suitable for a day at work. A quick stop at Tesco allows him to stock up on enough groceries to last a week, carefully placing them in the trunk of his car before setting off again. The scent of pine and moss fills the air as I drive deeper into the Scottish countryside, a place that feels ancient and wild, and I can't help but feel a thrill of excitement. This is much better than being stuck in a stuffy conference room with a bunch of old vampires who smell like dust and regret.

As I continue to track Caleb, his car disappears into a dense, secluded area that is mainly covered in thick, ancient forest. The trees loom tall and dark above me, their twisted branches reaching out like gnarled fingers. I can't help but think of the stories my father used to tell me about Scottish forests - tales of werewolves, will-o'-the-wisps, and fairies lurking in the shadows. He was more accurate about some of those creatures than he could have ever imagined. Caleb finally parks his car along the side of a rough dirt road, carefully concealing it among the dense foliage. He retrieves his shopping bags from the trunk before disappearing deeper into the forest on foot.

Meanwhile, I have to park my car miles away and make a cautious journey back on foot, making sure I'm not seen by anyone. I track his scent up a narrow, well-worn path that winds through towering trees and dense underbrush. The forest seems to stretch on forever, but eventually, the path leads me to a sprawling manor nestled amongst the greenery. Thick vines and ivy climb the stone walls, giving the impression of a fairytale castle abandoned long ago. It's the kind of place you'd expect to find a sleeping princess, or maybe a dragon. I'm hoping for the princess.

As I walk closer, I pull out my phone to check for a signal. To my dismay, there are none at all. Using the map feature, I place small markers on my location so I can send them back to Oscar when I regain a signal. The Manor that stands before me isn't as grand as some from my past, but it's an elegant structure that seems to have been recently restored. As I approach, I notice a soft glow emanating from the kitchen window. Through it, I can make out Caleb's figure wearing an apron and the faint outline of a woman with long dark hair.

My heart, a useless, still organ, gives a lurch. It's her. It has to be. The adrenaline surges through my veins, a heady, intoxicating rush that makes me want to rush inside and claim her as mine, to wrap her in my arms and never let go. But instead, I hold back, a rare moment of self-control. I watch from the shadows, a silent, unseen observer.

I watch her as she laughs and smiles alongside Caleb, their easy camaraderie a sharp, painful pang in my chest. And when he leaves, tears glistening in her eyes, I listen as he promises to return tomorrow with some books. Every detail about her captivates me, from the way she tucks a stray strand of hair behind her ear to the way her eyes light up when she smiles. I can't wait for our paths to finally cross.

As I watch Caleb disappear down a winding track to the left of the Manor, my curiosity is piqued. Without hesitation, I follow after him, my senses on high alert. The ground beneath my feet is soft and damp, covered in a layer of fallen leaves that crunches underfoot. The path leads deeper into the forest, surrounded by towering trees and overgrown foliage. Eventually, the track opens up to reveal Caleb's car parked at the end, hidden among the shadows and natural camouflage. It seems he has taken this alternate route to mask his scent, cleverly attempting to throw off anyone who may attempt to track him. A cunning move on his part, but one that will ultimately fail against my well-honed tracking skills. Though not completely foolish, Caleb is no match for my acute awareness and stealth. As I continue along the path with ease, I can't help but admire his strategic thinking and intelligence. After Caleb drives off, I turn on my heel and retrace my steps back to the Manor. As I approach, I can see the Woman through the window, her hands moving with practiced efficiency as she scrubs at the kitchen counters. But there's a sadness in her eyes that I hadn't noticed before. It makes me wonder what kind of life she has led up until this point, what secrets and sorrows she carries within her. My curiosity is piqued, and I can't help but want to know more about this enigmatic Woman and the life she has lived.

Emerging from my hiding spot behind the dense bushes, I made my way up to the door. My footsteps echo on the path, announcing my arrival. Suddenly, the door flies open, and she comes charging out to greet me. However, as soon as her eyes fall upon me, she freezes in place.

Her face pales at the sight of me, and a faint blush spreads across her cheeks as she speaks shakily. "Can I help you?" Her voice quivers, a delicate, fragile sound that makes me want to wrap her in my arms and protect her from the world.

A wave of her intoxicating scent flows over me, causing my knees to buckle and my fangs to snap out, ready for action. My dick starts to harden in my pants as I smile. My eyes scan her beautiful face, unable to contain my delight at being in her presence. It's like a spell has been cast over me, her mere presence enough to disarm any defenses I may have had. The sweet aroma surrounding her is like a drug, pulling me in deeper and deeper with every breath. It's the scent of rain-soaked earth, old books, vanilla, and ozone, a scent that promises to complete me, to make me whole.

She's quite tall for a woman, at least 5 foot 10, her height only adding to her allure, making her seem like a regal goddess among mortals. Her hair cascades down her back in rich, dark waves, resembling the finest chocolate. And her skin, so pale and delicate, seems to glow in the sunlight. From her soft features and well-defined curves, I can estimate she's around 19 or 20 years old. Her full breasts and curvy waist draw me in, just the way I like it. She's a masterpiece, a work of art, and she's mine.

"Yes, dear, I think you can," I reply with a slight smile, taking a step closer toward her. As I move closer, I can't help but notice the flecks of grey in her striking blue eyes and the soft pink blush on her cheeks. She's truly a sight to behold. As I step closer, she takes one back. I can't control the rush of concern as I witness her stumble backward, her foot catching on the uneven path. Her descent is swift, and I don't have a chance to catch her before she hits the ground. My heart races as I rush to her side, offering my hand to help her up.

"Let me help you up… Mate," I say to her, but as soon

as the word "mate" leaves my lips, I watch in alarm as her pupils dilate and a look of terror washes over her features.

Anxiety knots in my stomach as I approach her. The fear in her eyes is palpable, and it pains me to know that she sees me as a threat. With a quick gesture, I throw my hands up in the air, hoping to convey my non-threatening intentions. "I'm not here to harm you," I reassure her.

But her stammered reply reveals her doubt and mistrust. "Yes, yes, you are."

Desperate to gain her trust, I speak with sincerity in my voice. "No, I truly am not. I've come to save you and bring you home."

A gust of wind rustles the leaves around us, adding an eerie atmosphere to our conversation. Her wide-eyed gaze holds mine, searching for any signs of deception.

Her face has lost all colour, drained by the biting cold. Even her lips, once a rosy hue, now show hints of blue. I carefully approach her again and crouch down, my heart pounding in my chest. "Please don't panic," I whisper, gently sliding one arm under her knees and the other around her back. With a steady lift, I carry her into the warmth of the manor. The weight of her body against mine is both comforting and concerning. The cold must have been taking its toll on her.

As I cradle her in my arms, I can't help but notice how surprisingly light she is. Holding her feels like holding a feather, or a fragile porcelain doll. As a vampire, I know that I possess inhuman strength compared to humans, but this woman is lighter than any human I have ever held before. My mind immediately races with thoughts about feeding her more. I'll fatten her up, I think to myself, a thought that surprises even me.

With purposeful strides, I make my way into the manor, shutting the heavy door behind me. Gently setting her down on a plush armchair placed in front of the fireplace, I crouch down in front of her. Placing my hands on her cold knees, I begin rubbing them back and forth, desperately trying to transfer some warmth into her frozen body. The flicker of the flames cast an eerie glow on her pale skin, making her look even more delicate and vulnerable at that moment.

As my hand grazes her knee, she jolts and attempts to squirm deeper into the chair's cushions. Her voice trembles with fear as she asks, "Are you going to kill me now? Or mate me first, then fucking kill me?"

I can sense a newfound strength in her tone the longer I remain in her presence. A spark of defiance in her eyes that I find incredibly attractive.

"I'm not here for either of those things. I'm here to pack you a bag and bring you back home," I declare with a sense of finality.

She immediately protests, "I will not go with you."

"You've never had a choice," I reply, my voice a low, dangerous growl. I need to get her out of here and back to safety at Willows Peak. The air hangs heavy with tension as we both prepare for what is to come next.

As I stand and cross my arms in front of me, I ask the woman in front of me her name.

"Willow," she replies, causing me to stop dead in my tracks.

"Willow?" I repeat, staring back at her with a newfound curiosity. "My castle is called Willows Peak."

At my words, her eyebrows furrow together and she meets my gaze with confusion. "Okay, but what does that have to do with me?" she huffs impatiently.

"I just find it fitting," I respond with a small smile.

"Now, where is your room? We must get you a coat and be on our way," I say, my voice a soft command.

"No," she stubbornly crosses her arms in front of her. "I already told you, I'm not going."

I sigh in frustration and rub my temples. This is not how I imagined today going. I thought there would be more… enthusiasm.

"And as I said, you have no choice," I sternly point a finger at her. She shrinks back slightly, fear evident in her eyes.

"I can't go," she pleads, pointing to her ankle, which is encircled by an ankle bracelet - the kind given to criminals who have been released from jail.

I let out a frustrated curse and examine the bracelet. "What happens if you take it off?" I demand.

"I don't know; I've never taken it off," she confesses with a hint of desperation in her voice.

Sinking back onto the floor, I study the bracelet closer. It has left faint marks on her skin, evidence of its long-term presence. "How long has this been on?" I wonder aloud as I run my finger along the raised skin under the band.

"It's been about three years," she replied, her voice trembling with fear.

"What the hell does it do?" I demand my anger building at the thought of someone harming my mate.

"I can only walk so far away from the manor before it zaps me," she answers, her words laced with pain and despair. I feel a surge of protectiveness toward her and fury toward Edmund, who would have placed it there. It becomes clear that Edmund has been torturing my mate for the past three years and has been keeping her trapped here. The thought of it makes me want to rip him limb from limb.

"Where is your coat?" I ask through gritted teeth, my tone menacing.

She points toward the door we walked through, and I can see a coat hanging there, alongside a pair of leather knee-high boots that look too big for her petite feet. Walking over, I grab them both and throw the coat over her.

"I'm going to break this off of you, then I'm going to carry you to my car and we are leaving here," I tell her, my voice a low, dangerous promise.

A look of resignation washes over her face, knowing that she is no match for me. I can see the fear and helplessness in her eyes as she realizes she is only a mortal in a battle against a supernatural being. There is little she can do to fight back. As I help her place on her coat, I crouch down and grab onto her ankle with a firm grip.

"This may cause you pain, but we have to make a run for it as soon as I remove this," I warn her, unsure of what will happen when the monitor comes off. The material is warm under my fingers, properly warmed from her skin, and I feel an electric current pulsing through it. For a brief moment, I wonder if this is a mistake. But there's no turning back now. We must escape before it's too late.

With a soft voice, she requests, "May I take my book, please?" Moving swiftly, she snatches the well-loved copy of Wuthering Heights from the table next to her chair. Looking to face her, I notice the creased pages and worn edges, evidence of countless hours spent lost in its story.

"Do you enjoy reading?" I inquire curiously.

"Yes," she responds in a whisper, holding her ankle steady as I gently wrap my hands around both sides of the brace.

"Are you ready?" I ask, meeting her gaze with determination.

"Okay" is the only response she offers as I pull both sides of the brace, applying pressure and stretching it apart.

As soon as I pry the object open, a piercing alarm echoes through the room. I quickly snatch her shoes and slip them onto her feet, barely taking time to tie them before attempting to fling her over my shoulder in a fireman's hold. But she's not having it. She twists in my grip, her fists pounding against my back, her legs kicking wildly. "Put me down!" she shrieks, her voice a mixture of fear and fury. "I saidPut me the fuck down!" One of her flailing hands catches me in the jaw, a surprisingly solid hit that makes my head snap to the side. I can't help but feel a surge of pride at her spirit, even as I tighten my grip on her. She's a fighter, my mate. I like that.

"Stop struggling," I command, my voice a low growl as I adjust my hold on her, pinning her arms to her sides. "I'm trying to save you, you stubborn woman." She responds by trying to bite my shoulder through my jacket, her teeth scraping against the material. Adrenaline rushes through me as I sprint toward the door I came in from, yanking it open and leaving it gaping behind me, her protests and struggles continuing the entire way. My heart pounds as we fly down the same path Caleb had used to leave. Every step takes us closer to safety, but with each passing second, the risk of getting caught increases.

I bound over jagged rocks and ducked under low-hanging branches, emerging into a clearing where Caleb had parked his car. With a sharp pivot on my heel, I sprint up the winding road toward my vehicle, berating myself for having parked it so far away. Every second counts as we need to escape before anyone comes looking for her. The air is dense with the smell of pine and damp earth, filling my lungs with each breath as I push myself harder. My feet pound against the rough pavement, sending vibrations through my entire body. We cannot afford to get caught now; we must make our getaway.

As I near my car, my heart is pounding, and adrenaline is coursing through my body. I press the button on my keys, and the engine roars to life, and I fling open the passenger door to place her inside, though "gently" might be a stretch given her continued struggling. She immediately tries to scramble out the other side, her fingers fumbling with the door handle. I race around to the driver's seat, quickly buckle myself in, and hit the child lock button before she can escape.

"Really?" I mutter, hitting the gas, tires screeching as I speed off. She's pressed against the passenger door, her eyes wild, her chest heaving. "Let me out," she demands, her voice shaking. "Let me out right now!" "Not a chance, sweetheart," I reply, my eyes fixed on the road. We make it about five miles down the winding road when she does something I don't expect. She unbuckles her seatbelt and lunges for the steering wheel.

"Jesus Christ!" I shout, swerving to avoid a tree as I wrestle her hands away from the wheel. "Are you trying to kill us both?" "Better than whatever you have planned!" She shouts back, her nails digging into my wrists. I manage to pull over to the side of the road, the car skidding to a halt. Before I can stop her, she's somehow managed to unlock the door, and she's out, stumbling into the darkness of the forest. I'm out of the car in a flash, chasing after her. She's fast, I'll give her that, but she's no match for vampire speed. I catch up to her within seconds, my hand closing around her wrist. She spins around, trying to wrench herself free, and we tussle for a moment, her pulling away, me pulling her back.

"Let go of me!" she screams, her voice echoing through the trees.

"You're coming with me," I say firmly, trying to keep my voice calm even as my patience wears thin. She tries to kick me, her boot connecting with my shin. It doesn't hurt, but the audacity of it makes me laugh. "You're adorable when you're angry," I tell her, which only seems to make her angrier. She tries to run again, but she only makes it a few steps before she trips over a root and goes sprawling. I'm there in an instant, helping her up, and this time she doesn't fight me. She just sags against me, her breath coming in ragged gasps.

"Stupid vampires," she mutters, her voice thick with

frustration and exhaustion. "Stupid vampire strength. Stupid vampire speed. I just want to go home." Her voice cracks on the last word, and I feel a pang of guilt.

"I know," I say softly, scooping her up in my arms. This time she doesn't struggle, just lets her head fall against my chest. "I know, Willow. But you are going home. You just don't know it yet." I carry her back to the car and place her gently in the passenger seat. She doesn't try to run again, just sits there, her arms crossed, glaring at me with those beautiful, furious eyes. I buckle her in, and this time she doesn't protest. Fumbling with my steering wheel controls, I command my car to navigate us to the closest motorway. After a tense 30 seconds, a route appears on the map - we're back in an area with reception. Jabbing the button again, I instruct my car to call Oscar.

The car is filled with the noise of ringing, and Oscar answers on the 3rd ring.

"Jas," he says, his voice a mixture of relief and anxiety.

"I got her! Oscar, I fucking have her right now!"

"Well hello there, Mate," Oscar's voice fills the car, a warm purr that sends a shiver down my spine. And for the first time in a very, very long time, I feel a flicker of something that is forbidden, too.

CHAPTER 14

WILLOW

The voice of the second king, Oscar, I presume, speaks through the car speakers, his deep, commanding tone sending a shiver down my spine. "Mate," he says, the word a possessive, proprietary claim that makes my skin crawl. But I know it's just a ploy to manipulate me, to make me feel special and chosen. These men don't truly care about me or our supposed bond. All they want is power—to conquer and control the vampire world. And I can't let that happen. Caleb had warned me that one day something like this might happen. He explained to me that if it ever did, I wasn't to struggle. A vampire is stronger, faster, and a lot more witty than I'll ever be. I feel like rolling over and playing dead. Pity I'm not an opossum like the ones they have in America.

"Where are you?" The booming voice from Oscar fills the car, his voice deep, raspy, and surprisingly melodic, as if he could easily become a professional audiobook narrator. It brings back memories of my old life before Caleb had taken me to the manor—listening to audiobooks on my iPhone, enjoying the soothing voices of male narrators. But now, in this situation, Oscar's voice takes on a new meaning and sends shivers down my spine. It's the voice of a predator, and I'm his prey.

"I'm in Scotland," Jasper answers Oscar's question, his voice a casual, almost flippant contrast to Oscar's intensity.

"Scotland? But that's not even Edmund's territory," Oscar replies incredulously.

"No, it's not. I'm just jumping on the M6 now," Jasper explains, his tone suggesting that this is all just a casual road trip, not a kidnapping.

As we drive, I can't help but stare out at the passing scenery. The cars and buildings are all so unfamiliar to me after being locked up for so long. The trees blur into a green streak outside my window, and the sky seems impossibly vast. A small part of me is relieved to be out of the manor, and I instinctively rub at my ankle where the weight of the monitor had rested for years. It's strange how quickly I had become accustomed to its presence, and now without it, my leg feels oddly light and empty. But the freedom is a lie. I've just traded one cage for another.

"I'll be home in about 10 hours," Jasper tells Oscar and hangs up the phone.

"So Willow, seeing as we have 10 hours to kill, I would love to ask you some questions," Jasper says with an eager smile that I don't trust for a second.

I eye him warily, not sure what kind of questions he has in mind. "Do I have to answer?" I ask cautiously.

"No, but I would love to get to know you," he replies,

genuine curiosity in his voice. It's the kind of curiosity a cat has for a mouse right before it pounces.

"Do you normally talk to your food before you eat it?" I ask, my voice dripping with sarcasm.

To my surprise, Jasper bursts out laughing, a wide, genuine grin spreading across his face. "Are you always this sassy?" he asks, still chuckling.

I shrug nonchalantly by way of an answer.

"But yes," he replies, his voice laced with a darkness that sends a chill down my spine. "To answer your question, I always have a conversation with the people I bite. But you, Willow, you are not my food. You are my Mate." His eyes glimmer with pride as he emphasizes the word "Mate."

I can't help but shiver at the intensity of his gaze. "Please stop calling me Mate," I whisper, my voice barely audible.

"Why?" He asks, his tone curious and almost innocent, as if he can't possibly understand why I wouldn't want to be claimed by a creature of the night.

"Because it's not a good thing," I explain, my voice gaining a bit of strength.

His expression turns puzzled, and he tilts his head to the side. "Willow, you are the other half of my soul. The missing piece of my life that I have searched for, for the last 190 years." His words hang heavy in the air, a weight that threatens to crush me. "To me, it is a good thing."

Fury boils within me as I face him, my voice raw and seething. "How the fuck is being your mate a good thing?" I yell, flinging my words at him like daggers. "I have heard the prophecy; you're going to ruin the entire world.

Do you know what that means? It means my giving you power that will allow you to destroy your kind and rule over mine." My accusation hangs in the air, heavy and charged with emotion.

But he just sits there, cool and collected, as if this is all some twisted game. "That's not a good thing," I spat, shaking with anger. "It's a terrible thing. And here you are, acting like this is some sort of romantic affair. Let me tell you, it's not!" My chest heaves as I struggle to control my emotions.

"I have lost my whole life for this," I continue, my voice trembling with grief and desperation. "My ancestors all died trying to stop your reign of terror from coming to fruition. And now here we are at this very moment where everything could fall apart. I never asked for this; I don't want to fucking die!" A single tear traces a path down my cheek as I pour out my heart to one of the people who holds the fate of the world in their hands.

Jasper's knuckles clench tightly around the steering wheel as he abruptly turns on his blinker and veers the car off the road onto the shoulder.

Twisting in his seat to face me, he takes a deep breath before speaking. "Willow, you've been fed a bunch of falsehoods. I have no intention of harming you, or forcing you to complete the bond with me," he says earnestly, studying my face intently with his piercing gaze.

I want to believe him. God, I want to believe him. But how can I? Everything Caleb has told me, everything I've been taught, says otherwise.

"Do you know how long we've been searching for

you?" he asks, his voice soft, almost vulnerable. "190 years, Willow. 190 years of chasing shadows and dead ends. We followed every rumor, every whisper of your bloodline. We traveled to every corner of this country, and beyond. We searched through records, through graveyards, through forgotten villages that had been abandoned for decades."

He runs a hand through his hair, a gesture that seems so human, so tired. "Oscar spent decades in libraries and archives, pouring over birth records and death certificates, trying to trace your family tree. Theodore interrogated every vampire who might have had information, threatened every contact we had. And me?" He lets out a bitter laugh. "I hunted down every rogue vampire who might have been involved in your family's disappearance. I put down dozens of them, thinking maybe, just maybe, one of them had taken you, had hurt you."

My breath catches in my throat. I can see the exhaustion in his eyes, the weight of nearly two centuries of searching. But is it real? Or is he just a really good actor?

"We had no idea you were locked up," he continues, his voice gaining intensity. "We had no idea Edmund had you hidden away in some manor in the middle of nowhere. If we had known, Willow, we would have come for you. We would have torn down every wall, broken every chain, to get to you."

"Why?" I ask, my voice barely a whisper. "Why would you do all that?"

He looks at me like I've just asked him why the sun rises. "Because you're ours," he says simply. "Because the prophecy you were told is wrong. We don't want to rule the world, Willow. We don't want to destroy anything. We just want you. We want to protect you, to love you, to give you the life you deserve."

I shake my head, tears streaming down my face. "That's not what I was told. I was told you'd use me, that the bond would give you power to—"

"To what?" he interrupts, his voice gentle but firm. "To conquer? To destroy? Willow, we're already powerful. We're already kings. We don't need more power. What we need is you. What we need is to feel whole again."

He reaches out slowly, giving me time to pull away, and when I don't, he gently wipes a tear from my cheek with his thumb. "The prophecy Edmund told you is incomplete. We believe he's been manipulating you, manipulating us, for his own gain. We think there's more to it, something he's not telling anyone. And we need your help to figure out what that is."

I stare at him, my mind racing. Could it be true? Could everything I've been told be a lie? But why would Caleb lie to me? He's been my only friend, my only companion for three years. He's protected me, cared for me. Hasn't he?

But then again, he's also kept me locked up. He's also put that monitor on my ankle. He's also isolated me from the world.

"I don't know what to believe," I whisper, my voice breaking.

"I know," Jasper says softly, "And I'm not asking you to believe me right now. I'm just asking you to give me a chance to prove it to you. Come home with me. Meet my brothers. Let us show you that we're not the monsters you think we are."

Overwhelmed with emotion, I bury my face in my hands and allow tears to flow freely down my cheeks. This is all too much. Too much to process, too much to bear. What if he's telling the truth? What if I've been lied to this whole time? But what if he's the one lying? What if this is all just a trap?

Jasper tries to reach out a gentle hand to comfort me. "Please don't cry, Willow," he pleads softly. But how can I not? The weight of his words and the implications of the missing pieces of the prophecy are almost too much to bear. My heart races as I try to process it all.

Instead of allowing his touch, I scramble to the edge of my seat, desperately trying to put as much distance between us as possible. I feel his fingers brush against me and shudder involuntarily. "Please," I plead, "don't touch me."

"Okay," he replies, his voice smooth and calculated. "I won't touch you."

"I don't want to talk anymore," I declare, my voice firm despite the fear that coils in my stomach like a twisted serpent.

"Anything you want, Willow," he coos, his words dripping with a sincerity that I don't trust for a second. "It's all yours."

But deep down, I know the one thing I truly want—freedom—will never be mine as long as I'm trapped by this curse. I need to get away. I need to find Caleb. He'll know what to do. He'll protect me. But how do I get away from a vampire who can move faster than the speed of sound? I need a plan. A smart plan. Fighting him is useless. I've already learned that. I need to outsmart him. I need to play the long game. I need to make him think I'm starting to trust him, that I'm starting to accept my fate. And then, when he least expects it, I'll run.

Jasper sighs and pulls the car back onto the road, and we fall into an uncomfortable silence, aside from the sound of my occasional sniffles. I can't wrap my head around it all, but one thing is for sure: I have to find a way to stop the prophecy from coming true. And I have to do it without getting myself killed in the process.

As we continue on our journey, Jasper remains quiet, occasionally glancing over at me with a look of concern. I can tell that he's trying to figure out the best way to approach me, but I don't want to have anything to do with him. I just want to go home. But where is home anymore?

Then, Jasper speaks. "Willow, I know that this is all new to you, and I understand that you're scared. But I want you to know that I would never force you to do anything that you don't want to do. You have my word."

I look away from him, not wanting to be swayed by his words. "I don't know if I can trust you," I reply, my voice barely above a whisper.

"I understand that," he says, his voice gentle. "But I want to earn your trust. I want to show you that I'm not the monster that you think I am."

I turn to face him once more, studying his features. He's handsome, I'll give him that. But so are a lot of monsters. "What do you want from me?" I ask, trying to keep my voice steady.

"Nothing, nothing at all, just come home with me," was his only reply.

It wasn't like I had any other option, anyway. But that doesn't mean I'm going to make it easy for him. I'll play along for now. But the first chance I get, I'm gone.

CHAPTER 15

OSCAR

Every inch of my body is buzzing with anticipation since I hung up the phone with Jasper. Our Mate is finally in the car with him, after endless years of searching. A wave of emotions crashes over me all at once—happiness, excitement, nerves, and terror. What if she doesn't like us? The thought twists my stomach into knots as we wait to meet her. My palms are damp with sweat, and my heart feels like it's going to burst out of my chest. But deep down, a tiny flicker of hope burns bright—maybe she will accept us as her mates after all this time.

As soon as the call ended, I dashed straight to Theo's office. His usually composed demeanor has been replaced by a frantic energy, his steps pacing back and forth so rapidly that he's almost walking on air. The carpet behind my desk bears deep grooves from his anxious footprints, evidence of the stress we are both feeling. We exchange a knowing look, our minds in sync as we prepare for what is to come next.

With a deep breath, I pull up the tracker app on my laptop, grateful that it is attached to all of our cars. The last 10 hours have been spent following him home, his movements carefully monitored from afar. The only breaks he has taken during his journey were a brief pit stop on the motorway and a quick visit to a gas station. But now, as I watch his car turn onto the main road leading to our castle, I know he will be arriving in just 20 minutes. Panic sets in as I realize I need to quickly get changed before meeting her. There is no way I can greet her in my sweaty clothes.

I quickly instruct Theo to keep his eyes on the moving dot on the horizon. With a sense of urgency, I rush off to my room to take the quickest shower I have ever taken. The anticipation of her arrival is palpable, and I don't want to miss a single moment of it. As hot water cascades down my body, I can hear the sound of my heart racing in excitement. I scrub my skin until it's raw, trying to wash away the centuries of dust and grime that have accumulated on me. I need to be clean for her. Perfect for her.

As I step out of the shower, I feel the butterflies in my stomach flit around uncontrollably. This is it. This is the moment I have been waiting for, and I don't know whether to laugh, cry, or throw up. I push those thoughts aside, quickly drying off and slipping into one of my tailor-made suits, one that isn't super lavish, but also fitted to my frame. I run a comb through my hair, making sure every strand is in place. I check my teeth for any imperfections. I need to be perfect.

I practically sprint down the stairs, nearly tripping over my own feet in my haste. Theo is waiting for me, his eyes trained on the dot on the screen. "He's getting closer," he says, his voice low and steady.

I nod, trying to keep my breathing even. "Are you ready for this?" I ask him, trying to keep my voice from shaking.

Theo looks at me, his eyes gentle. "As ready as I'll ever be," he says. But I can see the tension in his shoulders, the way his jaw is clenched. He's just as nervous as I am.

With eager anticipation, we rush down the grand staircase to greet her. As we reach the bottom, we halt at the top of the smooth stone steps, our eyes fixed on Jasper's car as it pulls up in front of the ornate entrance. The sun glints off the polished exterior, adding to the dazzling display. Jasper gracefully emerges from the car, his confident gait bringing him around to open the door for her.

As the door opens, a delicate figure emerges. Her dark hair cascades down her back in gentle waves, glinting in the sunlight. Her skin is pale and porcelain-like, as if she spends more time indoors than out in the sun. My eyes are immediately drawn to her hourglass figure, accentuated by her full breasts. And yet, she stands tall and confident, defying societal norms for women's height. She is a vision of perfection. I want to lick her clean, to taste every inch of her, to make her mine.

I find myself unable to tear my gaze away from her as Jasper introduces us. "This is our Mate, Willow," he says with an undeniable sense of pride in his voice. She radiates beauty and grace, and I am completely captivated by her presence.

"Willow," I repeat her name, with a look at Jasper. Her

name, the castle's name, they belong together. It's a sign. It has to be.

"It's nice to finally meet you," I say, extending my hand for her to shake. But she just stares at it, her eyes hesitant and curious. I can see the fear in them, the mistrust. And it breaks my heart.

I can tell she is withdrawn, it bothers me to see her like that. I want to see her smile, to hear her laugh. I want to make her happy.

I can't help but feel drawn to her, my body reacting in ways that I can't explain. I want to touch her, to taste her, to claim her as my own. But I have to be patient. I have to let her come to me in her own time.

"Would you like a tour?" I offer her my voice, soft and gentle.

"No thank you," she states, her voice a soft whisper. "I would like to go to bed, please," she says with a huge yawn.

I nod, understanding that she must be exhausted after her long journey. "Of course, let me show you to your room," I say, gesturing for her to follow me.

As we make our way up the winding staircase, I can feel her eyes on me, studying me intently. I try not to let it affect me too much, but I can feel my body responding to her gaze. I can feel the heat rising in my cheeks, the way my heart is pounding in my chest. I want her so badly it hurts.

We finally arrive at her room, a spacious and elegant suite that overlooks the gardens. I had it prepared for her years ago. I had the walls painted a soft, calming blue. I had the furniture custom-made to match the room. I had the bed dressed in the finest Egyptian cotton sheets, so she would be comfortable. I wanted everything to be perfect for her.

"I hope you'll be comfortable here," I say, turning to face her.

She nods. "Thank you," she says softly.

I can't help but feel a surge of desire as I look at her, the way her lips curve into that small smile, the way her eyes sparkle in the dim light of the hallway. I want her more than anything I've ever wanted before. I want to push her against the wall and kiss her until she's breathless. I want to tear off her clothes and make love to her until the sun comes up. I want to claim her, to mark her, to make her mine forever.

But I know I have to be patient. I have to let her come to me in her own time.

I watch as she walks into the room and closes the door without another word.

As I turn to leave, I can't help but feel a pang of disappointment. I had hoped for some sort of interaction, something to give me hope that she was interested in me too. But I remind myself that this is only the first meeting and that there will be plenty of time for us to get to know each other.

Heading back down the stairs, I find Theo waiting for me, a knowing look in his eyes. "She's beautiful," he says simply.

I nod, unable to deny how captivated I was by her. "But she's also our mate; we can't rush things with her," I remind him.

Theo nods in agreement. "I know, but that doesn't mean we can't show her how much we care for her."

A warm smile spreads across my face as I glance at Theo. "You make a good point," I say, nodding in agreement. Jasper, now seated in a nearby chair, speaks up with a hesitant tone. "I'm not entirely confident that our plans will succeed," he admits. "She completely lost control on the way back here, shouting at me until her face turned red." He pauses, taking a deep breath before continuing. "She's been fed a false story about us, believing that we intend to rule over the mortals with an iron fist. And let's not forget the fact that she thinks we're planning to kill her."

I feel a surge of anger and frustration about the lies that have been told to her. It's not fair that she's been led to believe that we're some sort of tyrants. But I know that we have to be patient and show her through our actions that we're nothing like what she's been told.

"We'll show her the truth," I say firmly. "We'll prove to her that we're not who she thinks we are."

Theo nods in agreement. "We'll do whatever it takes to make her feel safe and loved," he says.

I smile at him, feeling grateful for his unwavering support.

"And how do you expect us to do that?" Jasper asks, his voice laced with skepticism. "She won't even let me touch her."

"We'll start by giving her space," I say, my voice calm and steady. "We'll let her get used to us, to our home. We'll show her that she's safe here, that she's loved. And then, when she's ready, she'll come to us."

I can only hope that I'm right.

CHAPTER 16

WILLOW

As soon as Oscar's face disappears behind the door, I feel a pang of guilt. How could I close the door on someone I had just met? But then again, how could I not? The universe is cruel and gave me the most handsome man I have ever seen. Three men I can't touch. They're like gods, with chiseled jawlines, strong noses, and eyes that seem to see right through me. It's almost too much to handle, and I can't help but feel that there must be some mistake. Why would three perfect men be interested in me?

But as I look at them, I can see the similarities between them. They are all tall, with broad shoulders and muscular arms. Their features are like puzzle pieces, fitting together in a way that makes it clear they are brothers. It's as if someone had taken the best parts of each of them and combined them to create the ultimate male specimen. I can't help but wonder what it would be like to be with them, to touch those perfect bodies and feel their lips on mine. But at the same time, I know it's dangerous. I have no idea who they are or what they want from me. And as much as my body craves their touch, my mind warns me against it.

Their hair is a striking shade of midnight black, each styled in a way that only enhances their chiseled jawlines. They are all dressed impeccably in suits that seem to have been tailored specifically for them. Despite their similar appearances, I can distinguish slight differences among the Kings—Jasper has dark brown eyes with glints of golden flecks, while Oscar's eyes are a deep, alluring blue. I have yet to see Theo's eyes, but I know they will be just as mesmerizing as the other two. The universe is cruel in its design. Why give me three mates who look as if they have stepped straight out of a GQ Magazine? The suit that Oscar wore clung to his body with precision, highlighting every muscle and curve. His defined arms and strong legs are accentuated by the garment, making it clear that he took good care of himself before he was turned. And just like Jasper, I can see glimpses of tattoos peeking out from beneath his sleeves and collar, adding an edge to his polished appearance.

I try to shake the thoughts from my head, but the Kings are like a gravitational force, pulling me toward them. I feel a sudden heat spread through my body at the thought of being with them, and I can't help but feel a twinge of desire in my core. My mind is in chaos as I grapple with the realization that these people, whom I have been taught to see as enemies, are kind and compassionate. How could this be? On one hand, I know I need to find a way to escape before they kill me. But on the other hand, their actions and words show a different side of them. A part of me wants to trust them and believe that maybe they aren't the monsters Caleb had portrayed them to be. But I can't ignore my fears and doubts. What if it's all just an act? What if they are just biding their time until they find the perfect opportunity to harm me? My inner thoughts are a jumbled mess as I try to figure out what to do next. Should I run, or should I stay and see where this strange relationship with my captors will lead? The thought of giving in and allowing them to take over the world makes my stomach churn, but at the same time, a part of me can't help but feel drawn to their mysterious ways. I am torn between my instincts and my curiosity, unsure of which path to choose.

feeling utterly drained, I decide to call it quits for the day. After enduring a grueling 10-hour car ride, the clock approaching 2 pm and my eyelids are heavy from the lack of sleep for over 24 hours. My thoughts are muddled and my mind feels like mush, desperately in need of rest and rejuvenation. I long for a deep, restful slumber that will bring clarity to my mind. Slowly taking in the room around me, I am struck by its elegant and spacious design. The walls are adorned with intricate patterns and rich, soft colours, while large windows allow natural light to stream in and illuminate every corner. Plush furnishings beckon me to sink into their softness and unwind as if I were a treasured guest in a luxurious hotel. This room feels like a sanctuary, a haven from the chaos of the outside world where I can find solace within myself.

Every detail has been chosen and placed—delicate gold accents dance alongside soothing shades of pink, creating an atmosphere straight out of a fairytale. A four-poster bed stands majestically in the center of the room, draped with sheer lace hangings that seem to shimmer in the sunlight. In any other circumstances, I would never want to leave this enchanting space. But this isn't any other circumstance. This is a gilded cage, and I'm the bird they've trapped inside.

There was a set of clothes folded on the bed, men clothes by the looks of it, but they were something to sleep in, as I quickly changed and I lay down on the plush bed and nestle my head into the soft pillows, my mind continuing to race with thoughts of the Kings. My heart pounds in my chest as I try to ignore the desire that still lingers within me. But it's impossible to forget the way their eyes roamed over me or the heat that spread through my body when they were near. I force myself to focus on the present moment, on the comfort of the bed beneath me, the sound of the wind rustling through the trees outside, and the warmth of the sunshine on my skin that is streaming through the windows. My eyelids grow heavy as I breathe in the sweet scent of the flowers that adorn the room. But even as I drift off to sleep, I know that this is just the beginning. The calm before the storm. I'm going to have to play along, be docile until I can work out a way out, or a way to contact Caleb.

CHAPTER 17

THEODORE

After Willow ran off to her room to sleep, Jasper, Oscar and I sat down in the drawing room and talked. Jasper explained how Willow had been lied to about the prophecy; she thought we were going to kill her. She was our mate; we were physically unable to hurt her. Caleb's explanation of vampirism to Willow had been riddled with falsehoods, and she had been deceived about the prophecy — the prophecy that only Edmund had witnessed. From the first moment I met him, I could tell that sly dickhead had something up his sleeve. His eyes would dart around, never making direct contact, and his words always seemed to have a hidden agenda. He was shifty and untrustworthy, like a snake slithering through the shadows.

As Jasper spoke, I could feel my blood boil. The thought of someone manipulating and lying to our mate made me want to rage. I knew we had to put an end to Edmund's games, and soon. Edmund had broken the carefully crafted accords I had painstakingly written, giving me a long-awaited reason to finally put him down. As the years passed, the others expressed their desire to remove Edmund from our midst, and this final transgression only strengthened my resolve to execute my right to kill him.

As we sat in the drawing room, discussing our next course of action against Edmund, Jasper voiced his concern about the other members potentially voting against removing him for good.

I shook my head, confident in my conviction to present concrete evidence of his deception and treachery. "No, I don't think they will," I replied firmly. "But we have to make sure we do this properly. We can't approach them without proof."

"Simply having Willow here is proof enough," Oscar states, his voice a low, dangerous growl.

"Yes and no, we can't prove that Edmund had her, we can't prove that Caleb was working on Edmund's word either," I explained. "At the moment, the most we can prove is that Caleb had her hidden away, and we have the right to take Caleb out." I sigh, running a hand through my hair.

"That is true," Oscar said. "But now that I have names, faces, and locations, I'll be able to go back through footage and bank transfers etc. and see if I can find a trail to link them together." He saidwith a hopeful glint in his eye.

The sun had long sunk beyond the horizon, leaving a soft orange glow in its wake. After hours of deliberating with Jasper and Oscar about Edmund, I suddenly realize that night has fallen once again. Frowning, I glance down at my watch and see that it is already 8 pm. In my distraction, I also notice that I haven't consumed any blood in the past 24 hours.

"I'm going to order in," I announce to the room, my stomach rumbling at the thought of food.

"How many should I call up?" I asked, my voice a low growl.

"I'll have one," Oscar replies with a tired yawn.

"Yes, please," Jasper agreed with a smile, his eyes shining in the dim light.

With a quick jerk of my hand, I reach into my pocket and retrieve my phone. My fingers flew over the screen as I dialed George's number.

"George," I spoke crisply into the receiver, my voice carrying an air of authority, "please make arrangements for three to be brought in."

"Of course, Sir," came George's prompt response before he ended the call.

Nodding to myself, I turn sharply on my heel and strode purposefully toward the back of the house. There, tucked away in a private room, is where we take blood donations from willing volunteers. With a gentle but firm hand, George leads the donors into the dimly lit room. The scent of old leather and stale blood filled the air as he carefully guided them to their designated chairs.

Today, as I entered the room, I noticed George leaving a blonde-haired female in the chair reserved for me. She was one of my favorites; her blood always carried a sweet hint of cinnamon that never fails to make my mouth water. But today, as I stared at her form, I felt a strange twinge of guilt and hesitation about using her as a donor. Is this what it feels like to have your mate around, leaving me always questioning my choices that I hadn't had an issue with in the past?

Sitting down next to her, I gently took hold of her wrist, feeling the delicate bones beneath my fingers. I had decided to forgo using her neck as it now felt improper and too intimate for a mere meal. Instead, I chose to use her arm, tracing the prominent veins with my fingertips before lifting it to my mouth. As I sank my fangs into her skin, I could hear a soft moan escape from the woman's lips. The rush of endorphins and the sweet taste of blood fill my senses. I found for the first time I was annoyed by her moaning. I suddenly felt wrong. With a few swift tugs, I retracted my fangs from her delicate skin and licked the wound to seal it. The taste of her blood lingered on my tongue, filling me with a sense of wrongness.

As she placed her hand back in her lap, I thanked her for her contribution and gracefully exited the room. Just as I reached the hallway, Oscar walked in and took a seat to my left, eagerly awaiting his turn with his donor. A sense of guilt washed over me as I made my way down the hall. Although I know what we do is necessary for our survival, it still feels dirty and cheap. Perhaps I'll make arrangements for some blood bags to be delivered to the house, and I'll rely on them for the time being. Until I can overcome this unsettling sensation that has washed over me like a tidal wave.

As I passed by the kitchen, the soft patter of tiny feet echoed down the stairs toward me. Looking up, my breath caught in my throat as I saw Willow descending the staircase. Her hair was tousled and wild, a perfect mess that framed her delicate features. Even with bed hair, she was utterly stunning. She was wearing a pair of my old pajama pants and a t-shirt that was so big on her it was practically a dress; I had placed them inside her room before she arrived, knowing full well we had no female clothes for her yet. She looked so small, so vulnerable, and so incredibly sexy. I wanted to throw her over my shoulder, carry her back to my room, and fuck her until she screamed my name.

"Good morning, Willow," I called out to her from where I stood.

She let out a small yelp, startled by my voice. "Oh shit, you scared me," she exclaimed, placing a hand over her heart.

I couldn't help but smile at her reaction. "Yes, I can hear your heart racing," I teased. "Are you hungry?" I asked, gesturing toward the kitchen. "I can whip something up for you."

Her shy demeanor melted into gratefulness. "Um… yes please," she responded softly.

"Come in, have a seat," I waved her toward the kitchen.

As she approached, my heart raced, and I could feel a rush of adrenaline coursing through my veins. In a moment of impulsiveness, I leaned forward and tenderly placed a quick kiss on her cheek. My cheeks immediately flushed with embarrassment as I stammered out an apology.

"Sorry," the words tumbled out of my mouth incoherently. "I have no idea how to act around you now that you're finally here." My eyes met Willow's, and I could see that she was silent, watching me intently. The tension between us felt thick and palpable, like a heavy fog settling between us. It was strange and unfamiliar.

As the tension hung heavy in the air, I attempted to break through it with a simple question.

"What would you like for breakfast?" I asked softly, trying to keep my voice light and calm.

Her response was quick and confident, with a hint of frustration underlying her words. "Eggs, please," she replied, her tone more assertive than before. "I have eggs every morning for breakfast." The determination in her voice hinted at a routine she held onto tightly, perhaps as a way to maintain some sense of control in her world.

I reached into the cold depths of the fridge and retrieved the carton of eggs; my fingers grazed against the smooth, shell-like surface. "How do you like them?" I inquired, already anticipating her answer.

"Sunny side up on toast with Vegemite," she declared confidently.

"I'm not sure about the Vegemite, but I can certainly whip up some eggs and toast for you," I replied, grabbing a pan from the drawer and expertly lighting the gas stove.

"What's this about Vegemite?" A new voice interrupted as Oscar sauntered into the room. He nonchalantly rolled up his sleeves as he spoke, showing off tattoos that moved with the shift of his arms.

I flipped a spatula in my hand and pointed it toward Willow, who sat at the kitchen counter with her legs crossed. "Willow here prefers her eggs served sunny side up, on toast with Vegemite," I announced proudly. Oscar opened the pantry door and reached toward the back, expertly retrieving a jar of the dark brown spread. He sat it down on the marble countertop next to the shiny chrome toaster. The sizzle of butter and eggs filled the air as I cracked open two eggs onto the hot pan. The aroma of toasted bread and savory Vegemite wafted through the kitchen, making my stomach growl in anticipation. Maybe I'll give the eggs and Vegemite and try myself. Anything to get closer to her, to understand her, to make her mine.

Chapter 18

WILLOW

I wake up to the feeling of being smothered in a giant, fluffy marshmallow, the kind that would make those fancy hotel commercials look like budget motels. The bed is so soft I think I might have actually sunk into it overnight, and for a terrifying second, I'm convinced I'll have to dig my way out like some kind of deranged mole person. The room is bathed in a soft, golden light that streams through windows so tall they could probably double as portals to another dimension, and I have to blink a few times to make sure I'm not still dreaming, that I haven't somehow stumbled into one of those period dramas my mom used to watch where everyone wore corsets and spoke in British accents. Nope. Still here. Still in the ridiculously opulent, straight-out-of-a-fairytale bedroom that looks like it was decorated by a princess with an unlimited budget and a serious addiction to gold leaf and pink and blue everything.

My stomach lets out a growl that sounds less like a human and more like a small, angry bear who's been denied breakfast for the third day in a row, reminding me that I haven't eaten since… since Caleb. The thought of him sends a sharp, painful pang through my chest, a confusing mix of anger and a deep, aching loneliness that makes me want to curl up in this ridiculously comfortable bed and never leave.

He lied to me. For three years, he fed me a steady diet of half-truths and outright fabrications, all while pretending to be my friend, my only friend, the one person I thought I could trust in this weird, isolated existence. And the worst part? I miss him. I miss his stupid, calming presence and the easy way we'd fall into conversation about books and cheese and the birds that nested in the trees outside. I hate that I miss him. I hate that part of me still wants to believe he had a good reason for lying, that maybe he was protecting me, even though the rational part of my brain is screaming that he's just another manipulative asshole who kept me locked up like some kind of pet.

I swing my legs out of bed, my feet sinking into a rug so plush it feels like I'm walking on a cloud made of unicorn hair and the dreams of small children. I need to find the kitchen. And an escape route. Preferably both, though I'm starting to suspect that escaping from a castle full of ancient, powerful vampires might be slightly more difficult than escaping from Caleb's manor in the middle of nowhere, Scotland. As I wander out of the room, I'm assaulted by the sheer, unapologetic grandeur of the place. Stone floors so worn down I can see my own horrified reflection staring back at me, complete with bed hair that looks like I've been electrocuted, hand-carved wooden doors that look older than most countries and probably cost more than a small island, and chandeliers that are dripping with so many crystals they're probably visible from space. It's all a bit much. Like, I get it; you're rich. You're stupidly, obscenely, probably own-several-countries rich. You can stop showing off now.

My internal monologue is cut short by a voice that seems to materialize out of the shadows like some kind of sexy, well-dressed ghost. "Good morning, Willow."

I let out a shriek that is probably illegal in several countries and definitely violates some kind of noise ordinance, clutching my chest as my heart tries to beat its way out of my ribcage and make a run for it. "Oh shit, you scared me," I gasp, glaring at Theodore, who is leaning against a doorway with a smirk that is equal parts infuriating and unfairly attractive. He's wearing another one of those perfectly tailored suits that probably costs more than my entire life, and his dark hair is artfully tousled in a way that suggests he either spent an hour on it or just rolled out of bed looking like a model. I'm betting on the former.

"Yes, I can hear your heart racing," he teases, his eyes glinting with amusement, and I have the sudden, overwhelming urge to throw something at his stupidly handsome face. "Are you hungry?" he asks, gesturing toward the kitchen with a casual wave of his hand. "I can whip something up for you."

And he does. I get my routine eggs with Vegemite toast, a small comfort in this sea of chaos and confusion and stupidly attractive vampires who keep appearing out of nowhere and scaring the crap out of me. Theo, in a move that I can only describe as either brave or incredibly stupid, makes a plate for himself, claiming he wants to try it. I watch with barely concealed glee as he takes the first bite, and the look on his face is priceless. It's a mixture of confusion, disgust, and a deep, existential regret, like he's just made a terrible life choice and is now questioning every decision that led him to this moment. I can't help but laugh — a genuine, belly-deep laugh that feels foreign after so long.

Oscar, who has since joined us in the kitchen, is doubled over, his whole body shaking with silent laughter, and I notice that he's rolled up his sleeves, which seems like a small thing but somehow feels significant, like he's letting his guard down just a little bit. "You're lucky we even have Vegemite in this house," Theo grumbles, pushing his plate away with a look of betrayal. "Oscar here is our resident grocery shopper and meal planner. He follows a strict diet and expects the rest of us to follow suit." He says it with a teasing edge, but there's an underlying affection there that makes my chest tighten.

"Are you one of those animal rights activists?" I ask, pulling a face at Oscar. He's so… pristine. so perfectly put together. It's hard to imagine him getting his hands dirty or doing anything that might mess up his perfectly pressed shirt.

"There's nothing wrong with eating ethically," he says, his voice a smooth, calming baritone that makes me want to curl up and take a nap, which is a weird reaction to have to someone who's technically my captor. "The way animals and food are treated before it reaches our plates would make anyone cringe." He then launches into a surprisingly detailed and passionate explanation of his ethical meat company, complete with statistics and anecdotes about visiting farms and ensuring humane treatment, and I find myself listening with a morbid curiosity. It's a weird flex, but I'll take it over being murdered any day. At least he cares about something.

"I guess this is one of those controversial discussions Caleb warned me about having at the dinner table," I say, trying to keep my tone light and not think about how much I miss those conversations, even the awkward ones.

Theo lets out a hearty laugh, the sound rich and warm. "Oh, Willow, you couldn't be more right. This is exactly one of those conversations."

Jasper saunters into the room then, a whirlwind of cheeky energy and designer clothes that probably cost more than a car. "What's so funny?" he asks, his eyes dancing with mischief, and I'm struck again by how different the three of them are, how they each have their own distinct energy.

"Willow asked Oscar about food," Theo replies, and Jasper groans dramatically, throwing his head back like he's in a Shakespearean tragedy. "Ah, did you get a lecture?" he teases, and I can't help but smile. After three years of talking to birds and having one-sided conversations with myself, the easy camaraderie between them is both comforting and exhilarating, like I've been invited to join some exclusive club that I didn't even know existed.

But the lighthearted mood doesn't last. After I've finished my meal, scraping up the last bits of Vegemite with my toast, Theo turns to me, his expression serious, all traces of his earlier amusement gone. "Willow, we need to talk about what happened yesterday," he says, his voice low and tense, and I feel my stomach drop.

My heart begins to race, and I'm sure they can all hear it, which is both embarrassing and terrifying. "What about it?" I ask, my voice barely a whisper.

"The prophecy," he says, his eyes searching mine like he's trying to read my thoughts. "Do you still believe it to be true?"

I hesitate, my mind racing through everything Caleb told me, everything I thought I knew. "I don't know," I finally admit, and it feels like a confession. "Everything I thought I knew about it feels like a lie now."

Jasper lets out a sigh, running a hand through his dark hair. "I can recite it in my sleep," he says, his voice cold and methodical, so different from his usual playful tone. And he does. His eyes glaze over slightly, like he's transported back to the moment he first heard it, and his voice takes on an almost robotic quality as he recites:

With the ascension of the three kings, a fourth will rise to join them.
However, it will not be another king who stands beside them.
No, a queen will step into their midst.
With her arrival, a great divide shall be created.
She carries within her a power so immense.
It will shake the very foundations of the world.
Her mere presence can incite fear and awe in equal measure.
This queen holds within her grasp.
Ability to fracture the vampire world as she transfers this power to her very mates.

Her existence threatens to tear apart everything that once seemed stable and unshakable.

The silence that follows is heavy, oppressive, and I feel like I can't breathe. My mind is racing, trying to reconcile what I just heard with what Caleb told me. "That's not what I was told," I say, my voice trembling, and I hate how weak I sound. "Caleb… he told me something completely different."

"What did he tell you?" Oscar asks, his voice gentle but urgent.

I take a deep breath, trying to remember the exact words that have haunted my nightmares for three years. "

He said:

With the ascension of the three kings, a fourth will rise to join them.

However, it will not be another king who stands beside them.

No, a queen will step into their midst.

With her arrival, a great divide shall be created.

She carries within her a power so immense it will shake the very foundations of the world.

Her mere presence can incite fear and awe in equal measure.

This queen holds within her grasp the ability to fracture the vampire world, and with her death at the hands of her mates, they will absorb her power, using it to enslave humanity and rule over both the mortal and immortal realms with an iron fist.

Her sacrifice will be the catalyst for a new world order, one where the king's reign supreme and unchallenged.

The three of them go completely still, and the look on their faces is a mixture of shock, rage, and something that looks almost like pain. "He added the part about your death," Theo says, his voice low and dangerous. "And the part about enslaving humanity. That's not in the original prophecy."

"The prophecy still doesn't sound great though," I say, because it doesn't. Even without the death and enslavement parts, it sounds ominous and vague and like the kind of thing that could be interpreted a million different ways.

"We can either rip everything apart or we can choose to repair and improve it," Jasper says, his eyes glinting with a fierce determination that makes me believe, just for a second, that maybe they're not the monsters Caleb painted them to be.

"We never sought to be kings," Theo adds, his voice tinged with regret, and I can see the weight of it on his shoulders. "It was a burden that was forced upon us."

"Thank goodness we didn't pass it to Edmund; he's a cunning and deceitful dickhead," Oscar spits, and the venom in his voice sends a shiver down my spine. I've never heard him sound so angry, so… violent.

"What, like kill him?" I ask, my voice dripping with sarcasm because that's my default setting when I'm terrified. "Do you resort to murder when someone angers you?" The thought is both horrifying and, if I'm being honest, a little bit thrilling in a messed-up way.

Oscar laughs, a sound that is both beautiful and terrifying, like wind chimes made of knives. "No, of course not. But if it comes down to protecting our kind and the greater good, we will do whatever is necessary."

My mind is reeling. I don't know what to believe, who to trust. Caleb lied to me, but are these three telling the truth? Or are they just better liars? It's all too much, and I can feel the panic starting to rise in my chest, making it hard to breathe. Just as I'm about to have a full-blown panic attack, Oscar claps his hands together, the sound sharp and sudden, breaking the tension. "That's enough morbid talking for today," he declares, and I could kiss him for it. Turning to me, he asks, "Willow, would you like a tour of your Castle?"

I raise my eyebrows, my brain struggling to process the words. "My Castle?"

A proud smile appears on Oscar's face, softening his features in a way that makes him look younger, less intimidating. "Yes, this is all yours now too." He says it with such sincerity, such… adoration, that it throws me for a loop. "You are our mate; there isn't anything we won't give you."

I stare at him, my mouth hanging open like a fish. My castle? My mates? What the actual fuck is happening? I feel like I've been dropped into some weird, twisted fairytale, and I'm not sure if I'm the princess or the dragon. And honestly, at this point, I'm not sure which one I'd rather be. Being a dragon sounds way more fun, but being a princess comes with a castle, apparently. A whole damn castle. This is insane. They're insane. I'm insane for even considering that maybe, just maybe, they're telling the truth.

CHAPTER 19

WILLOW

My castle. The words echo in my head like some kind of ridiculous, impossible mantra, the kind you'd find in a cheesy romance novel with a shirtless guy on the cover and a title like The Vampire King's Captive Bride. I stare at Oscar, half expecting him to burst out laughing and tell me it's all a joke, some kind of twisted vampire humor that I'm not privy to, like "ha ha, got you, you actually live in the dungeon." But he doesn't. He just stands there with this expression that's equal parts hope and adoration and something else I can't quite decipher, something that makes my stomach do weird little flips, and I realize he's completely, utterly, one hundred percent serious. He actually thinks this giant, gothic, probably haunted-by-at-least-twelve-ghosts castle is mine. Well, ours. Which is even weirder, because I'm pretty sure you can't just share a castle like you share an apartment. There have to be property laws about this kind of thing, right?

"A tour sounds... nice," I manage to choke out,

because what else am I supposed to say? No thanks, I'd rather stay in my gilded cage and have a panic attack? I'm pretty sure that's not an option, and honestly, the idea of getting out of this massive, overwhelming building and into some fresh air sounds like exactly what I need right now. So, I follow him, my legs feeling like they're made of jelly and my brain feeling like it's been put through a blender set to "maximum chaos," as he leads me out of the kitchen and through a series of hallways that are so long and grand I'm convinced we're going to need a map, a compass, and possibly a search and rescue team to find our way back.

We step outside through a pair of massive wooden doors that look like they were carved by someone who really, really loved dragons, and the cold night air hits me like a slap in the face, a welcome shock to my system that helps to clear some of the fog from my brain. The sky is a vast, inky black canvas, dotted with what has to be a million tiny, glittering stars, the kind of stars you never see in the city because of all the light pollution, and the moon hangs low and heavy like a giant silver coin, casting this ethereal, almost magical glow over everything. It's beautiful. so stupidly, breathtakingly beautiful it almost makes me forget that I'm technically a prisoner here, a pawn in some ancient, supernatural game that I don't understand and didn't ask to be a part of.

"Wow," I breathe, stopping in my tracks to take it all in. "Okay, I'll give you this. The view is pretty spectacular."

Oscar smiles, and it's a genuine smile, not the polite,

carefully controlled one he had at breakfast. "I'm glad you think so. I've always loved it out here at night."

We start walking along a cobblestone path that winds around the side of the castle, and I can't help but gawk at the sheer size of the place. It's massive, with towers that seem to stretch up into the sky, turrets that look like something out of a medieval fantasy, and walls made of dark grey stone that are probably thick enough to withstand a siege. There are ivy vines creeping up the sides in some places, giving it this romantic, slightly overgrown look, and gargoyles perched on the corners that are either really cool or really creepy, depending on how you look at them. I'm going with creepy, because they have these weird, leering faces that seem to follow you as you walk.

"So," I say, trying to sound casual, even though my brain is still doing somersaults, "how old is this place, exactly? Like, are we talking a few hundred years or full-on ancient?"

"The original structure was built in the 13th century," Oscar says, his voice taking on this almost professorial tone that's kind of endearing. "Though we've added to it and renovated it over the years. The east wing is relatively new, only about a hundred years old."

I let out a laugh that's more of a snort. "Only one hundred years. Right. Because that's totally normal and not at all insane."

He grins. "You'll get used to vampire timescales, eventually. A decade feels like the blink of an eye when you've lived as long as we have."

We walk in silence for a bit, the only sound the crunch of

our feet on the gravel path and the distant, rhythmic roar of the ocean. I can feel Oscar's presence beside me, a warm, solid weight in the darkness, and it's both comforting and terrifying in equal measure. He doesn't say anything, just walks at this slow, leisurely pace, as if he has all the time in the world. And I guess he does. He's a vampire. He has forever. Meanwhile, I'm over here with my finite human lifespan, trying to figure out what the hell I'm supposed to do with the rest of it.

My mind starts to wander, and before I know it, I'm mumbling to myself, my voice a low, barely audible whisper. "So, Caleb lied. He lied about everything. The prophecy, my death, the kings being evil overlords who want to enslave humanity… all of it. But why? To protect me? That's what he said, right? But protect me from what? From them? Or from something else? And what about them? Are they telling the truth? Or are they just better liars? More convincing? And this whole mate thing… is that even real? Or is it just some kind of vampire mind trick, like hypnosis or pheromones or something, to get me to do what they want?"

I glance over at Oscar, fully expecting him to tell me to shut up, to stop my incessant, neurotic muttering. But he doesn't. He just keeps walking, his eyes fixed on the path ahead, a small, almost imperceptible smile playing on his lips. It's like he knows I need to do this, to work through it all out loud, and he's giving me the space to do it. It's… nice. Nicer than anyone has been to me in a long time, except for Caleb. And he was lying to me. So, there's that.

"You can keep going," Oscar says gently, not looking at me. "I don't mind. Sometimes it helps to say things out loud."

"Thanks," I mutter, feeling oddly grateful. "I must sound like a crazy person."

"You sound like someone who's had their entire world turned upside down," he says, and there's no judgment in his voice, just understanding. "That's perfectly reasonable."

We reach a stone terrace that juts out from the side of the castle, and the view from here is even more spectacular. The castle is perched on this rocky cliff that drops down to the ocean below, and I can see the waves crashing against the rocks with this wild, untamed fury, sending up sprays of white foam that catch the moonlight. In the distance, there's a dark, shadowy forest that stretches as far as I can see, and a winding path that leads up into the hills, disappearing into the trees. It's all so… dramatic. so epic. Like something out of a fantasy novel. My fantasy novel, apparently.

"It's beautiful," I say, my voice filled with genuine awe. "But it's also a little bit terrifying. LikeLike one wrong step and you're plummeting to your death."

"There are railings," Oscar points out, gesturing to the stone balustrade that runs along the edge of the terrace. "And we'd catch you before you fell."

"Vampire reflexes?" I ask, raising an eyebrow.

"Vampire reflexes," he confirms with a nod.

I lean against the railing, careful not to get too close to the edge, and stare out at the ocean. "So, what's down there? Besides rocks and certain death?"

"There's a small beach," Oscar says, coming to stand beside me. "It's accessible by a path that winds down the cliff face. We used to go swimming there, back when… well, back when things were different."

There's a sadness in his voice that makes me look at him, really look at him. In the moonlight, I can see the lines of his face, the sharp angles of his jaw, and the way his dark hair falls across his forehead. He's beautiful, in that same otherworldly, almost unreal way that Theo and Jasper are, but there's something softer about him, something more approachable. Less likely to murder me in my sleep, maybe.

"Back when you weren't searching for your prophesied mate?" I ask, and I'm aiming for sarcastic, but it comes out more curious than anything.

"Back when we had hope," he says quietly. "And then we lost it. And then we found you."

The weight of his words settles over me like a blanket, heavy and warm and suffocating all at once. I don't know what to say to that, so I just stand there, staring out at the ocean, listening to the waves crash and the wind whistle through the trees.

"Can I ask you something?" I finally say, breaking the silence.

"Anything."

"This mate bond thing. The pull I'm feeling toward you guys. Is it real? Or is it just… I don't know, vampire magic or something?"

Oscar turns to face me, his expression serious. "It's real, Willow. It's the most real thing I've ever felt in my entire existence. The bond between mates is… it's hard to explain. It's not magic, exactly. It's more like… recognition. Like your soul recognizes ours, and ours recognizes yours. It's a pull, yes, but it's also a choice. You can fight it if you want to. But it will always be there."

"And if I choose not to fight it?" I ask, my voice barely a whisper.

"Then we get to spend the rest of eternity making you happy," he says simply.

I let out a shaky breath, my mind racing. "That's a lot of pressure."

"I know," he says, and there's that gentle understanding again. "And I'm not asking you to decide anything right now. I just want you to know that we're here. And we're not going anywhere."

We stand there for a long moment, the silence between us comfortable now, companionable. And then I ask the question that's been nagging at me since we stepped outside.

"So, what's the Wi-Fi password?"

Oscar blinks, clearly not expecting that. And then he laughs, a genuine, hearty laugh that makes his whole face light up. "You want the Wi-Fi password?"

"Well, yeah," I say, grinning. "I mean, Caleb had me cut off from the world for three years. I miss being able to search things, or Google 'what to do when you're the prophesied mate of three vampire kings.' I'm sure there's a wikiHow article about it."

He's still laughing, shaking his head. "I'll set you up with access tomorrow. I handle all the tech stuff around here."

"You?" I ask, genuinely surprised. "I would have pegged Jasper as the tech guy. He seems like the type."

"Jasper can barely operate a smartphone without

breaking it," Oscar says, rolling his eyes. "No, I'm the one who keeps everything running. Servers, security systems, the works."

"A vampire IT guy," I say, grinning. "That's actually kind of awesome. Do you have, like, a secret lair full of computers?"

"I have an office," he says, trying to sound dignified, but I can see the amusement in his eyes. "With computers, yes. But it's not a lair."

"I'm going to call it a lair anyway," I inform him.

"I wouldn't expect anything less," he says, and there's this warmth in his voice that makes my chest tighten.

We start walking again, following the path as it winds around the castle and toward the forest. Oscar points out different features as we go—the old stables that have been converted into a garage, the greenhouse where he grows herbs for cooking, the training grounds where Jasper apparently likes to spar with Theodore. It's all so normal and domestic and weird, and I find myself relaxing bit by bit, my guard slowly coming down.

"So, the forest," I say, nodding toward the dark line of trees ahead. "Is it safe to walk in there, or is it full of, like, werewolves and other supernatural nasties?"

"No werewolves," Oscar assures me. "Just deer and the occasional fox. There are some trails that lead up into the hills. Beautiful views during the day."

"And at night?"

"Even more beautiful," he says. "If you're not afraid of the dark."

"I've spent the last three years in the middle of

nowhere, Scotland," I point out. "I'm pretty used to the dark."

We reach the edge of the forest, and I can see the path disappearing into the trees, winding up into the hills. The trees are tall and ancient, their branches reaching up toward the sky like gnarled fingers, and there's this sense of timelessness about the place, like it's been here forever and will be here long after we're all gone.

"I think I'd like to explore those trails sometime," I say, surprising myself. "When it's light out, maybe."

"I'd be happy to take you," Oscar says, and there's this hopeful note in his voice that makes me smile.

We turn and start walking back toward the castle, and I find myself thinking about everything that's happened, everything I've learned. Caleb lied to me. The prophecy isn't what I thought it was. These three vampires—these three kings—claim I'm their mate, and they've been searching for me for 190 years. It's insane. It's impossible. And yet… here I am, standing on the grounds of a castle that's apparently mine, talking to a vampire who seems genuinely kind and patient and understanding. And I realize that I have a choice to make. I can keep fighting, keep questioning, keep holding onto my anger and fear. Or I can let it go. I can take a leap of faith and see where this goes.

Because what do I have to lose, really? My freedom? I never really had it, anyway. Caleb kept me just as locked up as they are, just in a different location. My life? They could have killed me a dozen times over by now if that's what they wanted. My heart? Well, that's the scary part, isn't it? But maybe it's worth the risk.

I take a deep breath, the salty air filling my lungs, and make a decision as I look at the shy that is transitioning over to day now. We had walked through the castle for hours, but it felt like minutes. A reckless, probably stupid, definitely impulsive decision formed in my mind, but a decision nonetheless. I'm going to believe them. For now. I'm going to give this a chance to see where it goes. Because maybe, just maybe, they're telling the truth. And maybe, just maybe, this is where I'm supposed to be.

CHAPTER 20

OSCAR

I want to reach out and touch her, to pull her close and never let go, but I force myself to be patient. She's been through so much, been lied to for so long. She needs time, and I will give her all the time in the world.

"There's one more place I want to show you," I say softly, my voice barely above a whisper in the quiet of the night. "If you're not too tired."

She looks up at me, her blue eyes reflecting the moonlight, and I see curiosity there, mixed with something else. Something that makes my dead heart feel like it's beating again. "I'm not tired," she says, and there's a slight breathlessness to her voice that sends a jolt of desire straight through me.

I lead her through a side door and down a corridor I've walked a thousand times, but tonight it feels different. Tonight, every step feels weighted with possibility, with the promise of something I've waited 190 years to experience. We reach the glass doors of the sunroom, and I pause, my hand on the handle.

"I had this built about fifty years ago," I tell her, pushing the door open. "It's my favorite room in the entire castle."

The sunroom is a marvel of glass and steel, a modern addition to the ancient structure that somehow feels perfectly at home. The walls and ceiling are entirely glass, offering an unobstructed view of the night sky, and the room is filled with lush, green plants that I've carefully cultivated over the years. There are comfortable lounges with plush white cushions, soft rugs scattered across the floor, and the air is warm and fragrant with the scent of jasmine and lavender.

Willow steps inside, her mouth falling open in wonder. "Oscar, this is… this is beautiful," she breathes, turning in a slow circle to take it all in. "It's like being outside, but warmer."

"That was the idea," I say, closing the door behind us. "I wanted a space where I could be surrounded by nature without having to deal with the cold or the rain. And during the day, when the sun comes through the glass, it's… it's magical."

She walks over to one of the lounges and runs her hand over the soft cushions, and I watch the way her fingers trail across the fabric, imagining those same fingers trailing across my skin. "But you can't come in here during the day, can you?" she asks, looking back at me. "Because of the sun?"

"I can," I correct gently. "The sun doesn't kill us, remember? It's just… uncomfortable. But for this room, for the chance to sit in the sunlight and feel warm again, I'd endure a little discomfort."

She smiles at that, a soft, genuine smile that makes something in my chest tighten. "You really love this room, don't you?"

"I do," I admit, moving closer to her. "But I think I'm going to love it even more now. Because you're here."

The air between us shifts, becomes charged with an electricity that makes my skin tingle and my breath catch. She's looking at me with those wide, beautiful eyes, and I can see the uncertainty there, the fear, but also the desire. The pull of the mate bond is strong. I can feel it thrumming between us like a living thing, and I know she feels it too.

"Willow," I say softly, reaching out to tuck a strand of her dark hair behind her ear. My fingers graze her cheek, and she shivers at the touch. "I know this is all overwhelming. I know you're confused and scared. But I need you to know something."

"What?" she whispers, her voice barely audible.

"I have waited 190 years for you," I tell her, my voice rough with emotion. "190 years of searching, of hoping, of dreaming about the moment I would finally meet you. And now that you're here, standing in front of me, you're even more perfect than I ever imagined."

Tears well up in her eyes, and one spills over, trailing down her cheek. I catch it with my thumb, wiping it away gently. "I'm not perfect," she says, her voice breaking. "I'm just… I'm just me. I'm nobody special."

"You're everything," I tell her fiercely. "You're my mate. You're the missing piece of my soul. You're the reason I've kept going all these years. And I know you don't fully understand that yet; I know you're still working through everything. But I need you to know that I will wait as long as it takes. I will be patient. I will be gentle. I will be whatever you need me to be."

She lets out a shaky breath, and then, before I can react, she rises up on her toes and presses her lips to mine. The kiss is tentative at first, hesitant, as if she's testing the waters. But then something shifts, and she deepens the kiss, her hands coming up to grip the front of my shirt. I wrap my arms around her waist, pulling her close, and lose myself in the taste of her, the feel of her body pressed against mine.

When we finally break apart, we're both breathing hard, and I rest my forehead against hers, my eyes closed, savoring the moment. "Willow," I murmur, my voice hoarse. "Tell me what you want. Tell me what you need."

"I don't know," she admits, her voice trembling. "I'm so confused. I spent three years being told you were monsters, and now… now I'm here, and you're being so kind, so patient. And I feel this pull toward you, this need that I don't understand. It's like my body knows something my brain hasn't caught up to yet."

"That's the mate bond," I explain gently, pulling back slightly so I can look into her eyes. "It's your soul recognizing mine. It's natural, Willow. It's right. But that doesn't mean you have to act on it before you're ready. We can take this as slow as you need."

She bites her lip, and I have to resist the urge to lean down and capture that lip between my own teeth. "What if… what if I don't want to take it slow?" She asks, her cheeks flushing pink. "What if I want… I mean, I've never…" She trails off, embarrassed, and it's the most endearing thing I've ever seen.

Understanding dawns, and with it, a surge of desire so strong it nearly brings me to my knees. "You've never been touched before," I say, and it's not a question.

She shakes her head, her blush deepening. "Caleb kept me isolated. And before that, I was just… I was focused on school, on my future. I never had time for relationships."

The thought that I will be her first, that I will be the one to show her, to teach her what her body is capable of, is almost too much to bear. My cock hardens instantly, straining against the confines of my trousers, and I have to take a deep breath to steady myself.

"Willow," I say, my voice dropping to a low, rough growl. "If you let me touch you, if you let me show you what it feels like, I promise I will make it good for you. I promise I will be gentle. But you have to be sure. Because once I start, I don't know if I'll be able to stop."

She looks up at me, her eyes dark with desire, and nods. "I'm sure," she whispers. "I want this. I want you."

That's all the permission I need. I cup her face in my hands and kiss her again, this time with all the pent-up longing and desire I've been holding back. She moans into my mouth, and the sound goes straight to my cock, making it throb with need. My hands slide down her body, tracing the curves of her waist, her hips, and she arches into my touch, her body responding instinctively.

"You're so beautiful," I murmur against her lips, my hands roaming over her body, learning every curve, every dip. "So perfect. I've dreamed about this moment for so long."

"Show me," she breathes, her hands fisting in my shirt. "Show me what you've dreamed about."

I groan, my control slipping, and scoop her up into my arms. She lets out a surprised laugh, wrapping her arms around my neck, and I carry her over to one of the lounges, laying her down gently on the soft white cushions. She looks up at me, her dark hair spread out around her like a halo, her lips swollen from my kisses, and I've never seen anything more beautiful in my entire existence.

I kneel beside the lounge, my hands trembling slightly as I reach for the hem of her dress. "May I?" I ask, my voice rough.

She nods, biting her lip again, and I slowly, reverently, lift her dress up and over her head, revealing her body to me inch by inch. She's wearing simple white cotton under-wear, and the sight of her, so innocent and pure, makes my mouth water. I toss the dress aside carelessly, something I would never normally do, but right now I don't care about anything except her.

"Don't hide from me," I say softly as she moves to cover herself. "You're perfect. Every inch of you."

I lean down and press a kiss to her stomach, just above the waistband of her panties, and she gasps, her body jerking at the sensation. I smile against her skin and continue my exploration, kissing my way up her body, over her ribs, the valley between her breasts, her collar-bone, her neck. She's trembling beneath me, her breath coming in short, sharp gasps, and I can smell her arousal, sweet and intoxicating.

"Oscar," she moans, her hands tangling in my hair. "Please."

"Please what, sweetheart?" I murmur, nipping at her earlobe. "Tell me what you want."

"I want… I want you to touch me," she says, her voice barely a whisper.

"Where?" I ask, my hand sliding down her side, teasing. "Here?" I cup her breast through her bra, and she arches into my touch, a soft moan escaping her lips. "Or here?" My hand slides lower, over her stomach, and I can feel her muscles quivering beneath my touch.

"Everywhere," she gasps. "Touch me everywhere."

I groan, my cock throbbing painfully, and reach behind her to unclasp her bra. I slide it off slowly, revealing her breasts to me, and I have to take a moment just to look at her, to memorize every detail. Her nipples are already hard, peaked and begging for my mouth, and I lean down and take one between my lips, sucking gently.

She cries out, her back arching off the lounge, and I smile against her skin, using my tongue to tease and torment her. My hand slides down her body, over her stomach, and I hook my fingers into the waistband of her panties. I look up at her, seeking permission, and she nods frantically, her eyes glazed with desire.

I pull her panties down slowly, revealing her to me completely, and the sight of her, spread out before me, wet and ready, nearly undoes me. "You're so wet for me," I murmur, running a finger through her folds. "So perfect."

She whimpers, her hips bucking up to meet my touch, and I can't resist any longer. I lean down and press a kiss to her inner thigh, then another, moving closer and closer to where she needs me most. When I finally taste her, when my tongue slides through her folds and I taste her sweetness, I groan, the sound vibrating against her sensitive flesh.

"Oh God," she gasps, her hands fisting in my hair, holding me to her. "Oscar, that feels… oh God."

I devour her, my tongue exploring every inch of her, learning what makes her gasp, what makes her moan, what makes her body tremble. I slide a finger inside her, feeling her tight heat clench around me, and she cries out, her hips grinding against my face. I add a second finger, stretching her gently, and curl them inside her, searching for that spot that will drive her wild.

When I find it, she screams, her body convulsing, and I know she's close. I focus my attention on her clit, sucking and licking and teasing, my fingers pumping in and out of her in a steady rhythm. "That's it, sweetheart," I murmur against her flesh. "Let go. Cum for me."

And she does. She shatters, her body arching off the lounge, her inner walls clenching around my fingers as wave after wave crashes over her. I work her through it, prolonging her orgasm, until she finally collapses back onto the cushions, her body trembling with aftershocks.

I pull my fingers free and bring them to my lips, sucking them clean, savoring the taste of her. "You taste like heaven," I tell her, my voice rough with desire.

She looks up at me, her eyes glazed and satisfied, and reaches for me. "What about you?" she asks, her hand sliding down to cup the bulge in my trousers.

I groan, my hips bucking into her touch. "It's waited 190 years," I tell her, even though every fiber of my being is screaming at me to take her, to claim her. "It can wait a bit longer. That was about you."

She smiles, a lazy, satisfied smile, and I know I've made the right choice. I stand and scoop her up into my arms again, carrying her toward the door. "Let's get you cleaned up," I murmur, pressing a kiss to her forehead.

I carry her upstairs to my bedroom, to the bathroom that's attached, and set her down gently on the edge of the large bathtub. I turn on the taps, adjusting the temperature until it's perfect, and add some of the aromatic salts I keep on hand. The scent of lavender fills the air, and I watch as the tub fills, my mind still reeling from what just happened.

Once the tub is full, I turn back to her and gently lift her to her feet. She's still naked, still flushed from her orgasm, and I have to resist the urge to take her right here, right now. Instead, I guide her into the tub, and she sighs contentedly as she sinks into the warm water.

"Are you joining me?" she asks, looking up at me with those big, beautiful eyes.

I hesitate for only a moment before I start to undress, shedding my clothes quickly and efficiently. Her eyes widen as she takes in my body, the tattoos that cover nearly every inch of my skin, and I see the curiosity and desire in her gaze.

"You're covered in tattoos," she says, her voice filled with wonder.

"I am," I confirm, stepping into the tub behind her. "Everyone tells a story."

"Is there any part of you that remains untouched by ink?" she asks, and I can hear the smile in her voice.

I settle behind her, pulling her back against my chest, and point to the spot over my heart. "Right here," I tell her. "This spot has been waiting for your name."

She turns her head to look at me, her eyes shining with unshed tears. "Really?"

"Really," I confirm. "And here," I lift my left hand, showing her my ring finger. "This is where I'll tattoo your initials when I marry you."

She smiles, a genuine, radiant smile, and leans back against me. I wrap my arms around her, holding her close, and we sit there in comfortable silence, the warm water soothing our bodies, the scent of lavender filling the air.

"Thank you," she whispers after a long moment. "For being patient with me. For being gentle. For making me feel… for making me feel like I matter."

"You do matter," I tell her fiercely, pressing a kiss to the top of her head. "You matter more than anything in this world. And I will spend the rest of eternity proving that to you."

CHAPTER 21

JASPER

I'm sprawled on my bed, a study in calculated indolence, staring up at the ridiculously ornate plasterwork on my ceiling and trying my best not to listen. But it's impossible. Even three floors up, with my door shut and music playing softly from my phone, I can hear them. My vampire hearing, usually a gift, is a special kind of torture right now.

I can hear the soft murmur of Oscar's voice, low and soothing, like the rumble of distant thunder. And then I hear her. Willow. Her voice is a soft, hesitant whisper at first, and then it grows stronger, more confident. And then… then there are other sounds. A soft gasp. A shaky breath. A low, throaty moan that goes straight to my dick and makes it twitch with a life of its own.

"Fuck," I groan, rolling onto my stomach and burying my face in my pillow. This is a new kind of hell. I knew Oscar was taking her on a tour of the grounds, a gentle, patient introduction to her new life, her new prison. I should have gone with them, should have been there to charm her, to make her laugh, to see that look of wonder in her eyes as she took in the castle. But I couldn't. The thought of being that close to her, of smelling her scent, of feeling the pull of the mate bond, and not being able to touch her… it was too much. so I ran. I scurried off to my room like a coward, and now I'm paying the price.

I can hear them moving, their footsteps faint on the stone path below. They're in the sunroom now, Oscar's little glass sanctuary. I can picture it perfectly: the last of the moonlight streaming through the glass, the scent of jasmine and lavender in the air, the soft white cushions on the lounges. And them. Together. Alone.

My cock is hard now, a throbbing, insistent ache against the fabric of my pants. I try to think about something else, anything else. The rogue vampire in Camden. The security arrangements for the conference. The ridiculously expensive suit I bought last week and haven't even worn yet. But it's no use. Every thought, every image, is consumed by her. By the sound of her voice, the scent of her skin, the memory of her fighting me in the car — all fire and fury and life.

Another moan drifts up from the sunroom, louder this time, sharper, and my control snaps. I flip onto my back, my hand going to my cock, stroking it through my pants. It's not enough. I need more. I need to feel her, to taste her, to lose myself in her. But I can't. Not yet. So, I do the next best thing.

I close my eyes and let my imagination run wild. I picture her on the lounge, her dark hair spread out around her like a halo, her eyes wide with a mixture of fear and desire. I see Oscar leaning over her, his movements slow and deliberate, his voice a low, seductive murmur. He's good, I'll give him that. For a guy who hasn't been with anyone in 190 years, he still has the skills. He knows how to be gentle, how to be patient, how to build the tension until she's begging for it.

I can hear her breath catching, her heart rate quickening. I can smell her arousal, a sweet, intoxicating scent that makes my fangs ache. And then I hear it. The sound of her coming undone — a high, keening cry that echoes through the quiet night and straight into my soul. And it's the most beautiful, most agonizing sound I've ever heard.

My hand moves faster, my own breathing becoming ragged. I imagine it's my making her feel that way; my touching her; me tasting her. I picture myself pushing Oscar aside, claiming what's mine, burying myself so deep inside her that she can't tell where she ends and I begin. I imagine her legs wrapped around my waist, her nails digging into my back, her voice screaming my name as I fuck her until she can't think, can't breathe, can't do anything but feel.

The thought is so vivid, so real, that I come with a guttural groan, my release spilling hot and sticky over my hand and stomach. For a moment, there's nothing but blissful, mind-numbing pleasure. And then the jealousy hits, a cold, bitter wave that washes over me, leaving me feeling empty and hollow.

She's ours. She's my mate. And I'm up here, jerking off like a teenager, while my brother gets to touch her, to taste her, to make her feel things I can only dream about. It's not fair. It's not right. But what am I supposed to do? Burst in there and demand my turn? I'm not Theodore. I can't just take what I want, consequences be damned. I have to be the fun one, the charming one, the one who makes her laugh. But right now, I don't feel very fun or charming. I just feel… pathetic.

I lie there for a long time, listening to the sounds from the sunroom fade away, replaced by the soft murmur of their voices as they talk. I can hear the water running in Oscar's bathroom, and I know he's cleaning her up, taking care of her. The thought sends another pang of jealousy through me, but this time it's mixed with something else. Relief. Gratitude. He's being good to her. He's being gentle. And that's what she needs right now.

Eventually, I drag myself out of bed and into my own bathroom, the need to wash away the evidence of my pathetic little wank session suddenly overwhelming. The hot water cascades over my body, but it does little to soothe the ache in my chest, the emptiness in my soul. I scrub my skin until it's raw, but I can still smell her on me, the phantom scent of her arousal clinging to my skin.

Tugging on a fresh pair of sweatpants and a t-shirt, I head downstairs, my feet carrying me toward the kitchen on autopilot. I need something to do, something to distract me from the endless loop of thoughts and images in my head. Maybe I'll make a sandwich. Or raid the freezer for some of Oscar's fancy ice cream. Or maybe I'll just stand there and stare into the fridge until my brain shuts off.

I'm not surprised to find Theodore in the kitchen, sitting at the small table by the window, his phone in his hand and a scowl on his face. He looks up as I enter, and his eyes are dark and stormy, a reflection of my own turmoil.

"Couldn't sleep?" I ask, trying for a casual tone and failing miserably.

"The noises from the sunroom were a little distracting," he says, his voice a low, dangerous growl. "I thought I'd work down here until it stopped." He looks me up and down, a smirk playing on his lips. "I can see you enjoyed the show, though."

I flush, caught out. "Didn't you?" I shoot back, and the smirk on his face falters.

He lets out a sigh, running a hand through his perfectly styled hair and messing it up in a way that would probably give Oscar a heart attack. "Oh, I did," he admits, his voice heavy with a weariness that goes beyond just lack of sleep. "But it was too distracting to work. And it only ramped up my jealousy."

"I'm glad I wasn't the only one," I say softly, the confession a weight off my chest. "I was starting to feel like a real creep, hiding in my room and listening in."

"We're all creeps, Jasper," Theodore says, his voice laced with a bitter self-loathing that I know all too well. "We're monsters pretending to be men. And now we have this… this perfect, innocent creature in our lives, and we're all just circling her like sharks, waiting for our turn to take a bite."

He's right, of course. But hearing him say it out loud makes it feel even more sordid, more shameful. "I don't know how we're supposed to do this," he continues, his voice low and uncertain. "Share her, I mean. I know she's our mate, all three of us. But how does that even work? How do we make it work without tearing each other apart?"

"I honestly never put any thought into it," I admit, feeling foolish. "For 190 years, all I could think about was finding her. I never stopped to consider what would happen after we did. I just assumed she would come into our lives and… and fit. Like the missing piece of a puzzle."

"And what if she doesn't fit?" Theodore asks, his eyes boring into mine. "What if she doesn't want us? What if she chooses one of us but not the others? Then what do we do?"

The question hangs in the air between us, heavy and unanswered. Because we don't know. We have no idea. We're in uncharted territory here, and we're all just fumbling in the dark, trying to find our way.

I need to change the subject to lighten the mood before we both spiral into a pit of despair. "Oh, I almost forgot," I say, forcing a cheerful tone. "I did something."

Theodore raises an eyebrow, his expression wary. "What did you do?"

"I stole your beloved copy of Wuthering Heights from the library and put it on Willow's bed," I announce with a flourish.

He groans, running a hand down his face in exasperation. "Jasper, you do realize that's a first edition, right? A personally signed first edition from Emily Brontë herself."

"Oh, I know," I say with a grin. "But I also know that it's Willow's favorite book. She had this tattered, dog-eared copy with her when I found her at the manor. It was practically falling apart, but she was still clinging to it like a lifeline."

The look on Theodore's face shifts from annoyance to

something else, something soft and almost… hopeful. "It's her favorite book?" he asks, his voice barely a whisper.

"Her favorite," I confirm, my grin widening. "Maybe you should show her your library sometime. I have a feeling she'd appreciate it."

CHAPTER 22

WILLOW

My brain feels like a snow globe that's been shaken too hard, a chaotic swirl of thoughts and emotions that refuse to settle. One minute, I'm on top of the world, feeling a sense of hope and possibility that I haven't felt in years. The next, I'm spiraling into a pit of doubt and fear, convinced that I'm making a terrible mistake, that I'm walking into a trap that's even more elaborate and dangerous than the one I just escaped.

I pace my room, the plush carpet doing little to cushion the frantic energy that's coursing through me. I've been lied to. For three years, my entire reality has been a carefully constructed fiction, designed to keep me safe, to keep me hidden, to keep me… a prisoner. Caleb — my friend, my protector, my only link to the outside world — was my jailer. And the monsters he warned me about, the three kings who would supposedly kill me and enslave humanity, are… well, they're not what I expected. They're beautiful and terrifying and confusing, and they claim I'm their mate, the missing piece of their souls. It's all so insane, so utterly unbelievable, that I feel like I'm losing my mind.

I stop pacing and sink onto the edge of the ridiculously large bed, burying my face in my hands. What if Caleb was right? What if this is all just a game, a long con to get me to lower my guard? What if they're just waiting for the right moment to strike, to take my power and fulfil the prophecy? If I trust them, if I let them in, and they turn out to be the monsters Caleb described, can I live with that? Can I forgive myself for being so naïve, so stupid, as to believe their pretty words and handsome faces? The fate of the world, apparently, rests on my shoulders. No pressure or anything.

But then… what if they're telling the truth? What if Caleb was the one who was lying, who was manipulating me for his own reasons? What if these three kings really have been searching for me for 190 years, their souls incomplete without mine? What if this is where I'm supposed to be? The thought is both terrifying and exhilarating. For my entire life, I've been a bird in a cage. A gilded cage, maybe, but a cage nonetheless. First with my "parents," who were actually my handlers, and then with Caleb, in his isolated manor in the middle of nowhere. I've never been free. I've never had a choice. But now… now, maybe I do. Maybe this is my chance to fly, to be something more than just a girl in a tower, waiting to be rescued. Or, you know, sacrificed.

I take a deep breath, my decision made. I'm going to play their game. I'm going to let this unfold to see where it leads. Because for the first time in my life, I have a chance at something real, something more than just a life lived in the shadows. And I'm not going to let fear hold me back. Not anymore.

My new resolve doesn't stop the butterflies from doing a frantic tap dance in my stomach as I make my way down the dimly lit hallways of the castle. I've already figured out that Oscar's room is on the second floor, and Jasper's is on the third. I decided to start with Oscar. He seems the most approachable, the most likely to answer my questions without making me feel like I'm being interrogated. Or, you know, eaten.

I knock softly on his door, my heart pounding in my chest. After a few moments, the door creaks open, and there he is. A disheveled, sleepy-looking Oscar, his dark hair a mess, his boxers riding low on his hips, and his eyes glazed with sleep. He's still the most beautiful man I've ever seen, even when he looks like he just rolled out of bed. It's not fair, really. No one should be allowed to look that good first thing in the morning. Or, you know, in the middle of the night. Or morning — I don't know what you call it; it's technically morning, but he is just going to bed.

"What are you doing here?" he asks, his voice husky with sleep, and it does things to my insides that I'm not prepared to analyze right now.

"I couldn't sleep," I lie, trying to sound as innocent and damsel-in-distress-y as possible. "I thought maybe... maybe I could sleep in here with you?"

He hesitates for a moment, and I can see the internal struggle on his face. The desire to say yes, to pull me into his arms and never let go. And the fear of moving too fast, of scaring me away. It's a battle I'm all too familiar with, and for a moment, I feel a pang of sympathy for him. And then he steps aside, holding the door open for me, and the sympathy is replaced by a jolt of triumph. Game on.

I step into his room, my eyes quickly scanning the space, taking in the details I missed earlier. It's exactly what I would expect from Oscar: neat, tidy, and impeccably organised. The large four-poster bed is perfectly made, the pillows fluffed just so. The walls are adorned with framed pictures of landscapes and architectural drawings, and the shelves are filled with books, all arranged by size and colour. The air smells of sandalwood and old paper, a scent that's both comforting and intoxicating.

Oscar closes the door behind me, and the sound echoes in the quiet room, making my heart jump. He turns to face me, his expression a mixture of concern and confusion. "Why can't you sleep?" he asks, his blue eyes studying me intently, as if he's trying to read my mind.

I shrug nonchalantly, trying to appear calm and collected even though my insides are a tangled mess of nerves and excitement. "Just restless," I reply vaguely. "A lot on my mind, I guess."

"Is there anything I can do to help?" he asks, his voice soft and gentle, filled with a genuine concern that almost makes me feel guilty for lying to him. Almost.

I let out a heavy sigh, letting my shoulders slump, playing the part of the overwhelmed, emotionally fragile human. "I just need a hug, I think," I say, my voice raw and honest, because that part, at least, is true. I do need a hug. I need something to ground me, to make me feel safe in this crazy, upside-down world.

His expression softens, and he closes the distance between us in two long strides. He wraps his arms around me, pulling me into his chest, and I melt into his embrace, my head resting against his shoulder. He's so warm, so solid, and he smells so good, like sandalwood and soap and something else that's just… him. I could stay here forever, wrapped in his arms, feeling safe and protected. But I have a mission, and I can't afford to get distracted.

He guides me over to the bed, lifting the covers and inviting me to crawl underneath. I do, my body sinking into the soft mattress, and he climbs in behind me, enveloping me in his warmth. His embrace is strong and comforting, a shield against the world, and I have to fight the urge to just give in, to let myself be taken care of. But I can't. Not yet.

"You know you don't need permission to come into my room," he whispers into my ear, his breath hot against my skin. "You are always welcome here, Willow. If you need a hug, simply walk in and jump in, sweetheart." He presses a soft kiss to my shoulder, and I shiver, my body responding to his touch even though my mind is screaming at me to be careful. "Go to sleep now, sweetheart," he murmurs, his voice a low, soothing rumble.

I close my eyes, pretending to drift off, but my mind is racing. This is my chance. My chance to get some answers, to start piecing together the puzzle of my new life. I wait until his breathing evens out, until I'm sure he's asleep, and then I whisper into the darkness.

"Tomorrow, do you think you could show me your office?"

His arms tighten around me, and for a moment, I think I've made a mistake, that he was just pretending to be asleep. But then he replies, his voice soft and sleepy.

"Sweetheart, I'll do more than that. I'll give you a tour of the inside of the castle and even give you a set of master keys that can open every single door and space." He pauses, hugging me closer. "You're not trapped here, my dear. You have the freedom to do as you please. The only issue is leaving the castle."

I prop myself up on my elbow, turning to look at him in the dim light. "What do you mean? Why can't I leave the castle?"

He sighs, and I can see the pained expression on his face even in the darkness. "It's complicated, Willow. We share the limelight among the three of us, which means only one of us is allowed to leave the castle for 10 years at a time. It's a precaution against being seen by the paparazzi and risking exposure. Because we don't age, we have to rotate who goes out into the public eye. Right now, it's Theo and Jas. I'm not saying you can't go, cause you can; we just have to work out the logistics so when you go you don't get seen."

"Theo is the face of our family currently," he continues, his voice low and hesitant. "While Jas prefers to work more stealthily. He has a unique ability to change his appearance, like a chameleon, which makes him less likely to be recognized. so he gets to go out more often."

"What does Jasper do when he's out there?" I ask, my curiosity piqued.

"He specializes in hunting down rogue vampires and disposing of them," Oscar explains, and I can hear the gravity in his voice. "Whenever we receive word of a vampire that has gone feral, Jas goes in to track it down and eliminate it, ensuring the safety of our kind."

I sit up, my eyes wide with shock. "Wait, are you serious? Vampires can go feral? And does that mean you can too?"

He nods gravely. "Yes, it is a rare occurrence, but it can happen. When a vampire is first turned, they often turn out like Caleb—controlled and rational. But sometimes, very rarely, one comes out bad. These are pure vampires, consumed by insatiable bloodlust. They are no longer human, but feral creatures unable to be saved. Every human they bite will also turn into a feral being, which is why Jas takes it upon himself to eliminate them."

"Is it possible for a typical vampire to become feral?" I ask, my mind racing.

"Yes, in essence," he says, his voice cautious. "However, it is not permanent. It's more like a blood-induced haze that can occur when a vampire goes too long without feeding. In this state, they could unknowingly drain their donor dry and lose control. A regularly fed vampire would never face such an issue."

"How do you three sustain yourselves?" I ask, my voice laced with a morbid curiosity. "I haven't seen anyone walking around for you to feed on."

"We have a system of regular, screened donors who come here on a rotating roster," he explains casually. "We pay them generously and ensure they maintain a healthy lifestyle."

"And where exactly in this castle do you obtain your sustenance?" I press, eager for more information.

He smiles, a warm, inviting smile that makes my heart do a little flip-flop. "I'll show you tomorrow. You're welcome to stay and watch, so you understand."

"I would be interested in seeing," I reply eagerly, scooting back down on the bed.

His arm wraps around me, pulling me in tight against his body. I can feel the heat radiating from his skin and the hard bulge of his growing arousal pressing into my back. A shiver runs down my spine as I squirm in his embrace, curious about what he might do next.

"Stop wriggling, Willow," he chuckles, his breath hot against my neck. "It's time to sleep."

A sudden boldness takes over me, and I ask, "Do you not want me?" My words hang in the air, tinged with a desire and anticipation that I can't take back.

His warm breath tickles my neck as he whispers, "Sweetheart, I want nothing but you. But I won't rush into anything." A shiver runs down my spine at the feel of his lips on my skin. "I will not pressure you into bonding with me. I want you to make that choice."

At that moment, I knew what my answer would be. Yes, I want him. And I want him now.

With a sudden burst of confidence, I roll over so that my face is in front of his. My hand finds its way to his cheek, and I lean in to kiss him.

CHAPTER 23

OSCAR

The world outside my body ceases to exist. There is only her. Willow. Her name is a prayer on my lips, a mantra in my mind. When she turns to me, her eyes a swirling vortex of desire and uncertainty, and presses her lips to mine, it's like a lightning strike to my soul. For 190 years, I have been a ghost, a machine, a creature of logic and reason. And in this one single moment, she brings me back to life.

Her hand, so small and delicate against my chest. I can feel the heat of her skin, the soft flutter of her pulse, the way her breath catches in her throat. And I am lost. Utterly and completely lost in the sensation of her.

I wrap my arm around her, pulling her closer, our bodies melting together in a perfect, seamless union. It's like coming home after a long, arduous journey. It's like finding the missing piece of my soul, the one I didn't even know was gone until this very moment. And I know, with a certainty that shakes me to my core, that I will never let her go.

"I want you," she whispers, her voice a raw, desperate plea, and the words are like a brand on my skin, searing themselves into my very being. Her fingers, so tentative at first, now roam my chest with a newfound confidence, tracing the lines of my tattoos, sending shivers down my spine. I have to fight for control, for a semblance of the restraint that has defined my existence for centuries. She is a virgin, a fragile, precious thing, and I will not rush this. I will not be the monster she fears.

I capture her hand in mine, my thumb stroking the soft skin of her palm. I look down at her, and her eyes are wide with a mixture of wonder, desire, and a curiosity that is so quintessentially her. She is a beautiful creature, a work of art, a masterpiece of creation. And she is mine. The thought is so overwhelming, so powerful, that I can feel my cock growing harder, my control slipping. I need to feel her, to taste her, to lose myself in her. But I have to be patient. I have to be gentle. I have to be the man she deserves.

"I've never felt this way about anyone before, Willow," I whisper, the words a raw, honest confession that I never thought I would utter. "Not in all my years."

"Me too," she replies, her voice a soft, breathless whisper. "I can't control myself when I'm around you." And then she's kissing me again, her lips soft and yielding, her tongue tracing the seam of my mouth, and I'm lost all over again.

I roll on top of her, my body a dead weight, but she doesn't seem to mind. She arches up to meet me, her hands tangling in my hair, her hips grinding against mine. I can see her nipples, hard and erect, straining against the thin fabric of her shirt, and I have to fight the urge to rip it off, to take her right here, right now, with a ferocity that would terrify her. But I won't. I can't.

I place my hand on her cheek, my thumb stroking her soft skin, my eyes locked on hers. I want her to see me, to see the man behind the monster, the soul behind the centuries of loneliness and despair. A soft moan escapes her lips, and it's the most beautiful sound I've ever heard. It's the sound of her surrender, of her trust, of her desire. And it's all for me.

Our lips part, and I shift my weight back, my hands going to the hem of her shirt. I pull it up and over her head, my movements slow and deliberate, savoring every moment, every inch of her that is revealed to me. Her hair, a dark, silken curtain, cascades down, almost covering her breasts, and I have to resist the urge to bury my face in it, to breathe in her scent, to lose myself in her.

My hands find her hips, my thumbs stroking the soft skin of her stomach. I tug at the waistband of her tracksuit pants, and they slide down her legs, pooling at her ankles. She is naked now, completely and utterly bare to me, and she is more beautiful than I could have ever imagined. I stand up, my own sleep shorts falling to the ground, my cock springing free, hard and erect. I can see her eyes widen as she takes me in, a mixture of awe and anticipation on her face, and a surge of pride courses through me. I am the one who is making her feel this way. I am the one who will give her pleasure, who will show her what it means to be loved, to be cherished, to be worshipped.

I climb back onto the bed, my body hovering over hers, and she reaches for me, her hand closing around my cock.

Her touch is electric, sending a jolt through me that makes me groan. She pumps me slowly, her eyes wide with a mixture of curiosity and desire, and I have to grit my teeth to keep from coming right then and there.

"I want you so much, Oscar," she whispers, her voice a raw, desperate plea.

"I want you too, Willow," I reply, my voice thick with a desire that has been building for 190 years. "More than you could ever know."

I lean down, my lips tracing a path from her neck to her breasts, my hands exploring every curve, every dip, every inch of her perfect body. I suckle her nipples, teasing them with my tongue, my teeth, until they are hard, erect peaks. I move lower, my lips trailing kisses over her stomach, her hips, her thighs. She arches up to meet me, her hips grinding against my mouth, and I let out a low, guttural laugh. "Patience, Willow," I murmur against her skin, my voice a low, seductive growl.

I kiss the soft skin of her inner thighs, my tongue tracing a path toward the prize that awaits me. The scent of her arousal is intoxicating, a sweet, musky perfume that makes my fangs ache. I part her lips with my fingers, my thumb stroking her clit, and she moans, her hips bucking against my hand. I look up at her, and her eyes rolled back, her lips parted, her breath coming in short, ragged gasps. And I know in that moment that I will do anything, anything, to keep her looking at me like that for the rest of eternity.

I take her clit into my mouth, my tongue flicking against the sensitive nub, and she screams, one that echoes through the quiet room and straight into my soul. Her hands tangle in my hair, her fingers gripping my scalp, and I know she wants more, needs more. I push two fingers inside her, and she is so wet, so tight, that I groan, my own control slipping. I lick her juices off my fingers, and she moans, her hips bucking against my hand. "You taste so good, Willow," I murmur against her skin, my voice a low, seductive growl.

"Oscar, please," she begs, her voice a raw, desperate plea.

"I like it when you beg," I reply, my voice a low, guttural laugh. I take my cock and brush it against her wetness, her juices coating the head and shaft. "I'm going to fuck you with my tongue first," I growl, "and then I'm going to fuck you with my cock."

I lean back in, my tongue plunging into her, tasting her, devouring her. I lick her from bottom to top, my tongue tracing every fold, every crevice, every inch of her perfect, beautiful cunt. She is so sweet, so intoxicating, and I can't get enough of her. I suck on her clit, my fingers pumping in and out of her, and she screams, her body convulsing around me as she comes, her orgasm a tidal wave that washes over me, cleansing me, healing me, making me whole.

I continue to move my fingers inside her, riding the waves of her orgasm until she is completely spent, her body limp and pliant beneath me. I pull my fingers out of her and hold them up to her mouth. "Lick them clean," I command, my voice a low, guttural growl. Her tongue darts out, lapping at my fingers, and I groan, my own control slipping. "See how good you taste?" I murmur against her skin, my voice a low, seductive growl.

I pull her hips toward me, lifting her so that her ass rests on my thighs. "Now, Willow," I say, my voice a low, guttural growl, "I'm going to take your virginal pussy." I pause, letting the weight of my words sink in. "It will hurt, but I'll make sure to distract you."

I guide my cock to her entrance, the head slick with her juices. I push in slowly, inch by inch, and I feel the resistance, the tightness of her virginity. She gasps, a sharp intake of breath, and I see a flicker of pain in her eyes. I stop immediately, my heart aching at the thought of causing her any discomfort. "Shh, sweetheart," I murmur, my lips brushing against hers. "It's okay. Just breathe. I'll be gentle."

I wait, my body still, my own desire a raging inferno that I have to fight to control. I kiss her, my tongue tracing the seam of her lips, my hands stroking her hair, her face, her arms. I whisper sweet nothings into her ear, telling her how beautiful she is, how much I love her, how much I've waited for this moment. And slowly, I feel her begin to relax, her body melting into mine, her muscles unclenching. The pain in her eyes is replaced by a look of trust, of surrender, of desire. And I know in that moment that she is ready.

I begin to move again, my thrusts slow and deliberate, my body a gentle, rhythmic wave that washes over her, cleansing her, healing her. I watch her face, her every expression, her every gasp, her every moan. And as the pain fades, I know that I have done it. I have made her mine completely and utterly, and I will never let her go.

I push deeper until I am buried to the hilt, my balls resting against her soft skin. I pause, savoring the moment, the feeling of our bodies joined, our souls connected. I dip my head, my lips capturing hers in a deep, passionate kiss. "You take my cock so perfectly, Willow," I whisper against her mouth, my voice a low, guttural growl.

I begin to move, my thrusts slow and deliberate at first, and then faster, harder, deeper. I rub her clit with my thumb, and she screams, her body convulsing around me as she comes again. I can feel my own release building, a roaring inferno that threatens to consume me. I try to hold back, to make this last forever, but it's no use. I come with a guttural groan, my seed spilling into her, my body shuddering with the force of my release.

I collapse on top of her, my body spent, my mind a blissful, empty void. I roll onto my side, pulling her into my arms, my lips finding the soft skin of her neck. I sink my fangs into her, and her blood fills my mouth, a sweet, intoxicating elixir that is more potent than any drug, more addictive than anything else. It's the taste of her, of our bond, of our love. And I know in that moment that I will never want to feed from anyone else again.

As our souls bond, a warm, complete sensation that fills the emptiness inside me. I look into her eyes and say the words that have been burning in my heart for 190 years. "You are mine now, Willow."

She meets my gaze, her eyes shining with a love and adoration that I have only ever dreamed of, and replies, "You are mine too, Oscar."

CHAPTER 24

WILLOW

My eyes flutter open to the soft glow of sunlight filtering through the balcony doors, a gentle, hazy light that feels entirely out of place in a castle full of vampires. For a blissful, ignorant moment, I forget where I am. I'm just a girl, waking up in a ridiculously comfortable bed, the sheets a cloud of silk and cotton around me. Then, the memories of last night come crashing down, a tidal wave of sensation and emotion that leaves me breathless. Oscar. The sunroom. The bath. The bite. Oh God, the bite.

I'm in Oscar's bed, tangled in sheets that smell like him, like us. It's a clean, crisp scent, like fresh linen and old books, with an undercurrent of something uniquely him, something wild and ancient and utterly intoxicating. He's wrapped around me, his arms a protective cage, his breath warm against my neck. And I feel... safe. It's a strange, foreign feeling, one I haven't experienced in a long, long time. It's also completely insane. I'm feeling safe in the arms of one of my kidnappers. A vampire. A king. My brain is officially broken.

I carefully, painstakingly, extricate myself from his embrace, my body feeling like a lead weight. Every muscle aches, a deep, throbbing soreness that makes me wince. My head is pounding, a dull, persistent throb behind my eyes, and my stomach is churning like a washing machine on the fritz. I make my way to his ensuite to throw some cold water on my face when my stomach lurches, a violent, undeniable heave. I sprint to the toilet, my hand clamped over my mouth, and vomit into it, my body convulsing with a violence that surprises me. I'm empty, but my stomach doesn't seem to care. It continues to heave, to protest, to rebel against the foreignness of it all. It's like my body is trying to purge the last three years of my life — the lies, the confusion, the fear. It's not working.

"Are you okay, sweetheart?" Oscar's voice is a soft, gentle murmur, and I feel his hand on my back, his touch a soothing balm against my fevered skin. He pulls my hair back from my face, his fingers gentle, his touch so full of a tenderness that I don't know how to react. Part of me wants to lean into it, to let him take care of me. The other part of me wants to bite his hand off.

"I think I have the stomach flu," I grumble, my voice hoarse, my throat raw. I lean back on my heels, my body trembling, my head spinning. "Or maybe I'm allergic to ridiculously handsome, centuries-old vampires. It's probably a thing."

He chuckles, a low, rumbling sound that vibrates through my back. "I don't think that's it. I'll send for the doctor," he says, his voice firm, his eyes full of a worry that is so genuine, so real, that it makes my heart ache.

"No, no, I'm fine," I protest, my voice a weak, pathetic whisper. "I don't need a doctor." The thought of a doctor, of needles and tests and prodding, sends a fresh wave of nausea through me. I've had a lifelong, irrational fear of doctors, and I'm not about to let some strange vampire doctor poke and prod me.

"Are you sure?" he asks, his brow furrowed with concern. "He'll just give you a quick check-up."

I shake my head, trying to reassure him, but as I stand, the world tilts on its axis, the ridiculously expensive bathroom spinning around me. Tiny white spots dance before my eyes, and I have just enough time to think, "Well, this is embarrassing," before I'm falling, falling, into a black, bottomless pit of nothingness.

When I come to, I'm back in Oscar's bed, and all three of them are there, their faces a mixture of worry and relief. It's like a really weird, really hot boy band reunion. Oscar is holding my hand, his thumb stroking the back of my palm, his touch a lifeline in the sea of my confusion. Jasper is perched on the edge of the bed, his eyes wide with a fear that he can't quite hide behind his usual cheeky grin. And Theo, he's pacing, his movements a caged, restless energy that fills the room with a palpable tension. He looks like he's about to punch a hole in the wall. Or maybe just me.

"You fainted," Oscar says, his voice a low, gentle murmur. "The doctor is on his way."

I groan, my head throbbing, my stomach churning. "I

think I really do need that doctor," I admit, my voice a weak, pathetic whisper. "And maybe a bucket."

Oscar nods, his expression softening with an understanding that is so complete, so absolute, that it makes me want to cry. "It's going to be okay," he assures me, his voice a soft, gentle murmur. "We will take care of everything."

Jasper takes my other hand, his fingers lacing with mine. "You scared the shit out of me, Baby," he says, his voice a raw, honest confession that is so at odds with his usual playful banter that it takes my breath away. "I thought… I don't know what I thought. But it wasn't good."

"Theo," I call out, my voice a soft, breathless whisper, and he stops pacing, his head snapping up, his eyes locking on mine. He strides toward me, his movements a graceful, predatory glide, and Oscar releases my hand, giving him space. He looms over me, a dark, imposing figure, and for a moment, I'm terrified. Then he kneels by the bed, his face level with mine, and the look in his eyes is not anger, but a raw, desperate fear that mirrors my own.

"Willow, how do you feel?" he asks, his voice a low, intense murmur that sends a shiver down my spine. "The doctor is about 20 minutes out!"

"I'm okay," I say, my voice a weak, pathetic whisper. "I just have a stomach bug, I'm sure. Or maybe I'm pregnant with a demon baby. It's probably 50/50 at this point."

Theo's lips twitch, a ghost of a smile that's gone as quickly as it appeared. "I don't think it's a demon baby."

"Do you think mating caused this?" Oscar's voice is a quiet, hesitant question, and I can see the fear in his eyes, the worry that he has somehow hurt me, that he is to blame for my illness.

"This is all new to us," Theo says, his voice a low, intense murmur. "We have no idea if the prophecy was complete when Edmund told us. There could have been something at the end that we needed to know."

"We need to stop bonding," he declares, his voice firm, his eyes locking on mine. "Not until we know what will happen next."

I nod, my heart a leaden weight in my chest. I had already decided not to bond with the rest of them until I was certain of their intentions, but hearing him say it, hearing the finality in his voice, it still hurts. It hurts more than I thought it would. It's like being told you can't have dessert after you've already had a bite of the most delicious cake you've ever tasted.

"Have you gained any powers?" I ask Oscar, my voice a soft, breathless whisper, my curiosity getting the better of me. "Can you fly? Or turn into a bat? Or, like, do my taxes with your mind?"

He smiles, a sad, gentle smile that doesn't quite reach his eyes. "Not yet, sweetheart. But I'm not worried about it." He brushes a stray strand of hair from my face, his touch a feather-light caress. "I just wanted you," he continues, his voice a low, intense murmur. "Even if I never gain any supernatural abilities, I'll still consider myself the luckiest Vampire in existence."

"Eww, yuck, I'm fucking sweaty," I cringe, pulling away from his touch. "You do not have to touch me. I probably smell like a gym sock that's been left in a hot car."

"Sweetheart, you were glistening with sweat last night and it didn't bother me then," he whispers, his voice a low, seductive growl. "Why would it bother me now?"

I playfully swat at him, a small, genuine smile touching my lips for the first time since I woke up. "Shut up," I say, my voice a soft, breathless whisper. "You're gross."

"The doctor is here," Theo announces, his voice a low, intense murmur, and the tension in the room returns, thick and suffocating.

"That's our signal to disappear, sweetheart," Oscar says, his voice a low, seductive growl. He leans down, his lips brushing against mine, and then he's gone, a silent, graceful shadow that disappears into the adjoining room.

"I'll be in the adjoining room," Jasper says, his voice a low, intense murmur. He taps his ear, a silent reminder that they can hear everything, and then he's gone too, another silent, graceful shadow that disappears into the darkness.

Theo returns with the doctor, an elderly man with kind eyes and a gentle smile that seems a little too calm for someone who's just been summoned to a castle full of vampires. He's carrying a worn leather bag, and he smells faintly of antiseptic and old paper. Theo hovers by the door, his arms crossed, his expression a thundercloud of worry and impatience.

"This is Willow, Doctor Michael," Theo says, his voice a low, intense murmur that brooks no argument. "She's unwell."

"Good evening, Willow," the doctor says, his voice a soothing baritone. He pulls a chair up to the bed, his movements slow and deliberate. "Theodore here tells me you're feeling a bit under the weather. May I examine you?"

"Sure," I say, my voice a little shaky. "Just be warned, I bite."

The doctor chuckles, a warm, genuine sound. "I'll keep that in mind." He opens his bag, and I eye the contents warily. Needles. Oh God, there are definitely needles in there.

"Firstly, can you describe what happened?" he asks, his eyes kind and patient.

"Well, let's see," I say, ticking the points off on my fingers. "I was kidnapped, found out my whole life was a lie, discovered vampires are real and don't glitter, and then I fainted after throwing up my guts. So, you know, a pretty standard Tuesday."

Theo lets out a low growl, and the doctor shoots him a look. "And physically? Before you fainted?"

"Achy, tired, nauseous. Like the world's worst hang-over, but without the fun party beforehand."

He nods, taking out a thermometer. "Okay, let's take your temperature." He places it under my tongue, and I sit there, feeling ridiculous, with this little plastic stick in my mouth and three vampire kings listening to my every heartbeat from the next room. Theo is practically vibrating with anxiety, his eyes darting from me to the doctor and back again.

"Is it hot in here, or is it just the ridiculously attractive supernatural being eavesdropping on my medical exam?" I mumble around the thermometer.

The doctor just smiles. He takes the thermometer, reads it, and makes a note on a small pad. "No fever.

That's good. Now, let's check your blood pressure, shall we?"

He wraps the cuff around my arm, and I watch as he pumps it up, the pressure building, tight and uncomfortable. "Is it high?" I ask, my voice laced with a sarcasm I can't quite suppress. "I can't imagine why. It's not like my entire life has been turned upside down in the last 24 hours."

"It's a little elevated, but nothing to be concerned about," he says, his voice calm and reassuring. He listens to my heart with his stethoscope, his expression unreadable. He presses gently on my stomach, and I wince.

"Tender?" he asks.

"Just a tad," I say through gritted teeth.

"When was your last menstrual period?" He asks, and I see Theo's head snap up, his eyes wide with a confusion that is almost comical.

"Uh, a couple of weeks ago?" I say, my cheeks flushing. "Why?"

"Just ruling things out," he says, his voice gentle. "Have you eaten anything unusual in the last 24 hours?"

"Just the five-star meals provided by my captor," I say, my voice dripping with sarcasm. "And some cheese. It was really good cheese."

Theo lets out another low growl, and the doctor ignores him. "Okay, Willow," he says, his voice kind and patient. "From what you've told me, and from what I can see, it looks like you have a simple case of gastroenteritis. The stomach flu. It's going around."

"So, no demon baby?" I say, my voice flat.

"Nope, definitely not," he says, a small smile playing

on his lips. "I'm going to give you a prescription for some anti-nausea medication, and I want you to rest and drink plenty of fluids. Broth, water, tea. Nothing too heavy. And stay in bed until you feel better."

"I'll make sure of it," Theo says, his voice a low, intense murmur.

The doctor packs up his bag, his movements slow and deliberate. He gives me a warm, reassuring smile. "You're in good hands, Willow," he says, his eyes flickering to Theo for a brief, almost imperceptible moment. "He'll take good care of you."

And then he's gone, leaving me alone with my thoughts, and the knowledge that after all the drama, all the fear, all the confusion, I've been taken down by a common, boring, human stomach bug. It's almost funny. So. Anticlimactic.

Oscar and Jasper return, their faces a mixture of worry and relief. Oscar makes me some broth, his hands gentle, his touch so full of a tenderness that I don't know how to react. Jasper fetches me a book, a dark romance that he says he ordered just for me, and I can't help but smile at his thoughtfulness.

"So, what genre are you in the mood for?" he asks, his eyes twinkling with a mischievous light. "Theo has quite the collection, but I have a feeling your tastes might be a little… spicier."

I can't help but laugh — a real, genuine laugh that feels good after all the drama. "You have no idea." I prop myself up on the pillows, feeling a little more like myself. "Okay, hit me. What's the last book you read?"

He pulls out his phone, a sleek, black device that probably costs more than my car. "The last book I read? Uh, probably a 17th-century treatise on military strategy. Not exactly your cup of tea, I'm guessing."

"Definitely not," I say with a shudder. "Okay, my turn. The last book I read was… 'Chasing the Wolf King'."

Jasper throws his head back and laughs, a deep, rich sound that echoes through the room. "Of course it was," he says, his fingers flying across the screen of his phone. He pulls up the book, a cover with a shirtless, tattooed man and a woman in a torn dress. "Okay, 'Chasing the Wolf King'. I'm going to search for books like this."

He taps away, a look of intense concentration on his face. "Okay, let's see… 'The Shadow Beast', 'The Cruel Prince', 'King's Bride', 'St Ivy's'… these sound promising. Adding to cart." He rattles off a dozen more titles, his thumb a blur as he adds them to a virtual shopping cart. "What else?"

I'm grinning now, a wide, happy smile that feels completely out of place in this crazy situation. It's just so… sweet. He's so genuinely into this, so determined to get me the books I want. "Oh, um… some reverse harem college romance is always good," I say, my voice a little shy.

His eyes light up. "Reverse harem college romance. Got it." He starts searching again, a new torrent of titles spilling from his lips. "'The Royals of Winchester University', 'The boys of Hastings House', 'Pumpkin Spice Apothecary'… this is a whole new world for me. I'm learning so much." He adds another twenty books to the cart, his enthusiasm infectious.

I'm laughing so hard now that my stomach hurts — a

good, cleansing pain that has nothing to do with the flu. "You're ridiculous," I say, my voice filled with a warmth that surprises me.

"Okay," he says, finally looking up from his phone, a triumphant grin on his face. "I've ordered like 50 books for now. But we can get anything else you want. Anything at all."

I spent the rest of the day in bed, drifting in and out of a restless sleep. The kings take turns sitting with me, their presence a silent, comforting vigil. They don't talk much, but they don't have to. Their presence is enough. It's more than enough.

Chapter 25

Jasper

I watch her sleep, a strange, unfamiliar ache in my chest. She's so still, so quiet, her face a mask of peaceful exhaustion. It's vastly different from the fiery, sarcastic woman who's been turning our world upside down for the last three days. I should be relieved that she's finally resting, that the doctor has assured us it's just a stomach bug, but I can't shake the feeling that something is wrong. Something is very, very wrong.

I slip out of her room, my movements silent, my mind a whirlwind of worry and a strange, unfamiliar excitement. The conversation we had about books, the way her eyes lit up when she talked about reverse harem romance — it's stuck in my head. It's the first time I've seen her genuinely happy, genuinely excited about something since she's been here. And I want to see that look on her face again. I need to see it.

I pull out my phone again, my fingers flying across the screen. I find the closest bookstore, a quaint little shop in a nearby village, and I don't even hesitate. I bought the entire online store. Every single book. I don't care what they are; I just want her to have them. I want her to have everything. I add a note to the order: "Deliver to Willows Peak Castle. All of it. Now." Then I start searching for more. I search for every reverse harem college romance I can find, every dark romance, every book with a morally grey hero and a feisty heroine. I add them all to my cart, my thumb a blur as I tap and swipe. I ordered hundreds of books, thousands of books, a veritable library of smut and angst and happily ever afters. I don't even look at the total. It doesn't matter. Nothing matters but her.

I finally force myself to stop, my phone hot in my hand, my heart pounding in my chest. I've gone completely insane. I'm a centuries-old vampire, a king, and I've just spent a small fortune on romance novels for a woman who probably still thinks I'm a monster. I should be out hunting. I should be preparing for the inevitable confrontation with Edmund, but all I can think about is her. Her smile, her laugh, the way her eyes sparkle when she's happy.

I need to talk to Theo. He'll know what to do. He always knows what to do.

I find him in his office, staring out the window at the dark, churning sea. He looks as lost as I feel, his usual mask of cold, hard control gone, replaced by a raw, naked vulnerability that I've only seen a handful of times in our long, long lives.

"How much space does the library have?" I ask, my voice a little too loud in the quiet room.

He turns, his eyes dark and stormy. "Why?"

"I bought some books for Willow," I say, trying to

sound casual, like this is a normal, everyday occurrence. "I wasn't sure if we had what she likes, so I ordered the entire store."

Theo's eyebrows shoot up, a flicker of something that looks almost like amusement in his eyes. "The entire store?"

"And then some," I admit, a sheepish grin spreading across my face. "I may have gone a little overboard."

He lets out a low, rumbling chuckle, a sound that is so rare, so unexpected, that it takes me by surprise. "I don't think we have enough room for all of that. I'll make arrangements to have the library expanded and more shelving units installed." He pulls out his phone, his fingers flying across the screen as he sends off a text.

"Did she tell you what books she liked?" He asks, his voice a low, intense murmur.

I can't help but laugh. "She asked for reverse harem."

Theo's lips twitch, a ghost of a smile playing on his lips. "Ah, reverse harem. That's what we are to her, aren't we? One woman with many male lovers."

"Is that a common genre?" I ask, my voice filled with a genuine curiosity that I can't quite suppress.

He chuckles again, a deep, rich sound that echoes through the room. "To some readers, it is. Maybe Willow enjoys the genre, or maybe she was just pulling your leg."

"I like to think she enjoys the genre," I say, a wide, happy smile spreading across my face. "I just ordered like 300 books for her."

Theo's eyebrows shoot up again, his eyes wide with a surprise that is almost comical. "You're telling me you've never picked up a book in your life, but you ordered 300 for Willow without even flinching?"

I shrug, a wave of guilt washing over me. "What can I say? She loves books."

"I'm not judging," he says, his voice a low, intense murmur. "I just haven't seen you do something so kind for someone else before, without expecting something in return."

"There isn't much I wouldn't do for her," I admit, my voice a raw, honest whisper.

"I couldn't agree more," Theo replies, his voice filled with a warmth that I've never heard before.

We fall silent, the only sound the crackling of the fire and the howling of the wind outside. The worry, the fear — it's still there, a heavy, suffocating blanket that threatens to smother us. But for the first time in a long time, there's something else too. Hope. A tiny, fragile flicker of hope that maybe, just maybe, everything is going to be okay.

"Do you think the bonding with Oscar is what made her sick?" I ask, my voice a low, intense murmur.

"I'm not sure," he says, his brow furrowed in thought. "I can't see why. Vampires have had mates forever, and not once have I heard of this happening. I'm assuming she does have a stomach bug."

"Oscar also doesn't have any powers yet," I say, my thoughts racing. "Do you think he might not?"

"No one knows for sure," he says, his voice a low, intense murmur. "We have no idea if we get them separately or once she has bonded with us all. But honestly, I'm too scared to bond with her now."

"The doctor saidshe was fine, but what if it's more than that?" I ask, my voice filled with a worry that I can't quite suppress. "What if there's something wrong?"

"What if there is more to this?" I ask, my voice trembling slightly. "Edmund hasn't made any attempts to retrieve her either."

"She has been here for three days now, and not once has he sent anyone this way," Theo says, his voice a low, intense murmur.

"Do you think maybe he won't?" I ask, my mind racing with possibilities. "I mean, he broke the accords. He knows that we know. Perhaps he's gone into hiding?"

"That's a valid point," he says, his brow furrowed in thought. "But it just seems too quiet. Like the calm before the storm."

Suddenly, a loud crash echoes from Willow's room, jolting us out of our thoughts and into action. Our hearts pounding with fear and adrenaline.

I'm across the room in a flash, my body moving on pure instinct. I burst through the door to her room, my heart in my throat, and the sight that greets me makes my blood run cold. She's on the floor, face down, her body still and silent. Oscar is standing over her, an apron tied around his waist, a wooden spoon in his hand, his eyes wide with a shock that mirrors my own.

"What the hell!" I roar, my voice a raw, guttural sound that I don't even recognize as my own. I rush to her side, scooping her up into my arms, her body limp and lifeless as I settle her back into the bed.

"What happened?" Theo's voice is a low, intense murmur from behind me.

"I don't know," Oscar says, his voice a choked, strangled whisper. "I was in the kitchen making her some broth. Just standing at the stove stirring it when I heard a crash and then…pop! I turned around, and she was here on the floor."

"You can teleport?" I ask, my voice filled with a disbelief that I can't quite suppress. "That's your power?"

Oscar nods, his eyes wide with a confusion that I can't even begin to comprehend. The room smells of herbs and spices — a strange, incongruous scent that only adds to the chaos of the scene.

"What the fuck happened to Willow?" Theo exclaims, his voice a raw, panicked cry. He snatches the thermometer off the table, his hands shaking as he tries to take her temperature. I gently brush the hair back from her face, my heart aching at the sight of her so pale, so still.

"I think she has fainted again," Theo says, his voice a low, intense murmur.

"Shit," Oscar curses, his voice a choked, strangled whisper. "I need to go turn off the broth before it burns down our entire castle." He rushes out of the room, his movements clumsy, uncoordinated.

"Just teleport!" I call after him, my voice filled with a frustration that I can't quite suppress.

"I don't know how!" he calls back, his voice a desperate, panicked cry.

I let out a low, frustrated growl, my eyes fixed on Willow's still, silent form. She's starting to stir, her eyelids fluttering, a soft, low moan escaping her lips.

"Willow?" I whisper, my voice a raw, honest plea. "Can you hear me?"

Her eyes flutter open, her bright blue eyes wide with a confusion that mirrors my own. "What happened?" she asks, her voice a soft, weak whisper.

"You fainted again," I say, my voice a low, intense murmur. "Do you remember anything?"

She shakes her head, a soft, low moan escaping her lips. "No, everything just went black."

"We need to get the doctor again," Theo says, his voice a low, intense murmur. "This isn't normal."

"Believe it or not," she says, a small, weak smile playing on her lips, "but I feel better already." A faint blush spreads across her cheeks, a hint of colour returning to her pale, translucent skin.

I can't help but feel skeptical, but I don't want to argue with her. She's been through enough already. "Are you sure?" I ask, my voice filled with a worry that I can't quite suppress.

"I'm sure," she says, her voice a soft, weak whisper. "I just need to rest."

I nod, a wave of relief washing over me. "Alright, we'll let you rest. But we're still having the doctor come around tomorrow," I say, my voice a low, intense murmur.

She simply nods in response, her eyes fluttering closed as she settles back into the pillows.

I turn to leave the room, my heart a tangled mess of worry and relief. Theo catches my arm, his grip tight, his eyes dark and stormy. "We need to talk," he says, his voice a low, intense murmur.

I nod, my steps echoing in the empty hallway as I follow him. Anxiety gnaws at my gut, a sense of unease settling in with every passing moment.

"What's going on?" I ask, my voice a low, intense murmur.

He pauses, his eyes flickering with a concern that I've never seen before. "Don't you find it strange that Oscar suddenly has the ability to teleport, and that Willow instantly started to feel better once he gained his powers?" he asks, his voice a low, intense murmur. "So let me get this straight, Willow has to fall ill in order for us to receive our powers through bonding?"

"I cannot say for certain, but if her condition continues to improve, it is safe to assume," he says.

CHAPTER 26

WILLOW

I wake up slowly, like I'm swimming up from the bottom of a deep, dark lake full of expired NyQuil. The first thing I notice is the silence. Not the creepy I'm-being-watched silence of the manor, but a peaceful, heavy quiet that feels like a weighted blanket over my entire body. My limbs are heavy, boneless, but the ache is gone. The nausea, the bone-deep chill, the feeling of my own body staging a hostile takeover—it's all just… gone. I feel hollowed out, but in a good way. Like someone came in with a power washer and scrubbed me clean from the inside out. Which, given my current hosts, is a disturbingly plausible scenario.

The second thing I notice is the smell. It's him. Oscar. He smells like old books and expensive soap and something else, something uniquely him, a clean, crisp scent like fresh linen and a hint of spice. It's clinging to the pillows, the sheets, to me. I bury my face in the pillow, inhaling deeply. It's… nice. It's more than nice. It's comforting. It's safe. And that, more than anything, is what truly terrifies me.

I crack open an eye, the room bathed in the soft, silvery glow of moonlight. I have no idea how long I've been asleep, but the sun has long since disappeared, replaced by a sky full of stars. I feel a pang of disappointment that he's not here, that I woke up alone, and then I feel a flush of heat creep up my neck. God, I'm pathetic. A few days with my captor-slash-fated-mates and I'm already turning into one of those sad, lonely women from a black-and-white movie, pining away for a man. Or three men, in my case. What has my life become?

As if summoned by my melodramatic thoughts, the door creaks open, and Oscar slips in, a tray in his hands. He's wearing a soft, grey sweater that looks like it was made for cuddling, his hair a little messy, his eyes soft and warm as they land on me. He looks… domestic. It's a strange look for a centuries-old vampire king, but it suits him. It suits him so well that it makes my heart do a little flip-flop in my chest. Stupid, traitorous heart.

"You're awake," he says, his voice a low, gentle murmur. He sets the tray on the bedside table, the scent of warm bread and savory broth filling the air. My stomach growls, a loud, embarrassing rumble that echoes in the quiet room. Oscar just smiles, a genuine, crinkly-eyed smile that makes him look younger, less like a king and more like a man. A man who could probably kill me with his pinky finger, but a man nonetheless.

"I thought you might be hungry," he says, his voice laced with a quiet pride. "I made you some broth. And some juice. And some bread. I churned the butter myself. I have a secret stash in the pantry fridge. Just for you."

I stare at him, my mind struggling to process his words. He churned the butter himself? He has a secret stash of butter just for me? It's the most ridiculous, most endearing thing I've ever heard. I can't help but laugh — a real, genuine laugh that bubbles up from my chest and spills out of my mouth. It feels good. It feels so, so good.

"You churned your own butter?" I ask, my voice a little shaky. "What, was the store-bought stuff not up to your exacting standards? Did it have too many… germs?"

He nods, a faint blush colouring his cheeks. "I like to be prepared. And the emulsifiers in commercial butter are subpar."

Of course they are. Mr. OCD, Mr. I-need-everything-to-be-just-so, of course he churns his own butter. I should be annoyed, I should be rolling my eyes, but all I feel is a wave of affection so strong it almost knocks the breath out of me. This man, this strange, complicated, butter-churning vampire, he's one of my mates. And I think… I think I'm starting to be okay with that. Which is probably a sign of Stockholm syndrome, but I'm too hungry to care.

I sit up; the sheets pooling around my waist, and he helps me, his hands gentle on my back. He arranges the pillows behind me, his movements precise, efficient. He hands me a bowl of broth; the steam warming my face, and I take a sip, the rich, savory flavor exploding on my tongue. It's the best thing I've ever tasted. I devour the broth, the bread, the juice, every last bite, my body humming with happiness. Caleb's cooking was good, but this… this is something else entirely. This is food made with love. And I can taste it in every bite. Or maybe it's just the secret, hand-churned butter. Either way, I'm not complaining.

I sleep for another sixteen hours, a deep, dreamless sleep that leaves me feeling refreshed and whole. When I finally wake up, the moon is high in the sky, and Oscar is sitting in the armchair by the window, a book in his lap. He looks up as I stir, his eyes soft and warm.

"How are you feeling?" he asks.

"Good," I say, and I mean it. "Really good. Suspiciously good. What happened? Did you perform some kind of vampire voodoo on me while I was sleeping?"

He chuckles, a low, rumbling sound that vibrates through the room. "No voodoo. You just needed to rest." He tells me everything. About how he was in the kitchen, stirring the broth, and then he heard a crash and he was suddenly in my room, standing over my unconscious body. He tells me about the teleportation, how it was triggered by his fear for me, and how he hasn't been able to do it since. He tells me about the new side effect of our bond, how he can sense my location, my emotions, a built-in GPS that connects us, whether I like it or not.

"So you're like my own personal stalker now? Great. Just what every girl dreams of," I say, my voice dripping with sarcasm.

"We're going for a hike later," he says, completely ignoring my comment. "To see if it works across long distances. To see if we can trigger the teleportation again."

"How?" I ask, my heart starting to beat a little faster.

"We're going to scare you," Jasper says, his voice a low, playful drawl from the doorway. He's leaning against the doorframe, a wicked grin on his face, his eyes sparkling with a mischief that is both terrifying and thrilling. "We think if you're scared, Oscar will be able to do it again."

I stare at him, my mouth hanging open. "You're kidding, right? You want to scare me? Like, on purpose? What are you going to do, jump out from behind a curtain and yell 'boo'?"

He pushes off the doorframe, his movements fluid, graceful. He walks over to the bed, his eyes never leaving mine. He leans in close, his hot breath tickling my ear as he whispers, "Oh, I think we can do better than that. Don't worry, we won't do anything to hurt you. We just want to test out Oscar's teleportation ability."

I shiver, a thrill of something that is definitely not fear coursing through my veins. I should be terrified, I should be screaming, but all I can think about is how close he is, how good he smells, how much I want to close the distance between us and press my lips to his. God, I'm a mess. A horny, hormonal, completely out-of-my-mind mess.

Theo is sitting at the foot of my bed, his eyes glazed over, his expression dark and stormy. He's been quiet this whole time, a silent, brooding presence in the corner of the room. He looks like he's a million miles away, lost in his own world of dark, angsty thoughts. Probably composing a new symphony of suffering in his head.

"Are you okay?" I ask, my voice a little too loud in the quiet room.

He sighs. "Yes, I'm fine. I just think this idea is

stupid." He gets up, his movements jerky, agitated, and starts to leave the room.

"Where are you going?" I call after him, a strange, unfamiliar worry twisting in my gut.

"I'm hungry," he says, his voice a low, guttural growl. "I need to feed."

He's almost out the door when I call his name, my voice a raw, honest plea. "Theo?"

He stops, his head popping back around the doorframe, his eyes dark and stormy. "Yes, Willow?"

"Can I come with you?" I ask, my heart pounding in my chest. The words are out of my mouth before I can even think about them, before I can stop them. I want to go with him. I need to go with him. This is a terrible idea. A wonderful, terrible, no-good, very-bad idea. And I'm all in.

His eyebrows shoot up, a flicker of surprise in his dark, stormy eyes. "You want to join me while I make something to eat?"

I nod, a sudden, inexplicable excitement bubbling up inside me. "Are you heading to the kitchen or indulging in some blood?" I ask, my curiosity getting the better of me. "Because if it's the latter, I'm not sure I'm ready to see you slurp down another human just yet."

His brows furrow, a flicker of annoyance in his dark, stormy eyes. "I was planning on doing both, but don't worry, I won't be biting anyone tonight. I have some blood bags that I can drink from."

"Why are you not sinking your teeth into anyone?" I ask as we walk down the long, empty hallway. "Is there a shortage of willing necks in the area? Or are you just trying to be a good boy for me?"

"To be completely honest… it just feels weird doing it now that you're here," he admits, his voice a low, guttural growl. A faint blush colours his cheeks.

"Why is that?" I ask, my voice a soft, curious whisper.

"Because biting someone is an intimate act," he says, his voice a low, intense murmur. "And now that you're here, it feels wrong to do so. Especially if they happen to be female, and I would essentially be giving them pleasure, even if it's purely platonic."

His words hang in the air between us, heavy with a meaning that I can't quite decipher. I feel a wave of desire wash over me, so strong, so sudden, that it almost knocks the breath out of me. I can't help but imagine it — the intimacy of him biting me, his sharp teeth sinking into my flesh, his powerful arms holding me close. It's a dangerous thought, a forbidden thought, but it's a thought that excites me more than I care to admit.

We enter the kitchen, the room filled with the warm, comforting scent of Oscar's cooking. Oscar and Jasper enter behind us, as Oscar reaches into his pocket and pulls out a large, ornate ring of keys. They glint in the soft, warm light, each one unique, each one holding its own story.

"I promised I would show you around inside the Castle," he says. "But unfortunately you fell ill, and we didn't get the chance. But these are the keys to every room, and the skeleton key too…" He trails off, his eyes dark and mysterious. He places the keys in my hand, his fingers brushing against mine, sending a jolt of electricity through my body.

I stare at the keys, the weight of them heavy in my palm. There are so many — well over thirty — each one a promise of a new discovery, a new secret to unlock. "Thank you," I say, my voice a soft, grateful whisper. "I can't wait to go exploring. And maybe get lost. And then you'll have to come find me. It'll be a whole thing."

Theo disappears into the dark pantry, his footsteps echoing on the cold stone floor. He reappears a moment later, a crimson blood bag in one hand, a delicate glass cup in the other. "To be completely honest with you, Willow," he says, his voice a low, guttural growl, "I feel incredibly self-conscious drinking this in front of you." He takes a deep breath, his chest rising and falling, his eyes dark and stormy. "But I also know it's something you will eventually witness, and I need to just rip off the bandaid, as they say."

He cuts open the bag, the thick, crimson liquid pouring into the glass like a river of dark, forbidden secrets. His hand trembles as he lifts the cup to his lips, his fangs peeking out from behind his lips, long and sharp and deadly. He tries to hide them, but I see them. I see them, and I'm not afraid. I'm fascinated.

"Would you like me to turn away?" I ask, my voice a soft, curious whisper. "I can hum a little tune, if that helps. Or I can just stare. Whatever makes you feel less weird."

"No, Willow. I'm just being silly," he replies, his voice a low, guttural growl. He takes a sip, his eyes closing, a single drop of blood clinging to his upper lip. He licks it off, his tongue darting out, a quick, sensual movement that makes my stomach clench.

"Are you all drinking from bags?" I ask, my curiosity getting the better of me. "Or is Theo the only one on the juice box diet?"

"Only Theo," Jasper says, his voice a low, playful drawl.

"It wasn't until our bond was formed," Oscar admits, his voice a low, gentle murmur, "that I realized I couldn't bring myself to bite anyone else." He takes a deep breath, his eyes dark and mysterious. "I did try to feed from a blood bag today, but all I tasted was bitter ash."

"What does that mean?" I ask, my voice a soft, curious whisper.

"I believe it means that he can only feed from you now," Jasper says, his voice a low, playful drawl, his eyes sparkling with a mischief that is both terrifying and thrilling.

My mind whirls with questions, my heart pounding in my chest. "What happened when you tried to drink it? Did it just taste bad or were you physically unable to consume it?"

"I couldn't even swallow it," Oscar replies, his voice a low, gentle murmur.

"So…does that mean you will need to bite me every day?" I ask, my voice a soft, hesitant whisper. "Like, is this a contractual obligation now? Do I need to sign something? Will there be a punch card? Buy nine bites, get the tenth one free?"

"Yes," he says, his voice a low, gentle murmur. "But I

can try to bite someone or drink from a bag again. If the thought of being bitten terrifies you, I understand."

My heart races, with a surge of adrenaline coursing through my veins. I feel dampness between my legs, a sudden, unexpected wetness that makes my cheeks flush with heat. The thought of him biting me, of his teeth sinking into my flesh — it doesn't terrify me. It excites me. It excites me so much that I can't even breathe. My panties are staging a flash flood, and he's got a front-row seat to my emotional state. Fantastic.

Oscar smirks, a slow, sensual smile that makes my stomach clench. He leans in close, his voice a low, playful drawl as he teases, "Oh, little mouse, do you enjoy the idea of being bitten?"

I can't speak. I can only nod, my eyes wide with a mixture of fear and desire. He knows. He knows what I'm feeling. He can sense my arousal, my excitement, my desperate, all-consuming need. And he's enjoying it. He's enjoying it so much that it makes my head spin.

CHAPTER 27

WILLOW

It's been a few days since Oscar gave me the keys, and a strange, new routine has settled over the castle, one that feels both bizarrely domestic and utterly surreal. Every night, after I've showered and changed into one of the kings tracksuit pants and tshirt sets that magically appeared in my closet, Oscar slips into my bed. He doesn't try anything. He doesn't push or prod or demand. He just… holds me. His arm will wrap around my waist, pulling me back against his chest, his body a warm, solid wall behind me. He'll bury his face in my hair, his breath a steady, calming rhythm against my neck, and we'll just lie there. In silence. It's the most chaste, non-sexual sleeping arrangement I've ever had with a man who has, for the record, had his face buried between my legs. And it's without a doubt the most intimate I have ever felt.

It's nice. It's so, so nice to feel wanted. Not just desired, not just the object of a prophecy or a pawn in some ancient vampire game, but genuinely, truly wanted. Like my presence here, in this bed, is a comfort to him. It's a feeling that's so foreign, so unfamiliar, that it's cracking open parts of me I didn't even know were sealed shut. The ugly, dusty parts that I've kept locked away for years.

It took me three years, living in that lonely manor in Scotland, to come to terms with the fact that the people who raised me, the people I called Mom and Dad, weren't my real parents. To accept the even uglier truth: that after Caleb took me, they just… moved on. They sold the house. They changed their numbers. They disappeared. No frantic calls, no missing person posters, no desperate pleas on the nightly news. Just… nothing. A clean, quiet erasure. I was a problem, and then I was gone. And their lives got easier.

I brushed it all under the rug. I told myself it didn't matter. I told myself that Caleb was my family now, that he was all I needed. I built a fortress around my heart, a high, thick wall of denial and sarcasm. But now, in the quiet, dark hours of the night, with Oscar's arm wrapped around me, his steady presence a silent promise of safety and belonging, the cracks are starting to show. His simple, uncomplicated affection is shining a light on all the gaping holes in my life, the ones I've been so careful to ignore. The profound, soul-crushing loneliness of that manor. The way I clung to Caleb for any scrap of human interaction, convincing myself that his need for control was a form of love. I was a bird in a gilded cage, and I had forgotten what it felt like to fly. Or maybe I never knew.

So, yeah. I'm a mess. A walking, talking, snark-machine of unresolved abandonment issues. Fun times.

The kings, for their part, have slipped back into their routines. Theo is a brooding, mysterious shadow, always locked away in his office, with the faint sound of classical music seeping out from under his door. Oscar is a whirlwind of quiet efficiency, his fingers flying across keyboards, his eyes glued to screens, hunting for the ghosts of Caleb and Edmund. And Jasper… well, Jasper has a new hobby. And that hobby is trying, and failing spectacularly, to scare the ever-loving shit out of me.

It's all part of their grand plan to trigger Oscar's teleportation ability. Apparently, my terror is the key. So, for the past two days, Jasper has been channeling his inner B-movie monster, with all the subtlety of a foghorn. Yesterday, I was walking down the hall, and I heard this heavy, theatrical breathing coming from behind a suit of armor. I stopped, crossed my arms, and just waited. After a full minute of the world's least stealthy hyperventilating, he leaped out, arms raised, roaring like a constipated lion. I just stared at him, one eyebrow raised. He deflated like a sad balloon, muttering something about me having supernatural hearing. No, dude. You're just really, really bad at this.

This morning, he tried to hide behind a curtain in the dining room. A sheer curtain. I could see the entire outline of his body, his ridiculous, spiky hair a dead giveaway. He's not salty about it at all. Not one bit. He just stomps off, grumbling about how I'm "un-scare-able" and how this is all my fault. It's kind of adorable, in a pathetic, lovable-doofus sort of way.

But his failed attempts at horror movie stardom are nothing compared to his other grand gesture. The books. The literal, actual metric ton of books. They arrived yesterday, a parade of delivery trucks winding their way up the long coastal road to the castle. And now, he wants to show them to me. He wants me to see the library, a room I haven't dared to venture into yet, despite having the keys jangling in my pocket.

"Are you ready?" he asks, his voice a low, excited hum. He's practically vibrating with an energy that is both infectious and a little bit terrifying. "Are you ready to have your mind blown?"

"I don't know, Jasper," I say, my voice dripping with sarcasm. "Is it a room full of puppies? Because if it's not a room full of puppies, I'm not sure my mind can be blown."

He just grins, a wide, happy, completely un-self-conscious grin that makes my stomach do a little flip-flop. "It's better than puppies."

I follow him through the winding, endless corridors of the castle, my hand trailing along the cool stone walls. This place is a labyrinth — a beautiful, terrifying, magnificent maze. And for the first time, I'm not afraid of getting lost. I have the keys. I have a home. I have… them.

We arrive at a pair of massive, ornate wooden doors, carved with intricate scenes of dragons and castles and knights. Jasper pushes them open, the heavy wood groaning in protest, and steps aside, a dramatic flourish of his hand. "Welcome," he says, his voice a low, reverent whisper, "to your new happy place."

I step inside, and my breath catches in my throat. The room is vast, cavernous, the ceiling so high it's lost in shadow. And every single wall, from the floor to the ceiling, is covered in books. Not just the existing shelves, but the ones filled with ancient, leather-bound tomes. But new shelves. Stacks and stacks of them, lining the walls, creating new aisles, new corridors, new worlds to explore. And they're all full. Overflowing. With my books. The ones he bought for me. The ones I saw online, the ones I dreamed of reading. Dark romance, reverse harem, fantasy, sci-fi… it's all here. A universe of stories, a galaxy of words, a lifetime of adventures. All for me. Theo explained that he is going to expand the library cause Jasper has bought even more than what has arrived so far, and he will need to hire some workers to do some work, but the new shelves for now will work.

I walk forward, my feet silent on the plush velvet rug. I run my fingers along the spines of the books; the smooth, glossy covers stand out against the ancient, cracked leather of the others. I can't speak. I can't breathe. I can't do anything but stare, my heart a wild, frantic drum against my ribs. It's too much. It's too big. It's the most extravagant, most ridiculous, most wonderful thing anyone has ever done for me.

I turn to look at him, my eyes blurry with tears. He's standing by the door, his hands shoved in his pockets, a nervous, hopeful look on his face. He's not the cheeky, fun-loving vampire king right now. He's just a boy, standing in front of a girl, hoping she likes his gift.

And I do. I more than like it. I love it. I love him. And that, more than anything, is what truly terrifies me.

CHAPTER 28

OSCAR

I can teleport. The words echo in my mind, a constant, thrumming mantra that feels both utterly alien and as natural as breathing. I, Oscar Michaels, can bend space and time to my will. It's the most astonishing thing to happen to me in two hundred years of my ordered existence. Well, second most astonishing. The first was Willow. And now, the two are inextricably linked, a beautiful, chaotic knot in the center of my once-sterile life.

I should be ecstatic. I should be running tests, documenting variables, trying to replicate the conditions that triggered the event. But I can't. Because I don't remember how I did it. One moment, I was in the kitchen, the scent of thyme and rosemary filling my senses, my mind a maelstrom of fear for her. The next, I was in her room. The scent of her, all sweet, intoxicating woman, wrapped around me, her body a pale, fragile heap on the floor. It was instinct. It was terror. It was… her. And now, the power lies dormant, a sleeping beast in the back of my mind, and I have no idea how to wake it.

My brothers, in their infinite wisdom, have a plan. A stupid, ridiculous, Jasper-scented plan. They want to scare her. They think her fear will be the trigger, the key to unlocking my new toy. I hate it. I hate the idea of putting even a flicker of fear in her eyes. But I'm also desperate. I need to understand this. I need to control it. For her. For us.

For now, Jasper gets to play knight in shining armor, or more accurately, book-hoarding dragon. He's with her in the library, showing off the mountain of paper and ink he bought for her. I can feel her excitement, a bright, bubbly hum through our bond, and it makes my chest ache with a strange, unfamiliar jealousy. I want to be the one to make her that happy. I want to be the one to give her the world. Or at least, a library big enough to hold it.

I turn back to my monitors, the glow of the screens illuminating the dark room. I have work to do. Before Willow, my life was a quiet, orderly pursuit of a ghost. Finding her was a project, a complex algorithm with a missing variable. Now, it's a hunt. A visceral need to find the men who kept her from me, who hurt her, who dared to touch what was mine. The programs I'm running are no longer just lines of code. They are my hounds, my digital trackers, sniffing out the scent of our prey.

Caleb has vanished. Utterly, completely. It's as if he never existed. No digital footprint, no paper trail, nothing. It's a clean, precise excision from the world, and it's the most unsettling thing I've ever encountered. This wasn't a panicked flight. This was a plan. A long, carefully constructed plan. And that means he's not just a rogue vampire with a god complex. He's a pawn. Edmund's pawn. And Edmund… Edmund is a king. He knows how to hide. But he doesn't know me. He doesn't know the man I've become since I bonded with Willow.

I feel a surge of raw, untamed power, a feeling so foreign, so intoxicating, that it makes my head spin. For the first time in centuries, I feel… alive. The world is brighter; the air is sharper, my senses are on fire. And it's all because of her. She's awakened something in me, something possessive and so, so hungry. I'm constantly, painfully aroused. Every thought, every breath, is filled with her. The memory of her taste, the feel of her wrapped around my cock — it's a brand on my soul. I want to bend her over every piece of furniture in this castle, to take her until she's screaming my name, until she's so full of me that she can't think, can't breathe, can't do anything but feel. But she was a virgin. A sweet, innocent, untouched virgin. And I was her first. The thought sends a wave of pride through me, so strong it almost brings me to my knees. She needs to be cherished, to be worshipped, to be shown how precious she is. I will treat her like a queen. But that doesn't stop the constant, gnawing hunger, the need to rut, to claim, to mark her as mine in every way a man can mark a woman.

I push back from the desk, the frustration of the hunt and the fire in my blood making the room feel small, suffocating. I need to move. I need to get out of here. I need to see her.

I change into hiking gear, the rough fabric a welcome friction against my over-sensitized skin. I found them in the library, just as I knew I would. And the sight that greets me makes my breath catch in my throat. She's surrounded by books, mountains of them, a veritable fortress of paper and ink. She's sitting on the floor, a book in her lap, her face lit up with a joy so pure, so radiant, that it's like looking at the sun. And Jasper is with her, his long legs stretched out, a lazy, happy smile on his face. He's watching her with such open, unabashed adoration that it makes my fists clench.

"Look, Oscar!" she says, her voice a bright, happy chime that cuts through the fog of my thoughts. She holds up a book, the cover a lurid painting of a woman surrounded by three bare-chested men. "This one is about a woman with three lovers. Can you believe it? It's like they wrote it just for me."

I can't help but laugh, the sound a low, rumbling growl in my chest. "I'm sure they did, little mouse."

I walk over to her, my eyes never leaving hers. I can feel Jasper's gaze on me, a silent, watchful presence, but I don't care. Nothing matters but her. "I'm heading off for that hike now," I say, my voice a low, intense murmur.

"I'm not sure jump scares work when you know one is coming," she teases, her eyes sparkling with a mischief that makes my heart ache.

"Even if it doesn't, it'll give me a sense of how far I can go before losing a sense of you," I say, my voice a low, husky whisper. I lean down, my hand cupping her cheek, my thumb stroking her soft, warm skin. I can't resist. I have to taste her. I press my lips to hers, a soft, gentle kiss that is meant to be a simple goodbye. She gasps, her lips parting, and I deepen the kiss, my tongue sweeping into her mouth, tasting her, claiming her. She responds instantly, her body pressing against mine, her arms wrapping around my neck, her fingers tangling in my hair. She tastes of sweet, innocent desire, and I can't get enough.

I hear a low, guttural curse from Jasper, and I reluctantly pull away, my body screaming in protest. I'm hard. Rock hard. And I can see the bulge in Jasper's pants, the tense set of his jaw, the dark, stormy look in his eyes. I can't resist a smirk. "Just wait until you taste her, brother," I say, my voice a low, taunting whisper. "She'll leave you begging for more." And I watch a blush take over the whole of Willow's face as she gulps.

I turn and walk away, my own body a raging inferno of need. I can hear Jasper grumbling behind me, and I can feel Willow's eyes on my back, a mixture of confusion and arousal that is so potent, so intoxicating, that it's all I can do to keep walking, otherwise I'll head back and fuck her against the pile of books she currently looking at.

CHAPTER 29

WILLOW

I've been in the library for hours, and I'm still not convinced this isn't some elaborate, book-themed fever dream. I'm surrounded by so many stories that the air itself feels thick with them, the scent of old leather from Theo's collection mingling with the crisp, clean smell of the new paperbacks Jasper bought for me. It's intoxicating. I run my fingers along the spines, a thrill shooting up my arm with every title. Chasing the Wolf King. Bound to the Demon. My Three Vampire Dads. Okay, I might have made that last one up, but you get the picture. My own personal smut palace. It's the most thoughtful, most insane gift I've ever received.

Jasper is perched on a rolling library ladder, looking for all the world like a sexy, punk-rock version of a Disney prince. He's been watching me with a grin on his face for the better part of an hour, his eyes sparkling with a mischief that is both endearing and deeply suspicious.

"Find anything good, bookworm?" he asks, his voice echoing slightly in the cavernous room.

"I've found about a hundred books that would make a nun blush," I shoot back, pulling out a particularly lurid-looking novel with a shirtless, horned man on the cover. "This one looks like it could get me excommunicated just for holding it. What is your obsession with my reading habits, anyway? It's a little weird."

He slides down the ladder with a grace that is frankly unfair and saunters over, plucking the book from my hand. "I'm not obsessed with your reading habits," he says, his voice dropping to a low, conspiratorial purr.

"I'm obsessed with the way your cheeks get all flushed when you read the dirty parts. It's cute." He flips the book over, his eyes scanning the back. "Oh, this is a good one, I read the first chapter of this when I unpacked it. The main character gets spit-roasted by twin dragon shifters in the first chapter."

My jaw drops. "She what?"

"Spit-roasted," he repeats, his grin widening. "You know, like a rotisserie chicken. But with dicks."

I snatch the book back, my face on fire. "You are a menace to society," I say, trying and failing to suppress a laugh. "A walking, talking, HR violation."

"Only one way to find out if it's as good as it sounds," he winks, leaning in so close I can smell the faint, clean scent of his soap. "I dare you to read the first page. Out loud."

"Absolutely not," I say, my heart starting to hammer against my ribs. "There are ancient, priceless books in here. I don't want to offend their delicate sensibilities with your filth."

"They're books, Willow, not my great-aunt Mildred.

They can handle it. Come on," he cajoles, his eyes dancing with amusement. "Don't be a chicken. Unless you want to get spit-roasted, that is."

"Oh my God, fine!" I snap, the laughter bubbling up and spilling out of me. I open the book, my eyes scanning the first few lines, and the blush on my cheeks deepens to a full-blown inferno. This isn't just filthy. This is a five-alarm fire of literary smut. I take a deep breath and begin to read, my voice shaky at first, then growing more confident as I get into the rhythm of the prose. The words are hot and heavy, the descriptions so vivid I can almost feel the heat of the dragon's fire, the press of their bodies. My laughter mingles with Jasper's, a wild, joyful sound that feels like a sacrilege in the hallowed silence of the library.

When I finish the page, I'm breathless, my whole body thrumming with a strange, unfamiliar energy. I look up at Jasper, and the laughter dies in my throat. The playful glint in his eyes is gone, replaced by something deeper, something more intense. Something hungry.

"You know," he says, his voice a low, husky whisper that sends shivers down my spine. "You're absolutely beautiful when you're flustered."

He reaches out, his fingers gently brushing a stray strand of hair from my face. His touch is electric, like lightning that arcs through my entire body. My core clenches, a familiar, insistent ache that has become a constant companion since I arrived at this castle of ridiculously hot, tattooed, emotionally complicated vampires.

"Thank you," I manage to squeak out, my voice barely a whisper. "You're… not so bad yourself, for a walking HR violation."

He chuckles, a low, rumbling sound that vibrates through my chest. "Ah, but you're the one who lights up the room," he says, his eyes dropping to my lips. "I'm just the guy who wants to get burned by your fire."

He leans in, his face just inches from mine. I can feel his breath on my skin, warm and sweet. My heart is pounding so hard I'm sure he can hear it, a frantic, desperate drumbeat against my ribs. This is it. He's going to kiss me. And I'm going to let him. I'm going to kiss him back, and I'm going to enjoy every single, reckless second of it.

My eyes flutter shut, my lips parting in anticipation. And then, a flash of ice-cold terror. The library disappears, replaced by a dark, moonlit forest. I see Oscar, his face a mask of confusion, his body tense. And then I see Caleb, his face twisted in a snarl of rage and betrayal, a gun in his hand. The glint of moonlight on the cold, hard steel of the barrel is the last thing I see before the vision shatters, leaving me gasping for breath, my body trembling.

"Jasper…" I whisper, my voice a raw, choked sound. "I just had a vision… Oscar's in danger."

Jasper pulls back instantly, the playful, seductive man gone, replaced by a king, a warrior, his eyes sharp and focused. "What?" he demands, his hands gripping my shoulders. "What did you see?"

"Oscar was hiking," I say, the words tumbling out in a frantic, jumbled rush. "And Caleb was there. He had a gun, Jasper. He was pointing it at Oscar. It felt so real. I've never had a vision before, but I know what I saw. We have to do something!"

"Are you sure?" he asks, his voice a low, intense

murmur, his eyes searching mine, not for doubt, but for certainty.

"Yes!" I cry, my voice cracking. "I'm sure! We have to go now!"

"Alright," he says, his voice a low, guttural growl, a sound that is pure, undiluted predator. "Let's find Theo."

We race out of the library, my heart a frantic, terrified bird beating against the cage of my ribs. The image of Caleb, of the gun — it's burned into my mind, a horrifying, repeating loop. "I can't lose him," I say, my voice tight with a fear so profound it's stealing the air from my lungs. "Why would Caleb do this?"

"To get to you," Jasper says, his voice a low, angry snarl. "It's always been about you."

My mind is racing, a whirlwind of fear and confusion. And then, a new sensation. A strange, pulling feeling in my gut, like a hook has been sunk deep inside me, and someone is yanking on the line. The hallway around me begins to warp and stretch, the colours bleeding together like a watercolour painting left out in the rain.

"Willow!" Jasper cries out, his voice sounding distant, distorted. He reaches for me, his fingers just brushing against mine, but it's too late. The world dissolves into a nauseating, chaotic swirl of light and sound, and then, with a sickening lurch, I'm somewhere else.

My feet hit the ground, the crunch of gravel under my boots a shocking, solid reality. The air is cold, crisp, and filled with the scent of pine and damp earth. I'm outside. On the hiking trail. And a few feet away, standing in a pool of moonlight, is Oscar. My breath catches in my throat as I see him, and then my blood runs cold. In front of him, his face a mask of pure, is Caleb. And in his hand, raised and steady, is the gun.

"Oscar, watch out!" I scream, my voice a raw, desperate cry that tears through the quiet night. I don't think. I just act. I launch myself at Oscar, my body a shield, a desperate, foolish attempt to protect him from the inevitable.

He turns, his eyes wide with confusion that quickly turns to horror. "Willow, what are you—"

His words are cut short by a deafening crack that echoes through the trees. A searing, white-hot pain explodes in my chest, so real, so visceral, that I'm sure I've been hit. But it's not my body that crumples to the ground. It's Oscar's. He falls like a puppet with its strings cut, a dark, spreading stain on the front of his shirt.

"NO!" I scream, the sound a raw, animalistic cry of pure agony. I fall to my knees beside him, my hands hovering over the wound, my tears a hot, useless rain on his pale, still face.

"Willow, it's okay," he rasps, his voice a weak, strained whisper. He coughs, a trickle of blood at the corner of his mouth. "Bullets… don't kill me. Just… slow me down." He starts to push himself up, his movements slow, agonizing. The hole in his chest is already starting to close, the flesh knitting itself back together in a way that is both miraculous and horrifying. "I just need… some blood."

"Too late for that," Caleb sneers, his voice a low, triumphant growl. He raises the gun again, and the night explodes in a series of deafening cracks, each one a hammer blow to my heart. Oscar's body jerks with each impact, the healing flesh tearing apart again and again, until he lies still, a broken, bleeding mess on the cold, hard ground.

Caleb grabs me, his fingers like iron bands around my arm, yanking me to my feet. "Let me go!" I scream, my fists beating against his chest, my struggles as useless as a fly caught in a spider's web.

"Shut up!" he snaps, his voice a low, menacing hiss. "You're coming with me."

"They will find me," I spat, my voice filled with a venom I didn't know I possessed. "They will hunt you down, and they will make you pay for this."

"Your precious kings can't save you this time," he taunts, dragging me away from Oscar's still, silent form. Panic, cold and sharp, cuts through the fog of my grief. Oscar needs my blood. He can't feed from anyone else. He's going to die. And Caleb is taking me away from him.

Or is he? I teleported. I did it once. Maybe I can do it again. A desperate, crazy, probably going-to-get-me-killed plan begins to form in my mind. I stop struggling, my body going limp in his grasp. He's surprised, but he doesn't loosen his grip. I let him drag me a few more feet up the trail, my eyes never leaving Oscar's body. And then, I act.

I snap my arm back, yanking it free from his grasp. He's so caught off guard that he stumbles, and in that split second of surprise, I swing. My fist connects with his nose, the crunch of bone a deeply, profoundly satisfying sound. He's a vampire; it'll heal. Probably. I punch him again for good measure. He reaches for me, his face a mask of rage, and pulls me into his chest, his arms a cage of hard, unyielding muscle.

"Stop fighting me, Willow!" he yells, his voice a raw, desperate cry. "I'm trying to save you!"

"You lied to me!" I scream, my voice a raw, broken sob. I close my eyes, ignoring his words, ignoring the pain, and focus all my energy, all my will, on one single point. Oscar. I feel a strange tingling sensation in my feet, a low, humming vibration that seems to come from the very center of my being. It's happening again.

The world dissolves into a violent, chaotic swirl, and then, with a gut-wrenching lurch, I'm back. I stumble, my legs weak, my head spinning, but I'm here. I'm beside him. I fall to my knees, my hands frantically searching for his mouth. "Oscar, please," I beg, my voice a raw, desperate whisper. I thrust my wrist toward his lips. "Bite me. Please, you have to bite me."

His eyes flutter open, a flicker of recognition in their dark, hazy depths. His mouth opens, his fangs, long and sharp and beautiful, sliding into place. He sinks them into my wrist, and the world explodes in a supernova. A deep, guttural moan escapes my lips, my body arching, my hips bucking. My panties are soaked, my mind a swirling vortex of need and desire. He's taking so much, I can feel myself growing weak, lightheaded, but I don't care. I would give him every last drop if he asked.

Suddenly, he pulls away, his fangs retracting with a soft click. He leaps to his feet, his body a blur of motion. The world spins, my vision going dark. "Oscar," I whisper, my voice a faint, fading echo in the vast, silent night. And then, the darkness takes me.

CHAPTER 30

THEODORE

The numbers on the screen blur into a meaningless jumble of black and white. I've been staring at the same quarterly report for the better part of an hour, my mind a million miles away from profit margins and market projections. It's a useless endeavor. My focus is shot to hell, my concentration obliterated by a five-foot-four-inch hurricane of snark and sass and a body that was built for sin. Willow. She's a virus in my system, a fever in my blood, and I can't fucking shake her.

Every time I close my eyes, I see her. I see her laughing in the library with Jasper, a sound that is both infuriatingly joyful and achingly beautiful. I see her in my bed, her body a pale, perfect canvas against the dark sheets, her scent a permanent, intoxicating stain on my pillows. I see her looking at me with those wide, innocent eyes that hold a spark of defiance, a challenge that makes my cock twitch with need. I want to break her. I want to worship her. I want to bend her over this very desk and fuck her until she's screaming my name, until she's so full of me that she forgets her own.

The thought sends a jolt of lust through me, so strong it makes my fangs ache. I'm a king. A centuries-old predator. And I'm reduced to a horny teenager by a woman who owned my soul with one look. It's pathetic. It's infuriating. It's the most alive I've felt in a hundred years.

The door to my office slams open, the sound a cannon blast in the quiet room. It hits the wall with a crack that would make a normal man flinch. I don't even blink. I just look up, my eyes cold and hard, ready to eviscerate whoever dared to interrupt my brooding. And then I see him. Jasper. His face is pale, his eyes wide with a terror I haven't seen since the night our father died. And in that instant, I know. Something is wrong. Something is very, very wrong.

"Willow had a vision," he pants, his voice a raw, ragged gasp. "Oscar's on the hiking trail. Caleb has him. At gunpoint. She teleported, Theo. She's gone. I don't know where she is!"

A cold, sharp dread, colder than any winter's night, slices through me. The air in my lungs turns to ice. My world, which had just begun to find a new, chaotic center, shatters. Caleb. That fucking insect. He has Oscar. And he has my Willow. No, not my Willow. Not yet. But she will be. And the thought of that bastard's hands on her, of his voice in her ear, it ignites a rage in me so hot, so violent, that it threatens to burn me from the inside out.

I'm on my feet in a flash, the chair flying back, the papers on my desk scattering like fallen leaves in a hurricane. They're meaningless. Everything is meaningless but her. "Let's go," I snarl, my voice a low, guttural growl that is pure, undiluted predator. "Now."

We race through the castle, our footsteps frantic, echoing against the cold stone floors. My mind is a maelstrom of worst-case scenarios, each one more horrific than the last. Caleb with a gun. Willow, teleporting for the first time, disoriented, vulnerable. The thought of losing her, of losing either of them, it's a pain, a gaping, bleeding wound in my chest.

"Where do you think she went?" I bark, my voice sharp, clipped.

"I don't know," Jasper gasps, his voice laced with a frustration that mirrors my own. "Her first time. I just hope to whatever god is listening that she ended up on that trail. With Oscar."

I don't pray. I don't hope. I command. Be there, little one. Be safe. I'm coming. We burst through the castle doors, the cold night air a slap in the face. The forest is a dark, menacing labyrinth of shadows and secrets, but we don't hesitate. We plunge into the darkness, our bodies moving with a speed and a purpose that is born of desperation and rage.

We find them at the bend in the trail. And the sight that greets me is a beautiful, terrifying, magnificent tableau of chaos and love. Oscar is on his feet, his shirt a tattered, bloody mess of bullet holes that are already closing, the flesh knitting itself back together with a speed that is both miraculous and grotesque. And in his arms, limp and pale but breathing, is Willow. My Willow.

Relief, so potent, so overwhelming, washes over me,

leaving me weak in its wake. And then, the rage comes roaring back. "Oscar!" I call out, my voice a raw, guttural bark. I skid to a halt beside them, my eyes scanning Willow's still form, searching for any sign of injury, any mark, any bruise that would give me an excuse to hunt Caleb down and tear him limb from fucking limb.

"Are you both alright?" Jasper pants, his chest heaving, his face a mask of worry and relief.

"Fine," Oscar says, his voice a low, tight growl. He pulls Willow's limp body closer, his arms a protective cage around her. "I'm fine."

"Tell me everything," I demand, my voice leaving no room for argument. "What the fuck happened here? Where is he?"

Oscar starts walking, his strides long and purposeful, his eyes fixed on the distant, comforting silhouette of the castle. "Caleb was here," he says, his voice a low, simmering cauldron of rage. "He had a gun. Demanded we give him Willow."

"That motherfucker," Jasper mutters, his hands clenched into tight, white-knuckled fists.

My own anger is a living thing, a beast clawing at the inside of my chest, begging to be unleashed. But I force it down. I need to be calm. I need to be in control. For her. "She's waking up," I say, my voice a low, intense murmur. "Willow? Are you hurt?"

Her eyes flutter open, her bright blue eyes hazy with confusion and exhaustion. "J-just tired," she whispers, her voice so weak it's barely a breath. "I'll be okay."

Her voice — that soft, sweet sound, it's like a balm on my raw, frayed nerves. But it does nothing to quell the fire in my blood. "Once we're back," I say, my voice a low, cold promise, "we are going to have a serious discussion about Caleb. And then, I'm going to end him."

"Agreed," Jasper says, his voice a low, angry echo of my own.

We walk in silence for a few moments, the only sound the crunch of our feet on the gravel path and the soft, ragged sound of Willow's breathing. The fury is still a living thing inside me, a beast clawing at my ribs, but seeing her, feeling her presence, it banks the flames. For now.

"Talk," I command, my voice a low growl that cuts through the quiet night. "From the beginning. Every fucking detail."

Oscar adjusts Willow in his arms, his jaw tight. "I was about a mile in. I felt… something. A shift in the air. Then he was just there. Caleb."

"Just appeared?" Jasper asks, his voice sharp with disbelief.

"No," Oscar says, shaking his head. "He was just… standing there. Like he'd been waiting. He told me to give her back."

"He told you?" I spit the words dripping with venom. "The audacity of that fucking insect."

"I told him to go fuck himself," Oscar continues, his voice flat, devoid of emotion. "And then… everything went to hell. I heard her scream my name. One second she wasn't there, and the next, she was. Standing right in front of me, between me and Caleb."

"She teleported," Jasper breathes, his voice filled with a stunned awe.

"She tried to jump in front of me," Oscar's voice cracks, a fissure in his carefully constructed dam of control. "The little fool actually tried to take a bullet for me. I managed to push her away, but Caleb fired and got me right in the chest."

My blood runs cold. The image of her, so small, so fragile, trying to shield a centuries-old vampire with her own body… it's the most insane, reckless, beautiful thing I have ever heard.

"He shot you," I state, my voice a low, dangerous rumble.

"Once," Oscar confirms. "Then he emptied the rest of the clip into my chest before I could fully heal." He looks down at Willow, his expression softening. "He grabbed her. Started dragging her up the trail. She was fighting him, screaming…"

"That motherfucker put his hands on her?" Jasper snarls, his hands clenching into fists at his sides.

"She got away," Oscar says, a flicker of pride in his voice. "I don't know how. One minute he was dragging her, the next she was standing over me again. She teleported back."

"Twice," I murmur, my mind reeling. This tiny, fragile human. She faced down a vampire with a gun, teleported twice, and saved my brother's life. She's not a fragile flower. She's a fucking warrior. And she's mine.

"She punched him, too," Willow mumbles, her voice thick with sleep, her face still buried in Oscar's chest, gesturing with light punch into Oscar's chest with her hand. "Broke his nose. It was very satisfying."

Jasper lets out a short, sharp bark of laughter. "Of course she did."

I can't help the small, grim smile that touches my lips. "You bit her?" I ask, my eyes narrowing on the mark on her wrist that is now visible as she pretended to punch Oscar.

Oscar's jaw tightens again. "I had to. I was too weak. The bullets… they were silver-tipped. Healing was slow. She shoved her wrist in my mouth and told me to bite."

"Forced her blood on you," I say, the words a statement, not a question.

"I'm fine," Willow says, her voice a little stronger now, lifting her head to glare at me with sleepy, defiant eyes. "Just a little anemic. Nothing a good steak and a nap won't fix. Or, you know, a blood bag. Got any of those O-negative Capri Suns lying around?"

I stare at her, this impossible, infuriating, magnificent woman. Even now, after everything she's been through, she's still a smartass. It's infuriating. It's intoxicating. It's everything.

We reach the castle, the heavy wooden doors a welcome sight. "My room," I say, my voice a low, firm command. "It's the closest."

Oscar doesn't argue. He carries her into my room and lays her gently on the bed. "I'll go make you something to eat," he says, his voice a low, gentle murmur. "You need to get your strength back."

He leaves, the door closing behind him with a soft click, and then, we are alone. The air in the room is thick with unspoken words, with a tension so palpable it's a living, breathing thing. The silence stretches, heavy and fraught. I should say something. I should be a king, in control, commanding the situation. But all I can do is stare at her, this impossible creature who has turned my world on its axis.

I move without thinking, my body acting on a need so profound it bypasses thought. I slip into the bed beside her, the mattress dipping under my weight. She doesn't flinch. She doesn't pull away. She just watches me, her eyes wide and luminous in the dim light. I wrap my arm around her, pulling her close, my hand resting on the gentle curve of her hip. Her body is a warm, welcome weight against mine. I bury my face in her hair, the scent of her—sweet and floral and uniquely her—filling my senses, calming the raging beast inside me.

"I was so scared," I admit, the words a raw, honest whisper against her hair, torn from a place deep inside me I didn't know existed. "When Jasper told me… I thought I was going to lose you."

She turns in my arms, her small hand coming up to cup my cheek. Her touch is a brand, a spark that ignites a fire in my veins. "We're both here now, Theo," she says, her voice a soft, reassuring murmur that does more to soothe me than a century of solitude ever could. "That's what matters."

I pull back just enough to look at her, my hand covering hers, pressing her palm flat against my skin. "Tell me about the vision," I say, my voice a low, intense murmur. "Have you ever had one before?"

She shakes her head, her hair brushing against the pillow. "Never. It was… weird. It just happened. One minute I was laughing with Jasper about… well, about spit-roasting." A faint blush colours her cheeks, and I feel a ridiculous pang of jealousy. "And next, I was in the woods. I could see everything. Oscar. Caleb. The gun. It wasn't like watching a movie. It was like I was there. I felt cold. I smelled the pine needles."

"And the teleportation?" I ask, my thumb stroking the back of her hand. "What did that feel like?"

"Like being pulled through a straw," she says, a small, wry smile touching her lips. "A very fast, very violent straw. And then I was just… there. It wasn't a choice. It was a need. I had to get to him."

I frown, my mind racing, trying to piece together the impossible puzzle of her. "I think… I think your powers are connected to ours. To the bond."

Her brow furrows, her expression a mixture of confusion and dawning understanding. "But why now? I've only bonded with Oscar."

"Perhaps each bond is a key," I muse, my fingers absently tracing the delicate line of her jaw. "Unlocking a different door. Oscar's bond gave you the ability to teleport, to feel our emotions. Perhaps… perhaps my bond will give you something else."

"Or maybe it's triggered by something," she whispers, her eyes wide with a sudden realization. "Like danger. Or strong emotions. When I saw Oscar in danger, it was like… like a switch flipped. Something inside me just… woke up."

Her words hang in the air, heavy with a significance that we are only just beginning to understand. She is more than just our mate. She is something new. Something powerful. And she is ours.

As we lie there, wrapped in the quiet intimacy of the moment, I can see the exhaustion settling over her. The adrenaline has faded, leaving behind a bone-deep weariness. Her eyelids are heavy, her blinks slow, languid. Her words begin to slur, her voice a soft, sleepy murmur.

"Rest, little one," I whisper, my voice a low, gentle command. I pull the covers up, tucking them around her shoulders. "Just for a little while. Close your eyes."

She doesn't argue. She just melts against me, her body a warm, pliant weight in my arms, her breathing evening out into the slow, steady rhythm of sleep. She's so small, so fragile in my arms. And yet, she's the strongest person I have ever known. I watch her sleep, my heart a tangled mess of emotions I can't even begin to name. Protectiveness. Possessiveness. Awe. And a deep, aching love that is so profound, so overwhelming, that it terrifies me.

She sleeps for what feels like an eternity, but is probably only half an hour. She stirs, a soft, sleepy sound escaping her lips, and she snuggles closer, her face burrowing into the crook of my neck, her breath a warm, sweet caress against my skin. My entire body goes rigid, my cock instantly, painfully hard. And then, she wakes up.

Her eyes flutter open, her gaze soft, hazy, and utterly, completely unguarded. She looks at me, a small, sleepy smile touching her lips, a look so sweet that it shatters the last of my control. It's a look that says I am safe with you. And in that moment, I know. I can't wait. I can't be the patient, noble king. I am a predator, and she is my prey. And I am so, so hungry.

"Willow," I whisper, my voice a low, husky growl, a sound that is pure, undiluted possession. I lean in, my lips brushing against hers, a soft, tentative touch that is a question, a plea, a promise. She gasps, her lips parting, and I take it as the invitation it is. I capture her mouth in a deep, bruising kiss, my tongue sweeping in, tasting her, claiming her. She tastes of sleep and innocence and a sweet, intoxicating desire that drives me absolutely fucking insane.

She arches into me, her body a pliant, willing offering. My hands are everywhere, under her shirt, skimming the soft, smooth skin of her back, cupping the heavy weight of her breasts. I pull her shirt over her head, tossing it to the floor, and then I'm on her, my mouth devouring hers, my hands exploring every inch of her perfect, porcelain skin. I suck and bite and lick at her nipples, teasing them into hard, tight peaks, reveling in the soft, breathy moans that escape her lips.

I trail a path of hot, open-mouthed kisses down her stomach, my tongue dipping into the shallow curve of her navel. She's wearing a pair of my tracksuit pants, the soft, worn fabric a ridiculous, endearing contrast to the fire raging between us. I hook my fingers in the waistband and pull, sliding them down her long, slender legs, my eyes feasting on the sight of her in a pair of tiny, lace panties that are already soaked through. The scent of her arousal — that sweet, musky, intoxicating scent — it hits me, making my head spin.

"Theo, I…" she whispers, her voice a raw, breathless plea.

"I know, baby," I groan, my voice a low, guttural growl. I push her legs apart, my eyes devouring the sight of her, the soft, pink flesh, the glistening wetness that coats her folds. I run my tongue from her ass to her clit in one long, slow, deliberate stroke, and she screams. It's the most beautiful music I have ever heard.

She tastes like heaven. Like sin. Like everything I've ever wanted and never knew I needed. I lick and suck and devour her, my tongue relentless. I slide two fingers inside her, her walls clenching around me, hot and tight and wet. She's so responsive, so eager, her hips bucking against my mouth. I find her G-spot, that perfect, magic button, and I play it like a virtuoso, my fingers a steady, rhythmic beat against her clit. I feel her start to tremble, her orgasm building, a tidal wave that is about to crash over her. But I'm not done with her yet. Not even close.

I slide my fingers out, and she whimpers, a soft, frustrated sound that makes my cock leap. I slick a finger with her juices and my own saliva and slide it into her ass, the tight, virginal heat of her a brand on my skin. She gasps, her eyes wide with a mixture of shock. "Do you like that, little one?" I whisper, my breath hot against her clit. She can only nod, her body a trembling, quivering mess of need. I add a second finger, stretching her, filling her, while my other hand returns to her cunt, my thumb circling her clit, my fingers teasing her entrance. And then, I let her go. She shatters, her body convulsing. I hold her, my mouth still on her, my tongue lapping at the sweet, sticky evidence of her, until the last tremor has faded.

"Fuck, Willow," I pant, my voice a raw, ragged whisper. "You are absolutely stunning when you scream like that."

"Can I have more?" she asks, her voice a low, husky purr. She's on her elbows, her hair a wild, tangled mess, her eyes dark and stormy with a desire that mirrors my own. She's a goddess. A siren. A fucking queen.

"Oh, baby," I groan, my voice a low, guttural growl. "You can have anything you want."

"I want you, Theo," she says, her voice a low, firm command that makes my cock leap. "Fuck me. Please."

"Baby, I can't," I say, my voice a raw, honest plea. "You're weak. You need to rest."

"No," she says, her voice a low, angry snarl. She pushes against my chest, her strength surprising me, and rolls me onto my back. She straddles my waist, her eyes blazing with a fire that takes my breath away. Her hands, small and delicate but surprisingly strong, go to my belt, her fingers fumbling with the buckle. She gets it undone, and then she's on my zipper, pulling it down, her hands sliding inside my boxers, her fingers wrapping around my throbbing, rock-hard cock. I groan, my hips bucking, my control slipping.

"Oh, Willow," I moan, my voice a raw, desperate cry. "What are you doing to me?"

She doesn't answer. She just lifts herself up, her eyes never leaving mine, and then she sinks down, taking all of me inside her, her tight, wet heat a brand on my soul. It's the most exquisite, most agonizing, most perfect pain I have ever felt. "That's it, baby," I groan, my hands gripping her hips, my fingers digging into her soft flesh. I start to move, to push, to fuck, but she stops me, her hands on my chest, her eyes blazing.

"No," she says, her voice a low, firm command. "I'm in charge now."

And then, she starts to ride me. And I, Theodore

Michaels, king of the vampires, master of my own destiny, I let her. I lie back and I let her fuck me. And it is without a doubt the best fucking thing that has ever happened to me.

She moves with an instinct, a rhythm, that is pure sex. She's a natural. A fucking prodigy. I'm on the edge, my control shattered, my body a raging inferno of need. "I'm going to cum, baby," I gasp, my hands gripping her hips, my thumbs stroking the soft, sensitive skin of her inner thighs. And then, I feel it. The telltale clenching of her walls, the soft, breathy moans that escape her lips. She's close. so fucking close. I push up, my hips meeting hers, and we shatter together, a supernova that rocks the very foundations of the castle.

Her body is limp, boneless, a beautiful, sated weight on top of me. She leans down, her breath hot against my ear, and offers me her neck. "Bite me," she demands, her voice a low, husky whisper. And I do. I sink my fangs into her, the sweet, metallic taste of her blood on my tongue. I only take a drop, just enough to seal the bond, and then I lick the wound clean, my tongue a gentle, soothing caress against her skin. She shudders, a soft, breathy moan escaping her lips, and I feel it. The bond. A warm, golden light that wraps around us, connecting us, binding us, making us one.

She tastes like chocolate and honey and cinnamon. She tastes like home. She collapses onto my chest, her body a warm, welcome weight. "You're mine now," I whisper, the words a raw, honest truth that I can no longer deny.

She lifts her head, her eyes soft and warm, her lips curved in a small, secret smile. "You're mine too," she whispers, her voice a soft, sweet melody that is the most beautiful sound I have ever heard.

"God, Willow," I murmur, my voice thick with an emotion I can't even begin to name. "That was the sexiest thing I have ever seen."

She just smiles, a radiant, beautiful, breathtaking smile that makes my heart ache.

CHAPTER 31

WILLOW

I wake up to the feeling of being slowly roasted alive. My skin is slick with a layer of sweat that is definitely not all mine, and I'm tangled in limbs and sheets and the oppressive, delicious heat of a vampire furnace. A very large, very muscular, very naked human furnace. Oh, right. Theodore. The memories of last night come crashing back, a tidal wave of heat and a series of screams that I'm pretty sure were mine. My body aches in places I didn't know could ache, a deep, pleasant soreness that points to a night well spent. Or, you know, a night spent being thoroughly, comprehensively, and enthusiastically fucked by a vampire king.

My head, however, feels like someone has taken a jackhammer to it. A dull, throbbing pound behind my eyes that is in direct, violent opposition to the languid pleasure humming through the rest of my body. Ugh. Is this the vampire equivalent of a hangover? A bond-over? I groan, the sound a low, pathetic whimper in the quiet room. I try to disentangle myself from Theo's octopus-like embrace, a feat of engineering that requires the stealth of a ninja and the flexibility of a contortionist. He's draped over me like a weighted blanket made of a hot vampire, one arm thrown possessively over my waist, one leg hooked over mine. He looks so damn peaceful, his dark lashes a stark, delicate fringe against his chiseled cheeks, his mouth soft and relaxed in sleep. It's a far cry from the snarling, demanding predator of last night. It's almost… sweet. Which is a deeply disturbing thought.

I finally manage to slither out of his grasp, my feet hitting the cold, hard floor with a soft thud. The room tilts, the ornate patterns on the wallpaper swirling like a cheap acid trip. My stomach churns, a violent, lurching rebellion that has nothing to do with the acrobatic sex and everything to do with the magical bullshit that is my life. Oh, no. Not again. I bolt for the bathroom, my hand clamped over my mouth, my movements clumsy, desperate. I make it to the toilet just in time, my body convulsing as I empty the contents of my stomach into the pristine, porcelain bowl. The sound of my retching echoes off the cold, sterile tiles.

In the midst of my technicolour yawn, I hear the soft scrape of a chair against the floor. My head whips up, my eyes wide with surprise that is quickly followed by a wave of mortification. Oscar is sitting in a plush armchair in the corner of the room, a book in his lap, his face a mask of gentle, worried concern. He was just… sitting there? In the dark? Watching us sleep? What in the actual, creepy, stalker-ish fuck?

"Willow? Are you okay?" he asks, his voice a low,

soothing murmur that is in direct contrast to the violent, disgusting noises currently erupting from my body.

"Oscar?" I croak, my voice a raw, shredded whisper between heaves. "What… what the hell are you doing here? Were you watching us sleep? That is so much creepier than your new GPS-tracking ability, and that's saying something."

"Shit, I'm sorry, Willow," he says, his face flushing with a guilt that is almost comical. "I didn't mean to startle you. Or be creepy. I just… after you and I bonded, you got so sick. I came in after… after you and Theo fell asleep. I disinfected the chair, of course. And I just wanted to be here. In case it happened again. In case you needed help."

Oh, my heart, that stupid, traitorous organ, does a little flip-flop in my chest. He's not a creepy stalker. He's a sweet, thoughtful, OCD-riddled vampire with a heart of gold. And he was worried about me. "Th-thanks," I manage to choke out, my throat burning, my eyes watering. "That's… really sweet of you, Oscar."

"Anything for you, Willow," he says, his voice so full of sincerity it makes my chest ache. He's by my side in an instant, a cool, damp cloth in his hand. He gently wipes my face. His touch so soft, so careful, it's like I'm made of glass. He holds my hair back as another wave of nausea hits, his presence a steady, calming anchor in the storm of my misery.

"Fuck," I murmur, my head resting against the cool, smooth porcelain of the toilet. "I really hope this doesn't last as long as last time. Once was more than enough. I'm not built for this supernatural morning sickness bullshit."

"I hope so too, sweetheart," he says, his voice a low,

gentle rumble. He kneels beside me, his hand rubbing slow, soothing circles on my back. It's a simple, comforting gesture, but it means the world to me.

"Willow? What's going on?" Theo's voice, thick with sleep and rough with concern, calls out from the doorway. He's standing there, a glorious, naked vision of sleepy, tousled sex-god, covered in tattoos, his eyes wide with a confusion that quickly turns to alarm. He takes in the scene —me, a pathetic, puking mess on the floor; Oscar, the ever-vigilant nursemaid, kneeling beside me—and his brow furrows.

"Theo," I groan, my voice muffled by the toilet bowl. "I think… I think I'm sick again. From the bond."

"Does that mean…?" he starts, his eyes widening with a dawning realization, a flicker of something that looks suspiciously like excitement in their dark, stormy depths.

"Yep," I say, spitting into the toilet with as much dignity as I can muster. "Congratulations, big boy. You're about to get your party favor. Isn't that just fucking fantastic for you?"

Theo looks at Oscar, a silent, questioning look passing between them, and then he looks back at me, a slow, wicked grin spreading across his face. "Hey, at least we can suffer through this together, right?" he says, his voice a low, teasing drawl. "I can hold your hair back while you puke, and you can… well, you can just keep being beautiful and miserable. It's a good look for you."

"Ha, yeah," I reply, my voice dripping with sarcasm. "Misery loves company. And I'm sure my company is just delightful right now. I'm a real catch. I puke, I have abandonment issues, and I come with two extra boyfriends. What a prize!"

"You are a prize, little one," he says, his voice a low, intense murmur that sends a shiver down my spine despite the nausea. He walks into the bathroom, his nakedness a casual, unapologetic statement, and crouches down beside me, his hand warm and heavy on my shoulder. "And you're our prize."

"Guys," I whisper, my vision blurring, the room starting to spin again. "I don't know how much more of this I can take."

"Willow, we're here for you," Oscar says, his voice a steady, reassuring presence in the chaos. "Do you want me to call the doctor? He can check you over, make sure you're okay. Especially after the blood you lost yesterday."

"No," I groan, shaking my head. "No doctors. I just… I just want to go back to bed and wait for the sweet, sweet release of death. Or, you know, for this to be over. Whichever comes first."

"Want me to lie next to you and suffer in silence?" Theo quips, his voice a low, rumbling chuckle. "We can be miserable together. It'll be romantic."

I can't help it. A weak, watery chuckle escapes my lips. "Yes," I concede, my laughter quickly turning into another series of gut-wrenching heaves. "That sounds… just lovely."

"I feel like this is going to be a long day," I say grimly, my head resting against the cool, smooth porcelain of the toilet bowl, my two very handsome, one very naked, one very worried vampire kings flanking me like a pair of ridiculously hot guardian angels.

"Where's Jasper?" I manage to ask, my voice a raw, shredded whisper. "Shouldn't he be here, enjoying the show? He seems to get a kick out of my suffering."

"Jasper went back out," Oscar explains, his voice a low, soothing murmur. "He's trying to catch Caleb's scent, see where he went. He didn't want to be too far away, though. He should be back soon."

"Good," I mutter, a small, irrational surge of relief washing over me. My stomach churns, a violent, lurching rebellion, and I cling to the toilet bowl like it's a life raft in a sea of vomit. "Why does this have to be so goddamn awful?"

"Sorry, Willow," Theo says, his voice a low, rumbling purr that is surprisingly comforting. He's rubbing my back again, his large, warm hand a steady, reassuring presence. "But hey, at least we're all in this together now, right? One big, happy, magically bonded, puke-filled family."

"Great," I snark, my voice dripping with a sarcasm that is only slightly undermined by the fact that I'm currently hugging a toilet naked. "Just what I always wanted. A nauseating bonding experience with two of my mates, while the third one is out playing vampire-CSI. This is the fairytale I always dreamed of."

"Hey, it could be worse," Oscar chimes in, his voice cheerful. "At least you're not alone in your misery. We're sitting in here with you while you hug Mr. Porcelain. That's true love, right there."

"True," I agree, a weak, watery smile touching my lips. "Misery loves company. And you two are… well, you're definitely company."

"Thanks, guys," I whisper, my voice barely audible

over the sound of my own retching. "I don't know what I'd do without you."

"Probably puke your guts out in peace," Theo jokes, his voice a low, rumbling chuckle. Despite myself, I laugh, a weak, watery sound that quickly turns into another round of heaving. This is my life now. Puking, snarking, and falling in love with three ridiculously hot, emotionally complicated, and surprisingly sweet vampire kings.

CHAPTER 32

JASPER

The castle is quiet. Too quiet. The kind of quiet that follows a storm, or in this case, a night of earth-shattering, bed-breaking, probably structurally damaging sex. I can still feel the echo of it in the air, a low, thrumming energy that is one hundred percent Theodore and Willow. I slip out a side door, the cool morning air a welcome shock to my system. I should be happy for him. For them. And I am, mostly. But there's a bitter, ugly little knot of envy twisting in my gut, a feeling so foreign and unwelcome that it makes me want to punch something. Preferably Caleb.

Focus, Jasper. I take a deep breath, the scents of the forest flooding my senses—damp earth, decaying leaves, the distant, salty tang of the sea. I close my eyes, pushing aside the image of Willow in my brother's arms, the memory of her laughter in the library, the ghost of her breath on my lips before I got to kiss her. I push it all down and focus on one thing, and one thing only. The hunt.

I let my senses expand, reaching out, sifting through

the daily smells. And then, I find it. A faint, acrid note in the harmony. The scent of stale blood, old leather, and a particular brand of self-important dickhead. Caleb. It's weak, but it's there. "Gotcha, you son of a bitch," I whisper, a slow, predatory grin spreading across my face. The chase is on.

I follow the scent, my body moving with a silent, fluid grace that is pure instinct. The trail leads me down the hiking path — the same path where he attacked Oscar, where Willow saved him. The thought of it — of her courage, her fire — it sends a fresh wave of adoration through me, so strong it almost knocks me off my feet. She's not just beautiful. She's a fucking force of nature. And she's ours.

The scent grows stronger, and I can feel the thrill of the hunt, that exhilarating rush, coursing through my veins. He was careless. Arrogant. He didn't think we'd track him. He underestimated us. He underestimated her. And that is going to be his downfall.

The trail ends abruptly in a small, muddy clearing. The scent of Caleb is thick here, overwhelming, but it's mixed with something else. The acrid smell of gasoline and hot rubber. Tire tracks. Deep, angry gashes in the soft earth. He had a car waiting. The fucker drove away. The frustration is strong, a bitter, metallic taste in my mouth. I lost him.

"Alright, Caleb," I say, my voice a low, angry growl that is lost in the vast, silent forest. "You can run. You can hide. But we will find you. And when we do, I'm going to tear you apart with my bare hands." I stand there for a long moment, my fists clenched, my body thrumming with a useless, impotent rage. And then, I turn and head back to the castle. The hunt isn't over. It's just gone digital.

I slip back into the castle, my movements silent, my mind racing. I need to see it. I need to know what happened. I head straight for Oscar's office, the nerve center of our little kingdom. The room is dark, the only light the soft, blue glow of the monitors. I slide into his ridiculously ergonomic chair, the scent of him, of his obsessive cleanliness, a strange, comforting familiarity. "Come on, Oscar," I whisper, my fingers flying across the keyboard. "Show me what you've got."

I pull up the security footage from the hidden cameras on the trail. I fast-forward through hours of nothing, my heart pounding a frantic, impatient rhythm against my ribs. And then, I find it. The moment Caleb appears. He's a dark, menacing shadow in the moonlight, his arrogance a palpable, suffocating presence even on the screen. I watch as Oscar confronts him, as Willow teleports in, a beautiful, terrifying avenging angel. I watch as Caleb shoots him, again and again, and the rage, the fury, it comes roaring back, so hot, so violent, that I have to grip the edge of the desk to keep from smashing the screen.

I watch as he grabs her, as he drags her away, and I feel a helplessness so profound it's like drowning. And then, I see it. The moment she gets free. The moment she turns and swings. My breath catches in my throat. I rewind the footage, slowing it down, frame by painful, glorious frame. I watch as her small, perfect fist connects with his stupid, arrogant face. The crunch of his nose breaking. She hit him, her face a mask of pure, righteous fury. And I am completely, utterly, and irrevocably in love.

"Holy shit," I breathe, a wide, incredulous grin spreading across my face. "That's my girl." I watch the rest of it, my heart in my throat. Her teleporting back to Oscar. Her forcing her blood on him. His desperate bite. And then, his pursuit of Caleb, a blur of righteous fury, disappearing into the darkness. I save the footage, a small, triumphant smile on my face. This is better than any book, any movie, any story I have ever known.

A few hours later, the door to the office creaks open, and Oscar shuffles in, looking like a man who has been through a war and then been forced to disinfect the battle-field. He's wearing a pair of soft, grey sweatpants and nothing else, the tattoos on his body are vivid, something he rarely displays, his hair a mess, his eyes heavy with a weariness that has nothing to do with being shot and everything to do with being in love.

"Find anything?" he asks, his voice a low, tired rasp. He should be sleeping after being shot.

"Oh, I found something," I say, a wicked grin spreading across my face. I rewind the footage, cueing it up to my favorite part. "Prepare to be amazed." I hit play, and we watch in silence as Willow delivers her two-piece combo to Caleb's face. Oscar lets out a short, sharp bark of laughter, a sound of pride. "Ha! That's my girl!" he says, clapping me on the shoulder, his eyes sparkling with a mischief that mirrors my own.

"She's a fucking rockstar," I say, my voice filled with a reverence that is only half-joking. "I've never been more turned on in my life."

"Me too," he agrees, a wide, happy smile on his face.

"Now, let's use this to our advantage. I can run facial recognition, see if we can get a lead."

"Agreed," I say, my determination renewed. We are going to find him. And we are going to end him. For her.

"Jas," Oscar says, his voice suddenly serious, his smile fading. He leans against the edge of the desk, his arms crossed over his chest. "I was just with Willow. She's… she's not feeling well. Again."

My heart plummets, the triumphant elation of a moment ago replaced by a cold, sharp dread. "What do you mean, again? Is it the bond? Did Theo…?"

He nods, his expression grim. "They bonded. She's sick. Just like with me. Puking her guts out."

"Fuck," I breathe, the word a raw, helpless whisper. I run a hand through my hair, the knot of envy in my gut replaced by a new, even uglier emotion. Fear. A deep, soul-crushing fear for her. "Is she… is she going to be okay?"

"She's strong," he says, his voice a low, reassuring murmur. "But… it's hard on her. This whole thing." He looks at me, his eyes soft with a sympathy that I don't want, that I don't deserve. "She's been through a lot, Jas."

"I know," I say, my voice a low, choked whisper. I stare at the screen, at her beautiful, furious face, and a question, a fear, a desperate, pathetic plea — it claws its way up my throat. "Do you think… now that she's bonded with you, with Theo… do you think she'll want to bond with me?"

Oscar is silent for a long moment, his eyes searching mine. "That's up to her, Jas," he says, his voice gentle, but firm. "This isn't a checklist. It's not a race. It's… it's her heart. And you can't rush that."

"I know," I say, the words a hollow echo in the quiet room. "I just… I don't want to be the odd man out. The third wheel. The comic relief."

"You're not," he says, his voice a low, fierce growl. "You're her mate. You're our brother. And you're the one who makes her laugh. Don't ever forget that. That's just important."

I let out a short, sharp bark of laughter, the sound a little watery, a little broken. "Thanks, man."

"Just be patient," he says, clapping me on the shoulder again. "Let her come to you. She will. I know she will."

I nod, a small, grateful smile on my face. He's right. I need to be patient. No matter how badly I want to sink into that tight, wet pussy of hers. I have to be patient.

CHAPTER 33

WILLOW

I wake up to the smell of chicken soup and… expensive cologne? It's a weirdly comforting combination, a signature scent I'm coming to associate with the Kings: one part domestic god, one part walking, talking sex ad. My eyes flutter open, and the world is blessedly, beautifully still. The tiny, angry construction crew that was using a jackhammer on my skull has apparently gone on their lunch break, leaving behind only a dull, manageable throb. The violent, churning rebellion in my stomach has subsided into a low, grumbling protest, like a union threatening to strike but not quite having the numbers. I survived. Well, I think it's over? I should get a T-shirt made. 'I survived the vampire bond-over, and all I got was this lousy headache.' And maybe a robe. Because I'm still naked. Very, very naked.

I push myself up on my elbows; the move send a new wave of aches and groans through my body. It's a deep, pleasant soreness, the kind you get after a really intense workout. Or, you know, after being thoroughly, comprehensively, and enthusiastically ravaged by a vampire king who apparently has the stamina of a freight train and the flexibility of a Cirque du Soleil performer. A faint blush warms my cheeks at the memory, a full-body heat that has nothing to do with the fever I'm pretty sure I was running. Theo. The bond. The… everything. It was a lot. And apparently, it was enough to knock me out for… I have no idea how long. I could have been asleep for five minutes or five days. Time has become a very fluid concept in this castle.

"Hey, sleepyhead."

The voice, a low, rumbling purr from the doorway, makes me jump so hard I think I pull a muscle in my back. I whip my head around, clutching the silk sheet to my chest like a flimsy shield.

"Holy hell in a handbasket!" I yelp, my heart doing a frantic tap dance against my ribs. Theo is leaning against the doorframe, laptop in hand, a vision of casual, infuriating hotness. He's wearing a pair of low-slung grey sweatpants that leave very little to the imagination, and a smug, self-satisfied smirk that says he knows exactly what he did to me. And that he's very, very proud of himself.

He lets out a low chuckle; the sound vibrating through the room. "Handbasket? That's a new one. I'm impressed. You're expanding your folksy Midwestern curse repertoire."

I glare at him, which is less effective when I'm naked, disheveled, and pretty sure I have drool on my cheek. "Warn a woman before you scare her, Theo! I could have had a heart attack! And then you'd have a dead, naked human in your bed, and that's a whole other kind of paper-work, I assume."

He just grins, pushing off the doorframe and starting to walk toward me, his movements slow, deliberate, preda-tory. "Oh, I think I could find a way to bring you back," he says, his voice a low, husky promise that makes my toes curl.

And then, with a soft pop like a champagne cork being opened, and a startled yelp that is definitely mine, Oscar is standing by the bed, a steaming bowl of broth in his hands, his eyes wide with a mixture of shock and triumph.

My brain short-circuits. One second, there was an empty space next to the bed; the next, there is a six-foot-four, ridiculously handsome, fully clothed vampire holding a bowl of soup. I stare at him, my mouth hanging open, my heart now attempting to exit my body via my throat.

"Holy shit!" I yelp, my voice a high-pitched squeak. "What the hell was that? Did you just… poof into exis-tence? Are you a genie now? Do I get three wishes? Because I wish for pants. And maybe a sandwich."

"I did it!" he exclaims, his voice filled with a wild, incredulous joy. He looks down at the bowl in his hands as if to confirm it's real, then back at me, his eyes sparkling with a childlike wonder that is completely at odds with his centuries-old, stoic demeanor. "I actually did it! I was just in the kitchen, thinking about how you needed this broth, and then… whoosh! I was here!"

"Whoosh?" I repeat, a slow, amused smile spreading across my face as my brain starts to reboot. I look from Oscar's beaming face to Theo's stunned, slightly annoyed expression. "That's the technical term for it, is it? The 'whoosh'? Is that what they teach you in Vampire Teleportation 101?"

"I don't know how I did it," he says, shaking his head in a daze of disbelief. He looks like a kid who just accidentally discovered he can fly by jumping off the garage roof. "It just… happened."

"Well, try to un-happen it next time," I say, my voice dripping with a sarcasm that is only slightly undermined by the fact that I'm grinning like an idiot. I yank the sheet up to my chin, a flimsy barrier against two sets of very intense, very male eyes. "A girl needs some warning before a handsome man materializes in her bedroom. It's common courtesy. What if I was naked?"

"You are naked," Theo points out from his position, still lounging against the doorframe like he owns the place. Which I guess he does. His voice is a low, hopeful purr, and his eyes darken with a familiar, hungry look that makes my stomach do a little flip-flop. Oscar, bless his sweet, innocent heart, actually blushes.

"Fuck," I say, rolling my eyes so hard I'm surprised they don't get stuck in the back of my head. I pull the blanket up a little higher, as if that's going to stop a centuries-old vampire from seeing whatever he wants to see. "You know what I mean. Now, are you two going to stand there looking all smug and self-satisfied, or is one of you going to give me that soup before I die of starvation? And maybe that T-shirt there so I don't flash my tits while I eat? I have some dignity left. A very small, very tattered amount, but it's there." I point a shaky finger at a black t-shirt lying in a heap on the floor. It's probably Theo's. It probably smells like him. My traitorous body gives a little shiver of anticipation.

Theo chuckles, the sound a low, warm rumble that vibrates through my chest. He gracefully pushes off the doorframe and retrieves the shirt, his movements fluid and predatory. He holds it out to me, and then, instead of just handing it over, he helps me into it, his fingers brushing against my bare skin, sending little zaps of electricity everywhere they touch. The fabric is soft, worn, and smells intoxicatingly of him—a clean, masculine scent of soap and night air and something that is just purely, deliciously Theo. He pulls the shirt down over my head, his hands lingering on my shoulders for a fraction of a second too long. "For the record," he says softly, his voice a low, intimate murmur meant only for me, "you can sit there topless all day long, and there will never be a word of complaint from me."

I gulp. A loud, embarrassing, fucking gulp. My pussy gives a distinct, traitorous throb at his words, a silent, enthusiastic 'yes, please!' that I pointedly ignore. My eyes track his every movement as he leans back, a satisfied smirk on his face, and Oscar leans in with my soup, his own expression a mixture of concern and… is that heat? What the fuck. He hands me the bowl, his fingers brushing against mine, making electricity shoot up my arm. Jesus Christ. These vampires know how to turn on the charm. They make me want to forget I was a virgin only a few days ago and climb them both like a goddamn tree.

The broth is divine, though. Rich, savory, and filled with tiny, perfect pieces of chicken and vegetables that have been diced with a precision that speaks to Oscar's particular brand of beautiful, obsessive madness. It's a hug in a bowl, a warm, comforting balm to my battered, bruised body. I slurp it down, my moans of appreciation a little less than dignified, but I don't even care. It's the best thing I have ever tasted.

"You're a miracle worker, Oscar," I say, my voice thick with genuine appreciation as I hand him the empty bowl. "A culinary god. I would build a temple in your honor, but I'm a little busy being a vampire's plaything right now."

"I'm glad you liked it," he says, and his eyes are definitely sparkling with heat now. There's no mistaking it. He takes the bowl, his gaze lingering on me, a slow, lazy heat that makes my skin tingle and my nipples pebble against the soft cotton of Theo's shirt. "I like you in our clothes," he says, his voice a low, husky murmur that sends a fresh wave of shivers down my spine.

I blush, a full-body, five-alarm-fire blush, because this vampire can make me feel like I'm wearing a goddamn ball gown when it's just an oversized men's T-shirt that probably has a hole in the armpit. "Well," I say, my voice a little breathless, "I wouldn't mind some of my own clothes to… you know. Wear. Occasionally."

Theo smirks at me, a slow, wicked, Theo-worthy smirk that looks devastatingly out of place and yet perfectly at home on his handsome face. "Well, honestly, I like you like this," he says, his eyes raking over me in a way that makes me feel both naked and worshipped. "But I have this…" He places the sleek, silver laptop on my lap. "I thought you might like this. You can buy whatever you want. Clothes, books, a lifetime supply of chocolate… whatever your heart desires."

I stare at the laptop, my eyes wide with a disbelief that has nothing to do with teleportation or magic broth. It's a simple, ordinary object. A tool. A window. And it's the most beautiful, most precious thing I have ever seen. "Really?" I whisper, my voice thick with an emotion I can't even begin to name. It feels like hope. It feels like freedom. "I… I haven't used a computer in years. Caleb… he never allowed it."

Oscar's expression hardens. The gentle, smiling man gone, replaced by the cold, hard mask of the king. "That's going to change now, Willow," he says, his voice a low, firm command that brooks no argument. "You are free. And you will have access to everything the world has to offer."

His words, his intensity, the fierce, protective fire in his eyes… it's too much. But it's Theo who is holding the laptop, who is offering me this impossible, beautiful gift. He's the one standing there with that infuriatingly hand-some, smug look on his face, as if to say, 'Of course I'm giving you the world. I own it.' The combination of Oscar's fierce declaration and Theo's casual, arrogant generosity, it's a one-two punch straight to my already battered and bruised heart. I'm overwhelmed. By their kindness. By the simple, profound, terrifying gift of free-dom. Tears prick at the corners of my eyes, hot and sharp and embarrassing. And before I can stop myself, before I can make a snarky comment or roll my eyes or do any of the things I usually do to protect myself, I'm launching myself off the bed.

I don't aim for Oscar, the sweet, gentle soul who just fed me soup. I aim for the bastard. The arrogant, bossy, infuriating king who looks at me like he wants to both break me and worship me. I launch myself at Theo, my arms wrapping around his neck, my body colliding with his with a force that should send us both tumbling. But he's a vampire. He doesn't even budge. He just catches me, his arms wrapping around my waist, lifting me effortlessly as my legs instinctively wrap around his hips. My lips crash against his in a desperate, grateful, hungry kiss.

From somewhere behind us, I hear a low, guttural growl. It's a sound of pure, undiluted possession, an animalistic warning. Oscar. My pussy gives a distinct, traitorous throb at the sound, but I'm too far gone to care. Theo groans into my mouth, his hands finding my ass, his fingers digging into my soft flesh, pulling me tight against the hard ridge of his cock. The kiss is a storm, a whirlwind of pent-up emotion and a desire that has been simmering just beneath the surface for days. It's not gentle. It's not sweet. It's a raw, desperate claiming. It's a battle for dominance that I have no intention of winning.

"Willow," he murmurs against my lips, his voice a raw, ragged whisper that sounds like a prayer and a curse all at once.

"Theo," I breathe, my hands tangling in his thick, dark hair, pulling him closer, my body arching against his.

With a speed that steals the breath from my lungs, he pushes me back onto the bed, his body a warm, heavy weight on top of mine. He pins my hands above my head, his eyes dark and stormy with a desire that mirrors my own. "Such a needy little mouse," he teases, his breath hot against my ear, his voice a low, wicked purr that makes my entire body tremble. "But don't worry. I'll take very good care of you."

He rips the t-shirt off me with an efficiency that is both thrilling and terrifying. One second, I'm wearing his scent, the next, I'm completely exposed, my skin tingling in the cool air of the room. And then, he's on me, his mouth a hot, wet brand on my skin. He flips me over with casual, almost careless strength, my body trembling with a mixture of anticipation and a fear that is so intertwined with desire that I can't tell them apart. I'm on all fours, my head buried in the pillows, my ass in the air, a willing, eager, and frankly, shameless offering.

"Spread your legs for me," he commands, his voice a low, guttural growl that makes my pussy clench. I obey without hesitation. I'm a shameless, wanton mess, and I don't give a single solitary fuck. I want this. I want him. I want them.

From the corner of my eye, I see Oscar move. He's been standing there, a silent, watchful predator, his eyes dark and hungry, his body thrumming with a tension that mirrors my own. He moves with a slow, deliberate grace, his gaze locked on me, on the scene unfolding on the bed. Theo doesn't stop him. He doesn't even look at him. It's as if they have a silent, telepathic understanding, a shared language of lust and possession that I am only just beginning to understand.

"Take off your clothes," Theo says, his voice a low, rough command that is directed at his brother, but his eyes never leave my ass.

My breath catches in my throat. Oh, my God. Is this really happening? Am I about to be the filling in a vampire king sandwich? My pussy gives a violent, enthusiastic clench at the thought. Yes, please.

Theo straightens up, his hands going to the waistband of his pants. He shucks them off with a casual, almost careless grace, his thick, monstrously long cock springing free, already hard and heavy and pointing right at me. It's a beautiful, terrifying weapon, and I want it inside me. Now. Oscar is more deliberate. He unbuttons his shirt, his movements precise, economical. He shrugs it off, revealing a chest that is a work of art, a masterpiece of sculpted muscle and tattooed, perfect skin. He unbuckles his belt, the sound a loud, sharp click in the quiet room. He slides his pants down his long, powerful legs, and then he, too, is naked. And he is just as magnificent, just as terrifying, just as beautiful as his brother. Two kings. Two predators. And I am their prey.

Theo's hand comes down on my ass, a sharp, stinging slap that makes me yelp, a sound that is half pain, half pleasure. "Oh, Theo," I gasp, my voice a raw, breathless plea. "More. Please."

He obliges. He spanks me again and again, the rhythm a steady, hypnotic beat against my skin. I'm a mess of moans and whimpers, my body a trembling, quivering mess of need. I can hear Oscar's breath hitch, a low, guttural sound of approval from the side of the bed. They're both watching me. They're both getting off on this. And that, that thought, it's the most exquisite, most decadent, most delicious thing I have ever known.

"You're so wet for us, Willow," Theo growls, his fingers slick with my arousal. "Dripping for us."

"Only for you," I moan, my voice a raw, desperate cry. "Please… fuck me. Both of you. Now."

"Your wish is our command," Oscar whispers, his voice a low, velvety purr from beside my head. He kneels on the bed in front of me, his eyes dark and stormy with a desire that mirrors my own. He gently takes my chin in his hand, his touch surprisingly soft, and guides my mouth to his cock. It's a beautiful, perfect thing, thick and hard and impossibly long. I take him into my mouth without hesitation, my lips closing around him, my tongue tracing the thick, prominent veins. He groans, a low, rumbling sound, his hand tangling in my hair.

And then, from behind me, I feel Theo. His cock, hot and hard and slick with my own wetness, presses against my entrance. He teases me, nudging, circling, driving me absolutely insane with a need so profound, so all-consuming, that I think I might die from it. And then, he pushes in. Slowly. Deliberately. Filling me inch by glorious, agonizing inch. I cry out, my voice a muffled scream against Oscar's cock.

I am filled. Completely. Utterly. From both ends. Oscar in my mouth, his cock a hot, hard brand against my tongue. Theo is inside me, his cock a thick, powerful presence that stretches me, fills me, claims me. It's too much. It's not enough. It's everything.

Theo starts to move, a slow, steady rhythm that is pure, exquisite torture. Oscar mirrors his rhythm, his hips moving in time with his brother's, his cock sliding in and out of my mouth, my head moving with him, my body a willing, eager instrument in their orchestra of sin. I'm drowning in them. In the scent of them, the taste of them, the feel of them. I'm lost.

"Look at her, Oscar," Theo growls, his voice a low, vicious purr. "So beautiful. so tight. Taking us both like she was made for it."

"She was made for us," Oscar says, his voice a low, reverent whisper. He pulls out of my mouth, his cock slick and glistening. He looks at me, his eyes dark and filled with a love so profound, so overwhelming, that it takes my breath away. "My beautiful, beautiful queen."

And then, he's back in my mouth, his rhythm more urgent now, more demanding. Theo's pace quickens, his thrusts harder, deeper, faster. He's a relentless, merciless assault on my senses, his hands on my hips, his mouth on my back, his cock a battering ram against my cervix. I'm being fucked and worshipped and broken and remade all at once. I'm coming apart at the seams, my body a raging inferno of need.

"Bite me!" I scream, muffled around Oscar's cock. Theo doesn't hesitate. His fangs sink into my neck, a sharp, exquisite pain that is followed by bliss. The world shatters. My body convulses, my orgasm a tidal wave that rocks the very foundations of the castle. I come on Theo's cock, my throat contracting around Oscar as I scream, my body milking him, my mind a blank, white-hot explosion.

"Fuck, Willow!" Theo growls, his own release a hot, violent flood inside me. Oscar groans, his release a hot, sweet rush in my mouth. We collapse onto the bed, a tangled, sweaty, sated mess of limbs and lust. Theo pulls me into his arms, my head resting on his chest, his heartbeat a steady, reassuring drumbeat against my ear. Oscar wraps his arms around both of us, his body a warm, solid wall against my back. I am surrounded by them. I'm drifting in a sea of contentment, my body humming with aftershocks so profound it has rewritten my DNA. I feel safe. I feel… whole.

Theo's hand strokes my hair, his touch surprisingly gentle for a man who was just using it to pull my hair with a force that should have ripped it out. I can feel the low, rumbling purr of his contentment vibrating through his chest, a sound that is more soothing than any lullaby. I'm so blissed out, so boneless and relaxed, that I almost miss it. A voice. A thought. It's deep and familiar and sounds exactly like Theo, but it's not coming from his mouth. It's just… there. In my head.

I don't even care if I get a power from this. I don't need one. After two hundred years of being empty, she's made me whole. Just having her is enough.

"That's so sweet, Theo," I murmur, my voice thick with sleep and satisfaction. I tilt my head back to look up at him, a small, sleepy smile on my face. His hand is still stroking my hair, his expression one of pure, unguarded contentment. "But I'm still wondering what power you'll get, too. It would be kind of lame if you were the only one left out. The powerless, grumpy king."

Theo freezes. His hand stills in my hair, his entire body going rigid beneath me. He stares down at me, his dark eyes wide with a confusion so profound it's almost comical. "What?" he asks, his voice a low, rough whisper that cracks on the single word.

I giggle, snuggling closer into his chest, completely

oblivious. "I said, I'm wondering what power you'll get. Keep up, sleepyhead. Don't tell me I broke your brain."

"But… I didn't say that out loud," he says, his voice barely a breath. He looks over my head at Oscar, his expression a wild, chaotic mixture of shock, disbelief, and dawning wonder. "I thought that. In my head."

I push myself up, my heart starting to do that frantic tap dance against my ribs again. The sleepy post-coital haze evaporates in an instant. I look from Theo's stunned face to Oscar's, who is now grinning from ear to ear.

"Wait," I say, my voice a high-pitched squeak. I point a shaky finger at Theo. "You mean… I heard your thoughts? Like, you were thinking about how you don't care about powers because I make you feel whole, and I heard it? In my brain?"

Theo just stares at me, his mouth opening and closing like a fish. He's speechless. For the first time since I've met him, Theodore Michaels has absolutely nothing to say.

"It would appear so, little mouse," Oscar says, his voice filled with a delighted amusement. He leans over and kisses my forehead, his lips warm and soft against my skin. "Congratulations, brother. It seems your party favor has arrived."

Theo continues to stare at me, his mind obviously racing, the gears turning at a million miles an hour. And then, a slow, wicked, predatory grin spreads across his face. It's a grin that says he has just been handed the most dangerous, most delicious new toy in the world. A toy that he can't wait to play with.

"Oh, this," he says, his voice a low, dangerous purr that

sends a fresh wave of shivers down my spine. "This is going to be fun."

CHAPTER 34

JASPER

It's been four days. Ninety-six hours. Five thousand, seven hundred and sixty minutes. Not that I'm counting. It's been four days since the world shifted on its axis, since my brothers, my stoic, controlled, emotionally constipated brothers, fell headfirst into a pit of domestic bliss so deep I'm surprised they can still see the sun. Four days of watching them orbit Willow like she's the goddamn sun, a radiant, brilliant star, and I'm just a lonely, forgotten planet out in the Kuiper belt. A cold, distant, irrelevant rock. It's pathetic. And the jealousy is a bitter, ugly acid eating away at my insides.

I'm supposed to be working. I'm sitting in Oscar's ridiculously clean, ridiculously organised office—a room so sterile it makes a hospital operating theater look like a frat house after a rager. I'm staring at a bank of monitors that display every conceivable angle of the castle grounds, my eyes burning with a lack of sleep I don't technically need but feel deep in my soul. My mission, should I choose to accept it, is to find any trace of Caleb or Edmund. To be the good soldier. The diligent hunter. The fun one, who is also secretly a badass. But my focus is shot to hell. Every time I see a flicker of movement on the screen, a deer darting between the trees, my heart leaps into my throat, thinking it's her. Every rustle of leaves outside the window sounds like her laughter, a sound that is both my favorite music and a knife to the gut. She's a virus in my system, a fever in my blood, and I can't fucking shake her.

I see her every day. That's the real torture. It's not like she's avoiding me. Yesterday, we spent three hours in the library. She was curled up on the plush sofa, her feet tucked under her, a small, secret smile on her face as she devoured another one of the smutty books I bought her. I was sitting across from her, pretending to read some ancient, dusty tome, but really, I was just watching her.

Watching the way her eyes lit up, the way she bit her lip when things got good. I made a stupid joke about a dragon shifter's 'hoard,' and she laughed, a bright, beautiful sound that was the only thing that made this whole situation bearable. But then, the laughter died, and she looked up, her eyes meeting Oscar's as he entered the room. And the air changed. A silent, secret conversation passed between them, a whole novel's worth of emotion and understanding conveyed in a single, shared glance.

And just like that, a wall went up. A shimmering, invisible barrier made of shared thoughts and synced heartbeats and a level of intimacy I can only dream of. Oscar can feel her every emotion, a constant, thrumming presence in his mind. And Theo… Theo can hear her thoughts. The bastard can literally read her mind. And me? I get to watch from the sidelines. The court jester. The comic relief. The one who isn't bonded.

The thought is a bitter, ugly pill that I can't seem to swallow. It's not just that I want her. I do. I want her so badly, a constant, low-grade thrum of need in my groin. I want to be the one she comes to when she's sad. I want to be the one who makes her scream in ecstasy. I want to be the one who gets to feel that final, soul-shattering click of the bond falling into place. But it's more than that. It's fear. A cold, terrifying fear that I'm being left behind. That they've found their missing piece, and it's her, and I'm just… extra. The spare part. The one they don't really need. And I don't know if I'll ever be anything more.

"Anything?"

Theo's voice, a low, rumbling command from the doorway, shatters my pity party. He strides into the room, all arrogant, kingly grace, a mug of something that is definitely not coffee in his hand. He looks… happy. Content. He's got this infuriating glow about him, like a man who has just discovered the meaning of life and found out it's really, really good sex. It's disgusting.

"Just the usual," I say, my voice flat and tired. I gesture vaguely at the screens. "A whole lot of nothing. It's like they vanished off the face of the earth. No credit card pings, no cell phone signals, no sightings. They're ghosts."

"They'll slip up," he says, his voice a low, cold promise of violence. He comes to stand behind me, his presence a heavy, oppressive weight. "Amateurs always do." He takes a sip from his mug, his eyes dark and unreadable as they scan the monitors. "I've contacted the other four. The meeting is tomorrow night. Here."

"Good," I say, the word a hollow echo in the quiet room. We need to deal with Edmund. We need to end this. For her. But the thought of a formal meeting, of all the political bullshit and posturing that comes with it, it just makes me tired. I want to hit something. I want to break something. I want to feel something other than this gnawing, empty ache.

"You should get some rest," he says, and his voice is surprisingly gentle, a soft, concerned note that is so unlike him it's almost jarring. He places a hand on my shoulder, a brief, brotherly squeeze. "You look like shit."

I flinch away from his touch, a surge of irrational anger flashing through me. "Thanks, Mom," I snap, my voice dripping with a sarcasm I don't feel. "I'll be sure to get my beauty sleep right after I finish saving the world."

He doesn't rise to the bait. He just sighs, a long, weary sound. "Jasper…" he starts, but he doesn't finish. What is there to say? 'Sorry your life sucks right now'? 'Sorry, we're deliriously happy and you're miserable'? He just gives my shoulder another squeeze, a little harder this time, and then he's gone, leaving me alone with my thoughts, my jealousy, and the crushing, humiliating truth that he's right. I do look like shit. And I feel even worse.

"Fuck off," I say, my voice dripping with sarcasm I don't feel. He just grins, a slow, wicked, infuriatingly handsome grin, and then he's gone, leaving me alone with my thoughts, my jealousy, and my raging, useless hard-on. The silence in the room is deafening, broken only by the low hum of the computer and the frantic, pathetic thumping of my own heart.

I stare at the screens, at the endless, unchanging footage of the castle grounds, and I feel a wave of something so close to despair it steals the breath from my lungs. I'm useless. I'm a joke. The fun one. The one who makes everyone laugh. But who's there for me when I'm the one who needs to laugh? Who's there for me when the silence gets too loud?

"Fuck it," I mutter, the words a raw, angry growl in the quiet room. My frustration reaches a boiling point, a white-hot rage that has nowhere to go. I can't focus. I can't work. I can't do anything but think about her. About them. About everything I don't have. About the way she looks at them, the way she smiles at them, the way she melts into them. I open a new tab on the browser, my fingers moving with a practiced, shameful speed that makes me hate myself just a little bit more. If I can't have the real thing, if I can't have her, then I'll settle for a cheap, pixelated imitation. A hollow, empty, meaningless release that will only make me feel worse in the end. But right now, I don't care. I just need to feel something. Anything other than this gnawing, empty ache.

I find a video — something mindless and degrading, something that requires no thought, no emotion. I lean back in Oscar's ridiculously ergonomic chair, and I pull my throbbing, aching cock from the confines of my jeans. It's a sad, pathetic sight, proof to my loneliness, my desperation. I close my eyes, the fake, tinny moans from the speakers a poor, pathetic substitute for the real thing, and I picture her. Her mouth, her hands, her perfect, beautiful, magnificent body. I picture her laughing, her eyes sparkling with a mischief that is all her own. I picture her looking at me, just at me, with that same, all-consuming love I see her give my brothers. And I stroke, my movements rough, desperate, a pathetic, shameful attempt to find some kind of release from the tension that is coiling in my gut like a venomous snake.

"Jasper?"

The voice — her voice, a soft, curious melody from the doorway — shatters the fantasy. It's so unexpected, so out of place in my sad, lonely little world, that for a second, I think I've imagined it. A new, particularly cruel trick of my sex-addled, sleep-deprived brain. But then I hear it again. "Jasper? Are you in here?"

My eyes fly open. And there she is. Standing in the doorway, holding the set of keys Oscar gave her, her head tilted to the side, a small, confused frown on her face. She's wearing one of my t-shirts, a faded, worn band shirt that is way too big for her, and a pair of soft, fuzzy pajama pants. She looks soft and warm and so, so beautiful it makes my heart ache. And then, her eyes drop. To my hand. To my cock. To the very obvious, very embarrassing, very hard evidence of what I was just doing.

"Holy shit," I yelp, my voice a high-pitched squeak that is completely at odds with my centuries-old, badass vampire persona. My heart tries to beat its way out of my chest, a frantic, panicked bird trapped in a cage. I fumble with the mouse, my fingers clumsy and useless, trying to close the tab, trying to zip up my pants, trying to do anything to erase the last thirty seconds from existence. But it's too late. She's seen it. She's seen me. And I want to die. I want the floor to open up and swallow me whole. I want to turn into a bat and fly away and never, ever come back.

"Jasper!" she exclaims, and then, she does something I don't expect. Something that completely throws me for a loop. She laughs. A bright, beautiful, musical laugh that echoes in the quiet room. It's not a mean laugh. It's not a mocking laugh. It's a genuine, amused, and dare I say, delighted laugh. "Well," she says, her eyes sparkling with a mischief that is both terrifying and deeply, profoundly arousing, "this is quite an introduction to your office."

"It's not my office," I manage to choke out, my face so hot I'm pretty sure it's about to spontaneously combust. My voice is a strangled, pathetic whisper. "It's Oscar's. Which is somehow even worse. He probably disinfects the air in here. And now I've contaminated it with my… my shame."

"Hey, don't worry about it," she says, a wicked, teasing grin spreading across her face. She steps into the room, closing the door behind her, the soft click a death knell to my dignity. She saunters over to me, her hips swaying in a way that is probably illegal in several states, and leans against the desk, her arms crossed over her chest. "We all have our needs, right? I get it. A guy's gotta do what a guy's gotta do. No judgment here."

"Yeah, but you didn't need to see that," I groan, burying my face in my hands. I can't look at her. I can't face the amusement, the pity, the disgust in her eyes.

"Actually," she says, her voice a low, sultry purr that makes the hair on my arms stand up. I feel her move, and then, her small, warm hands are gently pulling my hands away from my face. I look up, and she's kneeling in front of me, her eyes sparkling with a mischief that is both terrifying and deeply, profoundly arousing. "I think it's kind of hot."

"Really?" I ask, my voice a pathetic, hopeful squeak that makes me want to punch myself in the face. I sound like a goddamn teenager. "You're not just saying that to make me feel less like a complete and utter degenerate?"

"Wouldn't dream of it," she says, her grin widening. She's a siren, a goddess, a beautiful, magnificent creature of chaos, and I am completely, utterly, hopelessly under her spell. "In fact… want some help with that?"

"Help?" I ask, my brain short-circuiting. The words don't compute. The situation doesn't compute. This has to be a dream. A very, very good dream. Or maybe a hallucination brought on by sleep deprivation and an overabundance of self-pity. Either way, I'm not complaining.

"Of course," she says, her voice a low, sultry purr that vibrates through my entire body. Her fingers, which have been resting on my knee, trail up my thigh, a slow, deliberate path of fire that makes my breath catch in my throat. They deftly reach into my pants, her touch surprisingly confident, and free my still-throbbing, still-aching cock. Her touch is electric, lightning that shoots straight to my balls, making them tighten until it's almost painful. "Let me take care of you, Jasper."

"Willow, are you sure?" I ask, my voice a raw, ragged whisper. I have to ask. I have to give her an out. Because as much as I want this, as much as my body is screaming at me to just let it happen, I can't be the guy who takes advantage of her. I can't be the guy who lets her do something she'll regret.

"Absolutely," she murmurs, her eyes dark and serious, all traces of mischief gone, replaced by a raw, honest sincerity that takes my breath away. Her hand wraps around me, a warm, firm, perfect fit. Her thumb strokes the sensitive head, sending a fresh wave of shivers down my spine. She looks down at my cock, her eyes wide with a genuine, unfeigned appreciation that makes my heart ache. "God, you're beautiful," she whispers, the words a soft, reverent prayer. "So beautiful."

"Thank you," I manage to choke out, my voice thick with an emotion I can't even begin to name. It's gratitude. It's relief. It's a love so profound, so overwhelming, that it feels like it's going to tear me apart from the inside out. She leans forward, her lips brushing against the tip of my cock, a soft, wet, open-mouthed kiss that makes me see stars. And then, she takes me into her mouth.

It's heaven. It's torture. It's everything I've ever dreamed of and a million things I never could have imagined. Her mouth is hot and wet and so, so skilled. It's not the frantic, desperate act of a novice. It's the confident, deliberate, masterful work of a prodigy. Her tongue is a work of art, tracing the veins, swirling around the head, driving me absolutely, certifiably insane. I groan, my fingers tangling in her soft, silky hair, my hips bucking, my control slipping, shattering, gone. I'm hers. Completely. Utterly. And I have been from the moment I first laid eyes on her.

"Fuck, Willow," I gasp, my voice a raw, desperate cry. "You're so good at this. Too good. It's not fair."

She just hums, a low, satisfied sound that vibrates through my cock and straight to my soul. She cups my balls, her touch gentle, reverent, her thumb stroking the sensitive skin, and I'm gone. I'm lost. I'm hers. I'm a dead man walking. A happy, happy, dead man.

"Willow, I'm getting close," I warn her, my voice a strangled, pathetic plea. I don't want it to end. I want to live in this moment forever. But my body has other ideas. It's a runaway train, a speeding bullet, a goddamn supernova, and I'm about to go critical.

She just smiles against me, a wicked, secret, all-knowing smile, and her pace quickens, her mouth relentless. She's a storm, a hurricane, a beautiful, magnificent force of nature, and she is going to destroy me. And I am going to thank her for it. And then, I'm coming apart at the seams, my body convulsing. "Shit, Willow!" I cry out, my voice raw. I explode into her mouth, and she holds me firmly, swallowing every single, goddamn drop, her throat working, her eyes never leaving mine.

I collapse back into the chair, my body a boneless, trembling, sated mess. My mind is blank. She looks up at me, her lips slick and swollen, her eyes sparkling with a triumphant, satisfied amusement. She looks like a cat who has just devoured a particularly delicious canary. "Wow," I pant, my voice a raw, ragged whisper. "That was… amazing. You're amazing."

"Anytime," she says, her voice a low, sultry purr that promises a million more moments just like this one. She rises to her feet, her movements fluid and graceful. "Now, I have some exploring to do." She winks, a quick, playful, devastatingly sexy gesture, and then she's gone, the door clicking shut behind her, leaving me alone in the quiet, sterile office, confused. Did that just happen? Or did I just have the most realistic, most satisfying, most soul-destroying wet dream of my entire, centuries-long existence? I look down at my still-tingling, still-damp cock, and I have my answer. It was real. It was all real. And I am so, so fucked.

CHAPTER 35

WILLOW

I'm on a mission. A very important, very serious, very horny mission. The lingering taste of Jasper on my lips is a sweet, decadent memory, a promise of more to come. I lick my lips, a slow, deliberate gesture, and I can still taste him, a faint, salty tang that makes my stomach do a little flip-flop. The thrill of what we just did, of the look on his face, of the way he came apart in my mouth… it's a heady, intoxicating drug, and I am already jonesing for another hit.

I'm a new woman. A sexually liberated, vampire-blowing, castle-exploring badass. I have a keyring that would make a medieval jailer jealous, and I am going to use it. I'm wandering through the castle, a stone labyrinth of endless hallways and forgotten rooms, my thighs rubbing together with a pleasant, friction-induced warmth that has nothing to do with the ambient temperature and everything to do with the fact that I am a walking, talking, HR violation waiting to happen.

I open door after door, my key ring a jangling,

triumphant soundtrack to my adventure. I discover about eighteen bedrooms, their beds still crisply made up, their sheets tucked in with a precision that screams 'Oscar was here.' They look like they're waiting for guests who never arrived. "Such a waste of good bedding," I mutter to myself, a wicked, teasing grin spreading across my face. I can think of at least three very specific, very naked ways to put these beds to better use.

Empty rooms give way to storage rooms filled with boxes, some covered in a thick, velvety layer of dust, others appearing to have been touched more recently. Curiosity, my old, unreliable friend, gets the better of me. I rummage through them, my fingers tracing the outlines of trinkets and oddities from times long past. A delicate porcelain figurine of a woman with a ridiculously small waist. A tarnished silver locket that refuses to open. A collection of what looks like antique medical equipment that is both fascinating and deeply, profoundly disturbing. "This place is like an antique shop's wet dream," I muse, my voice a low, amused murmur in the quiet, dusty air.

"Ah, what do we have here?" I say aloud, my voice echoing in the sudden, damp chill. I've opened yet another door, this one leading down a set of steep, stone stairs into what looks like a cellar. The air is cool and smells of damp earth and old wine. Intrigued, I descend the stairs, my hand trailing along the cold, rough stone wall, the temperature dropping with each step.

"Seriously, though, who needs this many rooms?" I ask myself, my voice a low, breathy whisper. My breath forms small, white clouds in front of me, dissipating into the darkness of the cellar. "It's like they were preparing for an apocalypse." I walk carefully, avoiding the cobwebs that hang from the ceiling like macabre chandeliers and the other debris that litters the floor. As I reach the bottom of the staircase, I notice that the room seems to stretch further back than I initially thought. Rows of shelves line both sides, holding dusty bottles of wine and spirits, their labels faded and peeling. "Now we're talking!" I exclaim, my grin wide and triumphant. My fingers dance over the labels, my imagination running wild with the possibilities. A forbidden tryst in a secret corner of the castle? A bottle of centuries-old wine and a willing vampire? The possibilities are endless.

"Oscar said these keys open every door," I murmur to myself, my voice a low whisper as I come across a heavy, wooden door at the very back of the cellar. Unlike the others I've seen so far, this one appears much older, much more mysterious, as if it holds untold stories, and probably a whole lot of dust, behind its sturdy, iron-bound frame. A quick glance at the collection of keys I carry confirms my suspicion. There's no key for this lock. It's different. Older. More complex. My thoughts race; my mind a whirlwind of questions. What's behind it? Why can't I open it? What are they hiding?

Frustration, a hot, angry wave, bubbles up inside me. I try key after key, my movements frantic, desperate. But each attempt is a failure. The door remains stubbornly, infuriatingly closed. "Dammit!" I mutter under my breath, my voice a low, angry growl. I try to reach out with my mind, to send a mental message to Theo, a psychic SOS. Hey, mind-reader. There's a locked door down here. What's the deal? But it's no use. The connection is one-sided. He can hear my thoughts whenever he wants — a constant, intrusive presence in my head — but I can't seem to make it work on my end. Not since that first time. It's like having a phone that can only receive calls. It's infuriating.

I run a hand through my hair, my mind already concocting a new plan. A more direct, less psychic plan. I'll confront Oscar. I'll demand answers. He's the sweet one. The reasonable one. He'll tell me. And if he doesn't, I'll… I'll… I'll pout. And maybe cry a little. And then I'll demand answers again. It's a solid plan.

I spin on my heel, my mind a whirlwind of righteous indignation and frustrated curiosity, and I march toward the stairs. And that's when I see him. A figure, emerging from the shadows — a dark, menacing silhouette against the dim light of the cellar. Before I can react, before I can scream, before I can even process what is happening, a rough, calloused hand clamps a smelly rag over my face, the overpowering, sickly sweet scent of chloroform filling my nostrils.

"Wha-…you…bastard…" I attempt to gasp out, my voice a muffled, useless plea. I struggle, my arms flailing, my legs kicking, but it's no use. The drug is fast, efficient, a chemical blanket that smothers my senses, my thoughts, my will. My vision begins to fade, the edges blurring into a dark, swirling vortex. My last thought before the darkness swallows me whole is of pure rage at being caught off guard in my own castle.

· · ·

I AWAKE with a throbbing headache that feels like a tiny, angry man is trying to escape my skull with a pickaxe. The world swims in and out of focus, a blurry, nauseating mess of light and shadow. My limbs feel heavy, unresponsive, like they're made of lead. I try to move, to sit up, to do anything, and that's when the first wave of real, ice-cold panic hits me. I'm bound. Tightly. To a bed. The coarse, rough ropes dig into my skin, a painful, chafing reminder of my predicament. Don't panic. Don't panic. Panicking is for people who aren't about to be murdered. Deep breaths. In, out. Oh God, I'm going to die.

"Fuck," I whisper, my voice a dry, raspy croak that doesn't sound like me at all. Panic, a cold, sharp, familiar friend, claws at my chest, its icy fingers tightening like a vice around my heart.

"Ah, you're finally awake," a voice drawls from across the room. It's a smooth, cultured, infuriatingly calm sound that makes the hair on my arms stand up. My eyes dart to the source, and I find a man lounging in a plush velvet armchair, an unsettling smug smirk plastered on his disgustingly handsome face. He's a Ken doll from hell, with perfect golden hair, piercing blue eyes, and broad muscular shoulders that are straining against the fabric of his ridiculously expensive-looking tailored suit. He looks bored. And dangerous. The combination is terrifying. "You know, for someone so mortal, you seem to cause a lot of drama. I can smell fear on you from here. It's quite… intoxicating."

My blood runs cold. He can smell my fear. Of course he can. He's a vampire. And I am his prisoner. The thought is a bucket of ice water to the face, a shock to the system that pushes the panic down and lets the rage, my old, reliable friend, bubble to the surface.

"You must be Edmund," I spit, my voice dripping with a venom I didn't know I possessed. "Let me go! You pompous, over-dressed, Bond-villain-wannabe! Did you practice that smirk in the mirror, or does the 'smug bastard' look just come naturally?"

He actually laughs, a short, sharp, humorless sound. "Oh, I like you," he says, his voice losing its bored drawl, replaced by a cold, sharp cruelty. "You've got spirit. It'll be a shame to break it." He rises from his chair, his movements fluid and predatory, and stalks toward the bed. He leans over me, his face just inches from mine, his eyes cold and hard as chips of ice. "But to answer your question, no. I'm not going to let you go. And these," he says, his fingers tracing the line of the rope digging into my wrist, sending a jolt of terror through me, "are not just ordinary ropes. They're enchanted by a witch. A very powerful, very expensive witch. so you won't be able to teleport your way to freedom. Or do any of your other little party tricks."

"Enchanted ropes?" I snort, a harsh, incredulous sound that I hope sounds braver than I feel. My heart is trying to beat its way out of my chest. "Really? What kind of kinky, fifty-shades-of-bullshit is this? Did you get them on Amazon? Do they come in different colours? I'd prefer pink if you're taking requests."

His eyes narrow, the amusement gone, replaced by a cold, hard anger. "You think this is a game?" he hisses, his voice a low, dangerous whisper. He grabs the rope, yanking it tight, and I cry out, a sharp, involuntary sound of pain. "You think you're clever, don't you? A little, snarky, human girl who has stumbled into a world she doesn't understand. You are nothing. A means to an end. A key, and I will not have you screwing up centuries of planning because you can't keep your legs closed."

The words are a slap in the face, a cruel, vicious blow that hits me right where it hurts. My bravado falters, the fear, cold and sharp and real, threatening to swallow me whole. But I won't let it. I won't give him the satisfaction.

"Fine," I grit out, my teeth clenched so tight I'm surprised they don't shatter. I meet his gaze, my own eyes burning with hatred. "What do you want, then? Why did you drug me and tie me up like some goddamn damsel in distress? Is this your idea of a first date? Because let me tell you, you're not getting a second one."

His lips curl into a malicious, cruel grin that doesn't reach his cold, dead eyes. "Simple," he says, and the word is a condescending pat on the head. "Even for a mortal mind to comprehend." He rises from his seat, his movements slow, deliberate, predatory, and approaches the bed. Every step is a silent, terrifying threat. "There are secrets in the prophecy that you are not meant to find out. I spent twenty years keeping you hidden, a precious little secret tucked away from the world, so I could break the curse. If you bond with those Kings, if you give them what is rightfully mine, it will be the end of my plans."

My plans. My curse. My, my, my. This guy has a serious case of main character syndrome. My heart is a hummingbird trapped in my ribcage, but my mouth, as usual, has other ideas. "Secrets?" I raise an eyebrow, forcing a casual, bored tone. "You mean there's more to it than you told them? More than just 'find the girl, break the curse, live happily ever after'? Is there a secret handshake? A decoder ring? A bonus round where I have to solve a riddle posed by a grumpy troll?"

He doesn't laugh. He stops at the foot of the bed, his eyes narrowing, a flicker of something that looks almost like uncertainty in their depths. It's gone in an instant, replaced by a cold, hard anger. "You think you're so clever," he hisses, his voice a low, dangerous whisper. "But you are a child playing with matches in a room full of gasoline. Now, play nice, so I don't have to hurt you. And believe me," he adds, his voice dropping even lower, a soft, terrifying caress of sound, "I am very, very good at hurting people."

Don't show him you're scared. Don't let him win. "Play nice?" I scoff, the sound a harsh, brittle thing in the quiet room. My mind is racing, sifting through possibilities, through escape plans, through all the ways I'm going to make him regret this. "Good luck with that. I don't even play nice with the people I like. And you, my friend, are not even on the list. You're not even in the same fucking book as the list."

"Your choice," he says, his voice a low, cold promise of violence. He takes a step back from the bed, his expression a mask of cool, detached indifference. "Remember, Willow. You brought this upon yourself. You couldn't just stay hidden, could you? You had to go and get yourself found. You had to go and ruin everything."

As he turns to leave the room, I can't help but wonder what part of the prophecy is missing. What secrets are so important that he would go to such lengths to keep them hidden? But first, I think bitterly, glancing down at the enchanted, probably-not-from-Amazon ropes binding me, there's the matter of getting the fuck out of here. With every ounce of frustration and rage I possess, I scream at him. "Release me, you fucking bastard!"

"Sorry, Willow," Edmund replies, his tone infuriatingly calm, his back still to me. "I cannot allow you to complete the prophecy."

My heart thunders in my chest, a wild, frantic drumbeat of adrenaline and rage. "Fuck your prophecy!" I spit, struggling against my restraints, the enchanted ropes digging into my skin, a painful, burning reminder of my helplessness. "I don't give a shit about your prophecy! I just want to go home!"

Edmund looks back at me, his eyes cold and hard as steel. "This is your home now. Until I decide otherwise." He turns back to the door, his hand on the knob. "I won't let you fulfill it."

"Fine," I retort, my voice a low, vicious snarl. "Keep me tied up here like some sick pervert. See if I care. But you should know, my boyfriends are very, very protective. And they're going to be very, very angry when they find out you've taken their favorite toy."

That gets his attention. He turns back, his eyes blazing with a sudden, white-hot fury. In two strides, he's back at the bed, his hands gripping the headboard, his face just inches from mine. "Toy?" he snarls, his voice a low, guttural growl. "You think you're their toy? You are a vessel. A key. A means to an end. And you are mine. Not theirs. Mine."

"Believe me, I take no pleasure in this," he says, his

voice a low, rough whisper, and for a moment, just a fleeting, infinitesimal moment, I think I see a flicker of remorse in his eyes. But then it's gone, replaced by a cold, steely resolve. "But you leave me no choice."

"Then why?" I demand, my voice a raw, desperate plea. "Why go to such lengths to keep me from the truth?"

"Because the truth is dangerous, Willow," he replies, his gaze locking onto mine, his voice a low, ominous whisper. "And some secrets are better left buried."

"Like hell they are," I mutter under my breath, my mind racing, my heart pounding. As he turns to leave, I call out after him, my voice a low, cold promise of my own. "You can't keep me here forever, Edmund! I'll find a way out, and when I do, you'll regret ever crossing me."

"Good luck, Willow," he says, his voice a low, mocking echo from the hallway. The sound of a heavy door slamming shut reverberates throughout the room, a final, definitive punctuation mark on my imprisonment.

I take a deep, shuddering breath, my mind a whirlwind of fear and anger and a fierce, burning determination. Oscar will come for me. He has to. He can feel me, can't he? We never got around to seeing if distance affected it. Can he teleport to me? I hope so. I really, really hope so. "Fuck your prophecy," I whisper to myself, my voice a low, vicious growl. I grit my teeth, my eyes burning with unshed tears of rage and frustration, and I struggle against the enchanted ropes once more. "And fuck you, Edmund."

CHAPTER 36

OSCAR

The book — a heavy, leather-bound tome filled with centuries of meeting notes and political bullshit — slips from my numb fingers. It hits the floor with a heavy, sickening thud that echoes the sudden, violent lurch of my heart. One second I was reading, my mind a calm, orderly sea of facts and figures. The next terror crashes into me, so powerful, so overwhelming, that it steals the breath from my lungs. It's her. Willow. Her fear is a physical thing, a shard of ice in my gut, a scream in my soul. And then… nothing. The connection, the constant, thrumming presence of her in the back of my mind — it's just… gone. The silence is a gaping, bleeding wound.

"Willow!" I shout, my voice a raw, ragged sound that doesn't sound like me at all. I'm out of the library, my feet pounding against the polished stone floor. My control, my order, my carefully constructed world of logic and reason — it's all gone, shattered into a million pieces.

I round a corner, my movements clumsy, desperate,

and collide with a solid, unmoving wall of muscle. Theo. His eyes are wide, his face a mask of concern and a rage. He grabs my shoulders, his grip a painful, grounding pressure.

"Oscar," he gasps, his voice a low, guttural growl. "I can feel her too. She was screaming in her mind… then it just stopped. Now I can't feel or hear anything other than you! What the fuck is going on?" His grip tightens, his fingers digging into my flesh, his own panic a mirror of mine.

"Fuck," I mutter, the word a useless, pathetic puff of air. I try to concentrate, to latch onto any lingering trace of her presence, to find that bright, beautiful spark in the darkness. But there's nothing. Only the cold, empty, terrifying silence where her vibrant, chaotic, wonderful essence should have been.

"Where is she, Theo?" I demand, my voice cracking, showing the terror that is coiling in my gut like a venomous snake. "We need to find her! Now!"

He shakes his head, a gesture of pure frustration. He pushes his dark hair out of his eyes, his movements jerky, uncontrolled. "I don't know, Oscar. I can't sense her location. It's like she just… vanished."

"Shit, this isn't good." Panic, cold and sharp and real, sets in. I run a hand through my own dishevelled hair, my mind racing, sifting through possibilities, through plans, through anything that will help me find her. We can't afford to waste time. Willow needs us, and every second matters.

"Come on," I say, my voice a low, urgent command. I grab Theo's arm, my touch a desperate, pleading gesture.

"Let's check the computers in my office. Jasper might be able to help too."

Together, we sprint through the winding hallways, our footsteps a frantic, pounding rhythm against the cold, unforgiving stone floors. As we reach my office, I send a silent, desperate prayer to a god I don't believe in. Please let us find something. Anything. Please let her be okay.

I grit my teeth, frustration threatening to consume me. Why the hell can't I teleport to her? The one time I need it the most, the one time it could actually be useful, and my powers have decided to take a goddamn vacation. "Damn it!" I growl, slamming my fist against the cold stone wall as we run. My knuckles ache, a dull, throbbing pain, but it's nothing compared to the agony of not knowing where she is, of not being able to get to her.

"Think, Oscar, think," I mutter to myself, my voice a low, desperate mantra. An image of Willow, her eyes wide with terror, flashes in my mind, and I shudder, a full-body tremor of fear and rage. She was scared out of her mind, and we were powerless to help her. The thought is a knife to the gut, a fresh wave of agony that threatens to bring me to my knees.

We burst through my office door, the force of our entry sending it crashing against the wall. Jasper turns toward us, his eyes wide with surprise, a half-eaten bag of chips in his hand. But there's no time for explanations. There's no time for anything but finding her.

"Willow's in trouble," I blurt out, my voice cracking, the words a raw, desperate plea. "We can't sense her location, and I can't seem to teleport to her."

"Shit," Jasper mutters, his face paling, the bag of chips

falling from his numb fingers. He's on his feet in an instant, his eyes wide with a fear that mirrors our own. "What happened?"

"When did you last see her?" I ask, my voice tight with a worry.

"About two hours ago," he replies, his eyes darting from the security footage to us with a faint blush on his cheeks. "She was in here with me and then left to explore the castle with those keys you gave her."

"Damn it!" I curse, my voice a low, vicious snarl. Frustration — hot and sharp and bitter — boils within me like molten lava. There are eighteen bedrooms, ten more random, forgotten rooms, a library, a ballroom, a goddamn dungeon… she could be anywhere.

Jasper doesn't hesitate. He's out of his seat, a blur of motion, and he's gone, his voice a faint, fading echo from the hallway. "She went this way when she walked out! I'll catch her scent and follow it!" As Vampires, we can all scent trace, but Jasper is a bloodhound, a master tracker. He can find a scent and tell you how long it's been there, what the person had for breakfast, and what their favorite colour is. If anyone can find her, it's him.

"Good," Theo interjects, his jaw clenched, his eyes dark with a murderous rage. "Let's find her before it's too late."

We follow Jasper, our movements a frantic, desperate dance through the corridors of the castle. The image of her terror-stricken face is burned into my mind, a constant, agonizing reminder of what's at stake. My chest tightens at the mere possibility of losing her. The moments we've shared, the taste of her skin, the sound of her laughter, the way she looks at me with a mix of innocence and a desire so profound it takes my breath away… those memories are a fuel to the fire of my rage, my fear, my desperate, all-consuming need to protect her.

"Her scent is strongest this way," Jasper calls out, his voice a low, urgent echo from a narrow, winding staircase that leads down to one of the cellars. The words are a beacon, a lifeline, and we follow him without hesitation, our movements a frantic, desperate dance through the corridors of the castle. "We haven't used these cellars on this side of the castle in years."

"Shit," Theo mutters, his voice a low, angry growl that seems to vibrate through the very stones of the castle. "What the hell could she be doing down there?"

As we descend the creaky, wooden steps, the air grows colder, damper, the smell of old wine and damp earth a stark contrast to the warmth and comfort of the upper levels. The temperature drops with each step, a physical manifestation of the ice-cold fear that is gripping my heart.

"Over here," Jasper calls out, his voice a low, tense whisper from the back of the cellar. He points to a heavy, iron-bound door, its rusted hinges proof to how long it's been since anyone has ventured down here. "There's a second scent… It's faint, but it's there. And it smells… Edmund."

"Fuck," I swear, the word a raw, ragged sound torn from my throat. My eyes widen in disbelief, my mind refusing to process what I'm seeing. I point to the door, my hand trembling rage. "That's the tunnel door! We sealed it up over a century ago—it doesn't even have a key!"

"Something's not right," Theo says, his brow furrowed,

his eyes dark with a dawning, terrifying realization. He runs a hand over the door, his touch a gentle, almost reverent gesture. "The seal is broken. From the inside."

"How is that possible?" Jasper asks, his voice a low, worried murmur. "No one has been down here in decades."

"Never mind that now," I snap, my patience worn thin, my control shattered into a million pieces. "We need to find Willow." I shove the door, my shoulder colliding with the heavy, unyielding wood. It resists at first, a stubborn, immovable object, and then, with a loud, groaning protest that echoes the agony in my soul, it gives way.

"Be careful, Oscar," Jasper warns, his voice a low, urgent whisper. "We don't know what we might find in there."

"Willow is all that matters," I reply, my voice a low, firm promise of violence.

We venture into the tunnel. The air cold and damp, the smell of freshly moved earth points to the fact that someone has been here recently. The darkness is absolute, a thick, suffocating blanket that swallows the light from the cellar. "Jasper," I ask, my voice a low, tense whisper, "how much farther does this bloody tunnel go? I can't even remember where this one led."

"Her scent continues down the tunnel, and the second one too," Jasper replies, his voice a low, worried murmur from the darkness ahead. "But this doesn't make sense. We collapsed this part ages ago. It should be impossible to use."

"Fuck," I mutter, the word a useless, pathetic puff of air. The thought of Willow, lost and with some stranger in the darkness, vulnerable and terrified, makes me sick to my stomach. The image of her face, her smile, her eyes… it's a constant, agonizing loop in my mind. I can't lose her. Not now. Not ever. "We have to keep moving."

"Oscar, I understand your worry," Theo says, his voice surprisingly gentle, a soft, reassuring presence in the darkness. "But we need to be careful. We don't know what's down here, or how Willow even got this far."

"Fine," I snap, my frustration boiling over, my control completely gone. "But if anything happens to her because we're too cautious…"

"Nothing is going to happen to Willow," Jasper interjects, his voice a firm, reassuring promise from the darkness ahead. "We're going to find her and bring her back safely."

"Without a doubt," I declare, my resolve rekindled, my fear and rage coalescing into a cold, hard thing. With each stride down the tunnel, the opening ahead grows larger, allowing beams of sunlight to pierce through the darkness. We burst out into the open air, the sudden brightness a jarring, painful shock to our eyes. And then, it dawns on me where we are. Just beside the hiking trail where Caleb was last seen. This was why Caleb's came out here in the first place. To dig his way back into the Castle. To gain access inside.

Edmund and Caleb have Willow.

She's gone.

CHAPTER 37

WILLOW

The rough, scratchy material of the ropes bites into my wrists, leaving angry red marks that are probably going to bruise. I struggle against them, a futile, pathetic gesture that only serves to make them tighter. Fuck! How did I end up in this godforsaken room? One minute, I'm a sexually liberated, castle-exploring badass on a mission to find out what's behind a locked door. The next, I'm a cliché, a damsel in distress, kidnapped by a smug, over-dressed bastard with a Ken doll haircut and a serious case of main character syndrome. If I could just get my hands on him…

"Willow?"

The door creaks open, and Caleb steps in, looking like he's been to hell and back. And then to hell again for a souvenir t-shirt. His eyes, once so full of life and laughter, are dull and haunted. They go wide when he sees me tied up, a wave of guilt and regret washing over his face.

"Oh Lord, Willow… I didn't know. I swear."

"Didn't know what?" I spit the words a harsh, angry volley in the quiet room. I glare daggers at him, my eyes burning with hatred. "That your sire, the man you've been following around like a lost puppy for the last hundred and fifty years, was planning to kidnap me again and tie me to a bed? Or did you just think he was redecorating and needed my input on the new drapes?"

Caleb's worried expression tightens, and he approaches me cautiously, as if I'm a wild, cornered animal. Which, to be fair, is not entirely inaccurate. "I didn't know he was going to do this. I promise you, Willow. If I had known, I would've done everything to stop it."

"Great," I mutter, my voice dripping with a sarcasm so thick it's a wonder it doesn't drip onto the floor. "That helps so much right now. Your retroactive disapproval is a real comfort."

"Look, I'm here to help you," Caleb insists, his eyes searching my face for any sign of the girl he used to know, the girl who used to trust him. "We'll figure this out."

"Right. You and me against the world." My voice is low, bitter snarl. But deep down, a tiny, stupid, pathetic part of me wants to believe him. Caleb had always been there for me. He was my friend. My only friend. Until he wasn't.

"Please, Willow. You have to believe me. I never meant for any of this to happen." Caleb's eyes — those beautiful, sad, traitorous eyes — plead with me, and despite my anger, despite the betrayal, a tiny, stupid seed of hope sprouts within me. Maybe he is telling the truth. Maybe he's not a complete and utter bastard.

"Fine," I say, the word a bitter, reluctant pill that I

force myself to swallow. "Let's say I believe you. For the sake of argument. What the fuck are we supposed to do now? Do you have a plan? Or are we just going to sit here and have a heart-to-heart while your psycho sire decides which one of my limbs to remove first?"

Caleb takes a deep breath, his chest rising and falling with the weight of his confession. "Edmund finally told me the second half of the prophecy," he begins, his voice a low, urgent whisper. "I understand now why he brought you here. Why he's so afraid of you. You're actually safer with the kings."

"Safer?" I scoff, the sound a harsh, incredulous bark of laughter. I tug at the magical ropes that bind me to the bed. The irony is so thick I could choke on it. "Do I look safe right now to you? Do I look like I'm in a goddamn safe space?"

"Willow, please," Caleb implores, his eyes filled with a desperation that is almost convincing. "I know how bad this is. I'm trying to protect you."

"Protect me?" My heart pounds in my chest, a wild, frantic drumbeat of anger and disbelief. "By kidnapping me and tying me up like some sacrificial offering? Are you seriously listening to yourself right now? Did you hit your head on the way in here? Or are you just naturally this stupid?"

"No, Willow, I'm not defending his actions. But I am starting to see why Edmund felt it necessary." He looks away for a moment, his gaze distant, as if he's searching for the right words in a language he barely speaks.

"The prophecy says:

With the ascension of the three kings, a fourth will rise to
join them.
However, it will not be another king who stands beside
them.
No, a queen will step into their midst.
With her arrival, a great divide shall be created.
She carries within her a power so immense.
It will shake the very foundations of the world.
Her mere presence can incite fear and awe in equal
measure.
This queen holds within her grasp.
Ability to fracture the vampire world as she transfers this
power to her very mates.
Her existence threatens to tear apart everything that once
seemed stable and unshakable.

"I've already heard this!" I yell at him, my voice a raw,
frustrated scream. "The Kings told me straight away! They
didn't hide it from me like some dirty little secret!"

"You have to understand, the version I told you was the
one I was told," Caleb pleads, his voice cracking with a
sincerity that is almost believable.

"But there is a second half:

The three powerful kings will stand at a crossroads.
They must choose between a friend turned foe.
The decision will be made with a pure of heart.
For the decision made will defeat their enemy, leaving the
kingdom of vampires in a delicate state — one between
peace and chaos.
The stakes will be high as the kings must navigate through

treacherous waters of loyalty and love, knowing that only one choice can secure their reign and bring true harmony to their world.

I stare at Caleb, my mind reeling, my heart pounding. "You're telling me this whole time Edmund knew the whole prophecy and chose to eliminate my bloodline cause he believed he was the enemy they would defeat using the powers I give them?"

"Yes," Caleb says, his voice a low, defeated whisper. He runs a hand through his hair, his movements jerky, agitated. "I wish I had known about all this sooner. I never would have let any of this happen to you."

"Really?" I ask, my voice a low, dangerous purr. I narrow my eyes at him, my gaze cold and hard as steel. "So where were you when Edmund was tying me up and dragging me here? Were you taking a nap? Enjoying a cup of tea? Or were you just standing by, watching, like the good little soldier you are?"

"Believe it or not, I was trying to find out the truth," Caleb replies, his voice earnest, pleading. "I knew something wasn't right, but Edmund kept me in the dark about his real intentions."

"Fantastic detective work there, Sherlock," I mutter, my voice dripping with a sarcasm so thick it's a wonder it doesn't drip onto the floor. "You're a real credit to the force."

"Willow, I'm so sorry." Caleb's voice is laden with a remorse so profound it's almost convincing. "You have no idea how much your friendship means to me. I would never intentionally hurt you or allow anyone else to do so.

I just got caught up in this whole prophecy bullshit, and now we're both paying the price."

"Friendship?" The word tastes like ash in my mouth. I consider everything he has done, and everything he has failed to do. "Some friend you turned out to be."

"Please, Willow, just give me a chance to make it right," Caleb pleads, his eyes searching mine for any trace of the girl who used to look at him with something other than contempt.

As I stare into those desperate, sad, beautiful eyes, I wish I could believe him. But trust, once broken, is a fragile, shattered thing. And the weight of betrayal still hangs heavy between us like an unspoken curse.

With a heavy sigh, Caleb looks me dead in the eye. "I promise you, Willow. I'll make this right. I'll help you escape from here."

"Great," I snort, my voice a harsh, incredulous sound. I'm not sure if I can trust him, but I also realize that I don't have many options. "What's the plan, then? Are you going to untie me? Or are we going to have another heart-to-heart while your psycho sire sharpens his knives?"

"First, let's get you out of these ropes." He approaches the bed, his movements cautious, as if he's afraid I'll bite him. He studies the magical bindings that hold me captive, his brow furrowed in concentration. His fingers trace the intricate patterns woven into the ropes, and then, with surprising dexterity, he begins to undo the knots. The ropes begin to loosen, and I feel the pressure around my ankles ease.

"Oh, finally," I hiss, the word a low, relieved sigh. The

ropes fall away from my feet, and Caleb moves up to my hands, his fingers working quickly, efficiently.

Just as my wrists start to loosen, the door suddenly slams open, revealing an enraged Edmund. His face is a mask of fury. He takes in the sight before him: me, nearly free from my restraints, and Caleb, the traitor, the fool, the dead man walking.

"What do you think you're doing?!" he bellows, his voice a roar of rage. He storms toward Caleb, his movements a blur of speed and violence.

"Edmund, listen to me," Caleb says, his voice surprisingly calm, his hands held up in a placating gesture. "She knows. She knows the second half of the prophecy. There's no point in keeping her here."

"She knows?" Edmund stops, his eyes, cold and hard as chips of ice, darting from Caleb to me and back again. "You told her?"

"I did," Caleb says, his voice firm, his gaze unwavering. "She deserves to know the truth."

"The truth?" Edmund laughs, a short, sharp, humorless sound. "You have no idea what the truth is, you foolish, sentimental boy. You've just signed her death warrant. And your own."

"I won't let you hurt her," Caleb says, his voice a low growl. He takes a step forward, placing himself between me and Edmund, a vamper shield against the storm.

"You won't let me?" Edmund repeats, his voice a low, dangerous purr. He takes a slow, deliberate step toward Caleb, his movements fluid and predatory. "You, who I made? You, whom I saved from a life of poverty and disease? You, who owes me everything?"

"I owe you nothing," Caleb spits, his voice dripping with a venom I've never heard from him before. "You used me. You lied to me. You made me a monster."

"I made you a king," Edmund corrects, his voice a low, vicious snarl. "And you threw it all away. For her." He glances at me. "For a mortal. A weak, pathetic, insignificant mortal."

"She's not weak," Caleb says, his voice a low, fierce whisper. "She's stronger than you'll ever be."

"We'll see about that," Edmund says, his voice a low, cold promise of violence. And then, he moves. so fast I can barely track him. In one swift, savage movement, he lunges at Caleb, his fingers like vices wrapping around his neck. My heart pounds in my chest, a wild, frantic drumbeat of terror and disbelief. I watch my mind reeling, unable to comprehend the sudden, brutal burst of violence. With a sickening, wet crunch and a sickening, hot spray of blood, Edmund twists Caleb's head with a brutal, casual force, snapping bones and tearing flesh until it is gruesomely, completely severed from his body. The room is now a ghoulish, abstract canvas, splattered in crimson and filled with the thick, metallic scent of blood.

"Jesus fucking Christ!" I scream. I can't tear my eyes away from the grisly, impossible sight. Edmund stands there, his chest heaving, his eyes wild with a triumphant, bloodthirsty madness, clutching Caleb's severed head by the hair like some sick, twisted trophy. The lifeless body crumples to the ground, a gruesome, boneless puppet, a final, definitive punctuation mark on a life that was wasted, a friendship that was betrayed.

"Remember this, Willow," Edmund growls, his voice a

low, guttural promise of violence. His eyes — those cold, dead, soulless eyes — lock onto mine with a chilling, terrifying intensity. "This is what happens to traitors." He storms out of the room, dragging Caleb's head along with him, the sound a soft, wet, rhythmic thud against the floor, leaving the grisly, headless remains behind.

CHAPTER 38

OSCAR

Five hours. She's been gone for five hours. Five hours, three minutes, and twelve seconds. Not that I'm counting. The world is a grey, silent, empty void. The vibrant, chaotic, beautiful presence of her, the constant, thrumming connection that has become as essential as breathing, is gone. And I am drowning in the silence. We're in the sitting room, the air thick with tension. The fire in the hearth crackles, a mocking, cheerful sound in the face of our despair.

"He's not answering," Theo says, his voice a low, vicious growl. He's been pacing back and forth for the last hour, a caged, furious animal, his phone a useless, silent brick in his hand. He's been trying to reach the other vampire lords, to tell them what Edmund has done, to rally the troops, to declare war. But no one is answering. It's like they've all vanished into thin air.

"They're scared," Jasper says, his voice a low, bitter murmur. He's sitting on the edge of his seat, his body a coiled spring of barely contained rage. "They're scared of Edmund. They're scared of what he'll do to them if they side with us."

"They're cowards," Theo spits, his voice dripping with a venom so profound it's a wonder it doesn't poison the air. "They'd rather let him burn the world down than risk getting their hands dirty."

And then, I feel it. A flicker. A faint, distant, barely there spark in the vast, empty darkness. It's her. It's Willow. It's a whisper of a feeling, a ghost of a connection, but it's there. And it's drenched in a terror so profound, so overwhelming, that it steals the breath from my lungs.

"I feel her," I gasp, the words a raw, desperate plea. My knees buckle, and I have to brace myself against the arm of the sofa to keep from collapsing. "She's alive. And she's terrified."

Theo's head snaps toward me, his eyes wide with a desperate, pleading hope. He's at my side in an instant, his hands gripping my shoulders, his touch a frantic, grounding pressure. "Where? Can you sense her location?"

I close my eyes, my mind on a frantic, desperate search for that tiny, flickering light in the darkness. I try to focus, to latch onto it, to follow it. But it's like trying to watch a television with the sound muted and the screen covered in static. I can feel the emotion, the raw, unfiltered terror, but the location, the details, they're a blurry, indistinct mess. "I… I can't," I say, my voice cracking with frustration. "It's like… like she's behind a wall of glass. I can see her, but I can't get to her."

"Keep trying," Theo commands, his voice a low,

urgent growl. He closes his own eyes, his brow furrowed in concentration. "I'm going to try to talk to her. Willow. Willow, can you hear me? We're coming for you. Just hold on. We're coming."

I can feel his words, a faint, distant echo in the back of my mind, a desperate, pleading mantra. I focus on the feeling of her terror, on the faint, flickering spark of her presence. I try to teleport, to pull myself to her, but it's like trying to grab smoke. There's nothing to hold on to, nothing to anchor myself to. "Damn it!" I growl, my frustration boiling over, my control completely gone. I slam my fist against the arm of the sofa, the impact and jarring, painful shock that does nothing to ease the agony in my soul. "It's not working! I can't get a lock on her!"

"Don't give up," Jasper says, his voice a firm, reassuring presence in the chaos. He places a hand on my shoulder, his touch a gentle, grounding pressure. "Keep trying. We're not leaving her."

I take a deep, shuddering breath, my mind on a frantic, desperate search for anything, for any detail that will help me find her. I focus on the feeling of her terror, on the faint, flickering spark of her presence. And then, I feel something else. A flicker of an image. A room. A bed. Ropes. And blood. so much blood. The image is a flash, a brief, terrifying glimpse into her nightmare, but it's enough. It's an anchor. It's a destination.

"I've got her," I say, my voice a low whisper. And then, with a soft, silent pop, the world dissolves into a swirling vortex of colour and light, and I am gone.

I reappear in a room that smells of blood and fear.

Willow is on the bed, her hands still bound, but loosely, as if someone was in the process of freeing her. Her eyes are wide with a mixture of terror and a disbelief so profound it's almost comical. She's staring at me, her mouth open in a silent, perfect 'o' of surprise.

"Oscar?" she whispers, her voice a raw, ragged sound that tears at my heart.

"I'm here," I say, my voice a low, soothing murmur. I'm at her side in an instant, my fingers working quickly, efficiently, to undo the knots. The ropes fall away, and I pull her into my arms, my touch a gentle, reassuring pressure. "It's okay. You're safe now."

She's trembling, her body a fragile, quivering mess in my arms. She buries her face in my chest, her sobs a raw, ragged sound that echoes the agony in my soul. I hold her tight, my hand stroking her hair, my voice a low, soothing murmur. "I've got you. I'm not going anywhere."

And then, I see it. A body. On the floor. Headless. The room is a gruesome, abstract canvas, splattered in crimson and filled with the thick, metallic scent of blood. "Fuck," I swear, the word a low, vicious growl. I pull Willow tighter, my body a shield against the horror of the room. "Don't look. It's okay. I've got you."

She's still trembling, her sobs a raw, ragged sound against my chest. But she's safe. She's alive. And that's all that matters. I will burn the world down to keep her safe. I will tear it apart with my bare hands. And I will start with Edmund.

"I already saw," she says, her voice a low, shaky whisper against my chest. She rubs her sore wrists, the angry red marks a stark, brutal reminder of what she's just been through. She can't stop shaking. "He's a goddamn psychopath."

"Willow," I say, my voice a low, firm command. I pull back, my hands framing her face, forcing her to look at me. Her eyes are wide, her pupils dilated with fear. "We need to get the hell out of here before Edmund comes back."

"Right," she nods, a flicker of her usual, fiery spirit returning to her eyes. Adrenaline, a powerful life-saving drug, begins to kick in. She doesn't want to be here when Edmund returns. I don't want her to be here. I doubt she'd survive another encounter with him.

"Can you stand?" I ask, my voice a low, worried murmur. Concern, a sharp, painful emotion, etches itself across my face.

"Let's find out," she replies, her voice a low growl. She grits her teeth, her jaw set in a stubborn, defiant line, and attempts to push herself up from the bed. Her legs are weak, trembling, but she manages to stand with my help, leaning heavily on me for support.

My arms wrap around her, and I lift her off the ground, cradling her against my chest. She's so light, so fragile, a precious, beautiful thing that I will protect with my life. The warmth of her body is a soothing balm against the coldness that has seeped into my bones during the last five hours. She shivers, partly from relief, but mostly from the lingering terror that still holds her in its icy grip.

"Thank you," she whispers, her voice a raw, ragged sound against my neck. She buries her face in the crook of my neck, inhaling my scent, her breath a warm, shaky puff of air against my skin. "I don't know what I would have done without you."

"Shh," I murmur, my lips pressing a gentle, reassuring kiss to her forehead. "You're safe now. Edmund won't hurt you again. I promise."

"Let's hope not," she says, her voice a shaky, watery laugh. The thought of Edmund returning sends another shudder through her, and she tightens her grip on me, her fingers digging into my back, her body a trembling, quivering mess in my arms.

As we stand there, a moment of stillness in the chaos, I feel a faint, distant tug at the edge of my consciousness. It's Theo. He's trying to reach out to her, to us, through the mental link.

"Wait," she says, her voice a low, urgent whisper. She pulls back, her eyes closing, her brow furrowed in concentration. She's opening up her mind to him, and his relief, a powerful, overwhelming wave of emotion, washes over me, nearly knocking me off my feet.

"Willow!" his voice echoes in my mind. "Thank God you're alive! We've been going out of our minds trying to find you."

"Sorry for causing such a fuss," she replies, her voice a wry, sarcastic whisper in my mind. I can feel the tears pricking at the corners of her eyes, the raw, unfiltered emotion of the moment. "But you can call off the search party—Oscar found me."

"Oscar?" Theo sounds genuinely surprised, a flicker of amusement in his voice. "Thank the gods He managed to teleport to you?"

"Yep," she replies out loud but also in my mind and sends it right all the way to Theo, and I can feel and see the smile in her voice, a bright, beautiful sound that is a balm to my battered, bruised soul.

"Edmund kidnapped me," she whispers into his thoughts, her voice trembling with fear and relief.

"We know, baby," he replies, his voice a low, soothing murmur in my mind.

The urgency in her voice is palpable as she turns to me, her eyes wide with a desperate, pleading look. "We need to leave before Edmund returns," she pleads, her heart racing, her body a trembling, quivering mess in my arms.

"Agreed," I reply, my grip on her tightening, my voice a low, firm promise of safety. "Let's teleport back to the safety of the castle."

She hesitates, a wave of exhaustion washing over her. "Oscar, I don't know if I have the strength left to teleport," she confesses, her voice trembling, her body a fragile, beautiful thing in my arms.

"Don't worry about it," I reassure her, my voice a low murmur. I meet her gaze, my eyes locking onto hers, my expression a mask of cool, calm confidence that I don't feel. "Leave it to me. Just focus on staying close to me."

She nods hesitantly, her body a bundle of frayed nerves, her energy reserves dangerously low. The rough rope burns on her wrists are a constant, agonizing reminder of our perilous situation.

"Here goes nothing," I mutter, closing my eyes, my mind a frantic, desperate search for the feeling of home, for the warmth and comfort of the castle kitchen. I channel my power, the energy buzzing around us, the hairs on my arms standing on end.

"Shit, that's intense," she mutters, her voice a low, awed whisper against my chest. She clings to me for dear life, her body a warm, solid presence in the swirling vortex of colour and light.

And then, just as abruptly as it started, it stops. We're back in the warm, comforting embrace of the castle kitchen. My knees buckle beneath us as we land, the familiar scents of cinnamon and vanilla washing over me like a balm. Theo and Jasper turn toward us, their expressions shifting from confusion to shock as they take in our appearances.

"Willow! Oscar!" Jasper exclaims. He rushes to our side, his hand on my shoulder, his eyes wide with worry and fear.

Theo hovers nearby, his face pale with concern, his eyes dark with a murderous rage. "What the hell happened?" he demands, his voice a low, guttural growl.

"Guess who's back, back again," she croaks, her voice a weak, pathetic attempt at humor. Theo sighs, and he scoops her out of my arms, holding her as close as he can, his body a shield against the horrors of the world.

"In summary," she explains, her voice a low, tired whisper against his chest, "Edmund kidnapped me, heartlessly ripped off Caleb's head, and my knight in shining armor, Oscar, came to my rescue."

Jasper's face twists in disgust. He shakes his head and wordlessly leaves the room.

"Jasper," she calls out, her voice a low, pleading whisper.

I sit up from my kneeling position on the floor, my body aching with a deep, profound exhaustion. Teleporting both of us has taken its toll. "Let him go, sweetheart," I say, my voice a low, gentle murmur. "He processes things differently than the rest of us."

"Theo, please put me down," she wriggles in his strong arms.

CHAPTER 39

WILLOW

"Theo, please put me down."

He hesitates, his eyes dark with worry. "Willow, you need to rest. You've been through hell."

"I know," I say, my voice a low growl. "But I can't let him go. Not now." I pull away from him, my bare feet slapping against the cold stone floor as I tear after Jasper. My legs, which could barely hold me up a few minutes ago, are screaming in protest. They feel like jelly, like they're about to give out from under me with every frantic step. But I don't stop. I can't. The image of his face, the raw, unfiltered pain in his eyes before he turned away — it's a brand on my soul.

"Jasper, wait!" I call out, my voice a raw, desperate plea. He doesn't slow down. He doesn't even look back. It's like he doesn't even hear me. Or maybe he's just choosing not to listen.

"Goddamn it, Jasper!" I pant, my breath coming in short, ragged bursts. My lungs burn, my body aches, but I push myself harder, faster. "You can't just walk away like this!"

The lights lining the walls give off a soft, warm glow, casting long, dancing shadows on the ancient stones as we race toward his bedroom. I can't let him shut me out. Not now. Not after everything.

He finally stops, his hand on the cold, iron handle of his bedroom door. He doesn't turn around, his back a rigid, unmoving wall of tension. "I need a minute, Willow," he says, his voice a low, strained murmur.

"You don't get one," I say, my voice a low, breathless gasp. I stumble to a halt, my hands on my knees, my body trembling with a deep, profound exhaustion. "You don't get to walk away from me. Not now."

He finally turns, and the look on his face, the raw, unfiltered agony in his eyes — it's a punch to the gut. "Edmund killed someone in front of you," he says, his voice a low, ragged whisper. "We lost you. For five hours, you were gone. And I... I was scared, Willow. I was so fucking scared. And I need a minute just... to calm down."

His words, his vulnerability, the raw, honest pain in his voice — it shatters the last of my anger, my frustration, my confusion. And in its place, a wave of love, of a compassion so profound it brings tears to my eyes, washes over me. Without a second thought, I launch myself at him, my arms wrapping tightly around his neck, my body a desperate, pleading offering. He's stiff at first, a rigid, unmoving statue of pain and fear. But I hold on, my fingers tangling in his hair, my face buried in the crook of his neck, my body a warm, solid presence against his. And then, slowly, tentatively, he melts. His arms wrap around me, his hands finding the small of my back, pulling me closer, his body a trembling, quivering mess in my arms.

And then, the floodgates open. "I was so scared," he whispers, his voice a raw, ragged sound against my ear. "I thought I'd lost you. I thought… I thought I'd never see you again." He pulls back, his hands framing my face, his eyes searching mine, a desperate, pleading look in their warm, brown depths. "And I'm so jealous, Willow. I'm so fucking jealous of them. They have you. They're bonded to you. They can feel you, hear you, know you in a way that I can't. And I… I'm just the fun one. The comic relief. The one who makes you laugh. But what if that's not enough? What if you don't… what if you don't need me? Not really. Not like you need them."

His words, his fears, his insecurities — they're a torrent of pain and a vulnerability so profound it breaks my heart. I just hold him, my hands stroking his hair, my body a warm, solid presence against his. I let him talk; I let him pour out all the pain and the fear and the jealousy that has been eating away at him for days. And when he's finally done, when he's standing there, a raw, open wound in front of me, I pull back, my hands framing his face, my eyes locking onto his.

"I'm so sorry, Jasper," I whisper, my voice thick with an emotion I can't even begin to name. "I'm so sorry you felt that way. I'm so sorry I didn't… I didn't show you. I didn't tell you." I take a deep, shuddering breath. "I want you, Jasper. I have this whole time. There just… there hasn't been a good time. Between the bond sickness and the kidnapping and the… the everything. There hasn't been a moment just… to be with you." I lean in, my forehead resting against chest. "I'm back. I made it back. And I need you. I need you so much."

And then, I kiss him. It's a soft, gentle, tender kiss, a promise of everything to come. It's a thank you. It's an apology. It's everything. And it's just the beginning.

He pulls back, his eyes searching mine, a silent question in their warm, brown depths. I answer with a small, shy smile, my heart so full of love it feels like it's going to burst. He takes my hand, his fingers lacing with mine, and leads me into his room. It's so… Jasper. It's a comfortable, lived-in mess, with stuff stacked on every available surface, a guitar leaning against the wall, and a faint, lingering scent of him that is both comforting and deeply, profoundly arousing.

He turns to me, his expression a mixture of awe and desire. He doesn't speak. He doesn't have to. His eyes say everything. He kneels before me, his movements slow, deliberate, a silent act of worship. One hand find the hem of my pants; the fingers of his other brush against one of my ankles. He looks up at me, a silent question in his eyes, and I nod, my breath catching in my throat. He slides them down my legs, his touch a gentle, reverent caress that makes my skin tingle. I step out of them, my body trembling, my heart pounding in my chest.

He stands, his hands finding the hem of my shirt, his movements slow, deliberate, a silent question. I nod again, my voice lost, forgotten thing. He pulls it over my head, his eyes never leaving mine, his gaze a hot, searing brand on my skin. I'm standing before him in just my bra and panties, my body a trembling, quivering mess of need and a vulnerability so profound it's almost painful. He reaches out, his fingers tracing the curve of my hip, his touch gentle, making my pussy clench on itself.

"You're so beautiful," he whispers. "So fucking beautiful."

He moves behind me, his body a warm, solid presence against my back. His fingers find the clasp of my bra, his touch a gentle, reassuring pressure. He unhooks it, his movements deft and sure, and it falls to the floor, a forgotten, irrelevant piece of fabric. He presses a soft, gentle kiss to my shoulder, his lips a warm, wet brand on my skin. And then, he turns me around, his eyes dark and stormy with a desire that mirrors my own.

He kneels again, his hands finding the waistband of my panties, his thumbs tracing lazy, gentle circles on my hips. He looks up at me, a silent question in his eyes, and I nod, my body a trembling, quivering mess of need. He slides them down my legs, his touch a slow, deliberate, agonizingly sensual caress. I step out of them, and I am naked. Completely. Utterly. And I have never felt more beautiful, more desired, more cherished.

My hands find the hem of his shirt, my fingers fumbling with the soft, worn fabric. I pull it over his head, my eyes widening at the sight of him. His chest is a canvas of intricate, swirling tattoos, a beautiful, magnificent work of art that tells a story I'm desperate to read. I reach out, my fingers tracing the lines of a dragon that curls around his shoulder, its scales a beautiful, intricate pattern of black and grey.

"They're beautiful," I whisper, my voice a low, awed murmur. "You're beautiful."

"Not as beautiful as you," he says, his voice a low,

husky whisper. He leans in, his lips brushing against mine, a soft, gentle, teasing kiss that sends a shiver through me. He cups my breasts, his thumbs tracing lazy, gentle circles around my nipples, his touch a gentle, reverent caress that makes me gasp. I lean into him, my body a trembling, quivering mess of need, my hands finding the waistband of his jeans, my fingers fumbling with the button, the zipper. He helps me, his hands covering mine, his touch a gentle, reassuring pressure. The button gives way, the zipper slides down with a soft, satisfying hiss, and I push the rough denim down his hips.

He steps out of them, and then his boxers, and he's naked. And he's perfect. So, so perfect. My eyes roam over him, taking in the sight of him — the broad, muscular shoulders, the chiseled, tattooed chest, the narrow, lean hips, the long, powerful legs. And the hard, thick, magnificent length of him. My mouth goes dry, remembering the weight of his dick on my tongue.

"Willow," he whispers, his voice a raw, ragged sound. He reaches for me, his hands finding my waist, his fingers digging into my soft flesh, pulling me tight against him. I can feel the heat of him, the strength of him, the desperate, frantic thrum of his heart against my chest. He kisses me, a slow, deep, searing kiss that is a promise of everything to come. It's a kiss that says, 'I'm yours. And you are mine.'

CHAPTER 40

JASPER

I walk her back to my bed, and lay her out like a feast. My hands explore her body with a reverence that borders on worship. Each curve, each contour, is a masterpiece, a work of art that I am privileged to touch. I trace the gentle slope of her breasts, feeling the softness give way to firmness as I tease her nipples with my fingertips. With every gasp and shudder that escapes her lips, a surge of pride washes over me. I am the one inciting such a response from her.

As I press my lips against her skin, I inhale deeply, intoxicated by the heady scent of her. I taste the salt of her sweat on my tongue, a flavor more exquisite than any wine, any blood, any mortal delicacy. "God, your breasts are perfection," I whisper, my voice husky with a desire that has been simmering just beneath the surface for centuries. She arches her back, a silent, desperate invitation to explore further. Without hesitation, I trail kisses down her abdomen, reveling in the softness of her flesh beneath my fingertips. Her skin is a canvas, and my lips are the brush.

"Lower, Jas," she pants, her voice a raw, desperate plea that makes my cock twitch with a need so profound it's almost painful. I can't resist any longer; I need to feel her completely. I need to taste her, to know her in the most intimate way possible.

With an almost reverent touch, I lower my face to her pink, swollen pussy, feeling the softness of her skin against my lips. The scent of her — a heady mix of arousal and her own unique, intoxicating fragrance — fills my senses. I press a soft, gentle kiss to her wet folds, a silent act of worship, before my tongue eagerly seeks out her clit. It's a perfect, hard pearl, and I relish the heat and wetness that greets it. As I gently lap and flick at her sensitive bundle of nerves, I can feel her shudder beneath me, a beautiful, magnificent tremor that vibrates through my entire body. A soft, breathy gasp escapes her lips, and I know then that I am addicted to hearing her scream. It's a drug more potent than any blood, any power, any mortal vice.

Her hands, which had been tangled in my hair, grip the sheets tightly, her knuckles white, her body arching and writhing beneath me, unable to contain the sensations that are coursing through her. I vary my rhythm, a slow, deliberate lapping that makes her whimper, a fast, frantic flicking that makes her cry out. I tease her, my tongue tracing lazy, gentle circles around her clit, my lips pressing soft, gentle kisses to her inner thighs. With each lick and tease, I savor her taste. It fills my senses, drives me wild. I can feel her getting closer, her hips bucking against my mouth, her breath coming in short, ragged gasps. And as she gasps out my name, her voice thick with a need that mirrors my own, I feel a surge of pride. I am the one making her cry out my name. I am the one making her unravel.

I slide two fingers inside her, her wet, tight heat a beautiful, magnificent embrace that makes me groan. She's so wet, so ready, so responsive. I move my fingers in and out, a slow, steady rhythm that makes her cry out, her hips bucking against my hand. I can feel her walls clenching around my fingers. I watch her, my eyes tracing the curve of her body, the flush on her skin, the sweat on her brow. She's a beautiful, magnificent mess, and she's all mine.

"I'm so close," she gasps again, her body trembling, her hips bucking against my mouth.

"Relax, Willow," I urge, my own desire intensifying with every passing moment. I can feel her, taste her, smell her, and it's driving me to the brink of madness. "Surrender to it. Let me have you."

"Jas… please…" she whimpers, her voice cracking.

"Let go for me. Come for me." And she does. Her body shatters, her orgasm a beautiful, magnificent wave, leaving her breathless and trembling. I feel her, taste her, smell her, and it drives me wild with desire. I drink her in, my tongue lapping at the sweet, sticky evidence of her, my heart so full of love it feels like it's going to burst. And in that moment, I know that I will do anything, anything, to keep her safe, to keep her happy, to keep her mine.

As she comes down from the throes of her orgasm, her body a trembling, I gently trace my lips back up her body, leaving a trail of kisses and goosebumps in my wake. I kiss her inner thighs, her hips, the soft, gentle curve of her stomach. Her skin is flushed, her breathing ragged, her eyes glazed over. I am the cause of this. This beautiful, magnificent mess is my creation.

Our bodies are still intertwined, our breaths coming in ragged gasps. As I reach her lips, I pause and let her taste herself on my tongue, savoring the sweet and heady flavor. She moans, a low, guttural sound, and her eyes flutter open, a beautiful, magnificent shade of green that is so full of love, of a trust so profound it breaks my heart. "You taste so good," I whisper, my voice a low, husky murmur.

"So do you," she whispers back, her voice a raw, breathless sound that makes my cock twitch with a need so profound it's almost painful.

With a firm grip on my throbbing, aching cock, I position myself between her legs. Her eyes widen, a mixture of anticipation and desire. I don't push in. Not yet. I just rest the tip of my hardness against her wet, swollen entrance, teasing her, tormenting her, making her wait. She bites her lip in anticipation, a small, shy, incredibly sexy gesture that makes me smirk. Her body is like a quivering flame, ready to ignite at any moment.

"Jasper," she breathes, her voice a low, pleading whisper. "Please."

"Please what, my love?" I ask, my voice a low, teasing purr. "Use your words."

"Please fuck me," she says, her voice a raw, desperate cry that shatters the last of my control. "I need you inside me. Now."

"Are you ready for this?" I ask, my voice deep and seductive, a low, guttural growl that makes her shiver.

She meets my gaze with an intense fire burning in her

eyes, a beautiful, magnificent blaze. "More than ever," she replies, her words filled with a need and a desire that matches my own.

I slowly push forward, just the tip, a torturous, glorious inch. She gasps, her eyes fluttering shut, her head falling back against the pillows. The sensation is exquisite, a mix of tightness and a wet, slick warmth that makes me groan involuntarily. I pull back, just as slowly, and she whimpers, a small, frustrated sound that makes me grin. I push in again, a little further this time, and she moans, a low, guttural sound. I continue this slow, deliberate torture, pushing in and pulling out, each movement a little deeper, a little slower, a little more agonizingly pleasurable than the last.

Finally, when I can't take it anymore, when the need to be inside her, to be one with her, is too much, I push in all the way. The sensation of her tight, wet heat enveloping me, of her body stretching to accommodate me — it's a beautiful. "Fuck, Willow… you feel incredible."

I gasp for breath, my entire body trembling with the effort it took to maintain control. I pull out slowly, almost to the tip, before sinking back into her, every inch a glorious feeling. Her hips meet mine in a seamless rhythm, our bodies moving together in perfect harmony. It's a slow, deep, deliberate dance. A claiming. A possession. Each thrust is a declaration, each retreat a promise. The sound of our bodies slapping together, the slick sound of our joining — it's the most beautiful music I've ever heard. Each movement sends sparks coursing through me, leaving me breathless and trembling.

"Is this okay?" I manage to ask, my voice strained. I

need to know. I need to be sure this is as perfect for her as it is for me.

She opens her eyes, and they're blazing with a fire that steals the air from my lungs. "Better than okay…" she breathes, her eyes locked onto mine with an intensity that left me reeling. "It's perfect. You're perfect."

Her words, her voice, her beautiful, magnificent face — it only fuels my desire, and I quicken my pace, losing myself in the heady rush. The slow, deliberate dance becomes a frantic, desperate rhythm. I'm a man possessed.

"Jas… I'm close again," she admits, her words punctuated by ragged moans and gasps as she clings to me. Her nails dig into my back, not with pain, but with a desperate, pleading urgency.

"Me too," I confess, feeling my arousal peak and my balls tighten. I can feel the climax building, a roaring inferno in my veins. But I hold back. I want to watch her. I want to feel her come apart around me. "Come with me, Willow. Let go for me. Come with me."

As we both hurtle toward the edge, I can feel her walls tightening around me like a vice. Her body trembles with anticipation as my pace quickens, my hips slamming against hers in a frantic, desperate rhythm. I'm lost in the feeling of her, the scent of her, the taste of her. She is my world, my universe, my everything. "Willow!" I cry out, my voice raw and needy, a desperate, pleading prayer.

The wave of ecstasy crashes over us, engulfing us in a frenzy of passion. I feel her first pulse, a tight, exquisite clench around my cock, and it's the most beautiful, magnificent sensation I've ever known. It's the trigger, the final push that sends me over the edge. I surrender to the overwhelming feeling, my hot, thick release spilling inside her as she clenches around me.

"Jas… Bite me," she gasps between ragged breaths, her voice a raw, desperate plea that makes my fangs ache.

With a nod and without hesitation, I bring my lips to her neck, sinking my teeth into the soft, warm flesh there. Her taste explodes on my tongue, a mix of sweetness and spice that drives me wild. The flavor of apples and cinnamon floods my senses — a beautiful, magnificent taste that brings back memories of lazy autumn days.

I can feel her body shattering once more, her pussy fluttering and clenching around my softening dick. Each movement is like a pulsating wave, sending shivers down my spine. Her breaths are ragged and uneven as she rides the waves of her orgasm, and I can't help but marvel at the sight of her in this moment - completely lost, completely mine as the bond snaps into place.

I collapse beside her, pulling her into my chest as we both struggle to catch our breath.

Chapter 41

Theodore

A profound, almost jarring sense of completeness settles over me as I wake. For the first time in centuries, the world feels… right. The bond, once fractured, incomplete thing, is now a solid, thrumming network connecting the four of us. It hums beneath my skin, a constant, low-level vibration of power and presence. I can feel Oscar's calm, a steady, rhythmic beat in the distance. I can feel Jasper's chaotic, buzzing energy, even in sleep, a firefly trapped in a jar. And I can feel her. Willow. A soft, warm glow that has finally, irrevocably, been woven into our existence. She is ours. Fully. The thought is a possessive, satisfying purr deep in my chest.

But the satisfaction is immediately tainted by a familiar, grating irritation. Jasper. That impulsive, reckless fool. He and Willow had their little dramatic chase, their tearful reunion, and then… this. The bonding. And while a part of me rejoices, the strategist in me is screaming in frustration. I had a plan. A simple, effective plan. We rescue Willow. I let her have a moment to breathe, and then I sit her down and extract every last detail of her captivity. The location. The layout. The number of guards. Edmund's habits, his weaknesses, his resources. Every scrap of intelligence that could give us an edge.

Instead, she ran off with Jasper, got herself thoroughly fucked, and now they're bonded. The window for a clean interrogation has slammed shut. I let her sleep, of course. Let them have their night. It was a calculated decision. She'd be more pliable after a night of rest and sated desire. But my patience is a finite resource, and it is wearing dangerously thin. This morning, we get answers. All of us.

I swing my legs out of bed, the cool morning air doing little to soothe the fire in my gut. A glance in the mirror shows a man who looks like he's barely slept. Good. Let them see it. I pull on a pair of tracksuit pants—my tracksuit pants, the ones Willow practically lived in for weeks —and a simple t-shirt. The fabric strains across my chest, and I catch a glimpse of the ink that snakes down my arms. She likes tattoos. A smirk plays on my lips. Let the little minx have something to stare at. It's a reminder of who is in charge.

I don't bother with gentle wake-up call. I stride down the hall, rapping my knuckles sharply on Oscar's door first. "Lounge. Five minutes." I don't wait for a reply. I do the same at Jasper's door. When I get to his room—the room where she is—I pause. The bond hums stronger here. A wave of possessiveness, so fierce it's almost painful, washes over me. I push the door open just enough to stick my head in. They're a tangled mess of limbs in the center of the bed, the sheets kicked to the floor. Her scent—that intoxicating mix of vanilla, books, and now, Jasper—fills the air. "Meeting. Lounge. Now," I say, my voice a low command that cuts through the morning quiet. I see her stir, a flash of dark hair against the white pillows, before I pull back and close the door with a decisive click.

I'm the first one in the lounge, of course. I stand by the fireplace, arms crossed, waiting. Oscar is next, looking as immaculate as ever, even in sleepwear. He gives me a nod, his mind already cataloging the day's tasks. Jasper and Willow are last, filtering in looking rumpled and thoroughly debauched. Good. As Willow's eyes land on me, her jaw goes slack.

"Are you wearing… tracksuit pants?" She stammers, her eyes wide with a comical level of shock.

A low chuckle rumbles in my chest. I let my gaze sweep over her, from her messy hair down to her bare feet, a slow, deliberate appraisal that makes a faint blush creep up her neck. "You can close your mouth now, little bird. I do, in fact, own clothing that isn't a three-piece suit. You should know. You wore these for a month straight before Oscar's credit card saved you from a life of sartorial crime."

"Just because I wore them doesn't mean I expected to see you in them," she retorts, crossing her arms, the blush on her cheeks deepening with indignation rather than embarrassment. "I thought you were allergic to comfort. Or anything that wasn't woven from the tears of your enemies."

Jasper snorts with laughter, draping an arm over her shoulder. "He looks almost human, doesn't he? If you squint."

I level a glare at him that could freeze hell over. "That's enough. Sit down. We have work to do. Edmund."

The mood shifts instantly. The easy banter evaporates, replaced by a tense silence. I turn my attention to Willow, my gaze sharp and uncompromising. "We have a significant gap in our intelligence, Willow. I had intended to rectify that the moment we got you back, but circumstances… changed." My eyes flick to Jasper, who has the good sense to look away. "So, we will rectify it now. I want to know everything. From the moment they took you from the cellar. Leave nothing out."

She flinches, the colour draining from her face. Oscar makes a soft noise of protest. "Theo, perhaps we can ease into this…"

"No," I say, my voice cutting through the air like steel. "We don't have time to 'ease' into anything. Edmund has her scent. He knows she's here. He will come for her, and we will be ready. That requires information. Now, Willow. Tell us."

She takes a shaky breath, her eyes darting between the three of us before landing on the floor. Her voice is a low, trembling whisper when she begins. "It was so fast. One minute I was in the cellar exploring, the next… there was this cloth over my face. It smelled sweet, cloying. My head felt fuzzy, and then… nothing." She wraps her arms around herself, a fragile, self-protective gesture that makes something unpleasant twist in my gut. "I woke up in a room. With Edmund and Caleb, he tried ... tried …"

Her voice hitches on his name, and a wave of her grief, sharp and raw, lances through the bond. I ignore it. "He was kind," she continues, her voice barely audible. "He said he was sorry. He said Edmund tricked him, then he told me about the real prophecy."

"What did he tell you?" I press, keeping my voice even, devoid of the sympathy that would only encourage her to break down. We need facts, not tears.

"He saidEdmund was obsessed with the prophecy. That there was second part that Edmund never told anyone." She looks up at me, her eyes shimmering with unshed tears.

"What did it say?" Jasper asks, his voice uncharacteristically gentle.

She takes a deep, shuddering breath.

The three powerful kings will stand at a crossroads.
They must choose between a friend turned foe.
The decision will be made with a pure of heart.
For the decision made will defeat their enemy, leaving the kingdom of vampires in a delicate state — one between peace and chaos.
The stakes will be high as the kings must navigate through treacherous waters of loyalty and love, knowing that only one choice can secure their reign and bring true harmony to their world.

A heavy, stunned silence hangs in the air. A friend turned foe. My mind races, connecting the dots with cold, brutal efficiency. He made himself the foe. The viper in the grass. The sheer, calculated audacity of it is almost impressive.

"He told me to run," Willow whispers, tears finally spilling over and tracing paths down her pale cheeks. "But when he tried to free me, Edmund found him." Her body begins to tremble violently. "He called Caleb a traitor. And then… he just… he killed him. Right in front of me. He snapped his neck like it was nothing and pulled his head from his body."

She breaks down completely then, a raw, keening sob tearing from her throat. In an instant, Oscar is by her side, pulling her into his arms, murmuring soft, comforting words. Jasper stands frozen, his face a mask of fury. And I… I stand apart, the cold, hard facts of her story solidifying into a plan in my mind. The emotional debris is irrelevant. The tactical information is priceless. We now know Edmund's entire motivation was based on a lie of his own making. A lie that has now been exposed. And that makes him predictable. It makes him vulnerable.

After a few minutes, her sobs subside into shuddering breaths. Oscar helps her back into the armchair, and she looks up, her eyes red and swollen, but a new, hard resolve in their depths. It is in this charged, emotional silence that Jasper's attention drifts. He's staring at the decorative orb on the mantelpiece. A smirk plays on his lips, and he points a finger at it. The orb wobbles, lifts a few inches into the air, and then drops back to the mantel with a soft thud.

"Holy shit," Oscar breathes, his eyes wide. "Jas, you just… you have telekinesis!"

Jasper's grin is wide and triumphant. "Looks like it! All that pent-up energy had to go somewhere, I guess." He wiggles his fingers at the orb again, and it floats a good foot in the air this time, spinning slowly.

"Wow, Jas," she says. "Moving a paperweight. Don't

strain yourself. Maybe next week you can work your way up to a pillow." She says with a smirk, and he just grins at her.

I watch my mind already recalibrating. Another weapon. A powerful one. It's a welcome advantage, even if the wielder is an impulsive fool. "Good," I say, my voice cutting through their excitement. "Another tool at our disposal. Now, let's focus." I begin to pace in front of the fireplace, laying out the framework of my plan. "The rest of the board members—Thomas, Isabella, Yvonne, and Edith—will be here in a few days. I summoned them the moment we knew Edmund had you." My gaze lands on Willow, a silent reminder of the stakes. "Once they arrive, we will convene a formal war council. We will use the intelligence you've provided. We will not be reactive. We will choose the time and place of engagement. We will remove Edmund from the board permanently."

As I speak, I notice a change in Willow. She's staring at Jasper, but her expression is… odd. She frowns, her head cocking to the side as if listening to a distant sound. Her brow furrows in concentration, then clears, replaced by a look of pure annoyance.

"Jasper, for fuck's sake, will you stop talking so loud! I can't hear what Theo's saying," she snaps suddenly, her glare shifting from me to a bewildered Jasper.

He blinks, holding up his hands in surrender. "I wasn't talking."

"Then how the hell did I just hear you saying about how you could use your new trick to get the remote without getting off the couch?" She accuses, her own

words catching up with her as her eyes widen in realization.

A slow, wicked grin spreads across my face. So, it wasn't just me anymore. The bond has opened her up to all of us. Before I can comment, Oscar, who has been watching this unfold with quiet amusement, leans forward slightly, his eyes fixed on Willow.

I watch her as a new wave of colour, a shade darker and hotter than before, floods her face. She makes a small, choked sound, her hand flying up to fan her cheeks. Her eyes dart to Oscar, wide with shock and something else… something flustered and aroused.

"Okay," she breathes, her voice a little shaky as she points a finger first at me, then Jasper, then Oscar. "Safe to say I can hear all three of you now. Without any issues. And for the record," she adds, narrowing her eyes at Oscar, "that is physically impossible, and you should be ashamed of yourself."

Oscar just gives her a slow, deliberate wink. He leans back, the picture of innocence, and a low chuckle escapes him. "Well now, little mouse," he says, his voice a low, smooth purr that sends a visible shiver down her spine. "This is gonna be a lot of fun."

"Fun for you, maybe," she mutters, sinking deeper into the armchair. "I'm stuck in a room with three walking, talking dirty thoughts."

Jasper erupts in laughter, the tension in the room breaking. "Oh, this is brilliant! No more secrets!"

"Don't get too excited," I cut in, my voice sharp, though the amusement is thrumming through me. "It just means she has three voices to obey now instead of one."

Willow's head snaps in my direction, her eyes blazing with defiance. "Or," she says, a slow, dangerous smile spreading across her face, "it means I have three sources of blackmail material. Don't test me, Theo. I know what you were thinking about five minutes ago."

My smirk widens.

CHAPTER 42

WILLOW

My head is now Grand Central Station for the thoughts of three ridiculously old, ridiculously hot vampires. It's less of a psychic gift and more of an unsolicited, 24/7 podcast featuring 'Brooding Billionaire,' 'Cheeky Bastard,' and 'Domestic God.' I'm just waiting for them to start running ads. The silence in the room is thick with unspoken thoughts, but the problem is, I can now hear the unspoken thoughts. It's going to take some getting used to.

Just as I'm contemplating if I can mentally mute them, my stomach decides to join the conversation. It's not a polite little rumble. It's a loud, ferocious, guttural growl that echoes through the silent room, a sound so monstrous it could have been a Wookie mating call. My face flames with a heat that has nothing to do with dirty thoughts. All three of them turn to look at me, their expressions ranging from Jasper's open amusement to Theo's irritated glare.

"Is that your stomach, or did we just awaken a cryptid?" Theo asks, his voice dripping with disdain.

"Feed me, or I might eat the furniture," I shoot back, patting my stomach. "That couch looks expensive. It would be a shame."

Before Theo can retort, Oscar vanishes from his seat with a soft pop. A second later, another pop sounds from behind me, and he's standing there, holding a silver tray laden with a mountain of sandwiches. They're perfectly cut, the crusts removed, arranged in a precise, alternating pattern that is so quintessentially Oscar it makes my heart ache.

"Look at him, the domestic god," Jasper says, leaning forward to inspect the tray.

"I made them all up last night. I wanted to make sure you had food this morning," Oscar replies smoothly, setting the tray in front of me.

"You're a lifesaver," I breathe, my eyes wide as I stare at the feast. I lunge for the nearest sandwich, my fingers closing around the soft, yielding bread. The scent of roasted turkey and fresh bread fills my senses, and I take a huge, unladylike bite.

The flavors explode in my mouth—savory turkey, the slight nuttiness of Swiss cheese, a tangy smear of mustard. It's the most incredible thing I've ever tasted. I moan, a low, guttural sound of pure satisfaction.

You know, if you keep making noises like that while you eat, I'm going to get the wrong idea, Jasper's voice, laced with laughter, slides into my mind. Or the right one.

I choke on my bite, my cheeks puffing out as I try not to spray half-chewed sandwich across the expensive rug. I manage to swallow, my eyes watering as I glare at him. Shove it, sparkly, I think back, as forcefully as I can.

He just winks, his grin wide and utterly shameless.

"Are you trying to inhale it?" Theo asks, his lip curled in a mixture of disgust and fascination. "There are more. No one is going to steal your food."

"You say that now," I mumble, my mouth already full of a second bite. I grab another sandwich, this one piled high with tender roast beef and sharp cheddar. It's pure heaven. I'm a woman possessed, a sandwich-crazed fiend, and I don't even care. Judge all you want, I haven't eaten since I was kidnapped. A girl has needs.

Is it weird that watching you devour that sandwich is kind of a turn-on? Jasper thinks, and this time I can't help the small smile that curves my lips. A little bit, yeah, I shoot back, and his grin widens.

"Seriously, thank you," I say to Oscar, pausing to wipe my mouth with the back of my hand, a gesture that makes him visibly flinch. "I don't know what I would do without you."

"Starve, apparently," Jasper mutters, and I kick his shin under the table.

"It's nothing," Oscar says, ignoring Jasper and smiling warmly at me. "Just making sure you're well taken care of."

"Still," I insist, taking another bite and savoring the mouthful, "you're the best."

"Only for you, Willow," he replies, his voice soft and sincere. A comfortable warmth spreads through my chest, and for the first time since I woke up, I feel... safe. Truly safe.

With my hunger finally sated, I lean back against the couch, feeling a slight heaviness in my stomach that is both comforting and unfamiliar. I glance over at the three kings, who have been watching me with a mixture of amusement and concern. Jasper is still sending me a running commentary of increasingly filthy thoughts, Oscar is beaming with pride, and Theo… Theo is just watching me, his expression unreadable, but I feel a faint, surprising thought brush against my mind, his voice a low rumble in the back of my head. Good. You need your strength. I can't help the small, secret smile that touches my lips, just for him.

As I'm basking in the warm, fuzzy feeling of being full and safe, a thought occurs to me. I've been so focused on my own needs, my own trauma, my own hunger, that I completely forgot about theirs. I sit up a little straighter.

"Hey," I say, catching their attention. "So, I just had a thought. While I was busy becoming one with a turkey sandwich, I realized I hadn't even asked. You guys… you eat, right? Or, you know… drink."

Theo raises an eyebrow, a slow, amused smirk curling his lips. "You mean for blood, little bird? Are you offering to be the main course now that you've finished your appetizer?"

A faint blush creeps up my neck, but I hold his gaze. "I'm serious. Don't you need it like daily? To not get all… dusty?"

"Normally, yes," Oscar chimes in, his expression thoughtful. "But it seems our… dietary requirements have shifted. The small amount we've had from you has been more than enough to sate us. We haven't craved it since… well, since you became our only source."

The revelation sends a jolt of something wild and

powerful through me. I'm their food. Their only food. The thought should be terrifying, but instead, it's… intoxicating. A heady mix of power and responsibility. I am their sustenance. I am enough for them.

"So, you're saying you're running on fumes right now? Because of me?" I ask, a slow smile spreading across my face. "Well, we can't have that. I can't have my three vampire kings fainting from hunger. It would be terrible for your reputations."

"Are you sure, Willow?" Oscar asks, his dark eyes searching mine for any sign of hesitation.

"Yeah," I murmur, biting my lip. "I want to. I want to make sure you're all taken care of, too." I look at each of them in turn, my gaze lingering on their lips, on the fangs I know are hiding just beneath. "So, who's first? Or do I have to choose?"

"I think we can form an orderly queue," Jasper says, his voice a low, sultry purr as he slides closer to me on the couch. The air crackles with a sudden, thick tension. The playful banter is gone, replaced by a need that I can feel humming from all three of them, a palpable wave of hunger and desire.

"Promise you won't drain me dry?" I joke, my voice a little breathless.

"No promises," Jasper whispers, his lips brushing against my ear as his hand lands on my thigh, his touch a brand of heat through the fabric of my jeans. His fingers begin a slow, deliberate journey upward, tracing lazy circles on my inner thigh, each touch sending a shiver of anticipation through me. My breath hitches as his hand reaches the apex of my legs, his fingers teasingly close to where I want him most.

You want this, don't you? He thinks, his voice a velvet whisper in my mind. You want me to touch you. To taste you.

I can only nod, my throat suddenly tight. He smirks, a flash of white teeth in the dim light, before his hand slides down, pushing into the waistband of my pants. My body tenses as his fingers slip inside, finding me wet and ready for him. "Fuck," I gasp, my back arching off the couch, my sandwiches long forgotten.

His fingers move slowly, deliberately, a torturous rhythm that builds a burning, coiling heat deep inside me. He knows exactly what he's doing, the bastard. His lips find the soft skin of my neck, and I feel the sharp points of his fangs press against my pulse point, a promise of the bite to come. The dual sensations are almost too much—the slick, clever movement of his fingers inside me, the sharp, predatory pressure on my neck.

"Jasper…" I moan, my voice shaking as I feel the wave beginning to crest. "I'm close…"

I know, he thinks, his own excitement a palpable wave through the bond. Come for me, Willow. Let me feel it.

He bites down, sinking his fangs into my flesh, and the sharp, exquisite pain is the final push. My orgasm crashes through me, a tidal wave of pure, overwhelming sensation. My body convulses, my vision whites out, and the only thing I know is the feeling of Jasper's fingers moving inside me, his fangs in my neck, and the sound of my own ragged screams filling the room.

My chest heaves as I try to catch my breath, the aftershocks still rippling through my body. While I'm still reeling, a boneless, trembling mess, I feel warm hands slide under my hips. Oscar. He pulls my pants off in one smooth, efficient motion, and a shiver runs down my spine as the cool air hits my exposed skin.

"Are you ready for more, little mouse?" Oscar asks, his voice husky with a desire that sends a fresh wave of heat through me. I can only nod, a nervous excitement bubbling in my chest as I look into his dark, intense eyes.

"Please," I whisper, feeling a blush creep up my cheeks. He doesn't need any further encouragement.

Oscar lowers his head between my legs, and the anticipation alone has me clenching my fists on the soft fabric of the couch. His tongue finds my clit, teasing it with gentle, reverent licks that send shivers up my spine. It's so different from Jasper's frantic energy. Oscar is slow, methodical, and a master of his craft. My moans fill the room, growing louder as he increases the pressure ever so slightly, his tongue a warm, wet, perfect torment. He's mapping me, learning me, and I am more than happy to be his territory.

"Fuck, Oscar…" I gasp, my fingers digging into the cushions beneath me. The tension inside me is building again, an inferno threatening to consume me completely. He seems to sense it — the shift in my breathing, the way my hips have started to twitch. Just as I feel the familiar coil tightening in my gut, he pushes two fingers inside me, curling them just right to hit that sweet spot deep within. My hips buck against his touch, a desperate, silent plea for more. And then I feel it—the sharp, delicious sting of his fangs sinking into the tender flesh of my inner thigh.

"Shit!" I cry out, the pain a bright, searing flash that dissolves instantly. It's the final trigger. The sensation sends me spiraling into another intense, shattering orgasm, my body convulsing as waves of heat wash over me, leaving me panting and drenched in sweat.

He pulls back, his lips stained red, his eyes gleaming with a satisfaction that makes my toes curl. "Did you enjoy that, my love?" he asks, his voice a low, rumbling purr.

"God, yes," I manage to breathe out, still trying to recover from the onslaught of sensations. "You have… a very particular set of skills."

He chuckles, a low, warm sound. "I aim to please."

My eyes flutter around, and my gaze finds Theo. He's been standing there the whole time, a silent, brooding statue of a man, just watching. But he's not impassive. There's a raw, predatory hunger in his gaze that sets my pulse racing all over again. He wants his turn. And he's not going to be as gentle as the others.

"Your turn, Theo?" I tease, my voice breathy and weak. "Or are you just going to stand there and glower all day? It's a good look for you, but I have other plans for your face."

The corner of his mouth twitches, the barest hint of a smile. "Impudent little thing, aren't you?" he says, his voice a low growl that vibrates through the floor.

"Come on then, Theo. Don't just stand there," I say, my voice dripping with a desire I'm not even trying to hide. "Show me what you've got."

He doesn't need any more encouragement. With a slow, deliberate movement that is pure, arrogant grace, he pushes his pants and boxers down his hips, letting them fall to the floor. He stands there proudly, his cock thick and hard and standing at perfect attention. My mouth goes dry. He's bigger than the others, more intimidating, and the sight of him, fully erect and ready for me, is both terrifying and exhilarating. I can't help but lick my lips in anticipation.

"Ready for me, Willow?" he asks, a devilish grin spreading across his face. He knows exactly what he's doing to me.

"Absolutely," I reply, my voice a hoarse whisper as I open my legs, an open invitation.

Theo steps forward and positions himself between my thighs. He doesn't enter me right away. He just rests the tip of his cock against my entrance, a heavy, hot pressure that makes me gasp. He leans down, his lips brushing against my ear. "You're mine now, little bird," he whispers, his voice a deep, proprietary growl. "All of you."

And then he pushes inside me. It's not a gentle slide. It's a slow, powerful, deliberate claiming. I cry out, a sound that is half pain, half ecstasy, feeling a delicious stretch as he fills me up completely. He pauses, letting me adjust to the feeling of him, the sheer size of him, before he begins to move. His thrusts are hard and deep, each one a branding motion that sends shockwaves radiating through my body.

"Fuck, you feel amazing," he groans, his fingers digging into my hips, tilting them to meet his every powerful thrust. He's not just fucking me; he's conquering me, and I am a willing captive.

I glance over at Oscar, who has taken a seat next to me on the couch. He's stroking his own cock, his eyes dark and glazed with lust as he watches us. Jasper isn't far away either; he's leaning against the fireplace, his hand working furiously on his own erection, his gaze locked on me.

"Jesus Christ," I say, my voice a strangled gasp. "I must be the luckiest girl in the world right now."

Oscar leans down and pulls my top up over my breasts, his lips closing around my nipple, and he begins to suck, his tongue flicking over the sensitive peak. A fresh jolt shoots through my chest, and I arch my back, pressing myself closer to his mouth, desperate for more of his touch, even as Theo continues his relentless assault on my senses.

"Does that feel good, sweetheart?" Oscar asks, looking up at me with lust-filled eyes.

"God, yes," I gasp, my entire body aching for release as I'm caught between the two of them, a willing sacrifice to their insatiable hunger. The tension continues to build within me as Theo relentlessly pounds into my core. I can feel the pressure coiling tighter and tighter, a supernova about to explode. Sensing I'm on the precipice, Theo's rhythm changes, becoming harder, faster, more desperate. He grabs my wrist, his grip like iron, and sinks his fangs into the delicate skin. The combination of the sharp, exquisite bite and the relentless pounding is electric. A scream rips from my throat as my orgasm tears through me, a violent, shuddering release that seems to go on forever. I feel a gush of wetness, a hot, slick flood as I squirt all over him, my body convulsing with the force of it.

Theo cries out, a raw, guttural sound. "Fuck, Willow!

You're such a good girl!" he praises, his voice thick with arousal.

His own climax follows a heartbeat later. He buries himself deep inside me, a final, powerful thrust that steals the air from my lungs, and I feel his hot seed flood my womb, a thick, heavy release that makes my own after-shocks tremble anew. He collapses on top of me, his body a dead weight, his breathing ragged against my ear.

For a long moment, the only sound in the room is our harsh, ragged breathing. I'm a mess. A beautiful, glorious, well-fucked mess. My body is humming, my mind is blissfully blank, and I am covered in the scent of him, of us. I feel Theo stir, pushing himself up on his elbows to look down at me, his eyes dark and possessive.

"Come here, you two," I rasp, my voice hoarse from all the moaning and screaming. I look past him to where Oscar and Jasper are still watching, their cocks still hard and throbbing, their eyes full of a desperate, hungry need.

"Damn, Willow… you look so fucking sexy dripping Theo's cum," Jasper says, his voice a low, gravelly growl as his hand strokes himself faster. He takes in the sight of me lying there, a mixture of sweat and Theo's seed glistening on my skin, and I see his control begin to fray.

"Please…" I whisper, a silent, desperate plea as I spread my legs wider. "I want to feel both of you. I want all of you."

Oscar and Jasper exchange a look, a silent communication that passes between them in an instant. They move in unison, positioning themselves on either side of me, as Theo reached down and rubs my clit with is swollen and over sensitive. They grip their cocks, their tips aimed at my already dripping pussy, and the sight of them, both so hard and ready for me, is almost enough to send me over the edge again.

"Are you ready for this, my love?" Oscar asks, his voice burning with a desire that mirrors my own.

"More than ready," I reply, biting my lip in anticipation, my pussy already tightening on Theo's softening cock as he rubs my clit still.

With that, they begin to stroke themselves in unison, their breathing growing heavier, their groans filling the room as they near the edge. I watch them, mesmerized, a powerful shiver running down my spine, knowing that I am about to be completely drenched in their hot, sticky cum. It's a filthy, decadent, beautiful sight, and it's all for me.

"Fuck!" Oscar cries out, his body tensing just before he releases a thick rope of cum that splatters across my stomach and thighs.

"Shit, yes!" Jasper follows suit, his own release painting my pussy with another layer of white streaks.

The sensation of their warm seed coating me, the sight of it, the smell of it, and Theo's circles — it pushes me over the edge one last time. I let out a deep, guttural moan as my entire body trembles with a final, blissful wave of ecstasy.

"God, you guys are amazing," I sigh, feeling utterly sated and spent. My limbs feel like lead, my mind a hazy, happy fog.

"Right back at you, babe," Jasper says, chuckling softly as he wipes his forehead. He collapses onto the couch beside me, his arm thrown over his eyes.

As I lie there, completely boneless and relaxed, I feel Theo gently pull out of me and rise from the couch. I hear the faint sound of water running from down the hall, a gentle, soothing sound that cuts through the post-coital haze. He's drawing a bath for me. The thought is so tender, so caring, it brings a fresh wave of emotion bubbling to the surface. I can't help the small, contented smile that spreads across my face. These three men — these powerful, dangerous, magnificent creatures — they truly care for me in every way.

CHAPTER 43

OSCAR

The sun has begun its descent, painting the sky in hues of orange and purple that I would normally find aesthetically pleasing. Tonight, however, the beauty is lost on me. My world has been reduced to the cool, sterile glow of the four monitors that dominate my office. For hours, I have been engaged in a tedious, frustrating, and utterly necessary task: finding Edmund.

My system is a digital dragnet, a complex algorithm of my own design that scours satellite imagery, traffic cameras, facial recognition databases, and heat signatures. It is methodical. It is precise. It is, in short, a digital extension of myself. I have already swept the entirety of England, a grid-by-grid search that yielded nothing but dead ends and false positives. The frustration is a low-level hum beneath my skin, a discordant note in the symphony of my usually well-ordered existence. Now, I am in Scotland. The progress bar at the bottom of the main screen inches along, a snail's pace that grates on my already frayed nerves.

Our sleeping schedule, once a synchronized and predictable pattern, has been utterly demolished. Ever since Willow's arrival, and especially since her abduction and return, our nights and days have bled into one another in a chaotic, unstructured mess. We sleep when she sleeps; we wake when she wakes. She has completely reoriented our world, but it is also deeply unsettling. I am tired. A profound, bone-deep weariness has settled over me, making my thoughts feel sluggish and my movements heavy. I am not accustomed to being tired. I am not accustomed to this… disorder.

My eyes drift from the screen, scanning the pristine surface of my mahogany desk. Everything is in its place: my pen is perfectly parallel to my keyboard, my notepad is aligned with the right-angle corner, my phone is centered on its wireless charging pad. And then I see it. A faint, off-white, perfectly circular ring marring the polished wood to the left of my keyboard. A coffee cup stain. My eye twitches. A wave of irritation washes over me, so potent it momentarily eclipses my fatigue. Jasper. It had to be Jasper. He's the only one who would dare bring a beverage into my office without a coaster. The sheer, unmitigated barbarism of it.

I open the top right drawer of my desk and retrieve a canister of antibacterial wet wipes. The crisp, clean scent of lemon and citrus fills the air as I pull one out, the familiar sound of the plastic seal a small comfort in a world gone mad. I begin to scrub at the offending ring, my movements precise and firm. "Coasters," I mutter under my breath, the words a low, angry hum. "They exist for a reason. A simple, elegant solution to a problem that has plagued humanity for centuries. Is it so difficult to grasp the concept? A small, flat object upon which one places a beverage container to protect the surface underneath. It's not quantum physics."

I fold the wipe, my movements sharp and angry, and continue to polish the spot long after the stain has vanished. The wood gleams under the desk lamp, restored to its former glory. I dispose of the used wipe in the bin beside my desk and retrieve another, just to be sure. As I give the area one final, satisfying polish, my eyes flick back to the main monitor. The search of Scotland is 98% complete. My frustration returns, a familiar, unwelcome weight in my chest. He's not here either. Where could he possibly be hiding? The man is a ghost, and it is infuriating.

I am about to start the process of expanding the search to Wales and Northern Ireland, a task that will take hours, when a sound cuts through the quiet hum of my computer. A single, sharp, high-pitched ping.

I freeze, my hand still resting on the polished surface of my desk. My head snaps toward the main monitor. The progress bar is gone. In its place is a satellite map, a blinking red dot pulsating over a remote, desolate stretch of the Scottish Highlands. And beneath it, a single line of text: Match Found. Edmund Whitten. Heat Signature Confirmed.

My fatigue, my irritation, my carefully controlled frustration—it all evaporates in an instant. A cold, sharp, and utterly delicious wave of adrenaline washes over me. The world narrows, my focus sharpening to a razor's edge. The ghost has been found. We have a location. And the hunt is about to begin. A slow, predatory smile spreads across my face. "Got you," I whisper to the empty room. "You're mine now."

My first instinct is to summon the others, to alert Theo. But a different, softer impulse overrides it. Willow. I want her to be the first to know. I close my eyes, focusing on the warm, bright thread of her presence in my mind. I found him, little mouse, I project, the thought a clean, precise arrow aimed directly at her.

The response is instantaneous. A chaotic swirl of surprise, excitement, and a touch of panic floods the bond, followed by a dizzying sense of movement. A split second later, the air in front of my desk shimmers and tears, and Willow appears with a startled yelp. Her teleportation skills are still… unrefined. She stumbles forward, her arms flailing, and I move without thinking, my chair gliding back as I catch her, my hands finding her waist to steady her before she can collide with my perfectly organised desk.

"Whoa there," I say, a chuckle escaping me as I hold her steady. "A little warning next time, perhaps? You almost gave me a heart attack. And more importantly, you almost scuffed my floor."

She looks up at me, her eyes wide and her hair a mess. "You found him? For real?"

Before I can answer, the door to my office bursts open and Theo strides in, Jasper hot on his heels. "What the hell was that?" Theo demands, his eyes narrowed. "I felt you teleport. Is everything alright?"

"Everything is perfect," I say, my smile widening as I gently set Willow back on her feet. I gesture to the main monitor, where the red dot continues its insistent, rhythmic pulse. "Gentlemen. Willow. I present to you, Edmund Whitten."

They crowd around the desk, their eyes fixed on the screen. I zoom in, the satellite image sharpening to reveal a large, isolated manor nestled deep within a forest in the Scottish Highlands, not far from the coast leading to the Isle of Skye. "It's a manor, almost identical in layout to the one he held you in," I explain, my voice calm and clinical as I point out the similarities on a secondary screen. "Just on the other side of the country. He's been hiding in plain sight, using the same blueprint."

"Well, at least he's consistent," Willow mutters, peering at the screen. "You know," she adds, a thoughtful expression on her face, "I've always wanted to visit the Isle of Skye. I hear that's where the fae live."

Jasper bursts out laughing, a loud, unrestrained bark of amusement. I see Theo's lips twitch, the corner of his mouth curling into a condescending smirk.

"What?" she asks, looking between them, her brow furrowed in confusion.

"Sweetheart," Theo says, his voice laced with the patronizing tone he reserves for explaining things he deems obvious. "The fae live all over Europe, not just the Isle of Skye. But yes, they do have a rather large settlement there."

Willow stares at him, her mouth slightly agape. The cogs in her brain are turning, and I can almost feel her disbelief through the bond. "Wait… what? They're… real? Like, really real?"

"Sweetheart," Jasper says, slinging an arm around her

shoulder and pulling her into a one-armed hug. "Vampires are not the only thing that walked out of a fiction novel. All myths, all legends, they all came from a kernel of truth. Werewolves, witches, shifters… you name it, they're probably out there somewhere, trying to pay their taxes."

Her face is a perfect picture of utter, gobsmacked shock. Her eyes are wide, her jaw is slack, and she looks between the three of us as if seeing us for the first time. The gravity of finding our mortal enemy, the man who tortured her, is completely lost, overshadowed by this new revelation.

"So… you're telling me," she says slowly, her voice a hushed whisper, "that fairies… are real?"

I can't help it. A low chuckle escapes me. We are on the brink of war, our reinforcements are on their way, and our mortal enemy is finally within our grasp. And all Willow can think about is Tinker Bell.

CHAPTER 44

JASPER

I'm sitting on the top step of the grand stone staircase that leads to our front door, an amused jailer to the most inquisitive, infuriating, and incredible woman I've ever known. It was her idea, of course. The moment Theo mentioned the other board members were arriving, her eyes lit up with a mischievous glint I'm coming to recognize as the precursor to chaos.

"We should wait for them outside!" she had declared, her hands clasped together with mock seriousness. "Like bellboys! We can take their coats and everything. It'll be a whole vibe."

Theo had just grunted and walked away, which is his version of a resounding 'no.' Oscar had twitched, probably imagining the horror of Willow manhandling a priceless cashmere overcoat. But me? I just laughed. An hour of sitting out here, breathing fresh air and listening to the beautiful, chaotic symphony of her thoughts was infinitely more appealing than sitting in Theo's stuffy office while he paced and brooded.

So here we are. And she has not stopped talking for a solid forty-five minutes. The revelation that the supernatural world is more than just vampires has completely short-circuited her brain. It's like watching a kid on Christmas morning who just found out Santa Claus also brought a puppy, a unicorn, and a lifetime supply of chocolate.

"Okay, so fae," she says, her legs swinging as she sits beside me, her voice full of a breathless, academic curiosity. "Do they have wings? LikeLike gossamer, sparkly wings? Or are they more like… moth wings? And are they tiny? Like, small enough to live in a flower? Or are they human-sized? And the whole 'granting wishes' thing — is that real? Because I have a few notes. And what about werewolves? Do they only turn on a full moon, or can they just do it whenever they get angry? Like the Hulk, but with more fur and less green. And do they have to be naked? Because that seems impractical, especially in winter."

I just listen, a slow grin spreading across my face. I'm not even trying to answer anymore. I just let the questions wash over me, loving the curiosity that is so uniquely her. She finally pauses, taking a deep breath, and turns to look at me, her eyes wide and shining.

"And you guys," she says, poking me in the arm. "Vampires. I have so many questions. Like, the food thing. You all eat all the time. What's up with that? I thought vampires just drank blood. Is food like a hobby for you?"

I can't help it. I burst out laughing, a loud, genuine bark of amusement that echoes in the quiet evening. "A hobby?" I shake my head, still chuckling. "Sweetheart, you have no idea."

"Well, explain it to me!" she demands, her voice full of indignant curiosity. "It doesn't make any sense. You drink blood for sustenance. so where does the sandwich go?"

I lean back on my elbows, enjoying this far too much. "Okay, think of it this way. We're not dead. We're just… paused. Our bodies are pretty much still human, just operating on a different power source. The blood is the electricity. It keeps the lights on, stops the aging process, gives us our strength and speed. But the house itself? The plumbing, the wiring, the foundation… that's all still there. It still needs maintenance."

She stares at me, her brow furrowed in concentration. "So, the food is… maintenance?"

"Exactly," I say, pointing at her. "We still have human needs. We still get hungry for real food. We still have to… you know." I wiggle my eyebrows suggestively. "Process it."

Her eyes go wide. "No," she whispers, a look of horrified fascination on her face. "You don't."

"Oh, we do," I say, grinning. "We still have to take a shit, sweetheart. The plumbing still works; it just works forever. Immortality isn't all brooding in castles and wearing velvet. Sometimes, it's just taking a really, really long dump."

She stares at me for a solid ten seconds, her mouth opening and closing like a fish, before she bursts out laughing, a loud, beautiful peal of laughter that makes my chest feel warm. "Oh my God," she gasps, wiping a tear from her eye. "You're telling me that Theo… that grumpy, terrifying, thousand-year-old vampire king… poops?"

"Like a champion," I confirm with a solemn nod. "It's the great equalizer."

She's still giggling when a more serious thought seems to strike her. The laughter fades, replaced by a somber, thoughtful expression. "You said… immortality," she says softly, her voice losing its playful edge. "But you're not. Not really. Caleb… he's dead."

The name hangs in the air between us, a ghost of a memory. My own smile fades. I reach out, taking her hand in mine, my thumb tracing circles on her soft skin. "You're right," I say, my voice quieter now. "Immortal isn't the right word. We can be killed. It's just… difficult."

"How?" she asks, her gaze intense, her mind clearly filing this away as crucial, life-or-death information. Because it is.

"Two ways," I say, meeting her gaze and holding it, wanting her to understand the gravity of this. "Decapitation is the first. A clean cut, severing the head from the body. That's permanent. The other is fire. Not just a little bit of fire, but a complete immolation. Burned to ash. That's it. Nothing else works. A stake through the heart will paralyze us, sure. It's incredibly painful, and I don't recommend it, but it won't kill us. Sunlight is an annoyance, not a death sentence. But lose your head, or get turned into a pile of dust, and it's game over."

She's quiet for a long moment, processing this. I can feel the shift in her thoughts, the playful curiosity replaced by a cold, hard pragmatism. She's thinking about Edmund. About the fight to come. About what it will take to end him for good.

"Good to know," she says finally, her voice firm, a new

resolve in her eyes. She squeezes my hand, a silent thank you for the grim lesson.

Before I can reply, the sound of tires crunching on the gravel driveway cuts through the evening quiet. A pair of sleek, black cars, their headlights cutting through the twilight, pull up to the front of the house. Showtime. Willow immediately straightens up, a bright, excited grin spreading across her face. She hops to her feet, brushing off her pants, ready to play her self-appointed role as official greeter.

The first car, a gleaming black Rolls-Royce, pulls to a smooth stop. A driver in a crisp black uniform gets out and opens the rear passenger door. A man and a woman emerge, both exuding an aura of old-world power and elegance. Thomas, with his impeccably tailored suit, looks every bit the ancient, formidable vampire he is. Isabella, his wife, is a vision in a deep crimson dress, her hair swept up in an elegant chignon. They are the picture of vampiric aristocracy.

Willow, however, is completely unfazed. She practically bounces on the balls of her feet, waving enthusiastically. "Hello!" she calls out, her voice bright and cheerful. "Welcome! so glad you could make it! Can I take your coat? Or your bag? Whatever you've got."

Thomas raises a silver eyebrow, a flicker of amusement in his otherwise stoic expression. Isabella just smiles, a slow, knowing smile that says she's seen it all. "Jasper," Thomas says, his voice a low, smooth baritone as he nods at me. "Good to see you."

"You too, Thomas. Isabella," I say, rising to my feet. "Theo's inside, in the boardroom. He's expecting you."

They nod and sweep past us, their movements fluid and graceful, and disappear into the house. As the second car, a sleek black Bentley, pulls up, Willow turns to me, her eyes wide with a new kind of awe.

The driver opens the door, and two more women emerge. Edith and Yvonne. And they are a sight to behold. Edith is wearing a stunning floor-length emerald green gown that shimmers in the twilight. Yvonne is in a chic black pantsuit that looks like it was sewn onto her body, her hair cut in a sharp modern bob. They look less like they're here for a war council and more like they're about to walk a red carpet.

Willow lets out a low, appreciative whistle. "Man," she says, her eyes raking over their outfits. "I should be buying clothes like this." She looks down at her own outfit—a simple pair of black slacks and a silk blouse. It's the most dressed up I've seen her since she arrived, but next to them, she looks like a stable hand.

"You know you can get whatever you want, sweetheart," I say, nudging her with my elbow. "Oscar's credit card has no limit. You could buy a small country if you wanted to."

"Oh, I know," she says, a slow, dangerous smile spreading across her face. "I just didn't think I could be walking around in ball gowns instead of pants. But I'm gonna fix that. Immediately."

"Do you know how many skirts are in a ball gown?" I ask, leaning closer, my voice a low, teasing purr in her ear. "I'll get lost under there trying to find the honey pot."

She laughs, a bright, beautiful sound that makes my

chest ache. "I'm most definitely buying one now," she says, giving me a playful shove.

I just grin, shaking my head as I turn to greet the newcomers. "Edith. Yvonne. Good to see you." I gesture to the woman beside me. "This is Willow."

Edith's eyes land on Willow, and her face breaks into a wide, friendly smile. "Oh, you look like fun," she says, her voice a throaty, infectious laugh. She hooks her arm through Willow's, pulling her into an impromptu side-hug. "Come on, let's go find the others. I'm dying for a drink, and I have a feeling you have stories to tell."

And just like that, Willow is swept away, chattering excitedly as Edith leads her into the house. I watch them go, a fond smile on my face. This war council is about to get a lot more interesting. I follow them inside, ready for the chaos.

CHAPTER 45

THEODORE

The boardroom table — a single, massive slab of polished obsidian — is covered in the artifacts of war. Satellite images of the Scottish Highlands, architectural blueprints of Edmund's manor that Oscar has already rendered, and personnel files on every known associate of our enemy.

The door opens, and they begin to filter in. Thomas and Isabella enter first, a silent, united front. They nod at me, their expressions grim and resolute. Then comes the chaos. Jasper saunters in with Yvonne, a cocky grin on his face, followed by Edith, who has Willow tucked under her arm as if she's a new, fascinating accessory. They are whispering and giggling like schoolgirls, and a muscle in my jaw tightens. This is a war council, not a tea party. Oscar is the last to enter, his presence a calming, orderly balm to the chaotic energy the others have brought with them. He gives me a subtle nod, and I know everything is in place.

"Sit," I command, my voice cutting through the low

chatter. The room falls silent, and they take their seats. Willow, looking small and out of place in her simple blouse, is seated between Edith and Jasper, who immediately throws a casual arm over the back of her chair. I file away my annoyance for later. "Let's get right to business. The sooner we have a concrete plan, the sooner we can eat and rest."

A few appreciative smiles flicker around the table. I point to a large crystal pitcher filled with a deep ruby-red liquid sitting in the center of the table. "There is blood for those who need it."

Yvonne, ever the pragmatist, pours herself and Edith a glass. She takes a delicate sip, and her nose wrinkles in distaste. "Bagged, Theodore? Really? I would have preferred something… fresh."

"We no longer keep a fresh supply," I state, my voice flat and devoid of apology. "Our needs have changed."

"Changed how?" Edith asks, her curiosity piqued.

I glance at Oscar and Jasper, a silent acknowledgment passing between us. "Since bonding with Willow, we find we can only tolerate her blood. Anything else," I say, gesturing to the pitcher, "tastes like ash. It provides the necessary nutrients, but it offers no satisfaction."

A ripple of surprise goes through the room. Yvonne and Edith look at Willow with a new, calculating interest. But it is Thomas who speaks, a slow, knowing smile spreading across his face. "Yes," he says, his eyes finding Isabella's. "We know the feeling well."

Every head in the room snaps in their direction. "What?" Jasper asks, voicing the question on everyone's mind.

Isabella lays a hand on Thomas's arm, her smile serene. "Thomas and I are mates," she says simply, as if announcing the weather. "We have been for over a century. We just never saw the need to make it public knowledge."

The revelation hangs in the air, a stunning, game-changing piece of information. It explains their unwavering unity, their silent communication, their shared strength. It also solidifies their position as our most powerful allies.

My attention is drawn back to Willow. She's whispering something to Edith, her shoulders shaking with silent laughter. A hot spike of irritation lances through me. She is in a room full of ancient, powerful vampires discussing the downfall of our greatest enemy, and she is giggling. I focus on her, letting my thoughts slide into her mind, a low, intimate whisper only she can hear. *They're all looking at you, little bird. They're all wondering what you taste like. But only I know. Only I know how you scream when you come apart.*

Her back goes ramrod straight. The laughter dies on her lips, and a deep, furious blush creeps up her neck, painting her cheeks a delightful shade of crimson. She doesn't look at me, but I feel her indignant thought like a slap. *Stop it, you asshole. I'm trying to have a conversation.*

I just smirk. My point has been made. She belongs to us, and I will not have her distracted.

"Now," I say, turning my attention back to the table. "The plan." I lay it out for them, my voice cold and precise. I point to the blueprints, detailing the entry points, the guard rotations, and the location of Edmund's private quarters. "We will strike at nightfall. A full frontal assault. No subtlety, no subterfuge. We overwhelm them with sheer brute force. We go in, we kill everyone who stands in our way, and we end Edmund. Permanently."

"A frontal assault is risky, Theodore," Thomas says, his voice a low, thoughtful rumble. "Oscar's scans gave us an estimate of the guards, but there could be more. Hidden ones."

"Let them come," I counter, my voice flat and final. "We have the element of surprise and superior force. We go in hard and fast; they won't have time to react."

"The west wing," Yvonne interjects, tapping a long, manicured finger on the blueprint. "Oscar's layout shows it has fewer exit points. If we can corner him there, he'll have nowhere to run."

"I can create a diversion?" Jasper offers, leaning forward, his usual playful demeanor replaced by a sharp, predatory focus. "Draw their attention while the rest of you breach the west wing."

"Good," I say, with a grim satisfaction settling over me.

A soft, respectful knock sounds at the boardroom door. "Enter," I call out, not taking my eyes off the map.

The door opens and George, our long-serving and only on-hand human helper, enters. He is an elderly man; his movements slow but deliberate, and he pushes a large, heated trolley before him. The scent of roasted meat and fresh herbs fills the air, a stark contrast to the sterile scent of war planning.

"Dinner is served, sir," he says, his voice a low, respectful murmur.

He moves around the table with a quiet efficiency that comes from decades of service, placing a plate in front of each of us. A plate is set in front of Willow, a perfectly cooked steak resting on a bed of watercress salad. She looks down at it, her eyes wide with appreciation, and as she takes the first bite, a low, involuntary moan escapes her lips. It's a soft, sensual sound that makes my cock stir.

If you make that sound again, little mouse, I will bend you over this table and fuck you right here, in front of everyone.

Oscar's thought — a clean, sharp, and utterly filthy promise — slices through my own haze. I watch as Willow freezes, her fork halfway to her mouth. A new wave of colour, even deeper than before, floods her face. She shoots a panicked, flustered look at Oscar, who just gives her a slow, deliberate wink before taking a calm, composed bite of his own steak. My smirk widens. It seems I'm not the only one who enjoys playing with our new toy.

CHAPTER 46

WILLOW

The heavy oak door of the boardroom clicks shut behind me, and I let out a breath I didn't realize I was holding. The air in the hallway feels lighter, cleaner, free from the suffocating weight of war planning and centuries-old politics. One minute, you're learning that fairies are real, and the next, you're listening to a detailed, step-by-step plan for a supernatural special-ops mission to decapitate your kidnapper. It's a lot to process. My brain feels like a browser with way too many tabs open. Not to mention the fact that Oscar seems to think we will just teleport there and back… I mean, shit, he has gotten so good at it now, but all 8 of us?

Theo's final words echo in my mind: "Get some rest. We move at sundown." Rest. It's like seven am right now, and the morning light is streaming through the windows. I miss having a routine. But before I sleep, before we go to war, I need to wash the day away. I need to soak until my skin turns pruney and my mind goes blissfully, wonderfully blank.

My room is a sanctuary, a quiet haven in this castle of beautiful, dangerous men. I bypass the enormous, cloud-like bed and head straight for the adjoining bathroom, a cavernous space of marble and gold that would make a Roman emperor weep with envy. I turn the taps, the sound of rushing water a soothing balm to my frayed nerves, and pour a generous amount of lavender-scented oil into the tub. Steam begins to fill the air, thick with the calming, floral scent.

I strip off my clothes—the simple blouse and slacks that felt so inadequate earlier—and sink into the scalding water with a sigh of pure bliss. The heat seeps into my bones, and I let my head fall back against the cool tub, my eyes drifting shut. For a few precious moments, there is nothing. No Edmund, no war council, no telepathic chatter. Just the water, the steam, and the scent of lavender.

It doesn't last, of course. The door to the bathroom opens without a knock, a silent, arrogant entrance that could only belong to one person. I don't even have to open my eyes. "Privacy is a concept, you know," I murmur, my voice lazy with contentment. "You should look it up."

"Everything in this castle is mine," Theo's voice, a low rumble, answers from beside the tub. "That includes your privacy."

I open my eyes to find him looming over me, a dark, imposing silhouette against the steam-filled air. He crouches down, his knees cracking in a surprisingly human way, and his intense gaze rakes over me, taking in my exposed shoulders, the curve of my neck, the way my hair is beginning to curl in the humidity. He reaches out, his fingers tracing the line of my collarbone, his touch sending a shiver through the warm water. He leans in and presses his lips to mine, a slow, deliberate kiss that is not a request, but a claiming. It's a reminder that even in my sanctuary, I am his. He pulls back, his thumb brushing against my lower lip, before he stands and leaves as silently as he arrived.

I'm still trying to get my heart rate back to normal when the door opens again. This time, there's a playful, jaunty rhythm to the footsteps. "Room for one more?" Jasper asks, his voice full of a cheeky, infectious grin. He's leaning against the doorframe, his arms crossed over his chest, his eyes filled with mischief.

"In your dreams, sparkly," I shoot back, though I can't help the smile that spreads across my face.

He just chuckles and walks over, perching on the edge of the tub. He dips his fingers in the water, his expression turning more serious. "You doing okay?" he asks, his voice softer now. "That was… a lot."

I just nod, my throat suddenly tight. He leans in, but his kiss is completely different from Theo's. It's soft, gentle, a sweet, reassuring pressure that speaks of comfort and affection. It's a question, and I answer by leaning into it, a silent thank you for his concern.

He pulls away with a wink. "Don't worry, I'll keep you safe tonight." He gets up to leave, and as he does, he passes Oscar in the doorway.

Oscar enters, his presence a calm, steadying force. He offers me a small, warm smile. "I trust the bath is to your liking; I had the cupboards filled with salts and oils," he asks, ever the perfect host.

"I noticed. Thank you," I say, my voice thick with an emotion I can't quite name.

He kneels beside the tub, his movements graceful and precise. "I had some things brought up for you," he says softly. "Jasper mentioned you liked something...." He leans in and gives me a chaste, tender kiss on the forehead, a gesture so full of care it makes my heart ache. "Get some rest, little mouse."

As he leaves, Jasper reappears, dragging a large wooden crate into my bedroom. "What is that?" I call out, my curiosity piqued.

"Presents!" he calls back, the sound of him setting it down echoing into the bathroom. "From Oscar. He's a keeper."

I soak for a few more minutes, my mind a swirl of kisses, gentle reassurances, and the mystery of the wooden crate. Finally, the water begins to cool, and I pull myself out, wrapping a thick, fluffy towel around my body. I pad into the bedroom, ready to investigate Oscar's "presents," but I stop dead in the doorway.

The crate sits in the corner, unopened. But it's not the crate that has my attention. It's the bed. My bed. All three of them are there. Theo, Jasper, and Oscar. They are sitting on my bed, their backs against the headboard, waiting for me. And they are all shirtless.

My breath catches in my throat. I've seen them shirtless before, even ran my hands all over those tattoos, but sitting there like this..... Not all at once, laid out before me like a feast. And it's not just the sculpted chests and the corded muscles that have me frozen in place. It's the ink. They are covered in it. From their necks to their toes, there is barely an inch of unadorned skin.

I clutch the towel tighter around myself, my knuckles white. "What… is this?" I finally manage to ask, my voice a hoarse whisper. My question is met with a low, rumbling chorus of chuckles. They knew exactly what they were doing. They knew the effect this would have on me.

Oscar slides off the bed, his movements fluid and predatory. He prowls toward me, his eyes never leaving mine, and my heart begins to hammer against my ribs. He stops just before me, close enough that I can feel the heat radiating from his skin. He reaches out, not to touch me, but to grab one of his own oversized t-shirts from a nearby chair. With a slow, deliberate movement, he pulls the soft cotton shirt over my head, the fabric falling to my mid-thighs. Only then, once I am covered, does he reach behind me and tug the towel free, letting it fall to the floor.

"We are going to watch television," he says, his voice a low, soothing murmur that is completely at odds with the hungry look in his eyes. "And then we are going to sleep. All of us. Together." He leans in, his lips brushing against my ear. "And don't worry, little mouse. We won't fuck you." My body gives an involuntary twitch of disappointment, and he chuckles, a low, knowing sound. "Oh no," he whispers, his hand coming up to cup my jaw, his thumb stroking my cheek. "We'll do that when we get back from ridding the world of Edmund. Call it a treat. A reward for winning this two-hundred-year-old battle."

His words, the promise in them, sends a shiver through me. I reach out, my hand trembling slightly, and press my palm flat against his chest. The skin is warm, the muscles beneath it hard as stone, and the intricate, inked lines of his tattoos feel like a living, breathing texture beneath my fingertips. I trace one of the geometric patterns, my fingers following the perfect, precise lines that disappear under the waistband of his pants. "How is it," I ask, my voice barely a whisper, "that you are all built like this? Like… like Greek gods fell out of the sky and landed in my bedroom."

"You like, baby?" Jasper calls from the bed, flexing his biceps in a ridiculous, over-the-top pose. The swirling patterns on his arm seem to ripple and flow with the movement.

"It's like a dream," I breathe, my eyes still fixed on the masterpiece that is Oscar's torso.

"We worked hard before we were turned," Theo says, his voice a deep, rumbling baritone that draws my attention. "Just be thankful we weren't turned with big bellies and skinny legs, my love. This is forever."

My head snaps up, my eyes finding his. "So your bodies… they don't change? At all? Once you're turned?"

"No, my love," he says, a faint, almost imperceptible sadness in his eyes. "This is what we looked like two hundred years ago."

The weight of that, of two centuries trapped in the same form, hits me with a surprising force. There are so many stories, so much history, etched into their skin and their souls. "One day," I say, my voice soft but firm, "I want to hear the whole story. How you were changed. And why?"

"We can do story time, or we can do movie time," Jasper says, patting the space on the bed between him and Theo. "It's up to you, sweetheart."

The choice is easy. My brain is too full, my body too tired, my emotions too raw for a history lesson right now. I need… nothing. I need to be surrounded by them, to feel their warmth and their strength, and to let my mind go quiet. I walk to the bed, and they part for me, creating a space in the very center. I crawl in, the crisp, cool sheets a welcome shock against my skin. I snuggle down, my head finding a home on Theo's chest, my legs tangling with Jasper's, and my hand finding Oscar's as he settles in beside me. The remote is pressed into my hand.

"Mind-numbing television, please," I murmur, my voice already thick with sleep. And as the first flickering images of some mindless reality show light up the screen, surrounded by the three most dangerous, beautiful, and tattooed men I have ever known, I finally, finally, let myself rest.

CHAPTER 47

OSCAR

I wake to a feeling of profound, unprecedented peace. For the first time in two centuries, my world is perfectly ordered, but it has nothing to do with polished surfaces. It is the woman sleeping soundly in the center of the bed, her head pillowed on Theo's chest, her leg thrown casually over Jasper, who is wrapped around her legs like a boa constrictor. It is the steady, synchronized rhythm of their breathing that I can feel against me. My arm is curled around her waist, and the simple, profound rightness of it settles a deep, abiding calm in my soul. This, I realize, is what true order feels like. This is what holding your soul mate feels like when the world is quiet, and all that's left is the simple things.

The sun has set, and the room is bathed in the soft, dim light of evening. It is time. The peace is a fleeting, precious thing, and the reality of what we are about to do descends like a shroud. I gently extricate myself from the tangle of limbs, my movements slow and silent so as not to wake them. I need a moment to prepare, not just for battle, but to ensure our most precious asset is properly equipped.

I retrieve the items I had delivered, and lay them out for everyone. For myself, Theo, and Jasper, it is simple: black tactical pants, black long-sleeved shirts of a durable, flexible material, and combat boots. But for Willow, I have been more careful. Black cargo-style pants made of a soft, silent fabric. A fitted, high-necked top. And soft-soled boots that will allow for silent movement. It is a uniform for a soldier, a shadow, and the sight of it, so stark and utilitarian, feels wrong in this soft light blue painted room with pink accents. But it is necessary.

I turn back to the bed to find her stirring, her eyes fluttering open. She blinks, a slow, sleepy smile gracing her lips as she takes in the sight of us. "Morning," she mumbles, her voice thick with sleep.

"Evening, actually," Jasper corrects, stretching like a lazy cat. "Time to go kill a monster."

"Right. That." She sits up, running a hand through her tangled hair. Her eyes land on the outfit I've laid out for her, and a slow, mischievous grin spreads across her face. "Ooh, are we playing dress-up?"

She hops out of bed, completely unselfconscious in my oversized t-shirt, and pads over to the clothes. She holds up the blacktop, her expression turning from amused to downright gleeful. "I'll look like a ninja," she declares, her voice full of a sudden, energetic excitement.

She quickly shimmies out of my shirt and pulls on the tactical gear. It fits her perfectly. Once dressed, she strikes a ridiculous pose, her hands held up in a clumsy approximation of a karate chop. "Hiiii-ya!" she whisper-shouts before dissolving into a fit of giggles. She starts doing a series of clumsy, exaggerated ninja moves around the room, complete with sound effects. It is the most absurd, most endearing, and most inappropriate thing I have ever seen, and I find myself smiling, a genuine, fond smile that reaches my eyes.

"Before you go on your secret mission to assassinate the dust bunnies," I say, my voice laced with amusement, "there is one more thing." I gesture to the large wooden crate that has been sitting in the corner of her room since this morning. "For you."

Her ninja act ceases immediately, her curiosity piqued. She approaches the crate, her brow furrowed. "What is it?"

"Open it," I say softly.

She kneels down and, with a bit of effort, pries the lid open. She peers inside, and then she freezes. A soft, sharp intake of breath is the only sound she makes. Slowly, reverently, she reaches in and lifts out a cascade of deep sapphire-blue silk. It is a ball gown, a stunning creation from the Roman era, with a corseted bodice, intricate beadwork, and a full, sweeping skirt. It is in perfect, pristine condition, as beautiful today as it was over two centuries ago.

"Oscar…" she breathes, her voice full of a wonder so profound it makes my chest ache. "What is this?"

"They were my mother's," I say, my voice quieter than I intend. "I have kept them in storage. I thought… you mentioned to Jasper you wanted to wear ball gowns around the castle. I can have them tailored to fit you, if you'd like."

She looks up at me, her eyes shining with unshed tears.

She is speechless. She gently places the blue gown back in the crate and pulls out another, this one a deep emerald green velvet, and another, a soft buttery yellow satin. They are a treasure trove of a bygone era, a collection of memories from a life I have long since left behind. And now, they are hers.

"Thank you," she whispers, her voice thick with emotion. She looks from the gowns to me, and the gratitude in her eyes is a gift more precious than any jewel.

Her attention, however, is fleeting. The solemnity of the moment is broken as she looks down at her all-black outfit and then back at the gowns. A wicked grin spreads across her face. "So, I can be a princess by day, and a ninja by night?" She asks before launching back into her ridiculous martial arts routine. "Best of both worlds!"

She does a clumsy spinning kick that almost sends her toppling over, and I'm about to step in and steady her when Theo stands up from the bed and reaches out, making sure she does not fall.

Her eyes land on him, and without a moment's hesitation, she launches herself at him. "Ninja attack!" She yells, her voice full of playful glee.

She is a blur of black, a chaotic whirlwind of flailing limbs. But Theo doesn't even flinch. He moves with a speed that is almost too fast to see, his hand shooting out to catch her wrist, his other arm snaking around her waist. He uses her own momentum against her, spinning her around and pinning her against the nearest bedpost, her back flush against the cool, carved wood, her arms trapped above her head in his grip.

She is left breathless, her chest heaving, her eyes wide

with a mixture of shock and arousal. He leans in, his lips brushing against her ear, his voice a low, dangerous purr that sends a shiver down my own spine.

"Now that," he says, his voice thick with amusement and a dark promise, "was fun, little bird."

He doesn't release her. Instead, he lowers his head and captures her lips in a hard, punishing kiss. It is not a kiss of affection, but of ownership. A branding. He devours her, his mouth moving against hers with a hunger that makes my own blood heat. When he finally pulls back, she is dazed, her lips swollen and red, her eyes unfocused.

Theo steps back, a smug, satisfied smirk on his face, and I take his place. I walk toward her slowly, enjoying the way her eyes track my movement. I cup her face in my hands, my thumbs stroking the soft skin of her cheeks, and I give her the kiss Theo did not. It is a kiss of tenderness, of reassurance, of a love so deep it frightens me. I pour every ounce of my affection for this infuriating, incredible woman into it, and I feel her melt against the bedpost, a soft, contented sigh escaping her lips.

I pull away, and she blinks, her mind clearly reeling. "Now… um… what was I doing?" she asks, her voice a dazed, confused murmur.

I chuckle, a low, warm sound. "So, the best way to shut you up is to just kiss you?" I tease.

She purses her lips, a spark of her usual fire returning to her eyes as she glares at me. Before she can form a retort, Jasper, who has finally finished putting on his shirt, comes up behind her. He reaches around, his hand splaying across her stomach as he pulls from the bedpost and right back against his chest. His other hand comes up, his thumb and forefinger finding her nipple through the thin fabric of her top, and he rolls the hardening peak between his fingers.

"Now, now, my queen," he whispers in her ear, his voice a low, sultry purr. "Are you a little turned on?"

I watch her swallow hard, a visible gulp that betrays her arousal. He leans in, pressing a soft, lingering kiss to the side of her neck. "That's so unfair," she breathes, her voice shaky.

What's unfair, little mouse? I send the thought directly to her, enjoying the way her eyes dart to mine.

"It's three against one," she says out loud, her voice a frustrated whine. "I'm never going to win."

"You're not meant to win, little bird," Theo says from across the room, his voice a cold, hard statement of fact. "You're meant to submit."

Jasper chuckles, his breath warm against her ear, and I can feel the satisfaction humming from all three of us through the bond. The moment is thick with tension, with promises of what is to come after this night is over. And then, the spell is broken. A sharp, insistent ringing cuts through the air. My phone.

I sigh and pull it from my pocket. "We have to go," I say, my voice clipped and all business. The good mood evaporates, replaced by the cold, hard reality of our mission.

"Oh, that's right," Jasper says, releasing Willow and stepping back. "We're killing a monster." He claps his hands together. "Okay, okay, serious mode." He quickly pulls on his boots, his movements now sharp and efficient.

Theo turns to me, his expression grim. "You're sure you can teleport all of us?"

I meet his gaze, my own resolve hardening. "I know I can easily do two at a time," I reply, my mind already running through the logistics. "If it comes to it, I'll make two trips. We're not leaving anyone behind."

CHAPTER 48

WILLOW

The lounge room is a sea of black. It's like a casting call for a spy movie, and I am absolutely living for it. Everyone is dressed head-to-toe in tactical gear, a silent, deadly army ready for war. And my kings... my God, my kings look like sin. The tight, long-sleeved shirts they're wearing cling to every corded muscle, every hard plane of their chests and arms, leaving absolutely nothing to the imagination. The intricate lines of their tattoos peek out from the neck and hands, and I have the sudden, overwhelming urge to trace every single one of them with my tongue.

Down, kitten, Theo's voice, a low, amused purr, slides into my mind, and I jump. *I'll let you lick me when this is over.*

My face flames, and I shoot a glare in his direction. He's standing by the fireplace, looking utterly relaxed and impossibly arrogant, a faint smirk playing on his lips. *Stay out of my head,* I think, as forcefully as I can. His smirk widens, and he lets out a soft, audible chuckle that makes my stomach do a little flip.

Edith, Yvonne, Thomas, and Isabella are standing together, a formidable, silent group. All eyes are on Oscar, who stands in the center of the room, his expression a mixture of intense concentration and nervous energy. He's going to try to teleport all of us—all eight of us—at once. He is bloody insane.

"I normally hold hands when I do this," he says, his voice a little tight. He looks around at the assembled group. "I think… I think everyone needs to be touching me in some way."

Immediately, they close in. Thomas places a firm hand on Oscar's shoulder. Isabella rests her hand on Thomas's, creating a chain. Edith and Yvonne each take one of his arms. Jasper comes up behind him, placing both hands on his back. They form a tight, interconnected circle around him. He looks at me, his dark eyes finding mine across the room. "Little mouse," he says, his voice soft but firm, holding out his free hand. "You come and hug me. I'm not losing you."

"Nice to know where the rest of us stand," Edith mutters, a dry, amused tone in her voice.

I don't hesitate. I walk into the circle, right up to Oscar, and wrap my arms around his waist, pressing myself against his front and resting my head on his chest. I can feel the hard plains of his chest on my ear. I am surrounded by him, by his scent, by the solid, comforting feel of his body. The world outside our small, tight circle seems to fade away.

"Hold on," he says, his voice a low rumble against my ear.

And then the world dissolves. It's not like the other times I've teleported. It's not a gentle pop or a quick shimmer. It's a violent, wrenching sensation, like being turned inside out and squeezed through a keyhole. My stomach lurches, and a wave of nausea washes over me. The air is torn apart with a sound like ripping fabric, and for a split second, I am nowhere and everywhere at once. And then, just as suddenly as it began, it's over. My feet are on solid ground, the scent of pine and damp earth filling my lungs.

I stumble back as the circle breaks apart, my head spinning. The others seem equally disoriented, shaking their heads and blinking as they adjust. But Oscar... Oscar is in a bad way. He's panting, great, heaving gasps of air that seem to offer him no relief. He leans over, bracing his hands on his knees, his body trembling with the sheer effort of what he just did. "Shit," he gasps, his voice ragged. "That... that takes a lot out of you."

My heart clenches at the sight of him, so depleted and exhausted. Without thinking, I'm moving back toward him. I know what he needs. I need to help him. I need to fix this. I stand in front of him and hold out my arm, my wrist upturned, the pale, delicate skin of my pulse point exposed. "Top up," I say, my voice soft but firm.

He looks up at me, his eyes dark and glazed with a mixture of exhaustion and hunger that makes my breath catch. He doesn't hesitate. He straightens up, his hand closing around my wrist, his grip surprisingly strong. He pulls me toward him, his other arm snaking around my waist to hold me flush against his body. And then he bites.

The sharp, exquisite pain of his fangs sinking into my flesh makes me gasp, my back arching. He pulls me even closer, his mouth hot and wet against my skin, and I moan, a low, guttural sound that is lost against his chest. I can feel him drinking, the gentle, rhythmic pull a strange, intoxicating sensation. I can feel his strength returning with every swallow, the tremors in his body beginning to subside. He takes a few deep pulls, and then he stops. He releases my wrist, his tongue darting out to lick the wound, the tingling sensation of his saliva healing the broken skin instantly. He looks down at me, his eyes clear and sharp again.

"You're mine, little mouse," he whispers, his voice a low growl.

A dazed, happy smile spreads across my face. I reach up, my hand cupping his cheek, my thumb stroking the skin there. "You're mine," I whisper back, my voice full of a certainty that settles deep in my soul.

The moment is intimate, perfect, a bubble of peace in a world on the brink of war. And then, the bubble pops.

"Well, that's all well and good," Thomas says, his voice a dry, impatient rasp that cuts through the quiet clearing. "But we are here for a reason."

And just like that, the spell is broken. Theo gathers us all in a huddle, his voice low and urgent, and I suddenly feel like I'm in a heist movie. All we're missing is a whiteboard, and some cool codenames. I call dibs on 'Nightshade.'

"Alright, everyone. Stick to the plan we laid out before," Theo says, his voice all business. "Willow, you're with me, Thomas, and Yvonne. We'll take the left side.

Oscar, Isabella, Jasper, and Edith - you guys are on distraction duty. Remember, timing is everything. Let's do this."

I nod, swallowing hard as I look through the bushes at the manor. It's a carbon copy of the one I spent the last Three years in. A few lights flicker inside, casting eerie shadows that dance across the lawn like drunken ghosts. My mind races with a delightful cocktail of adrenaline-fueled excitement and pants-shitting terror. I focus on my breathing, trying to stay calm. It's just a casual evening of storming a manor and killing a two-hundred-year-old vampire. Totally normal Tuesday.

"Willow," Theo whispers, placing a hand on my shoulder. "Nothing will happen to you." I meet his gaze, our eyes locking for a moment, and I see a flicker of something in their depths, fear maybe. Then, just as quickly as it appeared, it's gone, replaced by the familiar mask of command. "Okay, let's move out," he says, breaking our trance.

As we sneak around the left side of the manor, I feel the ground beneath me shift slightly. My boots sink into the damp earth, the scent of wet grass and decaying leaves filling my nostrils. I am acutely aware of every sound, every rustle of leaves, every breath that escapes my lips. Focusing on all this is keeping my anxiety in check. It's either that or start singing show tunes, and I don't think Theo would appreciate a rousing rendition of 'Defying Gravity' right now.

My eyes flit between the manor and the team as we inch closer to our target. I can't help but think about what awaits us inside—the danger, the unknown. But deep down, I know we're ready for whatever Edmund has in store. I'm not the same girl who was dragged out of a cellar … I'm a ninja now. A ninja with a support team of super-hot, ancient vampires. The odds are definitely in my favor.

"Hey," Yvonne whispers, her breath hot against my ear as we crouch behind a large, ornate fountain. "We got this, right?"

"Damn right we do," I reply, a surge of genuine confidence building within me. "He's not walking away from this. Not this time."

As I watch Oscar, Isabella, Jasper, and Edith melt into the shadows on the right side of the manor, a tingling sensation runs down my spine. They're going to be the distractions, drawing attention away from our side as we make our move. I can't help but feel a mixture of fear and excitement. I hope Jasper does something flashy. He's got a flair for the dramatic.

"Are you ready for this?" Theo whispers in my ear, his breath warm on my neck.

"Yes," I reply, trying to sound more confident than I feel.

The quiet of the forest is shattered by a deafening explosion from the right side of the manor, followed by a series of bloodcurdling screams. Jasper is not a subtle man. I grin. Showtime.

"Alright, let's do this," Yvonne says, her eyes narrowing with determination. We all nod in agreement, and I take one last deep breath before following her lead.

As we round the corner of the manor, they are already there, a welcoming committee of about a dozen vampires, their faces twisted in ugly, feral snarls. They look less like the sophisticated, ancient beings I've come to know and more like rabid animals. My job is to stay out of the way. To be the precious cargo they're all protecting. I hate it.

"Here they come," Thomas whispers, his voice tense.

"Get ready," I say, my voice a squeak. My heart is pounding in my chest, and I press myself back against the cold stone wall of the manor, trying to make myself as small as possible.

Think of me when you're hiding back there, sweetheart. Jasper's voice, a low, sultry purr, slides into my mind, completely out of place in the middle of this chaos. *Think of all the ways I'm going to find you when we get home.*

A hot blush creeps up my neck, and I shoot a glare in the general direction of the explosion. *Not the time, Sparkly,* I think, as forcefully as I can.

As the first vampire charges at our group, I focus, trying to do something. I extend my hands and concentrate on a loose cobblestone at the vampire's feet. It wobbles. It actually wobbles. The vampire stumbles, just for a second, but it's enough. Theo is there in a flash, his sword a blur of silver, and the vampire's head is rolling across the manicured lawn. It comes to a stop at the base of a ridiculously ornate birdbath. Classy.

"Nice one," I breathe, already scanning the ground for another loose rock. This is my contribution. I'm a professional tripper. The world's most well-protected telekinetic pebble-pusher.

"Shit, that's hot," Yvonne pants, her eyes glazed with a mixture of bloodlust and arousal as she decapitates another vampire with a flick of her wrist. "It's like a workout, but with more screaming."

"Stay focused," I whisper to myself, trying to ignore the intoxicating mix of danger and desire coursing through my own veins.

You're so beautiful when you're trying to be helpful, my love, Jasper's voice is back, a soft, intimate whisper in my mind. It's making me hard.

I lose my focus on the small rock I was trying to lift, and it clatters uselessly to the ground. A vampire, seeing an opening, breaks from the main fight and lunges for me. A scream catches in my throat, and I squeeze my eyes shut, bracing for the impact. But it never comes. There's a soft pop, and suddenly I'm ten feet to the left, stumbling into the side of a large, marble fountain. I look up to see Theo standing where I just was, his sword buried in the chest of my attacker.

"Sorry," I mutter, my heart hammering against my ribs. My teleportation is still more of a panic button than a skill. Theo just gives me a sharp, annoyed look before pulling his sword free and turning to the next enemy.

"Hey, fuckers!" he suddenly shouts, drawing the attention of the remaining minions. "Looking for a fight? You've got one!"

They charge at him, a wave of snarling, bloodthirsty rage. But Theo is a force of nature, a whirlwind of death and destruction. He moves with a lethal grace, his blade a blur of motion, and heads begin to fly.

"Keep 'em coming!" he yells, his eyes wild with the thrill of battle.

As the last of the guards fall, the sudden silence is

almost as jarring as the sounds of the fight. Theo stands in the center of the carnage, his chest heaving, his sword dripping with black, viscous blood. He looks at me, then at Thomas and Yvonne, and gives a sharp, decisive nod. It's time to go inside.

We slink through a side door, entering a long, dark hallway. The air is cold and still, the only sound the soft padding of our boots on the marble floor. We move like shadows, checking each room as we go. A dining room set for a banquet that will never happen. A ballroom, its crystal chandeliers dark and silent. A sitting room, the furniture covered in white sheets like a gallery of ghosts. The manor is empty — a hollow, lifeless shell.

Finally, we come to a set of large, oak doors at the end of a long hall. Theo pushes them open without a sound, and we step into a massive, two-story library. Books line the walls from floor to ceiling, and a large, roaring fire-place dominates one wall. And sitting in an opulent armchair in front of it, as if he's been waiting for us, is Edmund. He is smoking a pipe, with a faint, self-satisfied smile on his face as he watches the flames.

He doesn't even look at us as we enter. His icy blue eyes are fixed on me. "So," he says, his voice a languid, condescending drawl. "You bonded with them. All of them. Collecting kings now, are we?"

"It's over, Edmund," I say, my voice shaking slightly, but I hold his gaze, refusing to let him see my fear.

He just laughs, a low, humorless sound that echoes through the silent library. "Oh, my dear, sweet, naïve little bird," he says, finally turning his head to look at me fully. "It's only just begun."

As his eyes meet mine, the world seems to tilt on its axis. The fire in the fireplace leaps, it roars, it expands, consuming the room in a wave of impossible heat. The vision hits me. Fire. The manor exploding. Screams. The smell of burning wood and flesh. It's so real, so vivid, it steals the air from my lungs.

"Run!" I scream, my voice a raw, terrified shriek that cuts through the sudden tension in the room. "Everyone, get out of the house now!"

"What?" Theo asks, his face a mask of confusion. But he doesn't question me. He trusts me. He turns and bolts, the others following his lead without hesitation.

"Go, go, go!" I shout, pushing Yvonne and Thomas ahead of me as we sprint out of the manor. My heart is pounding, my breath coming in short, ragged gasps.

"Willow!" Theo yells, reaching back to grab my hand, his grip a solid, reassuring anchor in the chaos. The ground beneath us trembles, a low, ominous rumble that shakes me to my core.

Just as we clear the edge of the manor, a deafening blast erupts from within the manor. The force of the explosion propels us forward, sending us tumbling through the air. We hit the ground hard, a tangled mess of limbs and bodies, the sound of the manor collapsing in on itself echoing in our ears.

CHAPTER 49

JASPER

"Alright, Team Distraction," I say, rubbing my hands together with a grin. "Let's give them a show they'll never forget."

Oscar, Isabella, and Edith are crouched with me behind a ridiculously large, and frankly, quite ugly, cherub-themed fountain on the right side of the manor. The plan is simple: I make a very loud, very flashy entrance, and they provide backup, taking down anyone who comes to investigate. It's a role I was born to play.

"Just try not to level the entire forest, Jasper," Oscar mutters, adjusting the collar of his shirt. Even in the middle of a war zone, the man is obsessed with maintaining a perfect, wrinkle-free existence.

"No promises, Ozzy," I say with a wink. "I'm feeling creative."

I close my eyes, reaching out with my mind, my new, shiny telekinetic powers a live wire humming beneath my skin. I find what I'm looking for: a massive, ornate stone gargoyle perched on the corner of the roof, looking down at us with a smug, stony expression. Oh, you are perfect.

With a mental shove, I send it tumbling. It falls with a glorious crash, landing right in the center of a meticulously manicured rose garden. The sound is magnificent as it echoes through the quiet night. A few lights flicker on inside the manor. Showtime.

"That's our cue," Isabella says, her voice a low, dangerous purr.

We move, a blur of black against the moonlit lawn. The front doors of the manor burst open, and a half-dozen vampires pour out, their faces a mixture of confusion and rage. They see us, and they charge. The fight is a beautiful, brutal ballet. Isabella and Edith are a whirlwind, their blades singing through the air. Oscar is precise, dispatching his opponents with a clean, almost surgical efficiency. And me? I'm having the time of my life, using my powers to send stray bits of rubble, garden gnomes, and even a particularly unfortunate birdbath flying through the air, creating chaos and confusion. I'm a one-man wrecking crew, and it is glorious.

I'm in the middle of trying to levitate two vampires at once when it hits me. A raw, undiluted wave of pure terror that slams into my mind. It's Willow. And she is screaming.

Run!

The single silent word is a shard of ice in my brain. The playful energy, the thrill of the fight — it all evaporates in an instant. The two vampires I was holding drop to the ground, forgotten. Nothing matters but that single, terrified command.

"Everybody back!" I scream, my voice raw with a panic I don't have time to process. I spin on my heels and sprint back toward the relative safety of the forest, not even checking to see if they're following. I can feel their confusion, their questions, but there is no time.

"Jasper, what the fuck is going on?" Oscar yells, his voice tight with exertion as he keeps pace with me.

"Trust me!" I gasp out, the urgency in my voice unmistakable. We reach the tree line, diving into the relative cover of the bushes, and I have no time to explain further. The world ignites.

The manor erupts like a volcano. A deafening, soul-shattering blast rips through the night, and a wave of pure, searing heat slams into us, knocking us off our feet and hurling us backward into the brush. The world is a cacophony of sound and fury — the roar of the explosion, the splintering of wood, the shattering of stone. Debris rains down from the sky, hot and sharp, and the taste of ash and fear fills my mouth.

"Shit!" I curse, my ears ringing, my vision swimming. I struggle to my feet, my body a symphony of aches and pains that are already beginning to fade. "Is everyone okay?" I pant, my eyes frantically searching the darkness.

Oscar groans, pushing himself up from the dirt. He's covered in scratches, his perfect tactical shirt torn at the shoulder. He looks… disheveled. He is not going to be happy about that. Isabella is clutching her arm, a deep gash oozing crimson onto the forest floor before it slowly, stubbornly knits itself back together. Edith is on her hands and knees, shaking her head as if to clear it, but she seems otherwise unharmed.

"Who the hell did this? What happened?" Isabella demands, her voice a low, furious growl. The rage is practically rolling off her in waves.

"I don't know," I admit, my own anger and confusion bubbling to the surface. But beneath it, a cold, icy dread is beginning to form in the pit of my stomach. Willow was on the other side of that explosion. With Theo. The thought knocks the air from my lungs.

"We need to find Willow and the others," I say, my voice tight.

"Right." Oscar nods.

And then the dread gives way to pure panic. The kind that claws at your throat and squeezes your heart until you can't breathe. Willow. My Willow.

"Willow!" I scream, my voice hoarse with a desperation so profound it scares me. I stumble to my feet, ignoring the throbbing in my limbs, and sprint around the edge of the wreckage. The manor is gone, replaced by a twisted, skeletal ruin silhouetted against a backdrop of fire and smoke.

"Jasper, wait up!" Oscar calls out, but I can't slow down. I can't stop. Not now. Every second is an eternity. My legs burn, my lungs ache, but the thought of finding her, of seeing her, of touching her, is the only thing that matters. The world has narrowed to a single desperate need. Find her. Find her now.

"Fuck, fuck, fuck," I mutter, leaping over jagged rocks and dodging smouldering debris. Oscar's footsteps keep pace behind me, his own determination matching mine.

"Where is she?" I gasp, my eyes scanning the chaos for any sign of her. "Please let her be okay."

As we round the smoldering remains of the west wing, my heart seizes in my chest. There. A splash of black against the scorched earth. No, two splashes of black. My legs feel like lead, but I force them to move. As we get closer, the scene resolves into my worst nightmare. It's Theo, his body draped protectively over a smaller form. Willow.

"Willow!" I cry, my voice a raw, broken thing. I drop to my knees beside them, my hands shaking so violently I can barely control them. I gently, so gently, lift Theo's dead weight off her. He's unconscious, but he will heal. But Willow... she is bloody and motionless, her face pale and still beneath a mask of soot and grime.

"Jasper..." Theo whispers, his eyes fluttering open. "Save... Willow."

"Oscar, help me," I implore, tears blurring my vision as I carefully roll Willow onto her back. Her usually radiant face is marred with blood, her shallow breaths coming in ragged, hitching gasps. A piece of shrapnel is embedded in her abdomen, a dark, ugly wound that is bleeding sluggishly. She's dying. The word is a scream in my mind.

"Jesus Christ," Oscar breathes, his eyes wide with horror. "What do we do?"

"Willow, baby," I choke out, my heart breaking into a million pieces at the sight of her. I press my fingers to her neck, searching for a pulse. It's there, but it's faint, a butterfly's wing against my skin. "Stay with me. Please, baby, stay with me."

"Jasper," Theo murmurs, struggling to sit up. "We have to... turn her. It's the only way."

The words are a punch to the gut. "No!" I shout, the sound raw and animalistic. "We can't! We only make rogues, remember? Our line is cursed! I can't… I can't hunt down my own mate!" The thought is a physical agony, a vision of having to put down a feral, mindless version of the woman I love. It would destroy me. We learnt long, long ago our bite makes rouges, it's why we wrote the accords that all new vampires had to be recorded. We knew we cannot turn.

"Then what the fuck are we supposed to do, Jasper?" Oscar demands, his voice cracking with desperation. "Let her die?"

My mind races, scrambling for a solution, for any other option. And then, like a beacon in the darkness, a name comes to me. "Edith," I whisper, my head snapping up to look at her as she and the others arrive. She never turns humans, but hers are not rogue. "Edith can do it. She can save Willow."

I look at her, my eyes pleading, my soul laid bare. "Please, Edith," I beg, my voice cracking. "Change her for us. I can't… I can't hunt down and kill my own mate." My hands shake as I clutch at Willow's lifeless ones, praying for a miracle.

Edith looks from my desperate face to Willow's dying form, then to Oscar and Theo, who both nod their grim agreement. I see the conflict in her eyes, the weight of what I'm asking. But then it's gone, replaced with a smile and a simple single nod.

"Alright," she says softly, her gaze returning to mine. "I'll do it. I'll turn Willow."

A wave of relief so profound it almost brings me to my

knees washes over me. "Thank you, Edith," I whisper, my voice thick with unshed tears.

"Jasper, we don't have much time," she warns me, her voice gentle but firm. "We need to act now."

"Right," I say, steeling myself. Edith wastes no more time. She kneels beside Willow, and with a swift, decisive movement, she rips open her own wrist with her fangs. Blood, dark and rich, wells up, it's intoxicating scent filling the air. I watch, my heart in my throat, as she holds her wrist over Willow's mouth, allowing the crimson liquid to drip onto her pale, parted lips.

"Drink, Willow," Edith urges, her voice laced with a desperate, pleading intensity. "You have to drink if you want to live."

For a moment, nothing happens. The blood just pools on her lips, a stark, crimson stain against her pale skin. My heart plummets. It's too late. We're too late. But then, I see it. A faint, almost imperceptible flicker of her throat. She's trying to swallow. My heart clenches painfully in my chest.

Her eyes flutter open, their usual vibrant blue clouded by pain and confusion. "Jasper…" she whispers, her voice barely audible, a ghost of a sound. "What's happening?"

"Baby, you're going to be okay," I reassure her, my voice cracking under the weight of my emotions. I smooth a stray strand of hair from her forehead. "You just have to trust us, alright?"

"Okay," she murmurs, her eyelids growing heavy once more. "I trust you."

"Good girl," Edith encourages, tilting her wrist to

allow more blood to flow into Willow's mouth. "That's it, keep drinking."

We watch in silence, a tense, breathless vigil as Willow slowly, painstakingly, swallows the life-saving elixir. Every swallow is a victory, a tiny spark of hope. Finally, Edith pulls her wrist away, the wound already beginning to close.

"What do we do now?" I ask, my voice a hoarse whisper, I know what happens when you change a vampire, but my brain is filled with nothing but dust bunnies right now.

"Wait," Edith replies, her expression grave. "And pray we got to her in time."

And then, from the center of the rubble, a figure emerges. He rises from the ashes like a motherfucking phoenix, his clothes torn and bloodied, but his arrogant smirk firmly in place. Edmund.

"That fucker is still alive!" Oscar snarls, his voice filled with disbelief and rage that mirrors my own.

A red haze descends over my vision. All the fear, all the desperation — it all coalesces into a single, burning point of pure rage. He did this. He hurt her. He almost took her from me.

"Oh, I'm going to enjoy this," I growl, the sound low and animalistic. "I'm going to take you apart, piece by piece."

I'm on my feet before I even realize I'm moving, my body fueled by a rage so profound it eclipses everything else. Theo is right beside me, his face a mask of cold, murderous fury. He looks at me and gives a single, sharp nod. We are in perfect, silent agreement. This ends now.

We take off running toward Edmund, the ground

shaking beneath our feet. I can hear Oscar shouting our names, but it's a distant, meaningless sound. The only thing that matters is the look of surprise on Edmund's face as he sees the two of us coming for him, two kings united in their righteous fury. It's too late for second thoughts. It's time to end this. Once and for all.

"You should have stayed down, Edmund," Theo says, his voice a low, deadly rumble. "It would have been a quicker death."

"You think you can defeat me?" Edmund sneers, straightening his torn jacket in a pathetic attempt at dignity. "I am older, I am stronger…"

"You're a dead man walking," I scream, unleashing the full force of my powers at him. A powerful gust of wind whips around us, picking up stones, jagged pieces of metal, and splintered wood, and flinging them toward him. The rain of projectiles hurls toward Edmund like a storm unleashed.

He's fast; I'll give him that. He dodges and weaves, a blur of motion against the fiery backdrop of his burning manor. But he can't dodge everything. A large chunk of concrete slams into his shoulder, sending him stumbling back. Theo is on him in an instant, his sword a blur of silver. The clang of metal on metal rings through the air as Edmund parries the blow with a length of rebar he's ripped from the ground.

Oscar joins the fray, his face a mask of cold, precise rage. He moves with deadly surgical efficiency, his sword darting in and out, forcing Edmund onto the defensive. It's a beautiful, brutal dance.

"Having fun yet, Eddie?" I taunt, sending a shower of

razor-sharp glass shards flying toward him. He cries out as they slice into his arms and face, but he doesn't go down.

"You will pay for this!" he roars, his eyes wild with pain and fury.

"No, you will," Theo says, his voice calm and cold as he sidesteps a clumsy swing from Edmund and drives his fist into his gut. Edmund doubles over, gasping, and Oscar takes the opportunity to slice his sword across his back, a deep, clean cut that would have crippled a lesser vampire.

But Edmund is not a lesser vampire. He roars, a sound of pure, animalistic rage, and lashes out, catching Oscar with a backhand that sends him flying. He stumbles but doesn't fall, his face a mask of cold fury.

"My turn," I say, my voice a low, dangerous purr. I raise my hands, and the ground around Edmund begins to tremble. The large boulders and chunks of concrete that litter the ground begin to rise, hovering in the air like a crown of jagged, deadly stones. "You hurt my Willow. You made her cry. And for that, there is no forgiveness."

I bring my hands down, and the makeshift crown of rubble slams down on him, burying him in a tomb of his own making. He screams, a high, thin sound that is quickly cut off as the weight of the stones crushes him. I hold him there, pinned and broken.

Theo and Oscar walk slowly toward the pile of rubble, their swords held ready. Theo kicks a loose stone, revealing Edmund's battered, bloody face. He's still alive, his eyes filled with a mixture of hatred and disbelief.

"It's over, Edmund," Theo says, his voice devoid of all emotion.

Oscar steps forward, his face a mask of cold, hard

satisfaction. He raises his sword, the polished steel gleaming in the firelight. "This," he says, his voice a low, chilling whisper, "is for Willow."

He brings the blade down with a swift, clean motion, severing Edmund's head from his body. As if in a trance, Oscar leans down and picks up the head by its matted hair, his expression one of pure disgust. He turns and, with a flick of his wrist, tosses it into the heart of the burning manor. The stench of burning hair and flesh fills the air, a sickening, victorious aroma of death and destruction.

CHAPTER 50

WILLOW

Two Weeks Later

The first thing I'm aware of is the sheets. They're wrapped around my legs like a particularly clingy python with a thread count of a thousand. I groan, a low, guttural sound of pure irritation, and try to kick my way free. You'd think that becoming an immortal creature of the night would come with a few built-in perks, like, say, the ability to gracefully exit a bed. But no. I'm still the same uncoordinated mess I've always been, just with a newfound aversion to sunlight and a sudden, intense craving for O-negative.

"Fucking sheets," I mutter, finally managing to extricate myself from their clutches. The cool night air of the castle caresses my bare skin, and I shiver, a purely reflexive action. I don't technically feel the cold anymore, not in the way a human does. It's more like a memory, a ghost of a sensation that my body still insists on reacting to. Old habits, I suppose. They die even harder than I did.

I'm pretty much nude all the time these days. The kings ravish me when we all go to bed together, then disappear before I get up.

As I pad across the plush rug toward the bathroom, I can't help but notice how incredibly grumpy I feel. It's a deep irritation that just won't go away. It's like the worst case of PMS imaginable, but without the convenience of a monthly cycle to blame it on. Great. so I get to be immortal, but I'm also stuck with the emotional stability of a hormonal teenager for all eternity? Fantastic. Where do I sign up for the refund?

I make it to the bathroom, flicking on the light switch with more force than is strictly necessary. The sudden, brilliant light is a sharp, painful assault on my eyes. "Bloody hell," I mutter, squeezing my eyes shut. Right. Heightened senses. Another one of the fabulous perks of my new, undead life. You'd think after two weeks, I'd remember that turning on a light is now the equivalent of staring directly into the sun, but apparently, my brain is still running on human-level software.

"Ugh, whatever," I grumble, making my way to the toilet. And as I do my business, I find myself reflecting on the fact that this particular bodily function hasn't changed either. I'm a creature of myth and legend, and I still have to pee. There's a certain humbling absurdity to it. At least there's some semblance of normalcy in my life, I suppose. Even if it is the least glamorous one imaginable.

A soft sigh escapes my lips as I wash my hands, the water running over my pale skin like liquid silk. It's strange, really. so much has changed since I woke up on that cold, hard ground, the taste of Edith's blood still on my lips. And yet, somehow, everything feels exactly the same.

I stare at my reflection in the mirror, and for a moment, I don't recognize the woman staring back at me. Her eyes, my eyes, are brighter, almost glowing in the harsh light of the bathroom. My skin is smoother, flawless. The dark circles that have been my constant companions since my teenage years are gone, replaced by an unnerving, porcelain perfection. I look… perfect. And I hate it.

I was promised a transformation. A rebirth. I died, for Christ's sake. I went through the whole dramatic, life-altering, traumatic experience. And for what? To wake up as a slightly more attractive, eternally grumpy version of myself? It feels like a cosmic bait-and-switch. I'm still the same old Willow, with the same insecurities, the same anxieties, the same snarky, cynical outlook on life. I'm just… shinier now. Maybe that's what she meant when she wrote, his skin was like diamonds?

"Damn it," I mutter, running my fingers through my tousled hair. "This is bloody ridiculous."

I thought becoming a vampire would be… more. I thought I would feel different. I thought I would be different. But I'm not. I'm just me. A me that can now hear a mouse fart three floors down. The kings, my kings, they treat me like I'm made of glass. They're constantly fussing over me, asking me if I'm okay, if I need anything.

"Having one of those days, are we?" a voice calls out from behind me. I turn to see Oscar leaning against the doorway, his arms crossed over his chest, a single, perfect eyebrow raised in amusement. so much for hearing a mouse fart, I didn't even hear him come in. Of course, he's already perfectly dressed in a pair of tailored trousers and a crisp white shirt, looking like he just stepped out of a magazine. I, on the other hand, am standing here naked and radiating a moody attitude. The contrast is not lost on me.

"Easy for you to say," I shoot back, snatching a nearby robe and pulling it on. "You've had centuries to adjust to all this vampire-human crap. I'm still trying to wrap my head around the fact that I'm thirsty all the time, and not for a goddamn glass of water."

"Ah, yes, the blood," he muses, stepping into the bathroom and coming to stand beside me. "That can be a bit… disconcerting at first."

"Disconcerting? That's one way to put it," I huff, rolling my eyes. "You, Theo, and Jasper make it look so easy. You drink from me like it's the most natural thing in the world. Like I'm your own personal juice box."

Oscar chuckles, his breath warm on my neck. "You are very tasty, and we can't stomach those bag like we used to, but you seem ok."

It's true. My three kings can't drink blood from anyone but me now. They hate the taste of blood from a bag, claiming it tastes like ash and despair. But for some reason, I don't mind it. I can drink a glass or two each day without any issues. Maybe being their only food source gives me some perks in the drinking department? A little silver lining to the whole 'being a walking, talking buffet' thing.

"Ugh, yeah, I guess I should count myself lucky," I say, leaning against the countertop, feeling the cool marble beneath my fingertips.

Oscar's voice is soft and soothing. "You'll find your footing soon enough, Willow."

"Maybe you're right," I concede, looking back at my reflection. "Maybe I just need to give myself a chance to adjust to this new life. I mean, it can't be all bad, right? There's got to be some perks to being a vampire."

"Perks?" Oscar raises an eyebrow, his gaze flicking up and down my body in a way that makes my skin tingle. "Oh, I could think of a few."

"Really?" I smirk, feeling a familiar heat start to build in my core. "Care to show me?"

"Only if you insist," he replies, his fingers tracing the curve of my hip. And as his lips find mine, and our bodies press together with a hunger that only immortals could truly understand, I can't help but think that maybe—just maybe—there is a silver lining to this whole vampire thing after all. I mean I'm not gong to die on them now, so 'Perk' right?

"Come on," Oscar says into my mouth while squeezing my ass with his huge hands, "I'll make you some breakfast."

As we walk to the kitchen, the silence of the castle feels more pronounced than usual. It's been three days since Theo and Jasper left to deal with the… aftermath of Edmund's demise, and the castle feels hollow without them. The constant low-level hum of their presence is gone, and I'm left with a quiet that is more deafening than any sound.

"I miss them," I say, the words soft and small in the grand hallway. "It's too quiet. I can hear myself think, and frankly, I don't like what I'm hearing."

Oscar's arm comes around my shoulders, pulling me into his side. "I know, little mouse. I miss them too. But they'll be back soon. And in the meantime, you're stuck with me."

"I know," I say, leaning my head against his shoulder. "But you're the responsible one. You're the one who makes sure the bills are paid, and the castle doesn't fall down. I miss Theo's grumpiness and Jasper's stupid jokes. I miss the chaos."

"I can be chaotic," he says, his voice a low, suggestive purr as we enter the kitchen.

"Sure you can," I say, patting his cheek. "Now, what's for breakfast? I'm starving."

He just smiles, a slow, secret smile that makes my stomach do a little flip, and gets to work. He moves around the kitchen with practiced, graceful efficiency, pulling out pans and ingredients. A few minutes later, he places a plate in front of me. Scrambled eggs, perfectly cooked, and a piece of toast.

I stare at it for a moment, a wave of nostalgia washing over me. "You made me Vegemite toast," I say, my voice a little softer than I intended. "You make me smile."

"Anything for you, Little Mouse," he says, his eyes twinkling. "Now eat up. We have a busy day ahead of us."

"A busy day?" I ask, taking a bite of the toast, and moan. "Doing what? Polishing the silver? Alphabetizing the library?"

"Paperwork," he says, and the single word is enough to make me groan. "With Theo and Jasper away, we have to sort through the quarterly reports for all of our... legitimate businesses."

"You're kidding me," I say, my mouth full of eggs. "You're telling me that the glamorous, exciting life of a vampire involves… paperwork?"

"I'm afraid so," he says, a hint of sympathy in his voice. "Immortality isn't all fun and games, little mouse. Someone has to do the boring stuff."

"Great," I say, taking another bite of my toast. "Just great. So, while Theo and Jasper are out playing vampire politics and being all dark and mysterious, I'm stuck here with you, doing taxes. This is not what I signed up for."

Oscar just laughs, a warm, genuine sound that fills the kitchen. "Come on," he says, taking my plate. "The sooner we start, the sooner we can finish. And then… we can be chaotic."

I just roll my eyes, but I can't help the smile that tugs at my lips. Maybe a day of paperwork with Oscar won't be so bad after all. Maybe. But I'm still going to complain about it. A lot.

Chapter 51

Jasper

Three months. Three goddamn months of this shit. I kicked a dust bunny across the dusty floor of what was once the manor. I found Willow. This place — the very one where he held my Willow captive for three years — still gives me the creeps. It's a cold, soulless mausoleum, a monument to one man's obsession and cruelty. And for the past three months, it's been my own personal hell.

Dismantling an ancient vampire's empire, it turns out, is less about epic battles and more about mind-numbing, soul-crushing paperwork. We've liquidated his assets, sold off his properties, and relocated his terrified, leaderless clan members. It's been a whirlwind of meetings, negotiations, and endless, endless phone calls. Theo, of course, thrives on this shit. He's in his element, a king in his counting house, his face a mask of cold, calculating efficiency. Me? I'm about to lose my goddamn mind.

The only saving grace in this whole ordeal has been Oscar. Our own personal teleporting taxi service. He pops in, drops us off at whatever godforsaken location we need to be at, and then pops back to pick us up when we're done. It's a hell of a lot faster than driving, and it means we get to spend our nights at home, with Willow. The thought of her, of her snarky smile and her warm, soft body, is the only thing that's kept me from going completely insane.

"Are you done with your tantrum?" Theo asks, his voice a low, bored drawl from behind a stack of dusty ledgers. He doesn't even look up.

"I'm not having a tantrum," I say, kicking another stone. "I'm expressing my existential dread through the medium of interpretive dance. There's a difference."

"Right," he says, the single word dripping with sarcasm. "Well, when you're done with your… expression, we have one last room to clear. The attic."

"The attic?" I say, my interest piqued. "You think he kept his porn collection up there?"

Theo just gives me a look, a look that says, 'I am surrounded by idiots.' "I think," he says, his voice slow and deliberate, "that we should be thorough. We don't want any surprises."

He's right, of course. He's always right. It's one of his most annoying qualities. With a sigh, I follow him up the staircase, our footsteps echoing in the silence. The attic is just as creepy as the rest of the house, a vast, cavernous space filled with shadows and the ghosts of forgotten things. But it's not empty. Far from it.

Hundreds of boxes, all neatly labeled and stacked, fill the room from floor to ceiling. They're old, the cardboard soft and crumbling, the ink on the labels faded with age.

My heart sinks. More paperwork. I'm going to die of boredom. I'm an immortal creature of the night, and my cause of death is going to be paperwork. There's a certain tragic irony to it.

"What the hell is all this?" I ask, pulling a box from the top of a stack. The label is written in a neat, spidery script. 'Carrington, 1785-1805.'

"I don't know," Theo says, his voice a low, curious hum. He pulls another box. 'Carrington, 1805-1825.'

We exchange a look, a silent, dawning realization passing between us. We open the boxes. They're not filled with ledgers or deeds. They're filled with journals. Hundreds of them, all handwritten, all detailing the lives of Willow's ancestors. It's an obsessive, and utterly terrifying record of her entire bloodline.

We spend the next few hours in silence, each of us engrossed in the horrifying story laid out before us. Edmund's journals are the worst. He writes with a cold, detached precision, detailing his mission to kill off the bloodline so the prophecy wouldn't come true.

A journal from the early 20th century. Edmund's tone is different. It's triumphant. There is only one left in the bloodline, but every time he kills them, another pops up, like no matter what he does he can't kill them all, so he comes up with the plan to let her die naturally.

"Holy shit," I breathe, the words a prayer in the dusty silence. "He wasn't trying to kill her in the end. He was trying to keep her alive."

"He was hoping to use the loophole to win," Theo corrects, his voice a low, dangerous growl. "He was keeping her alive, a prisoner in her own life, so that he could be free. He was going to let her grow old and die, all for his own selfish gain."

The rage that had been simmering beneath the surface for the past three months comes roaring back, a hot, white-hot fire in my chest. I think of Willow, of her vibrant, beautiful, and now, eternal life. I think of what Edmund would have taken from her, from us. And I am so, so glad he's dead.

Theo pulls out his phone, his movements sharp and precise. He dials Oscar. "We have a situation," he says, his voice devoid of emotion. "The attic. It's full of… research. On Willow's bloodline." He pauses, listening. "No, not just research. It's a goddamn library. Hundreds of boxes. Journals, notes, everything. We need to get it all back to the castle. Now."

He listens for another moment, then nods. "Good. Get it done." He hangs up, his eyes meeting mine. "Trucks will be here in a few hours. We're not leaving any of this behind."

I nod, my mind still reeling. While Theo makes a few more calls, arranging for a crew to help with the loading, I find myself wandering out of the attic, a strange, morbid curiosity pulling me through the silent manor. I need to see it. I need to see where she was kept. I need to understand. Theo follows me, distracted by his phone, typing away.

I find her room easily. It's the only one that feels… lived in. It's small by my standards, but cozy. There's a worn, comfortable-looking armchair in the corner, a small piles of books on her nightstand, and a thick, soft-looking rug on the floor. It's a cage, a gilded one, but a cage none-theless. And yet, she made it a home. She found a way to make it hers. The thought makes my chest ache with a love so fierce it almost brings me to my knees.

I run my hand over the soft fabric of the armchair, imagining her curled up in it, reading, her mind a million miles away from this cold, lonely place. I can almost smell her — a faint, lingering scent of lavender and vanilla. It's a ghost of a scent, but it's enough to make my heart clench.

I leave her room, my feet carrying me down the hallway as I pop my head into every room, until I stumble across a library. After being with Willow for months now, I see this place for what it was to her. It's not just a room full of books. It's her sanctuary. It's where she found solace, where she escaped from the reality of her life. The shelves are filled with books, hundreds of them, their spines a rainbow of colours. I run my hand over them, the covers soft and spine's all cracked. These books were her friends, her companions, her only connection to the outside world.

"We're taking these too," I say, my voice hoarse. Theo looks up from his phone, an eyebrow raised.

"What?" he asks, his eyes dart around the room, the soften at the sight. He has come to the same conclusion I just did. "All of them?"

"All of them," I say, my voice firm. "She loves books. This was her sanctuary. She deserves to have it."

Theo just nods, a flicker of understanding in his eyes. He knows, just as I do, that this is more than just about books. It's about giving her back a piece of herself, a piece that Edmund tried to steal. It's also a bit of Caleb, the man she refuses to hate. No matter how we feel about it, she still cares, and his death still haunts her.

CHAPTER 52

WILLOW

One Year Later

I stare at my reflection in the mirror, a slow, wicked grin spreading across my face. "Well, damn," I say to the woman staring back at me. "You clean up nicely."

And I do. I really, really do. I'm wearing one of the ball gowns from the crate Oscar gave me, a stunning, blood-red creation of silk and lace that looks like it was stolen from a Victorian gothic romance. The bodice is tight, pushing my breasts up in a way that is both scandalous and spectacular. The skirt is a masterpiece of engineering, a cascade of silk and petticoats that is heavy as fuck, but man, does it make an entrance. I feel like a queen. A dark, dangerous, and ridiculously hot queen.

I smooth down the fabric, a shiver of anticipation running through me. Today is the day. The day I marry my three kings. The day I officially, legally, and irrevocably bind myself to the three most infuriating and incredible men I have ever known. And I can't fucking wait.

I remember glancing at the three identical, exquisitely tailored Armani suits hanging on the back of my door before I left to get dressed. I bought them myself, a little wedding present to my future husband's. They're simple, plain, all black, with no frills or fuss. I even got them matching red pocket squares and cufflinks, a little nod to my dress. I left them a note. 'Wear these. No arguments.' I have a feeling Theo probably grumbled about it, but I know they'll wear them.

I take a deep breath. It's time. I make my way out of the castle, the heavy skirt of my dress rustling around me. The wind whips at my hair, pulling a few loose strands from the intricate updo I spent the better part of an hour on. But I don't care. The wind feels good, a wild, untamed thing that mirrors the wild, untamed joy in my heart.

I see them then, standing at the edge of the cliff, their backs to me, looking out at the churning, grey sea. Three dark, imposing figures against the dramatic, windswept landscape. They look like something out of a dream, a myth, a legend. And they are all mine.

They're wearing the suits. Of course, they are. The black fabric stretches across their broad shoulders, the cut of the suits emphasizing their lean, powerful builds. They look… perfect. Absolutely, breathtakingly, and infuriatingly perfect.

I walk toward them, the sound of my footsteps lost in the wind. They don't turn, not yet. They're waiting for me. They know I'm here. I can feel it — a low, thrumming hum in my blood, a silent, invisible thread that connects us all.

I stop a few feet behind them, a mischievous grin on my face. "You know," I say, my voice a low, playful purr, "it's considered rude to keep your bride waiting."

They turn all at once, and the world seems to stop. Their eyes, all three pairs of them, are fixed on me, a mixture of awe, adoration, and a raw hunger that makes my stomach do a little flip. I see the way their eyes trace the lines of my dress, the way their jaws tighten, the way their hands clench at their sides. And I know with a certainty that settles deep in my bones that I have them. All of them. Wrapped around my little finger.

"Willow," Theo breathes, his voice a low, rough growl. He looks like he's been struck by lightning.

"Wow," Jasper says, his eyes wide with a mixture of awe and adoration. "Just... wow."

Oscar just smiles, a slow, secret smile that makes my heart do a little pitter-patter. "You look... exquisite, little mouse," he says, his voice a soft, caressing whisper.

"I know," I say, my grin widening. "I clean up nice, don't I?"

I walk toward them; the wind whipping my dress around me. I feel like I'm floating, like I'm flying. I reach them, and they part, creating a space for me in the center. I take their hands, all three of them, their skin cool and smooth against mine. I look at them, at my king, at my husbands. And I know, with a certainty that fills my entire being, that this is where I belong. This is my home. This is my forever.

Theo clears his throat, stepping forward with an air of

authority that is so quintessentially him. "Alright," he says, his voice a low rumble. "Let's get this show on the road. We'll start with Oscar."

He turns to face us, his expression serious, but with a flicker of amusement in his eyes. "We are gathered here today on this ridiculously windy cliff to witness the union of two souls. Oscar, my brother, my friend. And Willow, the infuriating, beautiful woman who has turned our world upside down."

He looks at Oscar. "Do you, Oscar, take Willow to be your wife, to cherish and protect, to make Vegemite toast for, and to love for all of eternity?"

Oscar's eyes never leave mine. "I do," he says, his voice thick with emotion.

Theo then turns to me with a wink. "And do you, Willow, take Oscar to be your husband, to tolerate his obsessive need for order, to appreciate his quiet strength, and to love for all of eternity?"

"I do," I say, my voice a little shaky. "And I promise to at least try to use a coaster."

Theo rolls his eyes. "By the power vested in me, I now pronounce you husband and wife. You may kiss the bride."

Oscar pulls me to him, his kiss gentle and sweet, a promise of a lifetime of quiet, steady love. It's perfect. One down, two to go.

Theo clears his throat again, a smirk playing on his lips. "Next," he says, turning to Jasper. "Your turn, you degenerate."

He faces us, his expression a mixture of amusement and exasperation. "We are gathered here again to witness another union. Jasper, the constant source of chaos in my life. And Willow, the only woman brave enough, or foolish enough, to take him on."

He looks at Jasper. "Do you, Jasper, take Willow to be your wife, to fill her life with laughter and adventure, to annoy her endlessly with your terrible jokes, and to love for all of eternity?"

Jasper's grin is a mile wide. "I absolutely do," he says, his eyes sparkling with mischief.

Theo turns to me. "And do you, Willow, take Jasper to be your husband, to tolerate his constant need for attention, to pretend to be surprised by his pranks, and to love for all of eternity?"

"I do," I say, laughing. "Someone has to keep him out of trouble."

"Good luck with that," Theo mutters. "By the power vested in me, I now pronounce you husband and wife. You may kiss the bride."

Jasper's kiss is totally different to Oscar's. It's wild, and passionate, and full of a playful, infectious energy that makes me laugh against his lips. It's perfect. Two down, one to go.

Then, Oscar steps forward, a small, knowing smile on his face. "My turn," he says, his voice a soft, gentle murmur. He turns to face Theo and me, his expression serene and calm. "We are gathered here for the final time, to witness the union of our king and our queen."

He looks at Theo. "Do you, Theodore, take Willow to be your wife, to protect and provide for, to cherish and command, and to love for all of eternity?"

Theo's eyes are dark and intense, a burning fire that

threatens to consume me. "I do," he says, his voice a low growl.

Oscar then turns to me. "And do you, Willow, take Theodore to be your husband, to challenge his authority, to soothe his temper, and to love for all of eternity?"

"I do," I say, my voice firm and unwavering. "And I promise to never, ever make it easy for him."

Oscar smiles. "By the power vested in me, I now pronounce you husband and wife. You may kiss the bride."

Theo's kiss is a claiming, a possession, a brand of fire on my soul. It's a promise of a lifetime of passion, of power, of a love so fierce it could burn the world down. It's perfect. And that's the hat-trick.

I pull back, breathless, and look at my three husbands. My three kings. My family. They all laugh, a real, genuine laugh that echoes in the wind. And in that moment, surrounded by my three kings, on the edge of the world, I know that I am home. I am finally, completely, and utterly home.

The End

Acknowledgments

Thank You!

Thank you so much for reading! I know there are a million books out there vying for your attention, and it means the world to me that you chose to spend your time with Willow, Theo, Jasper, and Oscar.

Writing this story has been a wild ride, and sharing it with you is a dream come true. Every read, every page turn, and every reaction makes the long hours of writing completely worth it.

If you enjoyed your trip to Willow's Peak, please consider leaving a review on the platform where you purchased this book. Reviews are like gold to indie authors —they help other readers find the story and allow me to keep writing more books for you to enjoy.

Thank you again for your incredible support.

Happy reading!

About Cassandra Doon

Cassandra hates writing about herself in the third person, but here we are. With over 33 novels penned and no signs of stopping, she writes across multiple genres. Unable to be pinned down by just one, you'll find Fantasy, Dark Romance, Young Adult, and even a Detective series in the mix.

Having grown up in a small country town and later lived in the city, Cassandra found a perfect spot she likes to call an 'in-between place'—complete with rolling hills and just a stone's throw from the Gold Coast in Queensland Australia.

While she may have had social media in the past, Cassandra has since declared it's not for her. Her website is now the best place to find out what's happening in her world and to see what upcoming books are on the horizon.

ALSO BY CASSANDRA DOON

The 4 Seats Series:

Matteo

Felix

Gabriel

Catcher

Ruhn & Frost

———

The 4 Seats Extended World:

Aces

Obsessed Shadows 🎧

Adrian Romano

The Moretti Brothers (Coming Soon)

Standalone:

The Kings of Willows Peak

Damaged Goods

Tuesday May

The Devils Cut

The Detectives Mate

Dark Dahlias Rite

A Field of Tulips and Bones

Follow Poppy

To Her

Blood moon

Unit 9

Broken Creek Ranch

Eclipsion (Coming Soon)

The Dead Zone (Coming Soon)

———

Oakland Harbour Series:

Missing

Found

Home

———

The Boys Series

The Boys Of Hastings House 🎧

The Boys of Bittersweet College

The Boys of Nightsbane Academy (Coming Soon)

The Boys of Winchester U (Coming Soon)

————

Second Chances Series:

The Waterfall 🎧

Wicked Bonds

Writhe (Coming Soon)

The Restaurant (Coming Soon)

————

Umbravivus Series:

The Lost Kingdom of Umbravivus (Coming Soon)

The Crowned King of Umbravivus (Coming Soon)

The Queen of Umbravivus (Coming Soon)

————

Butcher and the Witch Series:

Poison is always in the Prettiest Bottle

Candles make Great Alibis

Socials with a Slice of Pie

Also By C.L. Doon

The Rain Dang Detective Series:

Still Waters

Moving Waters (coming Soon)

Standalone:

Second Chances at The Riverbend Café

Lavender (Coming Soon)

Also By C. Doon

Standalone:

Ravenwood Manor

Phantom Navis